Whispers of Deceit

A Novel of the Djinn Chronicles
Book Three

Claudia Herring

WHISPERS OF DECEIT: A Novel of the Djinn Chronicles

Author: Claudia Herring

Copyright © 2018 by Claudia Herring

All Rights Reserved

Cover Design: Claudia Herring Design

Interior Design: Claudia Herring Design

Published in the United States by Caravanserai Publishing

ISBN 978-0-9909985-7-0

For Barry

Djinni

*Jinni. More commonly known in English as **Genie**.*
*(plural) **Djinn** or Jinn*
Arabic, North African, Egyptian, Syrian, Persian,
*   and Turkish mythology and folklore*

Any of a class of spirits, created at the same time as angels, capable of appearing in human and animal forms and influencing humankind for either good or evil.

Djinn are created from subtle fire — fire that is smokeless, that does not proclaim itself through smoke — thus they can easily conceal themselves from human senses. They have magic, can fly, can travel long distances in a short time, and live long lives.

Djinn appeared in *The Thousand and One Nights* where Al-Addin (Aladdin), his lamp and djinnis (genies) were first popularly introduced to the West in the French translation by Antoine Galland in 1704.

"Those who tread among serpents, and along a tortuous path, must use the cunning of the serpent."

— *Thomas Becket*

1

England, 1820

The Lady Lavinia had cursed him. For three years, Meylo felt the words fester inside just like a splinter he thought he'd dug out, but the little bit left kept doing its dirty work.

The first clue was the bruises from their rough-and-tumble over the bottle. A surprise, that. A rich, proper lady fighting him, a boy who had only thirteen years, over a fancy brass bottle that she herself had tossed in the river. He pictured himself as the Lady Lavinia must've seen him then, short and skinny, looking all of eleven years old (he'd scrapped with those who had taunted him so). That old leather belt cut to hold up raggedy pants from Bony Herman. He checked his arm, flexed his biceps. Now he was bigger with a bit of muscle, thin as one of those wheels on the fancy carriages they said, but looked closer to his sixteen years. Still had those freckles though.

After their fight, he'd been black and blue and yellow and purple, with pain shooting through his body, longer than bruises from any ruckus he'd ever gotten into. He pictured the lady by the riverbank, muddy and wet from their tussle, near skewering him with those witchy blue eyes when he said he'd tell her husband about the bottle. Meylo'd felt the evil eye all the way to his gut.

This last winter, he almost froze as he starved on the streets of Hertford. After spring came he'd been laid up with a fierce fever and nearly died; sacked from selling newspapers when his were stolen and made to pay for them; beaten up by a nasty gang of boys, his best friend, Bony Herman, killed.

Meylo's head spun with his long list of bad luck. But this last one . . . He breathed hard, imagining the hangman's noose rough around his neck. This last one. Accused of the murder of a gentleman. They were still after him. He looked back, down the dark country road, the wagon bumping along the ruts and potholes. Nothing and no one.

So far.

Today, he'd hopped in and out of the cart for what seemed like hundreds of times, fetching this and that bundle at each stop. Making his way to London, bit by bit, penny by penny, where his luck would change. Where he would make his fortune.

He stood on his knees, swaying on the sticky hay piled in between the parcels packages in the bed of the wagon and looked over the driver's seat to see if they were close to Little Wymondley. Meylo wiped the tangles of his hair from his eyes, and yawned. He glanced up.

In the sky, the full moon glowed just above the dark skeletons of the trees.

Blood red.

His muscles locked. He stared at that thing shining like the gore on the murdered gentleman. The wagon lurched. Meylo fell backwards into the pile of hay, eyes stuck on the sky.

"Criminy! Cursed me double is wot she did," he mumbled. He squeezed his eyes shut and opened them. *Cor,* the moon was still there, still redder than a drunk's nose.

He pushed up on his elbows. The driver needed to know about this bad-luck moon. Might want to hurry and set up camp for the night, not wait for the town. Swaying with the rough ride, Meylo took hold of the back of the driver's seat and rose halfway. He cocked his head. Horses galloping. Voices. Heart thumping, he sank back down in the hay.

Somehow the Watch or the murdered gent's men had tracked him.

He scrambled. Started to crawl to the wagon's edge. He'd drop onto the road and run. But a man jumped onto the driver's seat. Meylo stayed still. He wouldn't risk being caught.

The driver reached for his pistol. A flash of steel, a strangled gurgle, and the driver fell backwards onto Meylo, blood spurting from the wide slit in his throat.

Meylo could barely breathe under the weight of the driver's body. Warm blood dripped onto his face, into his mouth. Spitting, he squirmed out from under the man and burrowed into the hay. The coppery taste of blood made him sick, but he forced himself to lie flat and tried not to retch.

Strong fingers gripped his ankles. He stifled a screech as his heart just about drove into his throat.

S'blood. Those rascals got him.

"What have we here?" A gruff voice.

Meylo kicked and dug deeper into the hay. If he could break loose they might figure it wasn't worth the effort, but he was dragged out as quick and easy as if he were a mewling kitten. Someone held him by the ankles and shook. He tried to hold his pocket closed, but his arms swung out from his side, head wobbling, as a big man, face covered in a scraggly black beard, jiggled him back and forth.

"Will wonders never cease?" The bearded man dropped him in the dirt. "Look a here. A sovereign." He dragged Meylo upright. "Now where would a slip of a beggar boy get hisself a gold sovereign?" He slapped him across the face. "Where's the rest?"

Meylo shook his head and wiped his nose with his sleeve. These weren't men of the Watch. They were just robbers, plain and simple.

In the man's palm, Meylo's gold sovereign from the murdered gentleman glittered. He'd stumbled across the body in a smelly alley piled with rubbish. He didn't kill the man, but that hadn't kept him from looking through his fancy clothes. And lo and behold, what did he find but the sovereign in a secret pocket the murderers missed. He'd used the pennies he saved to live on, kept the sovereign for the big city London. Finally, his luck had changed.

But now . . .

"Farley, slit his throat and strip him. See wot other surprises you can find." The man shoved Meylo in the direction of a skinny chap who pulled a knife on him. The blade gleamed red from that evil moon.

Just as Farley reached for him, Meylo stumbled on a rock. He almost fell to the ground, which took him out of Farley's grasp. Regaining his balance, he whipped to the side and dove into the bushes.

Branches slapped his face and tore at his legs while he tunneled through the forest's thick brushy undergrowth. He didn't stop until their shouts died away.

The woods stood quiet in all directions. Exhausted, he lay on his back under a fat bush, and peered through the tangled branches at the moon. Still bloody red. He hadn't imagined it.

"Her's wot caused this," he whispered to the night. "Witched me fer good." He was double sure of it now. If only he'd run away with the bottle as soon as he'd fished it from the river. The brass would've fetched a nice price. Then that Lady Lavinia couldn't have cursed him. Well, maybe just a tiny curse. But it would've worn off fast, since he wouldn't have entered her witch house or eaten her witch food in the kitchen like he did.

He jumped at an owl's cry. The Bird-o-the-Dead speaking for the murdered gentleman: Who, who, who killed me? Well, it wasn't him, Meylo. Who, who, who? He shivered on the damp ground at the cries, wicked strange evil like the moon that bloodied the sky.

It had gotten worse, this curse. He reached for the sovereign in his pocket, his luck piece, but the robber had it now. Left him only greasy crumbs.

"Blimey. 'Ave mercy. I almost died back there." Meylo said low and soft to the trees. He pictured the skinny robber with the knife lunging for him. They would've murdered him. He saw the Lady Lavinia's witchy blue eyes looking at him, evil as the red moon.

He never told her husband about the bottle. She had no reason to curse him. Except that he knew the bottle meant a lot to her. Something about it. But what? He couldn't figure it out.

He spat to the side, the taste of the driver's blood still in his mouth. He had no choice. Not now. He almost got killed this time. There might not be a next time for him. He would go back to the Lady Lavinia. Beg her to take the curse away. Beg her for mercy.

And if that didn't work?

Then he'd have to make her.

2

A scream ripped through the silence of the night. Rakhshan turned toward the open doors of the terrace, then grinned at his rival's skull set in a golden stand on the ivory tabletop. He placed his blackthorn wand in the hollow eye socket. "Neba Dadarshi, your power is mine."

"Vanquished at long last." A tingle of heat shot through Rakhshan. Once again he pictured their meeting in the crystal pavilion and savored his enemy's surprised expression as his head was severed from his body.

"How does it feel, Nan Dasha? Your soul has no rest, your body scattered in pieces, eaten by dogs and crows. Your skull on my table, eternally bestowing your shaman's magic to me." Rakhshan raised his voice. "I am your overlord now."

From the terrace came murmurs of a restless crowd. Night. Yet the light pouring in through the doors belied the darkness. The hundreds of voices, shouts and screams increased like a wave crashing to the shore. They came from his palace's very doorstep. Where were his soldiers? Why had he not been informed of this, this . . . mob? Uprising? Celebration?

His fine silk robes rustled as he stepped onto the terrace. The dry air cooled his face. He walked the length of it, past fountains, flowering fruit trees in giant gilded pots, and placed his hand on the marble balustrade, the stone still warm from the long day. Below, hundreds of his subjects filled the street, restless, looking up and pointing. At his palace?

A noise behind him. His wand flopped through the doors onto the tiles. It flew to him, passing through his dark shadow. A moon shadow. He caught his wand, pivoted, and looked at the sky.

Clutching the balustrade, his fist tight around his wand, he stared at the full moon floating in the heavens.

Blood red.

"Bisho'ur, idiots!" He struck the balustrade with his fist. He, the Great Sultan, the Supreme Magician, had no indication of this, not a sign.

Astrologers. Fools. Why did they not predict this for me? He spat off the balcony. This moon, a dire message even a simple-minded peasant could understand. How I would have been revered had I proclaimed this before it took place.

He looked to the moon again. Clouds flew by the heavenly body, never once covering it. What omen was this?

He snapped his fingers. Restless while he waited, he settled his eyes on the gilded sculpture of Nergal, god of the plague, underworld, and fires. In a few heartbeats a servant approached, bending low to the ground, his dark teal linen robes pooling around him.

"Send my astrologers."

The servant hurried from the terrace in a blur of movement, a shadow passing over the black onyx tiles. Rakhshan lifted his wand. He would have his minions before him.

A bulky figure filled the doorway. "Great Sultan, whose boundaries lie far to—"

"I don't need your kowtowing, Saddani. Why did you not warn me?" Rakhshan gestured to the bloodied moon.

"Your Eminence, I have only just returned to this land from one which has not the same heavenly bodies. His Grace was surprised?" Saddani sidled to the balcony, his hooknose silhouetted against the white marble of the palace.

"Imbecile. I would not have questioned why you failed to warn me if I weren't taken by surprise. Gods." Rakhshan fisted his hand around his wand. At a slight movement, they both looked to the doorway. Saddani arced his arm in a prelude to a magic gesture.

"Ah, I see I am about to receive either curse or blessing." Mehadeh stepped onto the terrace, her red dress a sharp contrast to her black skin. She tossed her head. The red beads in her long braids clicked.

"Refrain from your curt remarks, you are still beholden to me. And you have failed to find the djinni or his body." Rakhshan scowled at the sorceress.

He beckoned them. "Inside, away from this aberrant moon."

He heard Mehadeh's exasperated exhale as they followed him through the doors. Ingrate sorceress. Was she faithful to his cause, or still allied with the djinni?

Inside, they approached a tapestry filling half the wall opposite the ivory table with Neba Dadarshi's skull. Out of nowhere, the silk weaving sparked like a fire. Rakhshan caught himself before he exclaimed in fear.

Amazingly, his minions didn't give any sign of seeing it.

The red moon had shaken him. More than he dared let on. He was human, not as strong a magician as the djinni, yet with Neba Dadarshi's shamanic powers and the djinni's secret name, he had managed to enhance his magic. If Yasir were still alive, Rakhshan would need to steal as much of the djinni's powers as he could manage. Then he would kill Yasir.

At the thought of this plan, he felt a sense of loss. The djinni was beautiful, powerful. When he imprisoned Yasir in the urn, the djinni had been young, vulnerable. He would have made a perfect son, but for his pride. Now the prophecy made him a threat.

Mehadeh slitted her eyes at him. She knew he had nothing to do with this message. He had turned the sorceress to his will with a clever trick, but before that she had been close to Yasir.

As he passed in front of the wall hanging, Rakhshan felt his arm move counter to his wishes. He fought it for a moment, but his guests must not see his wand forcing his hand to point to the tapestry. He assumed his haughty pose of power and, with a sense of dread, watched as stylized flowers in the weave elongated. Their silken stems and leaves unwound and interlaced, creating a knot of inconceivable complexity. A magic knot.

He was not controlling this.

Ingeniously concealed in the intricacies of the configuration, a Parthian script wended its way from the design, golden threads declaring, *Sezamdim en widebe, sezamdim iib.* Unbound am I, only when you are bound.

Behind him, Mehadeh gasped. The sorceress knew the phrase, knew where it came from.

Rakhshan gripped his wand as a wave of uncertainty passed over him. This was the very same inscription he had incised on the brass urn. The urn where he imprisoned Yasir, where he had bound the djinni for centuries. He grinned. Yasir's desperation and shock when he found that a paltry human magician had beaten a djinni never ceased to amuse him.

But with Yasir's death (or rumors of his death), the djinni had been freed from Rakhshan's servitude. Freed from Rakhshan's control, such as it was.

"Your Eminence, how clever of you to call on the tapestry to translate the omen of the moon." Saddani's voice dripped with sarcasm.

So no one was fooled. They knew the djinni could be his nemesis—their nemesis.

"Do not be simple. There is more to this than meets the eye." Rakhshan put his wand to the tapestry, absorbing the power in the countless intersections that trapped and intensified the knot's magic. The gold calligraphy dwindled before their eyes. He breathed in relief as the tapestry restored itself to the innocuous bright palette of stylized florals, surrounded by dense, elaborate botanical motifs.

No more messages. But this moment of ease ceased abruptly—even in absence, in supposed death, the djinni raised his presence.

This message, a portent.

In his own chambers.

The wand shivered in his hand. He eyed his rival's skull. Was Dadarshi finally taking vengeance as well? Impossible. And yet . . . He turned away from the yellowing skull. His chamber, palatial as it was, closed in on him. He fought to keep the illusion of his power.

"Surely His . . ." Mehadeh paused. For a moment, Rakhshan thought she might dare to use a pejorative. ". . . His Excellency did not cause this. I sense another power here." The light from the oil lamps reflected on her round forehead. Saddani frowned as she continued.

"An augury. In the heavens above, and inside His Eminence's palace. This exceeds all boundaries." Mehadeh watched them both.

Saddani's dark eyes flicked from Mehadeh to Rakhshan. "Is the djinni still alive?" he asked, his disquiet barely contained. There was a long silence while they studied one another. At the sharp chime of a bell, they startled as one.

"Enter," said Rakhshan. The door creaked open. A servant bowed.

At Rakhshan's nod, he announced, "The astrologers."

Like a herd of frightened sheep, the seven primary astrologers clumped together. Rakhshan could smell their fear. They bowed lower than his servant, hands over their mouths, a symbol of obeisance. Good, after the tapestry and the red moon, he needed something to impress his minions.

"Nemasver, why I was not informed of this?" Rakhshan pointed his wand to the heavens in the direction of the terrace where the sinister light of the blood moon gleamed.

The head astrologer prostrated, his lanky body flat on the floor, arms spread towards Rakhshan's feet. "Oh Lord of the Many, Lodestar of Exalted Presence and Lofty Rank," his voice thick, muffled by the lush carpet.

"Rise to your knees, speak." Rakhshan moved his palm up in rapid staccato movements. "I would hear your excuses before I have your tongue torn out."

"We have read the constellations." The head astrologer's voice started strong. "The charts, the celestial signs." Sweat beaded on his high forehead and his voice grew fainter. "This moon was not foretold by the stars."

"Seven of you. Seven. And that is the summation of your knowledge?"

Keresaspa, second lord astrologer, bowing low, hand over mouth almost covering his sparse beard, spoke. "O Lord of the Many, your humble servant wishes to share."

Rakhshan dropped his hand to his side, his wand pointing downward. "I await."

Keresaspa, watery eyes cast towards the carpet, swallowed. His fat neck rippled above his brocade robe. "This sign is merely shown in the heavens. Not caused by the heavens." He kept his gaze down. "There were no signs pointing to this event. Our careful calculations showed no heavenly bodies lined up to cause this . . . this effect. Powers greater than astrologers' are needed to predict this."

Rakhshan put his hand to his chin. The odd reddish light of the moon slanted in through the open doors. He motioned Mehadeh and Saddani to the side of his golden chair and sat, his hands on the mother-of-pearl arms.

"Cast the shells to answer my question."

In a flurry of robes, the astrologers brought out a polished sandalwood platform and set a golden box upon it. Nemasver bowed, folded into a seated position before the platform, opened the golden box, and chose seven cockleshells. He set the box on the floor and spread the small shells on the table with a pass of his palm. Sliding the shells on the smooth wood, he rearranged them, each move bringing a whispering *shish, shish*. He put his hands in his lap and gazed at the shell's spotted mounds.

"There is one forgotten, of a tribe forgotten. A scourge predicted, but believed eliminated. A curse foretold, a curse coming closer." Nemasver's voice quivered.

A wave of emotion flowed through the room. The eyes of the six astrologers behind Nemasver glistened. Nemasver looked stricken, as though this were his fault.

Rakhshan leaned forward in his chair. "Why this?" He gestured around the room, towards the men with their shining eyes. To his side, Mehadeh wiped her cheeks with a white cloth while Saddani sneered at her. "This atmosphere?"

Nemasver tucked his hands into his sleeves. "A great sadness comes through." The head astrologer shut his eyes.

"Do not fabricate a sugar-spun tale. I will not have it." Rakhshan rose, towering over him.

Nemasver swallowed, his pointed beard wobbling with the effort. "The sadness. The one forgotten had lived through great sadness. That is all. We felt it as one."

"I feel no sadness. Only annoyance. Tell me more of what you see in the shells." Rakhshan took his seat and rubbed his thumb against the gold cord of his belt as though it were a string of prayer beads. "You said the forgotten one had *lived* through great sadness. Does that mean this one is dead?"

"The shells indicate a presence long ago." The head astrologer examined the cockleshells once more. "Yet the same presence in recent times is shown. A long lifetime like that is impossible for a human."

Leaning forward, Rakhshan scowled. He did not care for the way the reading was going. "Who is the forgotten one, the scourge predicted, the curse coming closer?"

Nemasver studied the table in front of him. With his right hand, he covered the shells and pressed his palm on them, moving them right, left, then in a circle. He removed his hand. The shells had scattered in a random pattern. He looked up at Rakhshan, then down again.

His intake of breath could be heard throughout the chamber. "Lord of the Many. The shells have changed after they left my hand. They have now formed a circle, indicating the question is answered. This is most unorthodox. A first reading usually requires a second. And for this complication, even more readings. Yet the circle is closed. " Nemasver bowed his head. His lips moved silently.

"That is all?" Rakhshan's voice rang out as piercing as the muezzin's call to prayer. He rose from his chair and raised his wand in an arabesque movement. The golden box crashed onto its side and dissolved in ashes, cockleshells scattering across the floor.

Nemasver stood, stumbled and tottered to the side, his head bowed.

"The answer. I want the answer or you will never see the stars again. Return to your quarters. Work your shells. Peruse your charts. I will have my answer before this blood moon sets."

The astrologers scrambled from the room. A forgotten cockleshell gleamed in the corner under the moon's tinted light.

Rakhshan motioned Saddani and Mehadeh over. With his eyes he traced the trail Mehadeh's tears left on her face. Long ago, imprisoning Yasir in the urn had proved so simple. It kept his own daughter, Thalia, who had fallen in love with Yasir, from the Djinn, a people Rakhshan detested. And in the meantime, he tried to work out how to steal the djinni's amazing effortless magic.

Yasir had managed to find Thalia reincarnated in Lavinia. And before the djinni's death or disappearance, they were together.

Now the prophecy signaling his own defeat was beginning—that one of the progeny of his daughter and the djinni would overthrow him.

Rakhshan waved his wand. Saddani jerked back and Mehadeh stepped to the side. So they were still afraid of him. Yes, this pleased him.

He caught Mehadeh with his eyes. "Are the heavens mourning the djinni's death? Or is Yasir somewhere laughing at this lunar plot to disgrace me?"

Mehadeh didn't blink. She stared in front of her, her face lit from no source that Rakhshan could see. "This has nothing to do with the djinni, but everything to do with him," she said.

He could barely hear her. Her voice sounded softer, higher, as if it came from a different person in a distant place.

She meant the djinni didn't do this, but it was about the djinni. Was everyone conspiring against him? With effort, Rakhshan restrained his temper. He clutched his wand, his fingers on his free hand twitching. It would get him nowhere to hurt the sorceress. He needed her close relationship with Yasir to obtain what he wanted.

Mehadeh still stared in front of her, the light from her face stronger now, so that it cast shadows on Saddani who stood next to her.

Funneling his anger for effect, Rakhshan buried his trepidation and gathered his strength. "Mehadeh, you have failed me. The body, I need the djinni's body. Only then can I be sure he is dead. But if he is alive, bring him to me." He pointed to the doors with his wand.

"Go now. Find him."

3

*L*ord Peter Bramley had left dinner early, saying to meet him at nine o'clock in the garden. Before Lavinia had a chance to question her husband he was gone. Peter could be so secretive. But for all her searching, she never found that he had anything to hide.

Unlike her.

She had a few hours before nine, and strolled to her sitting room to rest and read a bit before seeing the children for a bedtime story. At the chimes of the clock downstairs, she closed *The Gentleman's Magazine* she had borrowed from Peter's study. What a lurid story: "1720's Hell-Fire Clubs Still Exist, The Scandalous Secret of the Gentleman You Think You Know." And to think, it was 1820, one hundred years later.

Yesterday, she had read an article in *The Tmes*, one of the many newspapers Peter received, entitled, "The Hidden Life of the Gentleman, Debauchery and Devilry in Exclusive Clubs."

After overhearing scurrilous snippets of the footman's gossip, the maids idle chatter, and her friends speculating on whether this lord, that duke or even the regent prince belonged to one of the secret clubs, she had happened upon these articles. The shocking scenes described such things as "sodomy" and "buggery," depraved relations with harlots, and animal sacrifices during club meetings. Some said there was a dwarf who was sacrificed as well. The members allegedly drank themselves senseless, set each other on fire, made pacts with the Devil, and did "whatever they wanted," at the expense of whomever they wanted.

Yet, day to day, the aristocracy carried on as normal, tending to their estates, participating in the House of Lords, giving balls, supping at their respectable clubs. They believed no one could touch them.

She felt her cheeks flush. Names had been mentioned—Lord Chalmers-Bowles, the Duke of Strathern. These were Peter's cronies. Why, Lady Chalmers-Bowles and the Duchess of Strathern swore they knew nothing about these clubs, that the press fabricated these things to make the upper class look bad. Their husbands were gentleman, members of Parliament. They would never commit such tawdry acts.

The stillness of the room didn't quiet her mind. Her thoughts kept running over the things she'd read until she couldn't suppress the question any longer.

Could Peter be one of them?

Lavinia made her way to the nursery. Reading to the children calmed her, and tonight she sensed a restlessness in the air. She stood just outside the open door. James, six, her middle child, set the last of the miniature ninepins in a pattern on the floor; his brow furrowed in concentration, just like his father, Peter.

"Good job, James. Now, Cybelle, give me your dolly." Stuart held out his hand to his little sister. She hugged her porcelain doll and patted the frilly pink bonnet, then offered it. She was a serious child, quiet, and seemed to have no magic, but Yasir claimed she was his offspring.

By some miracle, they all looked like Lavinia—lapis lazuli blue eyes, raven-black curly hair, fair complexion. And Peter believed they were all his.

Stuart set the doll in the middle of the pins. Cybelle stared. Honestly, you could never tell what that child was thinking. Why, when Stuart was three, the same age as Cybie, he had babbled incessantly and worked little tricks, which Yasir said was normal for half-Djinn children.

Now seven, Stuart gestured to the large rubber ball in the corner. It flew to him. He caught it with a flourish, held it in one hand and pulled his arm back in a classic bowler's pose.

Cybelle's eyes grew wide.

Lavinia sighed. Stuart would knock down the doll. She would step inside before he did any damage. But as she set her foot over the threshold, the doll wobbled to the ceiling and hung there, wavering like a kite. Stuart froze in mid motion—he had seen his mother watching.

Cybelle reached out, and the doll floated into her arms.

When Lavinia entered the nursery, all three children turned to her, each with a different expression. She saw exhilaration, guilt and puzzlement.

"Mummy!" James hurried over and hugged her legs.

Stuart straightened and looked at the floor, still clutching the ball. Not as cocky as his father, Yasir—yet.

"I came to read you a bedtime story." Lavinia addressed them as if nothing had happened. She walked over to Stuart and said in a low voice, "Thank you for saving Cybelle's doll."

Stuart looked at his feet, then raised his head, but didn't meet her eyes.

"I hope that you would have done so, even if you hadn't seen me by the door. You're the big brother and the only one with magic. I'm glad you remembered our talk about responsibility."

"Yes, Mum." Stuart looked at her, a glum expression souring his face.

Lavinia took Cybelle by the hand. "We'll be back in a moment. Stuart, you may choose the book for me." It had been difficult to keep Stuart's magic a secret these years. He knew not to do tricks when anyone could see, but just now he had forgotten to close the nursery door. She must have yet another little talk with him.

In Cybelle's room, Lavinia sat the child on her lap facing her. Yasir said he was hers. Perhaps she had magic. "Dear, did Stuart make your dolly fly to the ceiling?"

The child held the doll to her chest and turned her head away. Lavinia had never heard her speak. When asked a question, Cybelle would nod or look in the other direction. Even her brothers couldn't persuade her to say anything.

Lavinia tried again, making the question simpler. Perhaps Cybelle still had trouble understanding. "Did Stuart make Dolly move?"

The child set the doll in her lap, making sure the bonnet was straight, careful to have her looking at Lavinia. Yet Cybelle kept her eyes down. Her lips moved, but no sound came. Then she took a deep breath and exhaled. Her little chest heaved under her embroidered frock.

Cybie looked up at her. The child's eyes were even bluer than her own. Cybelle smiled. Her face shone.

Lavinia had the oddest feeling, a sensation she received when her bit of clairvoyance set into play. Stuart hadn't met her eyes, but admitted to doing magic. However, he could have been ashamed that his baby sister bested him. His admission might have been to save face and avoid a scolding.

Did Cybelle's brilliant smile mean yes? Or did the child have indigestion?

Quarter to nine read the long case clock in the sitting room near the garden. Peter would be waiting. Why all the mystery? But her assignation took second place to what had happened after Peter left dinner.

As she walked through the house, Lavinia couldn't shake her perception about Cybelle. The child hadn't said a word, only smiled, but that smile had a special glow. Yasir would take Cybelle's reaction as proof she was his and could do magic. And Lavinia's feeling would justify it. After all, the djinni respected Lavinia's talent, as he called her bit of clairvoyance. She had seen the worry in his golden eyes that Cybelle had nothing of the Djinn. The possibility that the child was Peter's had become a recurring thought in the turmoil of Lavinia's mind.

She paused as she exited the French doors, careful of the lamp in her hand. Odd that the garden lights weren't lit tonight.

She passed a shadowed bench almost hidden by overhanging branches. At the sharp, unnerving hoot of an owl, the oil lamp's flame wobbled with the jerk of her hand. She clutched her shawl about her shoulders and held the lamp level, the bright flame steadying in the quiet night, but it made no difference in the strange light that flooded the garden's flagstone path. A full moon. She looked up through the trees into the bright sky.

The moon shone blood red.

The shatter of the glass shade on the flagstones broke the quiet. Lavinia held still while the pieces clattered around her feet as if her stillness might make the lamp reassemble. The shards glistened, reflecting the red moonlight. Warm lamp oil trickled onto the smooth stones, a dark stain like the seep from a wound. She stared at the sky, her mouth agape. Her shawl slipped down her back.

Sensitive to portents of any kind since her time with the gypsies, her mind sought associations. Did the red moon have to do with Cybelle? Had the child made her own magic? Or with Yasir, her djinni returned to her three years ago? She went through the list of his enemies and, by association, hers: Rakhshan, Dark Magician, who had imprisoned Yasir in the urn, making him a slave to whoever opened it; Saddani, Rakhshan's minion; and, on occasion, her husband, Lord Peter Bramley. But that was in the past. Now, after Yasir's long absence, she and Peter were successfully husband and wife.

So far, she had managed to keep the djinni a secret from him.

She closed her eyes for a moment at the dull pain of a headache beginning in her temple. Yasir had spell-cast Peter to give her the urn, to forget he was master first, to forget he had found the djinni embracing her in the garden, and shot Yasir. But Yasir's spells could be erratic. Whenever she envisioned Peter remembering and finding the djinni in her possession, it was like this red moon—unpredictable, unimaginable.

Lavinia stepped around the remnants of her lamp and hurried along the path, the eerie moonlight illumining her way. She pulled her shawl close against the chill damp.

Her mind kept wandering, awakened into worry by this portent. She had forgotten to add Meylo, the boy from the river, to her list of enemies. He had learned there was something about the urn she wanted kept from her husband, and had threatened to tell Peter she had the vessel.

Why, the boy believed she could curse him. And she had encouraged it, to try and keep him quiet about the urn. This uncouth street urchin, given to saying anything he thought, could cause her trouble. But he was long gone. Perhaps even deceased. Yet Meylo stayed in her thoughts.

When the boy saw this moon, would he blame her? Like the servants at Bramley House, he could spread rumors of her supposed witchery. Rumors that would circulate through the countryside to the city, from lowly servants to the great English houses, all because of the djinni and the urn. The servants had gossiped when, in her temporary madness, she had roamed Bramley House and its grounds, the urn clutched to her chest like an infant, mourning her child, mourning Yasir. Both believed dead. Why, she had even stabbed her husband. She was thankful Peter survived, although at the time she wished he hadn't.

She hurried towards the replica of the Temple of Hercules Victor, one of Peter's obsessions a few years ago when he had sections of the garden redesigned. A compact Roman temple in the round, it had become her peaceful refuge.

An image of Stuart rose in her mind. Dark curly hair and blue eyes just like his brother and sister, just like her. Not golden eyes like Yasir's, thank the angels in heaven. Stuart, bless his mischievous heart, was not an enemy, but his magic . . . And now perhaps his sister's. If Peter found out, what could she possibly say? Her younger, James, Peter's son, was a loving little child with no magic.

She shivered in the night air and tucked both hands under her shawl. Refusing to look at the sky, she paid attention to the shrubs and night flowers, which were monotone with a red tinge from the moonlight. When she glimpsed the slender Corinthian columns and gleaming dome of the temple reflected in the lake's placid water, she exhaled in relief.

Lavinia stepped onto the lawn below the edifice and halted, stiff with horror. At the top of the hill near the front of the temple, shadowy against the white marble, was a creature, all legs and protuberances. *Saints and angels*, the Guardian from the urn. She ran her hand down her arm. No trace of the stinging wound the creature had inflicted. She picked up her skirts to flee.

A deep voice sounded in her ear as if someone were standing next to her. ". . . predictions and calculations for this event in an ancient scroll I purchased in the Cairo bazaar. Full of the most fascinating text. This scroll is genuine, untampered."

It was Peter, just ahead of her in the temple, his voice magnified somehow, a freakish combination of the acoustics of the building's marble, the damp air and the lake. The contraption that she mistook for a monstrosity must be part of his experiment. Peter, as usual, fiddling with the scientific as well as his beloved antiquities. She walked up the hill.

"Milady, his lordship asked if you would wait in the portico for a moment." Dobson, the butler, ushered her up the circular steps. From here the lake shimmered, the red moon playing on its surface. By now she had guessed Peter's surprise would be the red moon. How on earth did he expect her not to notice the thing hovering over her head like a bloody indictment?

She needed to settle. The odd night, the moon, the incident with Cybelle. The years of keeping the secret of Yasir from Peter. Her guilt about it. The way Peter had treated her after she opened the urn. Surely she had forgiven him? After all, his actions reflected Yasir's spells on him. Or had they?

"Milady, if you please to sit." Dobson set an ornate wicker lawn chair beside her.

"She won't need that now." Peter strode over and took her by the hand. "Lavy, come see." He led her across the lawn to the monstrosity. Just as she surmised, one of Peter's newfangled scientific contraptions. Sometimes she had to stifle a smile at his boyish enthusiasm. So now she would humor him.

"Whatever is that?" Lavinia indicated the insect-like apparatus on the lawn at the top of the hill.

"A telescope. An instrument to view the heavenly bodies at close range." Peter's voice rang with pride.

"It gave me a start. I've never seen one like this." She took Peter's arm.

Dobson lit the way with a lantern, and they walked to the long mahogany tube with brass fittings set upon a tripod. Behind them in the columned portico, a footman arranged cases and bags with the occasional bump ringing out over the lake.

Peter bent at the waist, looked through the cylinder, adjusted the angle slightly, then rotated the first ring at the front. "Perfect." He stood up from behind the telescope. "Please, take a look."

Lavinia put her eye to it, just as Peter had. "The moon. Oh! It has pocks." She stepped back and looked at the moon far away without the aid of Peter's contraption. "Why is it red?"

"A lunar eclipse, Lavy. The shadow of the earth hides the moon. Before the moon disappears and after it reappears, the atmosphere of the earth colors it." He motioned Dobson to set the flickering lantern on the ground and indicated when it was positioned as he wished. The brass and polished wood glimmered. "A unique event. I found no indication of it in the usual astronomical records, or even from my own measurements."

"Yet you knew the time of it." Lavinia looked at the moon again. Would that she hadn't. She flinched as though the icy hand at the back of her neck were real. The moon had grown redder, a bloody disk floating above them all. She could only guess at the meaning of all this, but it wasn't, couldn't be, good.

"I had help from ancient records. I do put my antiquities to work. They aren't all for show." Peter pressed his lips together. He sounded petulant.

"Of course not. You are advancing science and history with your discoveries." Lavinia brushed his cheek with a kiss. For some reason, Peter had the idea that she disdained his passion for antiquities, when it was the endless explorations in Egypt and India and other godforsaken places, the times he left her alone, that she hated. How could she feel anything but pleased at his love of antiquities?

It had brought her Yasir.

But in other moods, she had cursed the moment when the djinni had entered their lives. In a fit of pique, she had destroyed one of Peter's artifacts from Egypt. Apparently, she had taken one that he hadn't yet catalogued and he blamed the shipping company for losing it.

But Peter was being stingy with his information. What was he keeping from her? The lantern glow lit his face. His ice-blue eyes in the light looked almost erased but for the dark pupils, giving him an otherworldly stare. His pale complexion and flaxen hair contributed to his ghostly appearance this night. When in ordinary daylight, his features were handsome, his eyes a complement to his fair hair and complexion.

"Peter, I would . . ." But it somehow felt wrong to ask him to expound on the manuscript where he found the information about the eclipse.

"Do you want to view the moon again? You might see the first hint of the sun's shadow that will soon obliterate it," he said, excitement building in his voice.

She must have looked shocked.

"Not literally. It's just a shadow that blacks out the moon, then the shadow leaves. But it put native peoples who didn't know the secret in dire straits. Some thought the world was ending. Pretty frightening stuff. You can only just imagine."

She watched him open the chest by the telescope and rummage through, finally pulling out a piece that he used to fine-tune the instrument. Something about him tonight . . . She put her finger to her lips. She would be sure to look for this ancient record. Peter's study had a huge cabinet with all sizes of compartments, each with its own locked door, each with its own key. She could hardly lift the key ring to remove one. Ancient furniture for ancient pieces. The manuscript must be in there. Or if she went to his study soon, the text would be on his desk.

Most probably it was written in Greek or some other impossible-to-read script. But it shouldn't be a problem. After all, she had a djinni.

She forced herself to look through the telescope again. The scarred celestial body seemed to pulse like a heartbeat. She laid her hand on her chest. Her heart thumped faster. What other secrets had this manuscript revealed?

Things Peter shouldn't, mustn't know?

4

*M*eylo watched the river sparkle in the early morning sunlight, and kicked at the dried mud in front of him. He blew out a long breath. Hard to believe that after three years, it still looked like a hog wallow. He never figured out why the Lady Lavinia had thrown the bottle in the river if she wanted it so badly.

She'd stood just here, eyeing that bottle in his hands with those big blue eyes, the oh-so-proper lady of the great house. To his surprise, her face had contorted in a scream and she'd landed on top of him with a grunt. She wasn't so fancy streaked with mud, desperate for the bottle he held.

He shrugged his shoulders, trying to rid the damp that had settled on him. All he needed to do was go to the big house and beg the Lady Lavinia to take that curse off him. It had all seemed so simple when he thought of it, the red moon hanging over him like a threat.

"Lady." Meylo bowed his head. He'd combed his hair with his hands, wetted it down with river water nice and neat. "Could you spare a bit o' bread?"

The old lady called Cook wiped her hands on her apron and stared. He was lucky she was the one that opened the door.

"You look familiar. Hmm. Well, I can't rightly place you." She eyed him for a moment, then her face lit up all shiny. "You–you're the boy that saved milady. Only you're a strapping young lad now." She grinned. "But you still have those freckles."

Looks like the Lady Lavinia had told everyone that he kept her from drowning. She couldn't tell them she just walked into the water, her mouth open so wide a fish could have swum in. Those full skirts almost drowned her before she even went under for the bottle.

He nodded at Cook, all shy-like. She led him into the kitchen. A maid rushed by with a bowl of peeled potatoes. Another, her hands all floury, kneaded dough on a wooden board. Meylo jumped at a clatter in the hall, but it was only a footman holding a tray stacked with dishes. Pots boiled on the big stove, bubbling as the steam rose and hung on the ceiling. Meylo felt his shoulders go slack. He'd been holding his whole body stiff from the cool damp outside and the kitchen was warm as a sleeping dog.

"Sit here, breakfast is just finished." Cook pulled a chair from a table tucked into the corner and bustled away, but was back in a second, leaning her head to his ear, nearly scaring him out of his wits.

"Not a word, ye hear?" She set a plate of bread, butter, and a cup of milk before him. His stomach gurgled almost as loud as the talk of the maids.

He raised his eyebrows to thank her, and Cook rushed off. He would have to wait now. Be like one of those birds that you can't see until you almost step on them. He pushed his chair further into the shadows of the nook. Girls scarce out of nappies washed dishes, handling the plates like they were the Queen's. With her red hands on her hips, Cook was worse than a tavern wench, eyeing the kitchen maids already busy with fixing the midday meal, shelling peas, peeling potatoes and cutting and pounding meat.

Meylo smeared a piece of bread with butter. He chewed the morsel as slow as he could, trying not to cram it all into his mouth at once, and snuggled into his hidey corner, chuckling to himself. No one noticed him. The warmth from the ovens, the clangs from the pots and pans—it was like a real home. Safe. The sweet butter melted on his tongue.

Would the fancy lady of the house witch him with another spell for coming back?

He rubbed his ear, hearing her angry shrilling from that time. Seeing her fury build in the flush of her face, the crease between her brows, before she jumped on him at the river, grabbing for that bottle. He blinked as he took a bite of the warm bread, his thoughts arranging in an order he'd never figured before—If she was a witch, she would have witched him then. Made him disappear, or turned him into a frog that wouldn't even want the bottle. If she couldn't do any of those things, then how could she make the moon turn red, or sic the robbers on him?

He slurped the bubbly milk, the tight knot in his gut loosening. Leaning back in his chair, he propped his hands behind his head. The Lady Lavinia couldn't really witch him. Funny how this was the first time he'd thought it through. Here, in her house, where he felt strangely at home in the warm kitchen. The witching stories were hearsay. All the other just bad luck, like the rest of his life.

Maybe he could change it.

Now he didn't have to beg her to remove the curse, because there wasn't one. But he needed money and he knew how he could get more of it.

He licked his fingers and looked up. *Cor!* Is that scowley lady heading this way? He put his head down, but kept his eye on her as he thought up excuses for being in the kitchen of a great house. Keys jangling, she hurried past. Under the table, he bent two middle fingers to his palm, making the horn sign to ward off the evil eye with his index and little finger. Just then, the clump of maids in the corner hushed their giggles and gossip as a gravelly voice spoke. "Girls, mind that the mistress is keeping to her rooms, so do the first floor at tea time."

Without scraping the chair, he stood and slunk along the wall like a shadow, then slipped up the servants' stairs to the second floor. He swallowed a couple of times. *Criminy,* why did it feel like the last chew of bread stuck in his throat?

At the room with the fancy gold stuff around the white door, the latch released without a sound. He held it open just a crack to the scent of some kind of flowery smell. Heard a sigh and a rustle. Holding his breath, he opened the door wider. And there she was, sitting pretty as you please in a chair by the window. Looking different all dressed like a doll, her dark hair swirled on her head with pearl clasps, no mud on her pretty face or smeared on her clothes. She bent over to fetch something from a basket.

It was now or never. He straightened his shoulders and crept up behind her chair. When he laid his hand over her mouth, her body jerked like a scared rabbit.

"Don't scream," he said, and swiveled to her side, keeping his hand in place. "It's me, Meylo." Her eyes were blue, so blue, and wide as the sky. Too bad he scared her. "I'm back." He grinned. "I forgot something."

She frowned and tried to wrench away. He tightened his hand on her mouth. "That bottle." Her eyes widened. "I want it."

She exhaled hard, as if she were swearing at him.

"Or, I can have a little talk with that lord of yours. I know he'd like to hear 'bout the fun time we had at the river, 'bout the bob you give me. I can tell him all 'bout the bottle."

She stamped her foot, but missed him. Her eyes had grown bigger than the shooters in his games of marbles—she was scared of her husband, scared of him knowing.

"So you wanna fight agin?"

She shook her head, short tight jerks.

"If you scream, you'll make it easier fer me to talk to the man of the house. Bet you haven't told him you have that bottle."

The lady jumped out of the chair and he stumbled backwards. He spread his arms to keep his balance. *Criminy,* how'd she do that?

She grabbed his arm and twirled him around. "Get out, you little rat." She pushed him towards the door.

He turned and almost tripped over his own feet. "I'll tell the servants and everyone I see 'bout yer witchy powers." He would make her think she had him hoodwinked, that he still thought she was a witch. He stood straight and looked her in the eyes.

Still, no telling what she might do, the crazy lady. "I seen that red moon." He took a step towards her. "And I'll tell the master, tell him about yer witchy powers and that bottle."

"You won't be able to see him. You're just a peasant lad. Even if you managed it, he wouldn't believe you." She stood her ground.

"But the servants remember, don't they? They remember me—the hero. I saved you from drownding." He lowered his voice. If someone heard him, it would be over. "Wonder why you ever told them that? Guess you couldn't even tell *them* 'bout the bottle."

"So what. I helped a beggar boy, who saved me." She looked up at him, her eyes full of anger.

She wasn't scared any more. He had to be careful now.

"He'll believe me." He felt his cheeks burn when his voice came out squeaky.

"You have no proof. Nothing."

"I can tell him wot the bottle looked like. I saw it good. Bet he's seen it afore."

The lady paused, her eyes softened. Ah, he had her, but why would she be so scared for her man to learn about a dumb bottle?

"You're wrong. It's just a bauble." She was trying to make him think she didn't care. But her eyes still looked afraid. Bring up the switch now. Trade the dumb bottle for boodle.

"See I've got nothing." He turned out his pockets and a silver cylinder fell to the floor. "Was robbed the night of that red moon. Them men 'bout slit my throat." He gulped.

She was looking at the floor, her eyes wider than fried eggs. He looked down where she stared, a little to his side. On the floor lay the silver piece he'd found under the kitchen table.

She swooped down for it, but he got it first. Flaming fast was what he was.

"Where did you find that?" her voice had gone deep, with that tone that meant he'd done something blooming bad.

"I-in the kitchen under that little table in the corner." He held the thing in his palm and looked at it. Just a small silver bit with some rings on it and flowery designs. Pretty. He could sell—

She lunged for him, and almost snatched it from his palm. But he closed his fingers into a fist and held the silver bit to his chest.

"You want this little thing? It'll cost you five bob, plus the twenty I want fer not telling the lord 'bout the bottle." He bounced his fist up and down, the cylinder tingling his palm. Little shivers crawled up his arm. Was this silver piece some kind of luck charm?

"Wait here." The lady turned away.

"You little rat," she said under her breath.

In her dressing room, Lavinia stroked the ruby. Yasir appeared.

"Mastara." He bowed, a short stiff movement. She stepped back, trying to clear her head.

"The boy from the river. He's back and he, he—" She took a breath. "He has my talisman from the Chovihano." Lavinia put her hand to her throat, feeling the jittery buzzing from when she first touched the talisman on her necklace from the gypsy king.

"When I returned from the urn after your body vanished, Peter had Fleming sweep up the beads from my broken necklace. We never found the talisman. The boy, Meylo, wants money for it. A-and he's threatening to tell Peter about the urn." She crossed her arms over her chest and said in disgust, "The little rat."

"What does the boy know about the urn?" Yasir stood very still. She felt his energy gather, heavy and threatening like the oppressive atmosphere before a violent storm.

"He knows it means a lot to me. I gave him a shilling for it." Lavinia looked behind her at the closed door. "He's in my chamber now. Demanding money."

"My talisman. What does it mean that Meylo has it? Could it somehow cause Peter . . . oh Yasir . . . could it make him remember? You have to do something. I couldn't have him remember. Take it from the boy."

"I will see to the matter." As Yasir walked towards the closed door, his body blurred and faded into the wood.

"Criminy!" She heard Meylo's voice, almost a shriek.

Before Yasir vanished, his face had been fierce with anger. When the boy beheld the djinni in all his glory—his tunic and cloth of gold pantaloons, his jeweled headband and rings on every finger glittering as if illumined from within—Meylo would surely flee.

There was silence. Then Yasir spoke. His voice was low. She couldn't understand what he said, and she didn't hear Meylo. All went quiet. She waited. It seemed a long time. Lavinia put her ear to the door and heard a slight shuffling.

"Criminy!" Meylo blinked hard. He had seen a smudgy shape come through the door, but now a man, solid and real, stood before him in circus clothes all glittery with jewels. And those eyes, something odd about them.

"Give the lady the talisman." The man spoke in a deep voice with one of those accents. A foreigner.

"She has to pay me fer it. I told her. I got robbed." Meylo backed towards the door to the hall.

"It is hers and you found it in this house." The spangly man's eyes turned all golden, with a black slit in the middle. *Bloody hell*. Eyes like a goat's, like the devil's. Eyes that curse.

"Hey, let go." *Cor*, the man had him by the blooming collar. Meylo patted his pocket, the talisman was still there. It sent a fuzzy feeling through him, like he'd drunk bad beer. Why did he stagger? He looked down, his legs cramping so that he couldn't walk, his toes long, skinny and pink.

He screamed. Gray fur stuck through his pants as his legs shrank. He put his hands to his face to scratch the horrible itching.

"S'blood!" His fingers, his hands! Tiny claws with pink fingers like bones. He felt his nose—pointed with scratchy whiskers.

"Ahhh! Mister, I jus' want the money. Help me!" But the man frowned and looked at his hands, as if he had nothing to do with it. Just like one of those circus fellows, all show with people doing their tricks for them behind the curtain. A fake. But then w••hat was happening to his own body? This wasn't fake.

Meylo looked up. Why had the man grown so large, like a giant? And the furniture. One of the chair legs as big as a tree. He moved his body from side to side. Jerked his head back at a blur behind him. A hairless pink tail, like a thin worm. He grabbed it and flinched. *His* tail.

"Noooo. Help me!" But all that came out was a loud squeak.

The silver talisman lay in front of him, bigger around than his legs. He wouldn't let them have it. He clawed the talisman towards him. Opened his mouth as wide as he could. The silver. Cold. His teeth crimped into it, and he scampered away.

Lavinia turned the handle and slowly swung the door open to her bedroom. Yasir stood there looking at the floor, hands behind his back.

"Where is Meylo?" She peered around the room.

Yasir swiveled towards her, eyes glittering. Curling one hand into a fist, he placed it in his palm.

"Whatever happened?" Lavinia checked the room again. "He got away? How could you let him? He will threaten us."

"By the Djinn. The Chovihano's power is greater than I imagined. A Gypsy King. His humility the mark of a great soul, a magic unparalleled." Yasir walked to the window and opened it, the cool air chasing the stuffiness from the room.

"What are you talking about? Meylo has nothing to do with those gypsies. Why, he's just a street urchin." What had gotten into Yasir? Why all this talk about the Chovihano?

"Lavinia, Meylo had your talisman. *Your* talisman. You desired it, and he wouldn't let you have it."

"Yes, I told you that. So?"

"What was the last thing you said to Meylo?"

Lavinia put her hand to her chin and looked up at the ceiling. "Um. . .Wait here."

"Did you say anything else—or have a particularly strong thought before you came into your dressing room and called me?"

She gave him a sheepish look. "I was angry, so angry. He could ruin us. Ruin us. I . . . Under my breath, I called him a *little rat*." She crossed her arms over her chest and gave him a *so there* look.

Yasir steered her to a chair. "Sit down."

"I am perfectly happy standing."

He pushed her into the chair.

"Yasir!" She put her hands on the arms to rise.

"Listen to what I say before you stand."

She settled into the chair with a sigh. Yasir could be so taxing. He moved away from her and stood near the window.

"When the talisman came into your presence and you called to it, the person preventing it from going to you—Meylo—became the object of its spell. And the talisman obliged you." Facing her, Yasir leaned back onto the windowsill, light sparkling on dark strands of his hair.

"What do you mean?" Lavinia bent forward.

"The talisman transformed Meylo into a little rat. A mouse. He snatched it in his mouth and ran away."

Lavinia gaped at him. "Don't toy with me Yasir. This is an important matter. We can't have the boy go to Peter. We—"

Yasir suddenly stood by her side. She didn't see him walk to her. Only a blur, and he was looking into her eyes. He took her hands. "Lavinia, Meylo transformed into a mouse before my eyes. I cast no spell. I only conversed with him for a minute or less by your time. No one was more surprised—well perhaps the boy was—than I. To have magic occur in front of me, its source unknown. I was confounded."

"Until I realized the talisman was a gift from the Chovihano for protection when you lived with the gypsies. Now you know they were not your enemies, that they saved you from Saddani and the Dark Magician. I recalled the strength I found in the charm when I first saw it on your blue-bead necklace. It was then I knew that the talisman had worked the Chovihano's magic to protect you."

Lavinia stood up, wriggling from his grasp. "You mean I—" She clapped her hand to her mouth and sat back down. "I turned the boy into a mouse?" She looked up at Yasir, glaring at him. "If you are teasing me. If this is your idea of a humorous little trick. I am master, swear to me that it happened."

"No it is not a trick. I was as perplexed as you. I swear it happened. The boy changed into a mouse and ran off."

Lavinia took the djinni's hand. "He's a little scamp, but he doesn't deserve that. Change him back."

"Only the Chovihano can do that." Yasir spread his fingers as if he would cast a spell. "Unless we can obtain the talisman. That is the only way. The Roma king is our friend, but his camp and his gypsies are watched. I dare not chance alerting the Dark Magician."

5

The next morning, after a brisk ride through the meadow on Maze, her chestnut mare, Lavinia breezed into her room. Just inside she looked around.

"Meylo, come out. I won't hurt you. Bring me the talisman. I can help you." Had Yasir lied to her about the boy? Had he turned him into a mouse or just sent him away? But why such a tall tale? She was master and had challenged him. He swore it was the truth.

"Meylo, I'll make it right." The dead silence scared her. She would find the mouse and change Meylo back. She just hoped it would be before something bigger and fiercer found him.

She pulled off her leather riding gloves, tossed them on the receiving table by door and glanced at the mail tray, which was empty. Her fingers tangled in her hair as she swept it from her face. In the wind at full gallop, she'd lost some of her pins. It had been lonely riding without Peter, and she wouldn't risk riding with Yasir. There was always the possibility someone would see them together.

She missed Peter, who was checking his land holdings in Scotland, and wasn't expected back for days. Before her husband's departure, she had met with Yasir in the urn and voiced her suspicions about Cybelle's actions in the nursery.

His eyes had brightened. He agreed that Stuart could have owned doing the magic because he was embarrassed his baby sister bested him. Yasir knew Lavinia wanted their daughter to have his magic, that her wanting it made it so in her mind. The sadness in his voice hurt her heart as he explained that half-Djinn children sometimes received characteristics solely from their human parent, and had no powers.

A fuzzy sensation ran up her arms. Profound disappointment, a kind of defeat, made her bow her head. Her baby Cybelle, ordinary and perhaps a little simple. A beautiful child, but oh, how she wanted her only girl to be so very special, a djinniyi, like Lavinia's aunt Alice, half sister to Yasir. To work magic, to have that power.

His expression stony, Yasir had turned to watch the children play hide and seek in the park he had conjured for them in the urn. Sam was what they called Yasir. The same name as the friendly young under groom in the Bramley House stables who gave the children candy when they visited. Lavinia never used the name Yasir around them. The djinni was always Sam. If Peter heard them speak of Sam with fondness, he wouldn't give it a second thought.

Almost seven years ago, Peter had found her embracing Yasir in the garden and shot the djinni, thinking he was a gypsy. Now Lavinia was careful to call Yasir only when she was sure no one would see him. These three years since the djinni had returned, she had managed to keep the balance in her relationship with her husband, and with Yasir. She would allow nothing to upset it.

Lavinia walked into her dressing room and closed the door. She wanted no interruptions at what she was about to do. Fleming knew to knock and wait for permission to enter; if there was no answer the maid would leave. At her toilette table, Lavinia removed the pins that survived the windy ride and brushed tangles from her hair, keeping the urn, set amongst her bottles and jars, in sight.

With a last look in the mirror, she set the brass vessel—heavier than it looked—in front of her. Amazing that Yasir's huge palace could fit inside a container almost as tall and a bit wider than the wine bottles in the cellar. She placed her finger on the hinged lid, clasped by a latch rendered as a slender brass vine that curled along the top forming an exquisite knob of intertwined leaves. An engraved inscription in what looked like cuneiform spiraled around the body to the base.

When she first opened the urn, years ago, she had been terrified when Yasir appeared. Then she had become fascinated by his strangeness. The extraordinary way he transformed from a wisp of smoke into a solid, flesh-and-blood man. The most beautiful man she had ever seen or imagined, his body sculpted like a classical Greek statue, his skin dusky with a golden glow. Encircling his waist and hips were peculiar dark gold markings similar to a tiger's stripes, diminishing in points at his midsection. When he moved they shone with a tremulous light, reminding her he wasn't human, but a creature unlike any she had ever known, a creature as exotic as a unicorn or a centaur.

Now, she had grown less afraid and felt a tingle of anticipation when she touched the warm metal of the urn.

She unclasped the lid and raised it. Spirals of white smoke unfurled, rising into the air, falling onto the floor, then thickening in a dense column. A shadow marred the white billows. Her djinni appearing in answer to her summons—at times instantaneous as if he had slipped through an unseen door, other times doggedly slow, the smoke embracing him like a reluctant lover.

It always took her breath away.

How I chafe at the endless millennia of my enslavement in the urn.

I have heard naught from my father, Zamyad al Din the Supreme Djinni, Pearl of Sovereigns, but I suspect he sent Alice to aid me. I am making slow inroads. After centuries, at last I have found my lost love Thalia, reincarnated as Lavinia.

Still, I wait for her as always, wait for her summons, for now she is my master. By Lavinia's whim, I am freed from this urn until she orders me to return.

When I go to her, I transform from smoke into the human body she identifies as Yasir. But I am so much more.

So powerful.

But powerless.

I am the Great Djinni Yasir, imprisoned by Rakhshan, a human magician who, by some mysterious dark magic lives through the centuries. How he overcame my power, I can only surmise. The irony is that Thalia was Rakhshan's daughter. The magician became incensed when she claimed me as her betrothed. Jealous of my powers, hating the Djinn, and enraged at his daughter's defiance, he cursed me to the urn.

I am closer than ever to my freedom. The prophecy states that one of our children will defeat Rakhshan and liberate me. But when Lavinia realized it did not predict whether our child would survive the ordeal, I promised I would fight Rakhshan in our child's place. When the Dark Lord cursed me, I was young and foolish. Now I am older and wiser, with powers stronger than a mere human magician.

I can win.

There is a thorn in my side—Lavinia's husband, Lord Peter Bramley. At the moment he is traveling, giving us a respite. I would that he were out of my life, out of Lavinia's life, but he plays a part here, a decoy father to our children. Peter believes that Little Cybelle and Stuart are his. Under the protection of this influential lord, they are safe from Rakhshan.

Lavinia and I have escaped detection by the Dark Magician. So far.

He had almost forgotten about me, about the urn, until he heard of the prophecy.

She calls . . .

She couldn't move her gaze from his.

"Mastara, how may I serve you?" Yasir bowed, an expression of longing in his golden eyes.

She walked to him, though it seemed as though she glided on air.

The djinni held her in his arms. Enveloped in the fragrance of cinnamon, myrrh and bergamot, his soft lips on hers, she felt the power of his magic threading through her.

His black hair fell to his shoulders in thick curls, the upper part woven in intricate designs kept in place by a golden band inset with fiery stones. The thick golden hoops of his earrings gleamed by his jaw line. The beauty of the feminine mingled with the strength of the masculine in the flared nostrils of his straight nose and full curved lips.

The vertical slits of his pupils, like a serpent's, changed to round pools of black as he gazed at her.

She spoke in a breathless whisper. "Yasir. Take me to your urn. I have missed you so—"

That odd feeling of acceleration stole her words, a feeling that she flew impossibly fast, faster than her carriage, faster than when she spurred Maze to the mare's swiftest gallop.

The gilded door to Yasir's rooms in the urn blazed in front of her. She looked askance at the niche in the wall to the left. It wasn't there before. Neither was that sculpture of a hideous creature perching inside as though it might suddenly leap out if one made the wrong move. She peered closer at the crocodile head crowned in a lion's mane, its bulky hippopotamus body with lion's legs, the huge paws bristling with sharp claws. Her eyes followed the hieroglyphics inscribed in a turquoise faience arch above the niche.

What else did she expect? Each time she came to the urn it was different. But this was too familiar. She didn't like seeing something similar to what Peter might have in his Egyptian room at Bramley House.

Yasir held out his hand, balancing a miniature blue glass flask with a glowing crystal top.

"For you," he said.

Lavinia took it from his palm and lifted the stopper. A watery stream of silver curved into the air and vanished, leaving a fragrance of such delicacy and deliciousness that she didn't know whether to drink it or apply it as perfume. She knew she looked puzzled, because he laughed.

"A potion to enhance our experience. In a moment we shall indulge." He had a devilish gleam in his eye, and she was almost afraid of her eagerness.

Yasir gestured in a graceful arc. The door opened without a sound. He placed his arm around her waist and escorted her inside. Clasping the potion with care, she took a last glance at the niche. Perhaps the hideous creature would be gone when she left.

"Bloody hell. Where is Lady Bramley?" Peter twitched as his valet, Stevens, looped and tied his cravat. He put his hand up to tear it away. He didn't need the blasted thing. Lavinia wasn't a stickler for tradition. However, he let his hand drop to his side. He wanted to look his best.

"Milord, I sent her maid to fetch Lady Bramley." Stevens straightened his master's coat in the back. "There, that should do."

"About time." Peter strode from his room. Why wouldn't Lavy come running as soon as she heard he had returned? He was early. She should be thrilled. And he had missed her. He looked forward to her bringing the children to greet him as usual.

He opened the door to her room. Tidy. Her embroidery by her chair. No gowns laid out. Her dressing room door closed. She must've already dressed for the day. Perhaps she was in his study with the children as a surprise. He stopped and picked up her riding gloves on the table by the door. Tomorrow morning they would take the horses out together. She liked that.

As he set the gloves down, something fell out in a flash of light. Fumbling, he caught the thing, but dropped a glove. He opened his palm. Her gold ring with the bright red ruby. A fine stone. Belonged to her mother. Lavinia must've snagged it inside her gloves when she removed them. Peter held it in his palm.

"Where are you Lavinia?" he said aloud to the room. A buzz vibrated through his hand as though the ring were an insect caught inside his fist. He started to open his palm when the oddest feeling passed through him. The room darkened, then vanished as though he had sped away from it. He had the sensation of being on a ship, sliding down an enormous wave. He thrust his other hand behind him to steady himself on the table, but nothing was there, and he fell, head over heels into a void, clutching the ring in his palm.

Peter raised his head. He was sprawled on the floor of a vast hallway. The tiles under him were amalgamations of precious and semiprecious stones, blue sapphire, mother-of-pearl, carnelian—a countless variety of stones and combinations. He stood. Dizzy, he wobbled and placed his hand on the wall. He pulled it away, the stone chilling him to the core. Yet the odd sparkle and directional golden light, as if the sun were hitting it, promised warmth. To his left a sizable niche had been scooped out of the marble.

He looked inside and raised an eyebrow in disbelief at the painted sculpture of the Egyptian demon Ammit, the soul eater—part lion, hippopotamus, and crocodile—the three largest man-eating animals known to ancient Egyptians. He had seen her image in tomb statues and wall paintings on his many expeditions to Egypt. If a person's heart, weighed on the scales of justice, was found to be impure, Ammit would devour it and the person would die a second time, leaving his soul restless forever.

He read the hieroglyphics in the blue faience arch above the niche: *Ammit, Of the World, Not of the World.*

What the deuce did that mean? Ammit was supposed to live in the underworld. Peter moved away from the niche and looked around. A door down the hall, formerly closed, was now open. A red light flickered from inside. It was quiet. Had he died suddenly? Was he to be judged?

"Where the bloody hell am I?" he whispered. He had imbibed one brandy while he was dressing. One brandy didn't make him drunk.

A gilded door caught his eye. He walked to it, fingered the glittering gold and started to touch the handle, which looked like quartz or diamond. *By God*, he still clutched Lavy's ring in his fist. He slipped it into his pocket and pushed down on the handle.

The room was a good size, with higher ceilings than the hall, painted with exotic scenes from some epic mythology that he didn't recognize. Multi-hued silken carpets threaded with gold and silver lay on areas of the parquet floor of exotic woods and mother-of-pearl. He walked past chests of silver and gold, and dressers with ivory tops holding cloisonné vases and crystal coffers. Opaque blown glass oil lamps hung from the ceiling glowing like moons.

He heard voices and ducked behind a massive gold sculpture with the sinuous body of a snake. The coils spiraled high overhead, ending in a fierce horned head with a beak and egg-sized rubies for eyes. Wings lined with diamonds spread from its body, the glimmer almost blinding. Six paces beyond, on an ebony platform, sat a huge bed shrouded in heavy brocade and gauze curtains. He heard vague murmurings and rustling.

Someone was in there

He crept nearer. Might as well make himself known. Unless he was dead, he had arrived here by accident and wanted to leave. Perhaps whoever it was could help him.

He felt his pockets for a weapon, but he had dressed for the day, not for battle. All he had was Lavinia's ring. From a side table he picked up a crystal carved into a vase, and hefted it—solid, heavy. It would do. He strode toward the bed, armed with a polite question, but ready for a hostile encounter.

A flap of the brocade curtain had caught in its own folds, exposing the gauze beneath. He could barely make out a couple in the throes of love making. He wouldn't be such a beast as to interrupt. He would give them time to finish. The woman raised her head, her black curls falling down her bare back, pale skin like alabaster, her profile—

Lord in heaven.

Lavinia.

No, just a strong resemblance. Besides, he had been looking for his wife before he ended up wherever this was. Of course he would mistake any similar-looking woman for her.

She murmured, breathless, to her partner, a dusky man with long dark hair. Then spoke aloud. "The strangest feeling suddenly came over me."

By God. Lavinia's voice.

His own wife. In bed with some darky.

Peter clenched his jaw as he tightened his grip on the crystal vase.

6

*P*eter stood over them.

"Lavinia. Have you lost your mind?" Keeping his eyes on his wife, he set the heavy crystal vase—his makeshift weapon—on the bedside table and dragged her from the bed.

She grinned as if she didn't know him, as though she were trying to figure out what was going on. Drunk. More than soused.

He took off his coat and threw it around her, covering her nakedness.

She stood in front of him. He could see it in her eyes, each stage occurring inside her head. She tried to figure out who he was. She had a glimmer, but it didn't catch. Tilted her head. Her mouth dropped open.

"Peter!" She stared at him, the blue of her eyes like glistening sapphires. She was so beautiful. Even as angry as he was, he found himself almost in tears. Why, oh why, was she with this blackguard?

He pushed her behind him, facing the man. He wouldn't be a bloody cuckold. The cad was sitting up in bed, even more foxed than Lavinia. An odd one, large and muscular. Peter doubted he could take him if he were sober. A gypsy? That dark hair, earrings, jewels.

"Who are you and what are you doing with my wife?" Peter shook him, ignoring the sudden jolt of vertigo as he clamped his hand around the gypsy's biceps. By God, he expected an answer, an excuse. The man stared just as Lavinia had. He didn't seem too concerned. What the devil had they been drinking?

Still, the fool had seduced Lavinia.

"Stand up and face me, damn it." Peter hauled him out of bed, then let go of the man. Sharp jabs of pain jittered up his arms. By God, it felt as if long needles had been jammed into his muscles.

The fellow stood there, wavering in a daze, his bare skin dusky with darker stripes around his hips, something like the markings on a tiger. Deuced half-breed of some sort.

Peter twisted his lips in distaste and punched the darky in the face. The gypsy fell backwards, striking his head on a life-sized gold statue of a nude woman. Peter rubbed his palms together in satisfaction.

"No." A faint voice behind him. A hand on his arm. Peter turned. Lavinia peered beyond him to the half-breed who struggled to his knees, swaying, his nakedness pathetically vulnerable. Peter looked from him to Lavinia.

"This gypsy? Really, Lavinia, you could do better." Peter clenched his fists. How could she do this to him? He pulled his leg back and raised his boot. "Let's see how he fares after a clout to the family jewels."

"No!" Lavinia hurled herself between them, throwing off his aim so his boot glanced her thigh. His leg swung freely, almost toppling him. She bent double and emitted a strangled scream.

"Damn it Lavy, get out of the way." He pushed her onto the bed.

The darky staggered to his feet, eyes half open.

"Dirty gypsy." Peter struck him in the face just as Lavinia rose from the mattress. Blood streamed from the man's nose and he rocked backwards. The bastard deserved more than a bloody nose. Peter curled his fists and raised his arms.

"Stop!" Lavinia tottered in front of Peter, arms flailing. His coat slid from her shoulders to the floor. "He's not a gypsy. Stop!"

Peter jerked her to the side. "Have you no shame woman?" He glanced at the red welt on her bare thigh and crushed one of the bed's silk coverlets to her chest. "Cover up. Move along. I'll deal with you later."

Lavinia wedged herself between them and latched onto his arm. Confounded minx.

"Don't hurt him. He's not a gypsy. He's a djinni!" she shrieked.

"I don't give a damn which tribe of gypsy." Peter glowered, drew to his full height and pulled her hand from his arm. "I'll finish him if it's the last thing I do. Then I'm taking you home."

"No. A djinni!" Lavinia pushed Peter away.

"What the blazes, Lavinia?" He started towards her.

Straightening, she looked him in the eye. "Get back."

"Or you'll do what?" Peter lurched for her. She shuffled backwards into the gypsy, who groaned.

"Leave him alone. He's from the urn you gave me." Her words tumbled over each other. "From Egypt." She threw herself at Peter, banging his chest with her fists.

"Leave him alone." A sob tore from her throat. "He's a djinni." Lavinia stamped her foot as she screamed. "Stop. Stop. Stop."

Peter stood still, looking from the gypsy to Lavinia. His mouth gaped. "A g-genie?" His lips had trouble with the word. Not only was his wife unfaithful, she had gone mad once more. His heart sank—the struggle back from the last bout almost undid him, not to mention the household. If madness could come over her this quickly, perhaps she had never been normal all this time.

"Yes, a djinni." She pushed her hair from her eyes and stood her ground, careful to keep between them.

"Lavinia, I thought you were over this, but underneath it all you're just as damn crazy as when you stabbed me. Bloody hell, you won't ruin us again." He would maim or kill this fellow, and take Lavinia back to where she belonged.

But Lavinia held out her arms, attempting to keep him from the darky. "Yasir, s-show him," she called out.

In a blur, the cad she called Yasir moved in front of her. *What the devil?* He was fully dressed in cloth-of-gold trousers and long tunic. His jeweled headband glimmered. His rings glowed. A *blasted* genie?

"What?" Peter jumped away, his fists out. "So you think to fight me for her?" He moved toward the gypsy. "I'll have that pretty crown."

The *pikey* flicked his hand. Like a sudden gale at sea, a brisk wind gusted through the room.

Peter struggled to keep his balance, but his feet flew out from under him and he was thrown against the far wall, sliding to the floor. He shook his head and got up, brushing his clothes.

"What is this devilry? Come and fight like a man. Or is that the wrong term for a genie? Or a gypsy who has hoodwinked my wife, taking advantage of her—her madness, her vulnerability to—" Peter saw Lavinia gape as she stared behind him.

He turned around.

A massive form materialized from shadows darkening the area next to the gold door.

He peered through the gloom and saw an amorphous blob inside a roiling storm cloud. Appendages pinched from the shape. Fragments of white, like porcelain, flashed through the black haze.

A deafening hiss filled the chamber, the sound of massive billows of steam blown from a locomotive's boiler. The mist thinned. Long rows of gleaming teeth, like scimitars, shone through the shadows and swirling mist.

Lavinia screamed.

The fellow she called Yasir—why did that name sound so familiar?—clamped his hand over her mouth, silencing her. He grasped Lavinia by the waist and swept them to the other side of the bed.

From the dark cloud, paws the size of a serving tray emerged and hooked claws gripped the parquet floor. Taut muscles rippled under tawny fur only to be enveloped in shadow again.

"God in heaven." Peter backed towards the opposite wall, searching for a weapon.

A rapid motion dispersed the murk. To Peter's horror, a fierce mythical monster sprang, salivating, into the center of the chamber. Its massive reptilian head jerked back and forth, rippling a shaggy yellow mane tipped with black. The creature stamped its thickset rear legs, rocking the floor with a boom of thunder. Hissing, the beast raised its head. Terrible red eyes sighted him.

Peter stared, not believing.

By all the gods of ancient Egypt. It was Ammit. Come to life.

The demon lowered her enormous crocodile snout, and splayed her paws wide on the wooden floor, bulky backside crouched low. She flapped her flat tail. The dull thwack, thwack, thwack made it hard for Peter to think.

Hell and blast, what he would give to have a gun.

He felt something cold, heavy in his hand. As his finger found a familiar curved shape, he glanced down. *God in heaven.* A Flintlock Dueling pistol.

He raised it.

Ammit sprang at him and knocked him to the floor. The pistol slid away.

Lavinia whirled around to face Yasir. Peter heard her say. "Remove this monster."

Yasir gestured to Ammit. The demon turned its expressionless eyes to the djinni and stamped her hippopotamus legs. But she didn't move.

One moment Peter saw Yasir next to Lavinia; the next instant the genie was beside the creature. Peter blinked as he lay helpless on the floor, the monster's great paws splayed on either side of his hips. He dared not move.

"Hoa, hoabim, kazib Ammit, sevara wern baopem." Yasir's voice held a tone of reverence. He bowed. Ammit cocked her head, opened and snapped shut her mouth with a loud crack of teeth.

"Yames sevara tun Djinn." The creature's snout, grotesque with warts, moved as it spoke, its voice gravelly, yet strangely refined.

Yasir looked at Peter, then Lavinia, and said loud enough for him to hear. "The Revered Ammit refuses to leave. The Great Goddess sees into your husband's heart—dark aspects. He came uninvited, an intruder who offers violence. She will be released from her ancient duty to punish the darkness inside him, if he convinces her he will do no harm to anyone here."

Peter steadied himself by inhaling deeply. Damn that pistol. If only he could have pulled the trigger. He would have been out of here with his wife.

The genie reappeared next to Lavinia. Peter heard him say, "I cannot turn The Revered Goddess from her path. She must be obeyed in this."

"This wouldn't have happened if we hadn't taken the potion." Lavinia was whispering, but he could hear her as if she were beside him. "You were so drunk with it you didn't know Peter had come into the urn."

If they kept up this banter, distracting Ammit, he could squirm out from under the monster and perhaps reach the door.

Yasir pulled Lavinia closer. "Did you show your husband the way here?" He spoke in a low voice.

Lavinia wriggled from Yasir's grasp. "What? You dare accuse me of undermining you? After all—" She stopped and looked directly at Peter.

Peter cocked his head. Lavinia realized he was listening. That he had heard every word. What didn't she want him to know?

Lavinia and Yasir were quiet. The beast turned her enormous head away from them. Her red eyes bored into Peter as he lay before her like an offering. Her curved claws scraped the floor beside him, a harsh grating sound that twisted his gut in terror. Peter felt the blood leave his face.

He must undo his aggressive move. He had to convince Ammit he wouldn't harm the bastard genie who tried to steal his wife. Neck stiff, eyes fixed upon the creature, he took a breath. His words needed to be clear and strong and, he hoped, sincere.

"I honor the Great Goddess Ammit." That was true. He had known this goddess from many different images throughout the years of his expeditions.

The beast's snout swayed above him. Her stench almost made him gag. The goddess took his arm in her lumpy snout. Her teeth rested gently on his flesh, tender but lethal.

Peter spoke fast. "My quarrel with the genie Yasir is ended. Yasir is master here. I honor him." Almost true. He wanted to leave with his wife; if it took honor he'd offer it.

Ammit applied more pressure. Peter clinched his jaw. Trickles of red ran between the sharp white teeth embedded in his arm. He felt the beast move. Leave now. Just go.

Quick. He needed another fact to convince her. "I have knelt before your image in Egypt during these last years. I have the same reverence for the genie." Absolutely true. In the tombs he was frequently on his knees excavating antiquities, amazing items that were once in the Pharaoh's palaces. And as for the genie, if what Lavinia said was true, why Yasir was one of those very treasures.

Ammit squinted at him. Was she nearing a decision? He held his breath.

She jerked her head right and left. Peter saw gobs of blood and bits of flesh fly from his arm. The pain bloomed, then rocketed through his body. He struggled to stay conscious.

Peter called out. "I beg his forgiveness. I beg Your Grace Ammit's forgiveness." *Bloody hell.* Perhaps he should have mentioned Ammit first. Why didn't he use a more flowery address?

"*Yames sevara tun Djinn.*" The creature spoke, his arm in her mouth.

Before he could jerk it out, the beast clamped down again, just hard enough to hold it. Through a haze of pain, he heard Yasir's voice.

"The great Ammit says there is one left who needs to forgive this man."

Lord in heaven. What should he do? Who could he get to—?

"I, Lavinia, Lady Bramley, forgive this man." Lavinia's voice.

Peter could see her. She had on a gown now. She looked pale. Before his eyes, she faded as if she were whitewashed.

The creature's jaws opened. A fresh wave of agony cleared Peter's vision as his arm slid from her grip. His blood pooled inside her mouth, dripping red between her crooked teeth. He saw his flesh stuck in the crevices.

She backed away with a searing hiss, her hot breath carrying the copper stench of his blood. He felt himself sinking, the horror of what transpired worsening his agony. Ammit was the Eater of Souls. She had tasted his flesh and blood.

Had she taken some of his soul?

Breathing hard, he watched as the ancient demon stepped through a far wall of the chamber as if it were a wafer-thin crust of ice.

Peter saw stars. He'd heard the saying but never experienced it, yet there they were in the darkness of his peripheral vision, bloody bright twinkling stars. He heard Lavinia's soft, sweet voice call his name. He heard his own, weak, barely there, say, "Lavy." The relief in his words made him feel better.

He opened his eyes. Her deep blue ones, shone with concern, when she saw his. She turned and called, "Yasir," but the genie had already knelt beside them.

Peter forced himself to look at his arm. Oh, Lord. He squeezed his one good fist tight, but still almost lost the contents of his stomach. He could feel the warm blood flow over his mangled flesh, his lacerated muscles. He may never have the use of his arm again. Then what could he offer Lavinia?

He looked up at Yasir, but the genie only stared at the wound. Peter forced his eyes to stay open as Yasir brought his hands near. He braced himself for the pain.

The blood left first, leaving the damage clear. Wounds like these meant amputation. Peter felt his brain go blank. All he'd done was go into Lavy's room to find her. That's all he'd done. He'd wake up from this. Soon. He would.

Wait, how did Yasir wipe the blood away? H-he saw with his own eyes, the lacerated muscles knit together, flesh closing over them as though a sculptor were remaking his arm. His arm felt numb, then warm, then comfortable. Without thinking he moved it, then gritted his teeth, waiting for the excruciating pain.

Nothing.

Peter looked up at the genie. By God, his eyes were golden.

Lavinia peered over Yasir's shoulder. She smiled. "Oh, Peter."

He hung on to those words, the love in her voice. He sat up. The dizziness caught him completely unaware and he grasped at Yasir as the room spun faster and faster until it wheeled away into black oblivion.

7

*L*avinia rose, but sank back to the floor next to her husband. Her hands, of their own accord, took the silk skirts of her gown and wiped at the blood. She had to remove it, stop it somehow. That sharp, sickening smell, red everywhere, gushing from Peter like a fountain. Her husband had appeared in the urn, caught her with Yasir, then almost died. The pain he suffered. All because of her. An eerie moan floated through the urn. *Her* cry. And the blood, coming faster now.

She felt an arm encircle her waist. "Let me go!" She struggled to get away. "The creature. See what she's done? See?" She looked into golden eyes, the pupils black as a cave.

"My *del ara*, you are safe."

"But, Yasir. The blood." She gestured at her husband, but now her gown, her arms, the floor, even Peter, were pristine. Not a drop of blood anywhere.

Yasir pushed wisps of her hair from her face. "Lavinia, Peter is safe. The blood you saw was an illusion, merely a result of what you have been through. For that I am sorry." He kissed her cheek, her forehead, and smoothed her hair.

She glanced at Peter on the floor next to her. The only sign of the horrid event was his lacerated shirt sleeve. She leaned close to Yasir, enveloped in his magic. What if the monster returned? Could Yasir send her away, or would he have to wait until it suited Ammit? Would the creature finish her husband off then?

Peter's tailcoat lay bunched on the floor near her. She reached for it. Not a spot of blood marred the fabric. She draped it around her shoulders, over the silken gown Yasir had conjured for her. When? She didn't remember in all the horror and terror. Just that she felt a soft cloth covering her body and didn't feel so cold on the outside anymore—only on the inside. He didn't conjure anything for that.

She hugged herself, picturing Peter fumbling in his fury, wrapping his coat over her shoulders, pulling it closed in front to cover her nakedness. He had placed her behind him with a gentle push. Then he had faced Yasir. Then Ammit. For her.

She caught her breath and realized that she was breathing normally for the first time since the horrid creature vanished. And in that small void of relief she sat straight, staring ahead as the thought took hold of her: *How on earth had Peter found his way inside the urn?*

Lavinia wobbled to standing, Yasir steadying her. She faced the djinni. "Shouldn't you put him on the divan where he will be more comfortable?"

"He should stay where he is for a time, let the healing work itself in." Yasir waved his hand and she was on the divan beside him, silken pillows stacked around her.

"Couldn't you have done more to help Peter? He's only human. Why didn't you interfere with Ammit? You could have stopped this." She let out a sob and sat up, shocked, then found her voice again.

"He was so brave, was in so much pain. How much did that cost him? To be brave for me, for you? My god, Yasir. How could you be so heartless?"

The djinni winced. "You told him I was a djinni, that he gave you the urn."

"Don't take that blaming tone. I had to. You and your potion. You said it would be wonderful, that we would ride on—"

"Did not the potion enhance your experience in our love-making?" Yasir's expression remained stern.

She gave him a sidelong glance. She had eagerly drunk the fragrant liquid. "Yes, I almost forgot after the awful . . ." She gestured at Peter. "After Ammit . . . and Peter. . ." She tried to vanquish the images from her mind, but they became more vivid. "Yasir, yes, yes the potion. I felt as if I were flying. It was marvelous." She kissed him on the cheek.

"But the potion made me more than drunk. I didn't even recognize Peter. And you . . . you were out of your head. Why, Peter could have killed you." Lavinia heard her voice jump to a higher register.

"Precisely why Ammit appeared." Yasir crossed his arms. "She appeared solely for the purpose of protecting me. I only discovered that when I addressed her." He looked to the side as if pondering something. "I do not control all that happens in the urn. I know not who sent Ammit. Perhaps she came of her on accord, she would not say. I did all I could without offending the Goddess. There is a protocol."

Of course, a protocol. Exasperated, Lavinia took a long breath, then let it out. You would think Yasir was a member of Parliament. "When I asked you to show Peter that you are a djinni, I thought you might conjure a fine horse or make it rain and then conjure a rainbow. Something to astonish him, not kill him. Not a-a monster."

"As I said, I did not conjure her. I conjured the wind, quite effective actually." He eyed her in that way of his when he was perturbed. "You told your husband about me."

She turned to him. "Yes, and I saved you. He was about to severely injure that human body of yours, aiming at a part I happen to be fond of." She looked down and suppressed a smile.

"That is not humorous. Now your husband knows about me." Yasir narrowed his eyes at Peter.

"Surely you're not angry. You can just make him forget." Lavinia snaked one of her arms into the sleeve of Peter's jacket and rested her hand in the pocket. Her fingers closed on a small object.

Yasir shook his head. "I—"

"What's this?" Lavinia opened her hand. "My ring!" She turned to Yasir, and held it up between her thumb and forefinger, the ruby catching the light. "I had no idea it was lost." She raised her left hand, her ring finger bare.

"Ahh." Yasir slipped the ring onto her finger. "Peter found your ring when he was searching for you. Whatever he spoke aloud, the ring fulfilled. That is how he came here in the urn. He wondered where you were."

"But the ruby is supposed to summon you. I haven't used it for a wish. Why have a magic ring if anyone can wish on it?"

"A conundrum. True, it is specifically yours, for summoning me. Peter is your husband. Somehow the ring felt it should serve him as well. Perhaps the ring was confused since it was not on your finger. This is unprecedented." Yasir directed his gaze at Peter. Golden beams of light shone on her husband. The same incandescent gold as the djinni's eyes.

"That explains the appearance of the pistol." Yasir motioned to the gun lying on the floor far across the room. The pistol appeared in his hand. "Peter must have had a strong desire for a gun, and the ring obliged. When it appeared in his hand, he realized his mistake too late—that he shouldn't provoke Ammit."

Yasir examined the gun, the jewels on his headpiece glimmering. "That unfortunate happenstance infuriated Ammit. He is lucky the demon left when she did."

"But Peter *will* remember. He's seen us together." Lavinia put her hand on the djinni's arm.

She leaned toward Peter. "He's still unconscious. Make him forget." She gestured, indicating the urn's chamber. "All of this."

"Of course, consider it done. But . . ."

She closed her eyes. Another caveat? Yasir, the powerful djinni. But the ins and outs of spell-casting, of who protected whom, of who was more powerful and why and when, had become a tangle in her mind. Nothing proved simple.

"What this time?" She looked into the djinni's eyes, his pupils vertical slits. Usually that meant he didn't like what he was considering. But not always. She sighed.

Glaring at her, Yasir crossed his arms over his chest. "Peter is not easy to spell-cast. He has history with me. When he first possessed the urn and was my master, when I spell-cast him to give you the urn, when I made him forget he was master first. All these complicate matters. Now there is a great deal more for him to forget."

"I well know what he has to put out of his mind." Lavinia twisted a lock of her hair around her finger. "He must not remember that he caught us, or the monster, or his awful wound." She placed her hand to her forehead, once more seeing Peter's hurt expression as he stood over the bed scowling at her and Yasir cavorting in the nude. She closed her eyes.

Yasir put his hand under her chin and guided her face so she had to look him in the eye. "I know not how he will react to my memory spells, to the enchantments I must work on him to achieve these wishes of yours. We had best be on guard."

Lavinia sagged under his touch. If Peter recalled only half of what happened. She envisioned his cane slamming into her face, partly the result of a spell Yasir worked on Peter when she first opened the urn.

"But, Yasir, you are a djinni." She ran her hand down his cheek. "Double your magic. Make him forget permanently."

"What you told him. What he saw." Yasir shook his head. "He is intelligent. He is not some peasant easily enchanted." He placed his hand on hers, holding it steady. "I have put many spells on him. This would be but another."

"You want him to know about us?" Lavinia pulled away. "You don't want to do as I command? Besides, Peter has a temper and I have suffered for it. If he remembers—"

"I have obeyed. I have already made him forget. We must see if it has the total effect it should." Yasir rose, leaving her sitting alone. "We need Peter. We need you married to Lord Bramley. Our son and daughter, Lord Bramley's children to everyone. Everyone must believe me dead. We need this to continue until I defeat the Dark Magician."

Yasir stood over Peter. With a terse gesture, Peter vanished. "I have sent him to his room in Bramley House where he will wake up with a fever."

Lavinia sprang from the divan. "What? You gave him a fever? After what the poor man's been through." She put her hands on her hips and faced Yasir.

He returned her gaze, unruffled. "It is kindest. This will help him emerge from his experience gradually, and ingrain the memory spell." Yasir tilted his head, giving her that pleasant expression he wore when he thought he'd done a good deed.

"Besides, a fever is better than being dead."

8

Betrayed. Again. By one whom I never dreamt would violate my trust. My Thalia, my Lavinia.

I should have been more vigilant. This has happened before. I feel the sensation of warmth, the burgeoning desire as a vision of the witch Amarja appears, her silks squeezing her curves, her hair bright flames flowing around her like a cloak. She healed me from the fatal wounds of Rakhshan's poisoned bullet, then seduced me. Our son was born dead, the cord wrapped around his neck. A son that she planned would be the one spoken of in the prophecy.

I was a pawn in her search for greater power.

But I can see no gain in Lavinia's telling Peter that he gave her the urn, that I am a djinni.

I pace down the hall of the urn and arrive at my gilded door. The niche that was here when Lavinia visited is gone, the wall smooth over it, the statue of Ammit nowhere to be seen.

When I explained that Ammit came unbidden, Lavinia did not believe me. Observing my magic, she is dazzled by my power, then realizes I am enslaved in the urn against my will.

A conundrum, for how can I be seemingly omnipotent and still so flawed?

I am powerful, more so than she comprehends, but complex forces rule the world of Lavinia, the world of the Djinn, all the innumerable realms. It is nigh impossible to direct each strand in each weave of each force in a world. One strand missed, and a life or action or event can unravel into disaster.

With my magic gesture the gilded door opens. I collapse on the divan and stare at my bed, picturing Lord Bramley standing over us, invading our privacy and my urn. With a wave of my hand, the bed erupts in flames. I watch it burn, each tongue of fire like a balm.

Would that I had not woven Peter so intricately into Lavinia's and my world. Would that I could eliminate him as easily and with as little conscience as I destroyed this bed.

9

*L*avinia put her hand to her head. Just a slight dizziness, as if she had stood up too fast. The only evidence that she hadn't gone mad, that she hadn't imagined the entire episode in the urn. Only a few hours ago, Yasir had sent Peter back to Bramley House. And now, with a wave of the djinni's hand, she had returned, suddenly sitting in her chair by the window in her own room.

Yasir had said Peter needed to rest, that the fever would ensure it. She should check on him, have Cook send him soup and bread and stout beer. What he liked when he was ill. She stood up and toppled back into the chair, her vision blurring with black spots, her stomach heaving. Oh Lord, would she vomit? She held still until the spots left her vision. She stood again, wobbly, to call Fleming, but didn't think she could navigate to the bell pull.

Outside, the sun had just set, leaving a fading twilight haze. With a shiver, she looked around at the darkness assembling in the corners and spreading. Her dressing room door had been left open, the strings of amber beads pushed aside onto a gathering gloom. What was lurking there this night, her first night returned from the urn? The Egyptian goddess Ammit splattered with Peter's blood? Peter, now insane with jealousy from finding her with Yasir, deranged from his assault by Ammit, or crazed and drooling due to some fault in his healing?

She felt the pull of the red moon high above, shining blood light over Bramley House as it had a few months ago. But that moon was merely a chilling memory. It had waned and waxed once over and was now again a waning white orb almost eaten away. Yet the household was still stirring over the incident. And now that something horrible had happened to Peter, the servants would start again with their superstitions and rumors.

She ran her finger thrice over the ruby in her ring. At the djinni's appearance, she felt her heartbeat slow, her shoulders relax in relief. Then she pictured Ammit and Yasir's conversion in that incomprehensible language and wished she hadn't summoned him.

"Yasir, I am ill. Please check on Peter. Make sure Stevens is caring for him. He must have Cook's special chicken soup and bread and stout beer." She looked straight ahead, not seeing, considering. "Hmm, it's too late for Cook to make soup. Conjure some and make sure it will be enough for a good supper. Check that Peter's arm isn't hurting."

She rested her cheek on her hand. Could she trust Yasir, who thought giving Peter a fever was a good idea? "On second thought, heal me, so I can go myself."

As Lavinia made her way down the hall, thoughts crowded her head, like puppies tumbling over one another for a teat. Was the fever another way for the djinni to take revenge on Peter for finding them in bed? For being her husband? She felt hot, then cold. Had Yasir failed to heal her properly? She stopped for a moment, listened to the maids chattering as they left their duties for the servants' quarters.

She was stuck. Bound to Yasir with Stuart and possibly Cybelle. With the prospect of Peter's soul compromised by Ammit, for who else could deal with that except Yasir? With her past involving the djinni. With her love for him. And bound to Peter as well, with dear James. With Peter's claim on Stuart and Cybelle for their protection. With her marriage, her love for her husband—yes, she did love him.

She tapped on the door to Peter's bedchamber, but there was no answer. Please, let him be asleep, she didn't think she could face him this evening. What if he remembered, or wasn't healed properly, his arm festering, his mental state precarious? She didn't feel strong enough for yet another confrontation with Yasir.

She would look upon Peter, make sure his arm was still whole, his fever abated, and leave. Then she could assure the household he hadn't been cursed by the red moon. The telescope had frightened the servants. They said it brought the red moon onto the grounds, into the house, that even a normal full moon made humans insane, made them into werewolves.

There had been other rumors, about Peter's antiquities, about the mummies—him bringing the dead into the house. About her, stabbing Peter, going round the manor clutching the urn as if it were a baby. She almost laughed, but all of those things were true. Had they heard that she told Peter there was a djinni in the urn?

She tried not to think of poor Meylo, but an image of him as a mouse scampering around Bramley House lodged in her head. Did the servants remember him? Did they know he had returned? They knew she had given the lad a shilling. He had called her "that crazy lady, what makes spells." Had he told them she cursed him?

Lavinia ran her hands down her skirts. She gripped the door handle to Peter's room, and opened the door. A few lamps were lit and the curtains were open, letting in enough of the twilight. Peter was asleep, a solid shape in the bed. She wrinkled her nose at the stuffiness. A bitter smell wafted from the murky liquid in the crystal glass on the bedside table. As her eyes adjusted to the dimness, and she drew near Peter.

"Noooo!"

At Peter's sudden anguished howl, she jumped in fright. He thrashed under his covers and sat up, an abrupt move made macabre by his wide-open eyes.

"Lavinia." He sounded breathless, as though he had just rushed into the room.

She moved away from him, alarmed at the sunken shadows under his eyes.

He turned in a slow semi-circle, looked beyond her, then all around, moving like a wooden manikin. He leaned forward.

"Where is he?" Peter's voice trembled along with his body. He rested his right arm with deliberate care on a pillow placed on top of the bedclothes.

"Who?" Lavinia regretted saying it the minute the word passed her lips.

"The bloody djinni." Peter's forehead shone with sweat. He rubbed his head, fingers tangling his matted hair. He pointed at Lavinia.

"You. You made him do it." A moan escaped him. He sniffed and wiped his eyes with his left hand, his right arm still stiff on the pillow. Coughing, he pulled the bed sheet up to serve as his handkerchief.

"He healed you." Lavinia stood near the edge of the bed, unsure of what Peter might do next.

He looked up from under his eyebrows. *Angels in heaven,* his hollow stare iced her bones, the spark of intelligence snuffed out. His body looked shrunken. His arm lay like carved wood upon the pillow.

"Get rid of him." Peter sprang forward. Such a sudden movement that Lavinia stumbled to the side in fear he might leap upon her. He held his hand out as if pressing something away, then his features distorted. Fear? Rage?

She reached out, put her hand on his shoulder.

"Peter, I'm here to help you. It's just a little fever. You will be fine." She started to take his hand, when he raised his head and stared at the corner.

His vacant eyes widened and his mouth dropped open. "Get it out."

Peter's shriek was as loud and shrill as a trumpet blast. Lavinia looked behind her in terror, to find only an armchair and a table.

"The creature!" Peter screamed louder, eyes riveted on the empty corner. He cradled his arm. Then he screamed again and again and again, as if undergoing horrible torture.

Lavinia slipped out of the room. She slammed the door on his screeches and fled.

Peter's valet scurried past her in the hall. When Stevens gained entrance to Peter's suite, her husband's screams blared down the corridor, then as the servant closed the door, they muffled.

Inside her room, Lavinia collapsed, quivering from Peter's outburst. Seeing her had only reminded him of what happened. She had made him worse.

Yasir had defied her and done this to her husband in the guise of healing. But the djinni's spell hadn't made her husband forget—Peter mentioned Yasir, and blamed her.

Was Yasir lying about Ammit? He insisted that he hadn't summoned the goddess, that she had arrived on her own to protect him. In accordance with her ancient duties, Ammit had seen something dark in Peter. When Peter aimed the pistol at her, the goddess became convinced of his evil, and punished him as was her obligation.

To Lavinia it was simple—Yasir took revenge on Peter for fighting him, for simply being her husband. The djinni had resented Peter from the first, finally saw his chance and seized it with a vengeance.

Lavinia walked in circles, her thoughts going round like a carousel. At movement in the shadowy corner, she stopped short.

Just yesterday in the urn, Ammit had taken shape from a shadow. Now the echo of the beast's sinister hiss spewed through the room. As she clutched at her *guéridon* table, reliving Peter's tortured screams from earlier, realization surfaced. "He was bitten by a demon-goddess. A demon-goddess called the Soul Devourer."

Lavinia startled at her voice, thin and reedy, loud in the silence. She pressed her fingers to her mouth as if to push the words inside, as if that simple gesture could undo the horrific events from yesterday.

"Lavinia, my dear." A voice in the hall. "Nia, dearest, are you there?"

Aunt Alice. She had written she would visit. Had she heard Peter screaming? Lavinia hurried to the door. Finally, someone to talk to.

"Alice." She embraced her aunt. A new fragrance? In the urn she had caught a whiff of a similar scent. She turned away, not wishing to be reminded.

"Dear, it's called Aqua-Mellis, or The King's Honeywater, but it has not a drop of honey, even though it has twenty-two ingredients, one of which is from sperm whales. Lovely isn't it? From ancient Persepolis. A very beautiful and gracious Djinniye gave it to me."

Lavinia motioned her aunt to a chair. "Yes, I noticed your perfume. How unique." Alice had a knack for getting into Lavinia's mind, but Lavinia had discovered she could block her, when necessary and with focused concentration. Today her concentration was anything but focused.

Alice settled into a chair while Lavinia pulled the bell cord. They could have a light supper here in the privacy of her room.

"Whatever was Peter screaming for? Did you stab him again?" Her aunt looked up at her. She was serious.

Lavinia couldn't control the incredulous expression that she knew had settled on her face as she sat across from her aunt. "Oh. No. I am healed from that time. But Peter . . ." She couldn't tell Alice. It was so preposterous. And her fault for being careless. When she got to the urn, how could she not have noticed her ring was gone?

She coughed. She would have to tell Alice.

"Peter somehow found his way to the urn where Yasir and I were . . ." Lavinia felt her cheeks burn.

"Peter found you in bed with my half brother." Alice propped her elbow on the arm of the chair, leaned her head into her palm and exhaled with a loud sigh. "However did your husband manage it?"

"Alice, I wasn't careless. I discovered my ruby ring in Peter's coat pocket. Yasir thought he must have been in my room and found it, wondered where I was, and the ring answered by taking him—"

"—to the urn. Where he found you. With Yasir. Poor man." Alice rested against the back of the chair and waved her hand. A tray laden with a supper of roast chicken, potatoes and buttery asparagus settled onto a small table set with a white cloth and a bottle of white wine. "Nia. With this news, I feel depleted and must take refreshment."

A wineglass drifted into her aunt's hands, light bouncing off the delicate cut crystal. The smell of hot food made Lavinia salivate. Then she sat straight in her chair—she hadn't seen to getting Peter a meal. She had forgotten all about the soup. But surely Stevens or Dobson would see that he was fed.

A full plate accompanied by a wineglass alighted on the table beside Lavinia.

"I have called off Fleming. I noticed you rang for her," said Alice. So Alice had seen into her mind that she would order a light supper. What else had her aunt found there?

"Alice, could you make sure Peter has some soup and bread. I don't want to deal with Yasir now. And I-I hesitate to visit Peter again tonight. I think his seeing me made him worse."

Alice gave her a look of pity, the gold specs in her brown eyes glinting. "Surely Nia." Her aunt closed her eyes for a moment. "All taken care of, and dear Dobson didn't blink an eye when the tray appeared in his hands."

Lavinia bit into the chicken. "Mmm. Rosemary, thyme and . . ."Lavinia looked up at the ceiling. What was the name of that herb? Delaying, yet trying to decide how to tell Alice about Ammit.

"Yes, it has a bit of sage also. Delicious is it not?" Alice sipped her wine. "Now Nia, out with it. What else happened in the urn?"

Lavinia felt her shoulders droop. Did Alice already know? If so, it would be cruel to tease this from her. She started the tale with Peter being angry, hurt, and fighting Yasir. How Yasir had conjured Ammit or seemed to. How it all fell apart. By the end, tears rolled down her cheeks.

"Dear Nia, was it necessary to tell your husband that Yasir is a djinni? That whole thing?" Her aunt bit into a stalk of asparagus.

"Peter was about to seriously injure Yasir. I saved him. I've thought about it. When Yasir became sober from the potion's influence, he could've sent Peter out of the urn and made him forget at the same time. He didn't have to call that creature." Lavinia pierced a piece of potato with her fork. "Although Yasir swears that he doesn't know who sent Ammit. That the urn does things he can't control."

"But now Peter—oh Alice, you should see him, how he looks— he is wasting away just down the h-hall." Lavinia set her fork down. Suddenly, everything tasted like old paper.

"I fear the monster took some of Peter's soul."

She felt the warmth of Alice's arm around her. "We know how impulsive Yasir can be. And to have Peter appear in his urn with no warning. It has been Yasir's prison, but also, in a curious way, his refuge. We are lucky Yasir reined in his fury, remembering that he needs Peter to keep you and the children safe. Otherwise . . ."

Alice set her wine glass on the table. "Otherwise Peter would be dead."

She fluffed her brown shawl around her shoulders. Loosely woven, it resembled feathers. The image of a brown bird flitted through Lavinia's mind.

"Peter must not remember anything that happened in the urn," Alice said with force. "I will see Yasir. If my half brother spoke the truth, that Ammit saw darkness inside your husband, that vision should not be discounted." Spearing her niece with a stern look, she swirled her hand above her head.

In a flurry of fluff, Alice vanished.

10

*C*onfounded arm." Peter mumbled as he locked the door to his study. "Must've somehow wrenched it riding." He moved his right arm up and down and massaged it with his left hand.

At his desk, he slumped in his chair and pressed his fist against his temple. Would the throbbing not cease? Never had he experienced such a peculiar pain. He racked his brain to determine the cause. No blows to his head, but there was his recent illness. Damn knocked him flat, too. No one could say what ailed him, and he only recalled bits and pieces of the time he had been sick.

Leaning back in his chair, he exhaled long and slow.

He hadn't told anyone, not even Lavinia, especially not Lavinia, about the visions— hallucinations? Nightmarish things, and when he was wide awake.

At the sound of a maid's shrill voice, Peter faced the door, but the momentary distraction didn't bring him back to the morning or lessen the pain blooming in his temple.

Inside his head, shapes formed, dim and hazy, a menacing shadow, something monstrous glistening red. A ferocious snout snapped, teeth just missing him. Peter jumped from his seat.

"Bloody hell." He gripped the back of his chair, steadying himself.

Supplanting the first image, a second emerged. A vast space, glittering treasures, a scroll with ancient writing. He collapsed into his chair. Pressing his fists to his forehead, he tried to capture the fleeting vision, as beautiful as the first was horrific. But the beauty somehow carried a threat, like a purring black cat on the sill, claws contracted into soft fur, waiting to draw blood.

Peter raised his head, sniffing the air.

"Incense. The same as in that godforsaken shop." He yanked open a drawer, lifted up the lining and retrieved a square-handled brass key as large as his palm. The brass hoop holding it jingled with smaller keys. He fit the main key into one of the doors on the imposing walnut cabinet that took up most of the wall behind his desk.

The beautifully crafted piece of furniture had been in the family home so long its origins were forgotten. His grandmother had told him that the cabinet was old even when it was purchased from the estate of an unfortunate family whose lineage could be traced back to William the Conqueror. She thought the cabinet had come from Flanders with William's wife, Matilda. In Peter's safe sat documents that had been removed from a hidden compartment in the cabinet. The papers included letters written to Matilda from her home and from places as distant as Constantinople.

He had heard stories that other secret compartments existed, hiding forgotten books with great wisdom and ancient treasures of jewels and gold. The massive piece had been constructed so well and was so labyrinthian that it was almost impossible to find even the compartment that had held Matilda's letters.

He opened a door inlaid with mother-of-pearl lotuses, one of many making up the front of the cabinet. Inside this section, red-veined onyx columns framed rows of smaller doors and drawers and shelves. Drawer pulls in the shape of unicorns and dragons glinted gold. Peter twisted one of the small keys in the lock of an arched door of black ebony and pulled it open, revealing rows of diamond-shaped compartments containing about fifty scrolls. When he purchased a select few of these from Baruti, there had been a promise of a sort that came with them, and a warning that he would need the scrolls in the future. He had never truly believed, yet had been intrigued with these ancient writings. But now. . .

Flecks of dust crumbled from the scroll's frayed ends as Peter unrolled the brittle parchment on a special pad of pressed felt. He placed round brass weights, their bases flat and smooth, to hold the stiff scroll open. The tiny *Kharosthi* script seemed to leap and wriggle as it had in Baruti's shop, causing the parchment to look almost alive.

When he first investigated these curious writings, he found that the ancient region of Ghandara, around the area of what was now the Punjab, had been a crossroads of cultural influences from the West, India, China and East Asia. This area of desert and mountains, a vast and varied terrain, became a melting pot of descendants of the great Scythian horsemen, the Greeks, and merchants from every empire traveling the Silk Road. These writings were the fruits of their vast knowledge. Satisfied after discovering the script had been found on coins and in caves as early as the first century before Christ, validating his scrolls, he had set them aside for less fanciful studies and almost forgotten about them.

He squeezed his eyes shut, willing the embryo of inspiration that drove him to consult these scrolls to burst forth, fully formed, bearing answers. He banged his fist on the arm of his chair and winced from the pain in his head.

Blast! Something had happened to make him sick, to cause these hallucinations. Peter straightened in his chair and set his jaw. *By the gods of the pyramids*, the answer was surely there in the writings, if he could just get to it. He steepled his fingers, pushed them hard against his mouth, trying to recall the strange shop where he purchased the scrolls, his odd experiences there, and the peculiar merchant who helped him.

When had the scrolls come into his possession? On which of his many Cairo expeditions?

Yes, the first trip after he married Lavinia. He gave his new bride a present she didn't like. What was it? Hmm. His memory had been worsening, perhaps with his illness? But it was that first trip away from his bride, a journey full of incidents, when the little peddler Ne'bi had been stabbed.

Early that morning, which seemed so long ago, Peter had strolled along the edge of the great Khan El-Khalili Souk, enjoying a brief hiatus from his dig. The smell of tangy spices, strong dark tea and sweet *mavade mokhader,* smoke from the hookahs lured him further into the huge market. A sharp whiff of donkey dung, a deft sidestep, and he avoided an unpleasant encounter.

Strolling under the slatted roof in the deep blue shade of the buildings, he happened upon an odd shop. No shopkeeper accosted passers-by to exclaim on the wondrous goods inside, insisting that the victim come in and have a look or bear the agony of regret. A wooden sign above the door, inscribed large in Arabic, identified the business as Wonders of the Past.

The arched windows were crammed from top to bottom with antiquities from all eras, in no particular order. Peter opened the door and walked in. The shop seemed deserted. Light from the windows, in some measure blocked by the objects on display, shone dim and hazy. Far from the dusty, dank smell Peter expected, he inhaled the floral fragrance of incense, and something exotic that, familiar as it was, he could not place.

He paused a few steps inside the entrance, astounded by the vastness of the interior. Gaping at the endless rows of ceiling-high shelves filled with astonishing treasures, he considered he might choose a few items and walk out with them. The thought enlivened him, but stealing in Egypt could get a hand chopped off, or worse. And depending upon which magistrate, many of whom hated the British, the punishment might be disastrous.

He stopped before the first row of shelves, transfixed. To his right, stood a waist-high, painted wooden statuette of a slim servant girl in full stride, eyes dark with kohl, steadying a basket of food on her head with one hand and holding a duck by its wings with the other. He bent closer, delighting in the exquisite detail of stylized designs in blue and orange embellishing her dress. A prickling sensation on his neck signaled a different feel to the room. He glanced towards the door of the shop. No one was there. The shopkeeper's usual place behind the front desk with the abacus, still vacant.

"I see you found one of our treasures."

Peter almost toppled the statue as he pivoted, looking for the source of the voice. Short and round, with a deep brown complexion and long fleshy nose, the man had appeared behind the counter so abruptly that Peter would have sworn he materialized from nowhere.

The shopkeeper held Peter with his gaze, his limpid brown eyes scrutinizing, probing. Peter made an effort to turn away, but was held captive by the man's remarkable calm. Inside, Peter squirmed, but he could detect no threat—the shopkeeper's eyes radiated kindness and intelligence.

The merchant waved his hand, indicating the statue Peter had been examining. "I like to place the most remarkable all around, rather than lock them in a case." He chuckled under his breath. "I am Mr. Baruti."

Shocked as he was at the sudden appearance of the shopkeeper, Peter found his chortle infectious, and laughed with him. He stepped aside, exposing the statue fully, and said, "I discovered one similar in the Valley of Kings on my last expedition."

Mr. Baruti held out his hands in a gesture of welcome, giving Peter a wide smile with even, white teeth, unusual when most Egyptians' teeth were stained brown from chewing *khat* leaves.

"Aha, a true scholar and explorer. They all stumble upon my shop eventually." An amused grin lit his eyes as he glided from behind the counter and swerved to avoid an incised gold chest inlaid with lapis lazuli, garnets and carnelian.

What the blazes? Peter cocked his head. The man must weigh at least 15 stone, but he moved with a swan-like grace, as if he weren't touching the ground. When Baruti stood before him, his wavy black hair came even with Peter's chest. Yet this short, round shopkeeper possessed a quality Peter had only felt in the presence of great personages, such as the Queen, or famous poets, or those descended from illustrious families. Peter resisted the urge to give a slight bow.

"I have something that may interest you more than this rare wooden statue," Mr. Baruti said, raising his bushy black eyebrows. He started down a crowded aisle.

Distracted by the amazing objects, Peter barely missed colliding with the limestone canopic jars and waist-high stone sculptures stacked at the front of the row. Twice he lost Mr. Baruti, but managed to sight him through the treasures and hurried ahead. Peter stopped short at the translucent alabaster bust of the famed Egyptian queen, Nefertiti, her sightless eyes still bestowing a regal gaze.

"I am interested in this one." He tried to keep the awe from his voice. Awe meant less bargaining power.

Mr. Baruti suddenly stood beside Peter. "Yes, a beauty. Came in the other day, but old, many thousands of years."

Peter trailed the merchant around a corner, distracted first by a precisely painted ivory box, then by a gold rhyton, one of the rare, elegantly fashioned Persian drinking horns, its base formed by a fanciful beast, part mammal and part bird. Mr. Baruti disappeared around an upright body-shaped mummy case, crowded with colorful glyphs. Peter tarried a moment longer, then followed. They arrived at the back of the shop where polished wooden cabinets stood floor to ceiling.

"Ahh." The shopkeeper fitted a huge key, so swirled with silver curves and curlicues that Peter was surprised it proved functional, into an equally ornate lock. He opened a wooden door inlaid with mother-of-pearl. Inside, shelves and odd-shaped nooks were crammed with scrolls, wooden tablets, codices and books. The odor of aged paper and parchment, and a vague, moldy smell wafted out and mingled with the hint of incense in the air.

The shopkeeper chose one scroll after another, studying the small labels that appeared every several inches under each compartment. One label, in Arabic, noted: *Keep for M. Guillot, 1826*. A date? If so, it was fourteen years from now. Another, written in archaic Persian: *Gathering for MNS curator NY, 2002*. Who was this Mr. Baruti? Peter tried to decipher other labels, but the letters proved too small and the light reaching the inside of the cabinet was dim at best.

Mr. Baruti selected a plain wooden tray from a side table and, with the sureness of a connoisseur used to handling fragile manuscripts, placed the scrolls on the smooth surface. He carried the ivory-toned, and, to Peter's astonishment, peach, red, purple and green parchments to a table placed directly below an amber glass oil lamp suspended from the ceiling. One of the few areas in the store where the surface remained clear.

Motioning Peter to sit in the rattan chair beside him, the shop-keeper placed the tray out of Peter's reach. He unrolled a crimson scroll under the light, put pyramid-shaped weights of dark-veined lapis lazuli at each corner, and leaned back in his chair so Peter could see. Peter struggled to read the scroll's peculiar script and found it almost indecipherable. He looked away, turned back with a fresh eye, and pulled the scroll closer. It resembled Sanskrit, but was another language entirely, one with which he was unfamiliar. The scroll must be very, very old.

Mr. Baruti, in a casual gesture, passed his hand over the manuscript. Before Peter's eyes, the calligraphy came to life as legible words.

After a while, Peter stopped reading. His eyes burned. He turned to Mr. Baruti. "What is this tale?"

"Ah, it is a story of the Djinn, a very powerful race, which has been almost forgotten." His bright gaze rested on Peter. He seemed to expect something.

"But the Djinn are simply a legend," Peter said. He wrestled with his impressions of genies from folktales in *The One Thousand and One Nights,* in some translations of the Bible, and Mr. Baruti's assertion that there were truly in existence a strange people called Djinn. His stomach sank. He didn't belong here. An unaccountable fear clutched at him. Fear of the rumors of curses from the tombs he had discovered and relieved of objects, fear of the possible existence of all that he had deigned superstitious and magic.

"I assure you, the Djinn are most real." Mr. Baruti's eyes shone with a piercing brilliance that made Peter fidget in his chair like a schoolboy.

"In my extensive studies and travels, I've never found a shred of evidence to prove these quaint tales." Peter crossed his arms over his chest and smiled at the shopkeeper. "I have never met a genie."

"You will." Mr. Baruti held Peter's gaze, his voice, steady and confident.

A wobbling chill climbed up Peter's spine and tingled his scalp. He brushed his hand through his hair, sure that it stood on end.

Mr. Baruti turned his eyes to the scroll.

"Halfway down from where you stopped reading there are spells to keep you safe from the Djinn." The shopkeeper's broad square finger hovered over a particular text, careful not to touch the delicate parchment.

"And these over here counteract a djinni's hexes." He indicated an area of script set off by a rectangle enclosing seven symbols bright with gold leaf. One in particular fascinated Peter, three wavy lines contained in an octagon intersected by a diagonal rule. Peter's gaze followed the angles of the octagon to an intersection and sprang off, tracing an undulating line to its end, spinning and skidding until the symbol expanded, lines pitching like waves swelling in a stormy bay. He felt his tether to earth loosen and Mr. Baruti, surrounded by his sublime treasures, grew smaller and smaller as Peter, helpless, floated away.

Peter blinked at the sudden sharp pain in his arm, and looked straight into the dark eyes of Mr. Baruti, who kept a tight grip on Peter's upper right biceps. His head spun as though he were a twisting kite, and Mr. Baruti the kite flyer who held the string guiding him to a safe landing.

Queasy and dizzy, Peter pushed his chair from the table and peered at his feet as he struggled to focus, wishing the tingling numbness would leave his body. He raised his arms and held them out over the red scroll on the desk's surface. They seemed to extend unnaturally far, as if they were made of rubber, but all of him was there in one piece.

"Be careful with the symbols. They are very powerful." Baruti's voice blared in Peter's ear. Sweat beaded on his forehead. His breath came in shallow puffs.

Mr. Baruti took him by the shoulders, and guided him away from the crimson scroll to an upholstered divan sequestered in a cozy nook. A squat red goblet wavered into view on an octagonal side table.

The shopkeeper held the goblet until Peter grasped it with trembling hands, as if it could anchor him to earth now that he had returned. What had occurred in this odd shop?

Something very dangerous.

"It's all right. You are safe now." Mr. Baruti patted him on the shoulder. "I will show you how to keep from falling under the enchantment of the symbols. Then you can use them safely for what you were meant to."

Peter wrinkled his brow. *Was he hearing this correctly?* He rubbed his ear, felt a warm liquid and held his hand in front of him.

Blood.

Peter's hand shook. Trying to keep his whole body from quivering, he looked up at Baruti, eyes wide with fear, and showed him his hand.

"A little blood never hurt anybody." The shopkeeper laughed, a separate trill of three high-pitched giggles.

Peter stared at him.

With surprising strength, Baruti pulled Peter to standing. The shopkeeper placed his hands a palm's length from either side of Peter's shoulders, then, starting at the side of Peter's head, ran them in tandem down to his heels, then back up again. A feeling of warmth, as if he were being swathed in soft flannel, enveloped Peter. Each sweep held him in thrall, Baruti's broad palms moving down in a graceful pass, gliding through the air, swooping up without a pause—over and over like the hypnotic chorus of a song.

With a muffled thump, Baruti plopped both hands on his thighs and studied him. "That should be adequate."

Peter squeezed his eyes shut. He felt calm inside, his body mellow as if he had just awakened from a sound sleep. He opened his eyes. Baruti offered him a clear glass filled with honey-colored liquid. Peter reached for it, his hand steady. He drank. He hadn't realized he was so thirsty.

After a suitable amount of time resting on the divan and a refill of the restorative liquid, Peter settled into himself once more.

"I would like to see the scrolls again?" He hadn't meant to end his statement in a question, and gulped at his show of insecurity.

"Of course. I believe we are sufficiently recovered." Mr. Baruti helped him to his feet and they walked back to the table.

Peter fought a moment of panic when he sat in front of the red scroll once more, but the shopkeeper's brief clasp of his upper arm calmed him. The manuscript appeared more exotic on second perusal, the strange hue glowing like a sunset and the script glinting silver in the lamplight.

Peter glanced at the symbols from the corner of his eye. Would they do worse things to him if he gazed fully upon them?

"The symbols allow a mere mortal to work with the more powerful spells." Mr. Baruti, sitting next to him, opened his eyes wide, then blinked, slow and deliberate, like a bullfrog.

A subtle vibration wavered around Peter, emitting a thin whine, faint, then stronger, then faint again. An insect of some sort? He checked left and right, but saw nothing and the noise died away.

A stillness fell over the shop as though a heavy curtain had muffled the faint echoes of carts in the street, the vendors calling over the murmurs of the crowd and the even breathing of Baruti. The stifling quiet from thousands of years of buried darkness emanated from the hundreds of objects fashioned to accompany the dead on their journey. Afraid that the shopkeeper had vanished into the silence, Peter turned slowly from the scroll towards his left side, and jerked back at Baruti's dark eyes, staring hard at him.

Peter stayed still. The light behind the shopkeeper brightened. Dust motes floated like tiny planets in the fanning lines of orange rays. Peter put his hand to his eyes, squinting at the shadows playing in the light. A shape. The silhouette of a man? Peter's muscles tightened. The figure turned and faced him, golden light shining from his eyes.

Peter stayed still, afraid to move. Cold sweat beaded on his brow.

Something touched his fingers. He yanked them away as if he had been bitten. Baruti shrugged and set his hand on the table next to the scroll.

Peter stared around the shop. The sun slanted through the front widows, scattering bright spokes of light over the sightless statues, the glittering chests, the scrolls stacked on the table. A vendor's cry rose over the shrieks of street children. A cart clattered by. A camel rumbled its odd nuzzing sound.

"Please. I think, for sake of your health, we have studied enough." Mr. Baruti removed the corner weights from the scroll and gently rolled it up. "I have every confidence that you can continue on your own."

Peter eyed the scroll. What he must endure to obtain the objects of his desire. He shook his head.

"Lord Bramley, I ask for your patience." Mr. Baruti leaned towards him, head tilted, eyes full of empathy. "You will fully recover. The scrolls will not harm you anymore."

Peter shifted in his chair. He hadn't introduced himself. He had not given Baruti a card. He patted his pockets. *Bloody hell*, he should've brought a pistol instead of a knife.

Pointing to the gold-leafed symbols, Mr. Baruti said in a soft voice, "Do not doubt, Lord Bramley. You will soon be desperate for the knowledge in these scrolls."

11

*I*t had been a little over a week after Ammit appeared in the urn. Lavinia wrinkled her nose as her stomach squeezed out another queasy swell, convincing her that this was how her upset with Peter and Yasir had surfaced. She sank into her embroidery chair and gazed out the window at the cloudy day.

"Tea," she said to Fleming who hovered over her, practically wringing her hands. It made Lavinia more anxious when her maid fretted like this, but if she reprimanded her, Fleming would sulk the rest of the day. "And scones. And lemon slices, lots of lemon slices." That would be her meager breakfast.

Soft warm bread would fill her stomach and the lemon and tea would lessen the nausea. Her mouth watered at the image of a knife cutting into the tart yellow fruit. She placed her hand on her stomach and breathed long and slow. For a blessed moment, a peaceful calm settled upon her.

The bloody djinni—Peter's voice, in her head. *You. You made him do it. Get rid of him.* Peter accusing her, ordering her.

He had remembered.

Yesterday, Alice had reassured her that Peter had been delirious, talking out of his head. That what he said, what he hallucinated, would leave no imprint on his mind. And when Lavinia confronted Yasir, he reluctantly admitted that the strongest incidents might leak through, but Peter would interpret them as nightmares with no link to anything that actually happened.

What did the djinni mean by strongest incidents? The monster, Ammit, attacking Peter, almost severing his arm? Or Peter finding her in bed with the djinni? Or Peter noticing he was in a strange place—the urn? *Angels in heaven*, they were all strong incidents. And what if somehow Peter put it all together? Lavinia paled at the fresh surge of nausea that roiled through her body.

Scritch, scritch, scritch.

Her stomach lurched. She was alone in her room. Had Ammit come for her? She searched the dark corners. A small piece of shadow separated and shifted from the shadows, its shape defining as it scrambled from under the drapes, a thin string trailing behind like ballast.

She slumped in relief. Only a mouse. A tiny mouse. Yet it came right at her. Fast, faster. Would it attack? Lavinia jumped from the chair in a swift movement that surprised her. A queasy sick feeling surged up her middle. Flashes of pain sliced into her temples. She held onto the back of the chair while the sudden blackness shrouding her sight faded.

The mouse halted in front of her, raised its pink nose and glared with bright beady eyes.

"My God." Lavinia bent closer to the creature, hands on her thighs. "Is it you Meylo?" Her stomach sat hard, as if weighted by a stone.

The mouse squeaked, a high-pitched little cry, and froze. Fearful of scaring him more, Lavinia stayed still, and spoke in a softer voice, almost a whisper.

"Bring me the talisman, the silver piece you found in the kitchen. We might be able to change you back if we have it." She said *we*, but Yasir was adamant he had nothing to do with Meylo's becoming a mouse, that it was the Chovihano's talisman protecting her. Yasir knew Meylo had threatened her. The djinni wasn't forgiving that.

But this was real—a poor street urchin who had his life stolen for only a few pounds, his price for not telling Peter about the urn. The amount was as insignificant to her as a few pence. If she hadn't felt so insulted that Meylo had the gall to bribe her, if she hadn't told Yasir, if she had just given the poor boy the money, he probably would've gone on his way. Then all this mess wouldn't have happened, wouldn't be weighing on her conscience.

"Can you understand? Bring the talisman."

The mouse just stared. Of all things, here she was, talking to a rodent because she thought he was previously a boy. *These things didn't occur in real life. They were the stuff of horror that happened only in fairy tales.*

She looked into Meylo's eyes. Shouldn't he scamper off and bring back the talisman?

The door opened. Of course, Fleming bringing tea and scones. Her maid carried a tray into the room, leaving the door ajar.

Lavinia straightened, keeping her eye on the mouse, who jerked his tiny head and scurried back to the curtains. As Fleming set the tray, china and silverware gleaming, on the table by Lavinia's chair, a gray and white cat slithered around the doorframe.

"Shoo!" Lavinia placed herself between the cat and the curtains. Waving her arms, she tried to scare the animal back into the hall. The cat widened its hazel eyes and scampered past her in the same direction as Meylo. She lunged for it, but the creature slipped behind the curtains.

Meylo dashed out.

Before Lavinia could move, the cat whipped in front of her and pounced on the mouse.

"Meylo!" she screamed, springing for the cat. In a surprising burst of speed, it circled around her and ran for the door, the mouse clamped tight in its mouth.

She ran after them.

The creature sped down the hall, outrunning her in a blur, the end of its tail disappearing into one of the open doors.

"Help!" Catching her breath, she stared in disbelief where she last glimpsed the cat. Then she raced to her room and pulled the bell cord, summoning more servants. Ignoring Fleming's gaping mouth and astonished expression, she blurted instructions.

"Fetch as many footmen as you can. Tell them to capture that cat and save the mouse. It went into one of the rooms or down the servants' stairs."

For a second Fleming just stood there, then she nodded and hurried away.

Footsteps pounded up the stairs and Lavinia heard male voices, none of which were Peter's, thank the Lord. She watched her maid in the hallway, gesturing as she gave orders to the three footmen gathered around her.

The cat was probably long gone. Shaking her head, Lavinia closed the door, thought better of it, and left it open a crack in case Meylo returned.

At her washstand, she poured water from the pitcher into the washbasin, and splashed her face, closing her eyes to the image of the mouse's tail hanging from the cat's mouth. She looked into the mirror.

All this was her fault. Her stomach felt as if it had flipped upside down.

She had transformed Meylo into a mouse. She had killed a young boy.

Lavinia vomited into the basin.

She rinsed her mouth and looked up to see Alice standing just inside her room. Wrinkling her nose at the smell, Lavinia covered the basin with a towel.

"Nia, what is all this excitement?" Her aunt's puzzled expression changed to one of concern. "You are paler than the milk I use in my tea." Alice led her to the divan and sat beside her.

Lavinia rested her head on Alice's shoulder.

"Now what has you so upset, dear?"

She would make up something. She couldn't stand the thought of her aunt knowing she was a murderer.

"Nia, what is it? Give me permission. I can save you the trouble of telling the story."

Alice would find out anyway. She didn't have any big secrets from her aunt anymore. She'd best get it over with. Lavinia nodded.

Alice rested her warm hand on Lavinia's forehead.

When her aunt saw into her mind, Lavinia was relieved to feel only a slight, pleasant bewilderment, as if streams of tiny champagne bubbles were rising inside her and bursting with a soft pop in her head. She gave silent thanks that she wouldn't have to relive the awful experience with Meylo in the telling, and was surprised when she heard Alice's voice in what seemed like only a few minutes.

"Dear, you and Yasir have a most interesting life." Alice smoothed Lavinia's hair.

At the knock on the door, they both jerked to attention.

"Enter." Lavinia turned to Alice. "It's probably Fleming."

Alice's expression looked as worried as Lavinia felt.

Fleming curtsied. "Milady, they found the cat outside, grooming itself. But no one saw a mouse. One of the footmen said the cat must've eaten the mouse because—"

Lavinia heaved a sob. Fleming looked aghast.

"Did anyone find remains of the mouse?" Alice asked.

Lavinia made another sound, her hands against her mouth as she stared at the maid.

"No, milady." Fleming looked confused.

"Well, then, that will be all." Alice draped her arm around her niece. "See dear, no creature was killed. In my experience, cats leave remains of what they eat. Little Meylo is probably in Cook's cupboard sampling the cheeses. Do not worry, I will find him and bring him to you."

Her aunt placed a hot cup of tea in her niece's hands. "Chamomile. We shall both have some. Calms the nerves." The sweet smell of blossoms rose in the steam from the light yellow liquid and Lavinia gratefully sipped.

"Ah, hits the spot, as they say." Alice reached up, took several biscuits from the air, and offered one to Lavinia who bit into it with a crunch of crumbs. "I always thought that phrase rather alarming. Associated it with target practice, and not in a good way."

"Thank you, Alice." Lavinia savored the anise flavor of the biscuit. "Stay here a while longer. Until things settle down."

She met her aunt's eyes, alarmed at Alice's burgeoning smile. Then, to her surprise, she felt a smile spread across her own face.

Suddenly, they burst into giggles.

"As if anything would ever settle down . . ." Lavinia could barely get the words out between chortles. ". . .wh-what with Yasir living in Bramley House."

They graduated into full-fledged laughs, then guffaws.

Alice pulled a soft cotton handkerchief from the air and blotted the tears from her face.

Drying her eyes with the hem of her dress, Lavinia glanced at her aunt and envisioned herself, ridiculous with her skirt end raised to her face, her chemise and drawers laid bare. Her mouth twitched.

Alice's eyes lit up.

They both dissolved into fits of laughter again.

Lavinia settled into the cushions of the divan, feeling somehow purged. She glanced at Alice, who hunched beside her, hand to chin, emitting a few last strangled chortles, and realized she had never felt so close to her. Alice, somber, mysterious, half sister to Yasir, had always been unreachable. Lavinia couldn't help the broad smile that curved her lips when the word appeared from nowhere in her head—*human*—her aunt had seemed *human*.

Although Alice's reassurance had lifted her sense of doom regarding Meylo, she really had no proof that the little mouse in her room had been just a normal creature. But her aunt must know something.

"Now I must be serious." Alice dabbed her eyes and tossed the handkerchief into the air where it billowed into nothingness. She leaned away from Lavinia and regarded her, the gold flecks in her eyes glittering, a most disconcerting effect.

"How does Peter seem to you?" Alice asked.

Looking at the ceiling, Lavinia curled a strand of her hair around her finger.

"Well. They say time heals. Each day he becomes more like his normal self. But there is something about him, something different."

Peter had seemed off at tea in the garden yesterday, his manner unfamiliar, his eyes canny.

"He appears to have absolutely no memory of any of it, thank heaven." Lavinia gave a faint laugh.

Alice turned her body to face her, their knees almost touching.

"I talked with Yasir. He remarked that Ammit either reevaluated the darkness she saw in Peter, or purged it. Djinnis cannot see that particular flaw in humans as precisely as Ammit. It is the goddess's art. And the goddess always resolves it. If it were not solved, Peter would have died." She patted Lavinia's hand.

"Yasir is confident your husband will return to normal." Alice sat straight and folded her arms over her chest. "But Nia, I feel things in this house, stirrings that Yasir does not. Perhaps he is deliberately overlooking these, for what reason I have not a clue. You know how opaque he can be."

Lavinia clasped her hands. She looked down at the carpet where the bits of red in the design fuzzed together into a puddle, like Peter's blood pooled on the floor of the urn.

"Lavinia, something is amiss." Alice almost whispered the words, making them more eerie than if she had spoken in her usual voice.

Lavinia felt the blood drain from her face.

"But, Alice, you see, Yasir's spell is working. Peter has no recall. We are safe." Her earlier worries about Peter had disappeared with the horrid incident with Meylo, and she didn't care to revisit them.

"Dear Nia." Alice took her hand once more, eyes wide with that look people gave animals fattened for slaughter. Her aunt peered around the room as if she were waiting for something or someone to arrive. "Would you bring out the mirror I gave you?"

Mirror? Lavinia stared blankly at Alice.

Dear Lord, her aunt meant the *magic* mirror, Alice's parting gift years ago when she sent Lavinia back to Peter for her new life without Yasir. The mirror would have been her link with Alice. If Lavinia thought of her aunt when she looked into it, she could see her, see what she was doing. When anyone else looked into it, the glass became an ordinary mirror, but for Lavinia and a select few, it was always magic. She was warned to be wary and think only of who she desired to see.

In the carriage, waving goodbye to Alice, Lavinia had clutched the mirror in her other hand, until her aunt was out of sight. Fed up with magic, she had meant to throw the mirror out the window.

Had she?

She could have slipped it into her reticule. Lavinia had been forlorn and afraid as she left, smoothing her pink silk gown, running her hand over the pale blue lace at her neckline. She had sent the dress out of her life forever in a bundle to the home for wayward women. If only Fleming hadn't sent the matching reticule with it.

"It's here in my dresser." She didn't add, somewhere or possibly.

Lavinia rummaged in the drawer where Fleming arranged her reticules from recent usage front to back. Her stomach sank. Had her maid given it away with the dress? At the back, a shimmer of pink silk flashed between the black and lavender bags. She pulled out the reticule and unbuttoned the pearl clasp. A silver gleam shone from the dark inside.

Exhaling in relief, she returned to her aunt and plunked down next to her on the divan. "Do you know, Alice, I haven't given it a thought since you gave it to me." She paused and put her hand to her mouth. Her cheeks burned. "Uh, that doesn't mean that—"

"Dear, I take no offense." Alice smiled. "Besides, it is not as if it were dull around here." She raised her brows in mock consternation.

Lavinia laughed, open and easy. She unclasped the filigreed silver case. The glass shimmered. She didn't look into the eerily shining surface. Her fingers chilled. Then the cold seeped into her very bones, as if she had sunk into an iced-over pond, the water freezing in a thick crust over her head, trapping her with only a thin layer of air. Her breath came faster and faster, using up more air.

"Now, look in the mirror and tell me what you see." A voice. Someone to save her? She looked up. Alice, instructing her, chasing the cold away.

Why should she be frightened of the mirror? *Because it is magic,* a voice in her head spoke slowly, enunciating each word, making sure she understood.

But Alice was here, right beside her. If something happened, she could call Yasir. Why should she be so afraid?

Taking a breath, Lavinia peered into the round glass. She saw her reflection as in any other mirror. Her tense expression relaxed. She reached up, tucked a wayward curl into her hair, then angled the mirror further away to check her tresses. With a gasp, her fingers loosened from the silver frame. The mirror landed in her lap, cushioned by her voluminous silks. She groped for it, but Alice stayed her hand.

"Nia, what did you see?"

"Yasir." Lavinia bit her lip, trying to make sense of the scene. "I saw Yasir. With Peter." She turned her ruby ring on her left ring finger. Why would she see Peter and Yasir together? They weren't fighting, just standing companionably. What in the name of heaven was the mirror trying to show? And why would—

She let out a sharp screech. Yasir stood in front of them, hands behind his back, surrounded by a faint glow. Lavinia put her hand to her chest.

"Lord in heaven, Yasir. What are you doing here?"

"You summoned me, Mastara."

Of course, she must have stroked the ring thrice when she fussed with it as she mused about the images in the mirror. She would leave Alice and Yasir together, let them hash out Alice's premonition. Lavinia started to rise and caught the mirror as it slipped from her lap. She sat again and slid the gleaming edge of the looking glass under a fold of silk in her skirt.

"What is your command, Mastara?" Yasir put his hand on Lavinia's shoulder. She glanced down, making sure the mirror was hidden.

"That is a true looking glass. Is it not, Alice?" Yasir stared at Lavinia's lap. The mirror gleamed through the pale blue silk.

"Indeed, your accuracy is in top form." Alice, responding to the accusatory tone in his voice, squinted up at him, her mouth drawn down in disapproval.

He grinned back.

Lavinia cradled the mirror in her hands. She had no patience with their cavalier attitudes towards what she considered miracles. Besides, she was upset with what she had seen in the glass. She groaned in frustration.

Alice cocked her head. Yasir crossed his arms over his chest in a gesture remarkably similar to Alice's when she adopted the same pose. The concentrated focus of their power had Lavinia grasping the mirror to somehow hold her own.

"Yasir, I looked in the mirror." Lavinia held up the magic glass. "I saw you and Peter. Together. Without me." She looked from Yasir to Alice, attempting to read their inscrutable expressions. "I got the strangest feeling, one of . . . as though I were off-balance. Like I was falling." She caught Yasir's eye.

"Something is amiss." Alice's tone of voice made Lavinia flinch. Her aunt shouldn't have said it like that. She shouldn't have used those words. So certain. So absolute. Not around Yasir.

"I keep watch here. Are you implying my protection is insufficient?" Yasir peered down at Alice, his demeanor as royalty to a misbehaving peasant.

Lavinia drew up her shoulders, tucked her head and shut her eyes. No.

They couldn't start arguing again. It would end with Alice transforming into that bird as she did when the djinni first appeared in Lavinia's life all those years ago, and Yasir changing into God knows what. Both fleeing. She would be left behind, terrified that they had been eaten by something larger and stronger, or had torn each other apart.

"Remember what happened with Peter? When he found us?" Lavinia fixed her eyes on Yasir.

He leaned his head back—truly, he was most marvelous looking—and eyed her in that patronizing way of his. "Peter was adequately handled."

Her body quivered at the force of hatred in Yasir's voice.

"Peter is the same now as before, is he not?" Yasir slitted his eyes at her, the gold glinting sharp, like a partially hidden weapon.

Lavinia put her hand to her cheek, recalling years ago, her facial bones cracking with the blow of Peter's cane, her warm blood trickling through the cold numbness. Recalling when she stood quaking over Peter as she tried to take in his ghastly injuries from Yasir's beating— the consequence of Yasir's protecting her. Yasir asking her, oh no, not outright, but it was in his words, in his very stance. *"Why have me heal him, Lavinia? Why not let him . . . ?"*

And she had snapped back, *"No! I am not a murderer. I am not like him."* But Peter had beaten her as a result of Yasir's spells. Because of Yasir. And Yasir had wanted her to command him to let Peter die of his wounds. She looked up at the djinni, his hatred of Peter almost palpable, like some vicious aura. He waited for her answer to his question: *Peter is the same now as before, is he not?*

She stood and clutched the mirror. Her skirts rustled as the silk shook out around her legs. The word, *murderer,* displayed in her mind, then an image of poor Meylo transforming into a mouse. That image faded. Another appeared, one of Peter grimacing as Ammit clamped her teeth into his arm.

"No, Yasir, Peter is not the same as before. Not the same at all, thanks to you." Lavinia stared straight at Yasir.

"And neither am I."

12

His package from the Wonders of the Past tucked safely under his arm, Peter left the bright sun for the shade of stone arches and a noisy cafe packed with men in turbans and *tarbooshes*. They scooped meat and vegetables off kabobs onto large squares of bread and drank tea from tiny cups in their broad hands. The noise and sour smell of close bodies contrasted with the eerie quiet of the shadowy antique shop Peter had just left.

From the babble of languages, he picked out a thread in Arabic about pieces of eight, a conversation in Coptic, then a rather titillating discussion in Farsi on trading a camel for a wife.

He cocked his head. A differentiation in some part of his flesh, as if a sudden breeze ruffled a grove of hushed stillness. *Bloody hell*, the exact sensation as the start of the episode at Baruti's. He gripped the table. Peter held on, keeping his body in place, forcing his feet to the floor. Baruti wasn't here to draw him back. Would he lose his mind in this hole-in-the-wall cafe? He inhaled, almost choking in panic. The nutty aroma of baking bread and the rich smell of roasting lamb filled his nostrils. His body settled into its proper weight, his feet firm now on the hard tiles. Sweat beaded his forehead as the hubbub of the cafe closed around him, anchoring him to the earth.

He held the warm cup in his hands. The familiar peaty smell took him back to teatime at home when Lavinia chose his favorite savories. Peter sipped his tea. He shifted his feet, the floor still firm under them. Mr. Baruti had stated with emphasis that he would fully recover, that the scrolls wouldn't harm him anymore. Perhaps his little episode could be likened to the wave of fear that flooded one after waking from a nightmare, merely a residue. He relaxed into his chair and poured more tea.

Soon he was wielding bits of huge flatbread, *aish merahrah*, and sopping up *fuul madams*, fava beans mashed with tomatoes, onions, and bits of lamb spiced stronger than his Cairo cook's version. He would tell Qadir not to be so fussy. His cook's idea of Englishmen being averse to spices had been thoroughly ingrained. Mouth stinging pleasantly from the chili peppers, Peter slurped more of the sugared tea from a cup so small he found it comical.

Outside the open archways of the restaurant, crowds thronged through the souk, sunlight shining through the slatted roof on the passers-by like bright splashes of paint. Women, covered in black from head to toe, appeared as graceful shadows, while young girls clothed in the bright colors of wildflowers, shrieked around them, their legs and arms uncovered, hair flowing behind, free to run and play until they came of age and had to go under the veil. Men sauntered by in flowing galabayas, wearing turbans of white or indigo, or round knitted caps sitting on the crowns of their heads. He could have sat here in this very restaurant, hundreds of years before, and observed much the same scene.

Peter leaned towards the arches, eyes riveted on a heavy-set man gliding behind a group in red felt *tarbooshes* and striped kaftans—Mr. Baruti? A cart blocked his view. He tried to see through the rough twig cages filled with squawking chickens. As the cart pulled away, he located the group of men, their black tassels jiggling with their animated conversation, but Mr. Baruti was nowhere to be found.

Peter drained his second cup of tea, paid his bill and left a stack of bronze para coins on the table. Making his way into the midst of the crowd, he turned a corner and stopped, gripped with the strongest urge to return to Mr. Baruti's and buy several more scrolls. One in particular contained information pertaining to a new project for the Society of Antiquaries of London. He couldn't think why he neglected to ask for it.

Of course, he had bought the scrolls about the mysterious Djinn. After his frightening experience, he had somehow been bamboozled into believing he might need them in the future. He clenched his fist. Was Baruti a first-class swindler? Peter's foot hit something and he stumbled, just missing a woman balancing a clay pot on her head.

His stomach cramped. Something he ate? A peculiar fluttering in his belly. That feeling from when he saw the symbols on the scroll. As clearly as if it were before him, the red parchment glowed in the dim light of Baruti's shop. *My God*. He leaned against a cool stone wall, the crowd buzzing past like a swarm of locusts.

He headed back to the shop. If he had been cheated, so what? The scrolls were genuine, ancient. And the colors unusual. If nothing else they would add a bit of novelty to his collection. He moved out of the fast flow of the crowd and stopped short.

Wonders of the Past . . . where had the shop gone? It should have been before this carpet store on the right, the rugs laid out like flower gardens on the stone pavings. Rubbing his jaw, he looked around. A stone's throw after leaving Baruti's, he had passed the miniature white minaret with onion domes.

There, that was the turn he should make—the shadowed lane with the thin man selling baskets. The merchant caught Peter's eye, his weathered face brightening in a grin as he lifted the lid from a basket by his leg. A hooded black cobra, tongue flicking, rose in the shape of an S.

Peter hurried to the other side of the narrow street. Through the throngs of people and animals, he searched the lane from side to side. Ah, the last of the brass shops. Wonders of the Past should be just opposite. He waited for a line of camels, piled high with cloth-wrapped bundles, to saunter past.

"Blast." Through the settling dust he saw a small park with a fountain and trees tucked incongruously between buildings.

He stood on the brass store's open porch, dazzled for a moment as the sunlight changed angles and struck the huge brass caldrons, lighting like a blazing fire the engraved trays, curved pitchers, embossed chests, hanging lamps and a thousand other items that he would never have imagined in brass. He stepped through the arched entrance.

A small dark man, the pupil in his left eye barely visible for the white cast, rushed to meet him.

"Is Honored Sir, looking to find brass oil lamps? I, Onuris, will give you a prodigious bargain. We are having a bountiful selection. Our brass—the best in the souk." He opened his arms as if to embrace his merchandise.

"Yes, yes, but first I need your advice. Is an antiquities shop, Wonders of the Past, near here? It should be across the street, but I seemed to have missed it."

Onuris blotted sweat from his face with a fringed scarf folded over his shoulder. "I have heard of this place." He touched the chased silver amulet at his neck, his rheumy eyes narrowing. "Sir, you are knowing that business has not been there for over one hundred years."

Used to obfuscations of the oddest kind, Peter sighed inwardly.

"Are you certain?" He took the measure of the hawk-nosed merchant. Perhaps he wanted baksheesh.

"Sir, there are existing no antiquities dealers in this area of souk. I am sure." The brass seller waggled his head. "My great, great grand-father, Allah keep his soul, was telling me the tale, was knowing the shop and the owner." He gestured for Peter to sit at a small hammered-brass table in the middle of the store. At a clap of his hands, a young boy in a white kurta and *churida*r came running. He bowed. The brass seller nodded almost imperceptibly, and the boy scuttled away, sandals flapping.

Onuris took a seat across from Peter and leaned his arms on the table. The wares of his store gleamed behind him.

"The antiquities seller, a Mr. Baruti, as you are knowing, came from a long line of dealers in very, very old treasures. Where they found these treasures was a matter of gossip for all who knew the family. The treasures were fantastical and most valuable, each having a special history that Mr. Baruti would be telling you personally."

At a rattling noise, Onuris held up his hand. The boy set down a tray containing two brass teacups, a shapely brass teapot, a smaller brass pitcher of milk and a bowl of sugar crisscrossed by two spoons. The brass seller poured tea, then milk and shoveled three spoonfuls of sugar into each cup. With a satisfied smile, he set the steaming cup in front of Peter.

Onuris took a slurp of his tea and leaned towards Peter, his milky eye giving him the appearance of a classicist's idea of a seer or prophet.

"One day Mr. Baruti did not show up to open his store. My great, great grandfather, Baba Merkha, went to his house to see if he was ill, and found that he and his family had left. No one was knowing anything. When the silversmith looked through the window into Wonders of the Past shop he was astounded to find it as empty as Baruti's house. Finally, the landlord arrived with the key. Baba Merkha and the merchants gathered around him. When he opened the door a powerful force rushed out. So strong it knocked the landlord flat, bounced the door against the wall and held it open as the power streamed from the inside. My great, great grandfather said the sound was like a thousand souls wailing, that it was so unbearable he put his hands to his ears, helpless, while he felt his turban unwind from his head."

Onuris sipped his tea, then set his cup down, leaving his hand curled around it. He leaned back in his chair.

"The merchants stood rooted to the spot, and with trepidation removed their hands from their ears. They still hovered near the door. No one wanted to go inside. Finally, Baba Merkha, having fought in a war and still carrying that courage with him, took a deep breath, made a prayer to Allah, squared his shoulders, and entered Baruti's.

"All the shelves were empty, all the wondrous artifacts gone. No one knew how the hundreds of pieces of history had vanished. As Grandfather wandered through the building, he kept seeing movement out of the corner of his eyes. He thought he saw Mr. Baruti, a short heavy man who walked like a spirit, hurrying around a corner with a golden box in his hands. Another time he heard the swish of robes and saw a flash of white. Each time Grandfather turned to look, he saw only shadows and dust motes in the light coming through the windows."

The brass seller refreshed his tea and dumped in an overflowing spoonful of sugar. He stirred the full cup carefully. The tea seemed to solidify with each sluggish swirl of his spoon. He took a sip, smacked his lips and continued.

"After Baba Merkha inspected most of the store, finding nothing, he came to the last row of shelves. Way in the back, in the gloom on a bottom shelf, there was the one thing that was left." Onuris held up his hand, blotted his damp mustache with his shawl, and went to help a veiled woman wrapped in a black *milaya lef.*

Peter sat there, almost stupefied by the brass seller's tale. He eyed the teapot, the tea. Was Onuris drugging him, waiting for the effect by spinning this outrageous fable? Then what? Steal his parcels?

Peter felt his pockets. He had precious little money, having spent it at Baruti's, and nothing particularly valuable on him, a usual precaution when he went to the souk. The scrolls and what not from Wonders of the Past weren't easily sold for quick baksheesh.

He felt fairly normal except for his being a bit lost, but that happened before he took tea. Best thing was to see how this Onuris fellow would end his story.

Peter watched the woman choosing a brass oil lamp, and tried to imagine how she looked under the black drapes of her costume. Fairly voluptuous. If he watched closely, he caught a curve here and there as she bent to wipe her little boy's nose, to hand him a sweet from the brass seller. Her eyes, outlined in broad strokes with kohl, made her resemble the tomb drawings and statues, but she was a living breathing woman. He thought of Lavinia, her evening gowns cut low on her bust, the soft flesh of her breasts rounding above the ribbons or lace.

Onuris wrapped the woman's oil lamp in newspaper and tied the parcel with string, which he looped into an ingenious handle. She slipped her fingers through the loop and left the shop, clutching the hand of her chubby little boy who kept his head turned towards Peter as he was dragged into the sunlight.

Peter smiled at him. It must be startling to see blue eyes and yellow hair for the first time.

The brass seller seated himself with a screech of the chair legs on the stone floor and poured more tea for them both. "The only thing left in the Wonders of the Past shop was a brass vessel with strange markings and an ornate lid."

Devil take it. Peter sat straight and eyed the brass seller.

"There was a brother of Mr. Baruti's in town, and they saw to it that the urn went to him. It was a shame, he was being the poor brother, and of all the valuable things in the place, this was just a cheap trinket. However, the brother seemed glad to get anything. We later heard that he had suddenly become prosperous."

Onuris looked through the arched windows at the small park across the street, the old stone benches shaded by stout fig and tall sycamore trees, the bright red flowers lifting their colors like an offering to the sunshine.

"When Baba Merkha stepped over the threshold of the Wonders of the Past, his friends standing outside said he vanished. Foof!" Onuris gestured with both hands as if he were throwing something out. "Some thought they had lost him. When Grandfather appeared in the doorway with the vessel, they all rejoiced, relieved that the force that blew out of the building when it was first opened didn't consume him." The brass seller cleared his throat.

"After he emerged, they all toppled to the ground. They took their bearings and saw that the shop had disappeared. There was nothing there, that's why they fell, because the portico vanished and they had nothing to stand on." Onuris shrugged his shoulders and eyebrows in a single gesture.

"No one was building there. Nothing grew where the store had been. People talked of evil spirits. All this, bad for business. Merchants called a shaman. The man walked through the grounds. Then he raised his fee."

Onuris guffawed and shrugged once more. "Always the baksheesh, ah?" He rubbed his fingers together.

"The shaman had a—what you say—devil of time. Said an evil one had been thwarted. Something about a vessel of magic. He said, 'wait until tomorrow.' Then he left." Onuris scanned his place of business, pausing on each customer.

"The next morning the ground was still bare. The merchants swore they had been cheated. That afternoon the ground was covered in a strange green plant with red flowers. Different bushes and flowers started growing there, trees even. The merchants brought more plants. They were all anxious to bury the memory of the Wonders of the Past shop."

He tilted his head in the direction of the park across the street. "Now the red flower is only growing there, nowhere else."

Peter pursed his lips and frowned. He stared at the brass seller.

"Surely I must be on the wrong street. I must have gotten confused." He could have sworn the room vibrated as if someone were shaking it ever so slightly. Peter reached under his chair. With a dull thump, he placed the package from Mr. Baruti on the tabletop.

"I bought these items today, just a few hours ago." Peter pulled the card from under the twine securing the newspaper wrapping and handed it to Onuris who read the Arabic aloud. "Wonders of the Past, Antiquities from Tymes gone Bye, Mr. A. Baruti."

"There is the direction." Peter pointed to the bottom of the card.

The brass seller drew back from Peter, eyes wary.

"Forgive me, but I must attend to business." He rose from his chair. "Please excuse—" And strode to the back of the store, disappearing behind a curtain of amber-colored glass beads. The strands clacked together as they fell into place, the only sound in the now-quiet shop.

The brass items glinted at Peter like cunning, living things.

The curtains soon parted and a younger man with the strong nose and stout build of Onuris stood before Peter.

"My f-father, he is feeling ill," he stammered. "Please, you must be going now." He put his hand on the back of Peter's chair.

"Please for luck to you, Father suggests ridding yourself of your recent purchases. Best not keeping." The young man, with much bowing and smiling, ushered Peter out of the building.

"Good day to you, sir." He stood on the stoop and watched Peter with his deep-set eyes as if afraid Peter might change his mind and reenter the shop.

Peter joined the crowd streaming through the market, his head suddenly aching from the everyday noise and dust and bedlam. The cool tranquility of the beautiful little park across the street drew him. He held his bundle tight to his chest.

Under the tall sycamore and fig trees shading the red flowers, he sat on a stone bench, letting the music of the fountain soothe his nerves. He placed his hand on his knee, trying to steady it. Was he sitting at the very place where he had sat with Mr. Baruti in his store?

Everything around him looked and sounded normal: trees, flowers, fountain, people in bright robes passing by, dust from the road, the pungent smells of the bazaar—even the package resting on his lap. He fingered the twine. This package held proof of his sanity. Mr. Baruti had wrapped the purchases with care less than an hour ago.

"Pardon, sir. It appears you dropped this." Coptic language, the accent thick, but nevertheless, Peter understood. The black-robed monk held out his hand.

Peter stifled an exclamation and stared. The monk's black robe gave a fitting background to the object in his palm—a deep blue lapis lazuli pyramid, identical to the ones Mr. Baruti used to flatten and secure the curling edges of the scrolls. The brother kept his palm still, the ornate silver swirls of the Coptic cross hanging low on his chest reflecting light on the polished stone.

Peter took the pyramid, which retained the heat of the monk's hand, and motioned the brother to sit beside him on the bench. Gathering his robe under him, the monk obliged. He leveled his serene gaze at Peter. His black skullcap bore a single white cross on the front and small crosses grouped in sixes on either side. With his long face, thin straight nose and bushy whiskers, he had the appearance of an ancient icon.

"Where did you get this?" Peter's voice came out louder, more aggressive than he meant.

"Thou knowest where this originated." The monk's voice was soft and gentle. His black beard moved with his thin mouth.

Peter feigned ignorance. What kind of deceit was this? And from a monk?

The brother straightened the silver cross hanging around his neck, his hazel eyes steady. "I believe you conversed with him shortly before mid-day. Heed his words." He nodded at the package. "Study the scrolls. Get thee home and begin."

At a cat's eerie yowl, the monk turned away, then faced Peter. With a gasp, Peter drew back, clutching the pyramid and his bundle. His eyes locked on the brother's face— a fat hooked nose, sinister dark eyes, a sneer.

Mr. Saddani? As the monk rose, Peter stared. *My God*, could he be hallucinating this whole interminable day? He pressed his hand into the package. Still solid. Still in his lap.

The monk's face returned to its former appearance—long thin nose, hazel eyes, bushy whiskers. He bowed, swept his robes behind him and walked down the gravel path, disappearing in the deep shadows of the trees, appearing again in splashes of sunlight, as he strode towards the noisy, crowded street. A black cat leapt from the red-flowered vines and followed him.

13

*L*avinia stared out the window by her embroidery chair. She tilted her head, hands splayed on her cheek. This summer had been erratic. Warmer than usual, then cooler, but it hadn't affected the garden or the deep green foliage of the shrubs and trees. She couldn't put her finger on when she had first noticed Peter acting odd after his final healing by Yasir. A few weeks ago? Perhaps longer.

He locked himself in his study day and night, and when she encountered him, he behaved as though she were a stranger. Several times she had caught him regarding her with narrowed eyes and a rather irritated expression. What was he up to? The night of the red moon, Dobson mentioned a manuscript that told of the eclipse. What else did the document have buried in it?

Lost in thought, she sat on the bed, lifted a hatbox onto her lap and ran her finger over the blue roses twined on an airy white trellis decorating the lid. The fanciful deer flanking the nimble figure of a hound curving around the sides had always been her favorite. Until now, when, with a gasp, she realized the deer was fleeing for its life.

Lavinia pulled off the lid, lifted a bundle enveloped in several lacy chemises, and unwrapped the urn. The sewing box had proved an adequate hiding place, but she kept uncovering the urn when she searched for new colors of thread. Fleming, or, God forbid, Peter, might notice the gleam of brass through the stuffs and notions, so she had transferred the urn to the hatbox.

She piled her shoes from the bottom of the wardrobe onto the rug. When she first married, she had discovered this secret place, but in the tumult of her marriage, of discovering Yasir, she had forgotten. She pulled up a brass ring inset in the wardrobe's floor and removed the panel, which had been beveled on the bottom for a tight fit. The compartment looked deep and long enough.

She rewrapped the chemises around the urn as if swaddling a baby, and lowered it into the secret space. Would it fit? She let out her breath. Three finger-widths to spare lengthwise. With a grunt she refitted the floor section, replaced the shoes over it and stacked her hatboxes in a neat row. It looked normal.

Finally. The perfect hiding place.

14

As the days passed, Lavinia's thoughts turned more and more frequently to Peter. There were little things he did. Looks he gave her when he thought she was not paying attention, things he said without thinking, and when he was tired he unconsciously favored his right arm. Of course, it was nothing she could actually substantiate, just minutiae, but before when she had entertained these feelings they had been correct.

When she doubted, Lavinia envisioned her grandmother standing before her. Countess Spencer, her dark hair beautifully coiffed, streaked with only a few strands of gray, lace gloves closed with a single shining pearl button on each. She would straighten Lavinia's hair bows, saying: *Now, Lavinia, dear child, you must pay attention to that small voice inside your head, for it will be a most enlightening guide.*

Yasir had been true to his word. Two days after Peter's horrific injury, Lavinia steeled herself for a visit to his rooms and found him vigorous, pulling on his boots with his valet's assistance.

"Lavy, come for a ride. Palomar is literally champing at the bit."

"I promised the children I would play farm with them and their new animals."

Peter gave her an odd look as his valet finished pushing his boot in place.

"Oh, no, not real animals. I had the carpenter carve small wooden ones. He painted white sheep, spotted cows, even a red rooster and hens. The children love them." Lavinia scrutinized Peter for any odd signs and asked guarded questions, slipping them into their casual conversation. For all intents and purposes, Peter had no memory of the events from that dreadful day. For him, Yasir didn't exist.

She kept a pleasant expression until she was in the hall. Then she let the slow smile spread on her face. Finally, she and Yasir were safe again. All was as before.

A week later, she sent a note to Peter, inviting him to join her morning ride, regretting her inability to accompany him previously. She received no reply, and the groom said Peter hadn't ridden that morning.

Maze was excited to see her and acted a bit rowdy at the first of their jaunt, so they galloped until they reached the stream at the far end of the west meadow where Lavinia dismounted. Maze walked in the water, drinking and blowing air through her nostrils, creating noisy fountains.

Lavinia tried not to read anything into Peter's failure to respond to her note. He had been preoccupied with the Society of Antiquaries of London and the business of the estate. She had recently accompanied him to an increasing number of social engagements, but hadn't seen him in private that much. Putting her husband from her mind for a moment, she laughed at Maze, who stamped her hoof in the stream, making higher fountains.

These last weeks, the frequency of Peter's connubial visits had slackened remarkably, yet he showed her the greatest courtesy. Hmm, perhaps Yasir's healing hadn't extended to the whole of Peter's body and soul as she had asked. Of course, Yasir would have some rational excuse if she pursued a line of questioning. Didn't he always?

She bit her bottom lip. Had the excuses regarding Peter's club, the slack in his bedroom attention been by design, rather than mere happenstance? Was her husband purposely avoiding her?

After the ride, she left Maze in the stables happily munching hay while the undergroom brushed her coat. Lavinia was discussing the evening menu with the housekeeper when Peter came striding towards her and stopped, riding crop in his hand.

"Good morning. How are you this day?" he inquired politely, as if she were some passing acquaintance.

"That will be all." Lavinia dismissed the housekeeper, who slipped away. Taken aback by her husband's impersonal manner, Lavinia just stared. He gazed directly into her eyes and slapped the braided leather whip of his crop against his palm. *Thwack. Thwack. Thwack.*

She flinched inwardly with each blow. Was he threatening her?

"I–am . . ." She blinked each time the cord smacked his palm. "I-I am. Very well. Very well, thank you, Peter." She swallowed. Her cheeks burned.

He grinned. *Curse him, he knew when he had gotten to her.* He appeared healthy, a pink glow on his cheeks, after riding, she presumed, but she could no more read him than if he were those hieroglyphics of which he was so enamored.

"Peter." She smiled and met his eyes. He dropped his hand to his side, holding the crop loosely. "Would you give me the pleasure of dining with me tomorrow night? I have a special dinner in mind." She gazed at him with her best tantalizing smile. She needed time alone with her husband to see if he was truly healed. To check if he seemed suspicious of her.

"How thoughtful, Lavinia." He tapped his crop against his thigh, a quick staccato beat. "I'll see Dobson about my schedule. He will let you know . . . ah soon." Peter glanced around the hall. Staring into the distance, he rubbed his right arm, and, for a swift second, a fierce grimace distorted his calm expression.

Her body went rigid.

Peter looked her in the eye and something flickered between them, as if he had searched her and taken what he needed. The hardness in his expression loosened and a hint of a smile brightened his face. A display of triumph.

"Please excuse me, business to attend." He smacked his side with the riding crop.

Lavinia watched him walk away. His stride had changed. It wasn't obvious, but there was smugness in it.

Her skin tingled. The pounding of her husband's boots as he disappeared down the hall increased even as he retreated. She stood straight, offsetting the faint tremble in her muscles. Was her imagination playing tricks?

She heard her grandmama reminding her to listen, listen to that voice deep inside, the voice that was not so small at the moment. That voice that was screaming for her attention. She focused, her mind a prism for the chaos inside her. The white light of spirit burst through, a rainbow of sensations, a spectrum of voices.

A burst of brightness around her stilled her breath, then the mass of color and sound converged and, hand to her heart, she understood.

My God. Peter remembered something.

15

In his study, Peter adjusted the lapis lazuli pyramid that held the top left corner of the scroll. "Blasted parchment should have lost more of its curl by now." For weeks, he had been unfurling the document and laying it out, studying the odd passages, particularly the arcane spells Baruti said related to the Djinn. The red color, really more of a dull cinnabar, now felt easier on his eyes than the beige glare of most scrolls.

As for the odd circumstance of Baruti's shop, he couldn't find any logical explanation except to shrug, saying to himself, that's Egypt. Yet, he still possessed physical evidence he'd been in the Wonders of the Past shop, and that he had encountered a Coptic monk who knew more than he should.

He eyed the lapis pyramid and the three matching ones he'd commissioned. Why would he see Saddani's features in the monk's face? He hadn't heard from Saddani in years. The man never returned for the pistol he'd paid for, or contacted him about another expedition. And after Lavy returned from the gypsies, she swore that Saddani had tried to kidnap her the day she disappeared.

What role did this man play in this current business? He collected antiquities. Perhaps he was an associate of Baruti's, or more likely, had Baruti acquire items for him. But why would Saddani attempt to kidnap Lavinia? She had been out of her head when she spoke his name, but Peter had never mentioned Saddani to her. Perhaps one of the servants described Peter's unusual visitor, and Lavinia, in her burgeoning insanity, latched onto his name.

Mysteries. He ran his finger down the lapis pyramid. Testing fate? Or pushing it?

This morning he had started early, with a sense of urgency he couldn't ascribe to anything specific. He reread what he called "verse four." A few main words had several definitions depending upon sentence placement, and the meanings he had chosen didn't work. He retranslated, his pen scratching on the heavy note paper. The sound lulling him to dullness as it had time and again in Cairo while writing his expedition reports, the late night alive with the chirps of geckos and sweetened with the faint smell of incense.

His mind took him back to Egypt after Ne'bi, the little peddler, had been knifed and abducted by the Bedouins. In the pitch dark of the Cairo night, Peter had run down to the wagon in the stables and retrieved a mysterious bundle. Back in his city house, he unwrapped the cloth to find a brass urn with strange markings in a language he couldn't decipher. Peter opened the vessel's ornate lid. His room had filled with smoke and a marvelous man attired in opulent clothes materialized through the haze.

"How may I serve you, master," the stranger asked in a deep hypnotic voice. The odd phrase reverberated in Peter's head as the mist obscured the stranger.

Peter blinked.

The air had been clear and temperate, with none of Cairo's seaside dampness at that season. Now, years later, he sat at his desk in Bramley House, windows opened onto a sunny morning, curtains bowing inside the room with a chill breeze. His feet still felt the cold from the clay tiles on the floor of his Cairo house. From deep inside him a feeling emerged, responding to the magnetism of the man who had called him master. His senses sharpened. Were the colors around him brighter? The smells stronger? Confusion, elation, anticipation, anxiety, anger, even fear fought within him.

Had these memories really taken place?

"Damn daydreams. Haven't had one since I was a schoolboy." Peter spoke aloud as he stood and stretched, meaning to retreat to the garden for fresh air. But he was drawn back to the scroll and, against his better judgment, continued translating the same passage—a fascinating, if fanciful, treatise which elucidated how to overcome spells from the Djinn. He repeated aloud in the ancient language the odd phrases the scroll instructed him to say. Mr. Baruti had coached him in the exact pronunciation. "*Taiifi – aaiifi – yu – ursat – ifiiat – ifiiaa – uy.*"

The words conjured his room in Cairo, the exact furnishings, the glow of the rich inlaid woods, the pungent smells of food stalls in the street. A smoky haze had floated over his bed, his fine silken pillows, his antique writing desk. Through the mist loomed the same man in magnificent clothes studded with gems. His golden eyes bore into him, a predator's gaze. Peter had stood transfixed in awe and fear.

"I am a djinni, to serve you, master." The man's resonant voice rang in Peter's head, repeating like the clang of a gong, scattering his thoughts.

A loud rap startled him from his vision. He jumped from his chair. Gripped the edge of his desk to steady himself. Another firm knock at the door.

"Enter," he called, his voice thin and wobbly.

"Milord, the door is locked."

Peter shook his head to clear his thoughts, strode to the door, unlocked and opened it.

"*Master,* tea is served. Shall I bring it here? Or do you prefer to take tea in the parlor, or perhaps the garden?" A familiar-looking man held a tray with a magnificent silver tea service.

This man had called him Master? Struggling to lose the grip of his vision, Peter stared at the man. Had he heard this servant correctly?

"How did you address me?" Peter didn't mean to sound so angry, but . . . He put his hand to his temple, hoping to dispel his sense of disorientation.

"Mi-Milord, sir. The salutation that Milord prefers." The tray rattled in the servant's hands.

Peter stepped backwards, the rich woods, the tile floor, the incense-laden air of his Cairo house surrounded him once again, then dissolved into the vivid carpets, sunny windows, and rose-scented breeze of his Bramley House study.

Peter blurted, "In the garden. Ah . . ." He stared at the portly man standing in front of him. *Blast,* he couldn't remember his butler's name.

Peter breathed in the fresh, brisk air, glad to be out of doors. He would take tea, and afterwards indulge in a short walk to clear his head. Things had been passing strange these last few months, and it all seemed to have to do with Lavinia, though why he had that impression he could never figure out.

Peter halted when he saw his wife seated at the dark green wrought-iron table, surrounded by deep green foliage and haloed by flowers. He didn't want company, and had forgotten that Lavinia, on sunny days, liked to take tea in the fresh air. She said it would help her health. Where these women got their notions he had no idea. Dash it all, she could catch a chill.

"Lavinia, how are you feeling?" He dragged a chair along the flagstones and took a seat.

"Peter, what a pleasant surprise." She poured tea and assembled a plate of savories for him. He noticed she skipped over his least favorite, treacle. "I hate to think of you cooped up in your study when the day is so beautiful. And I'm feeling fine. Why do you ask? Do I look pale today?"

"No, you look beautiful and healthy." There, that should quell her alarmed expression. Peter settled into the garden chair, the metal cold through his clothes, and sipped hot tea, the steam warm on his skin. He tapped his fingers on his leg. Damn this fixation with the Djinn and spells. Decidedly unhealthy. He would forget his daydream, set aside the study of Baruti's scrolls. After all, the incident with Mr. Baruti, wherever he may be, had happened probably eight years ago.

The air in the garden, so clear and fresh, wavered in front of him, blurring Lavinia and the flowers into a fog of color. Mr. Baruti's voice, intensified in the quiet of the huge interior of his shop, blared through Peter's head, " . . . because you, Lord Bramley . . . you will most likely find yourself in need of the knowledge these scrolls impart."

The sweet odor of warm bread and sugar drifted through the air and a voice came from over Peter's shoulder, startling him. "Milady, Cook made these especially for you and his lordship." Dobson presented Lavinia with a tray held level in his gloved hands. Lavinia plopped a small pastry into her mouth and her eyes lit up.

"Oh, Peter, do taste this." Ignoring Lavinia's prattling about pastries and Cook, Peter's mind drifted to another garden scene soon after he had returned from Egypt. His first trip after marrying Lavy. It was in the spring, the rhododendrons blooming in fluffy clouds of pink. Dobson had stood at Lavinia's side. In his gloved hands, he held a brass urn. "Milady, you left his lordship's gift on the dining table."

Peter envisioned the little peddler, knife protruding from his back, thrusting the urn at him. His daydream from earlier in the morning replayed, clear in his mind—a man who said he was a djinni calling him 'Master,' a shadowy glimpse of fantastic magic.

It slammed into him with the force of a physical blow. Stunned, Peter sat in his chair, birds chirping all around, Lavinia chattering on.

He had been master of a djinni.

And forgotten.

A djinni who came from an urn.

Peter had given the urn to Lavinia and forgotten about it.

How could he fail to recall something so extraordinary? How could he give away this remarkable object? And to Lavinia? He propped his elbows on the table, threaded his fingers together and collapsed his head onto his double fist.

Did she know about the urn?

A faint glimmer disturbed his mind, something about Lavinia, but he couldn't remember. The delicate perfume of incense tinted the breeze. He became aware of a fleeting presence, eminently powerful, which faded as a terror took hold of him. His skin grew cold and clammy. The birds' songs ran together into a mesh of sound, growing in intensity, surrounding him. He must—

"Peter." Lavinia's voice cut through his agitated thoughts. Her warm hand pressed on his cheek. She materialized out of his vision, a stranger with deep blue eyes and a halo of dark hair. "Peter, are you all right? You didn't hear me."

He closed his eyes and fought for composure. "Yes. I'm fine. Bully. Smashing." He heard his answer from far away, muddled as if he were underwater, drowning in deceit.

16

eter dropped into the armchair in his study. His head swam. Somehow, Mr. Baruti, isolated in his strange Cairo store, had known Peter would encounter a djinni. What else did Mr. Baruti know? He clenched his fists in frustration at the peculiar occurrences the last time he attempted to find the Wonders of the Past shop.

It is not existing for one hundred years. The brass seller had held Mr. Baruti's card as if it were a live bomb, then let it fall onto the brass table. Mr. Baruti had been adamant that Peter acquire the scrolls reversing the Djinn spells. He had placed them last in the thin wooden box so they would be on top, making sure to catch Peter's eye as he laid one next to the other.

"God's blood." Peter shot from his chair and hit his hand with his fist. "The damned djinni hexed me." Seething in anger, Peter twisted his mouth as he paced back and forth in front of his desk. Did Lavinia have a hand in this? He would say the words again, make sure he was fully released from the hex. He placed his hands on the massive desktop, leaning forward.

What was he doing? Paying credence to daydreams, to scrolls sold by a charlatan? Had he completely lost his mind? Yet . . .

He lowered his gaze. The cinnabar-tinted scroll lay on his desk, unrolled and secured with the lapis lazuli pyramid weights. Peter found the place in the text, set his finger at the start of the strange words and repeated, *"Taiifi – aaiifi – yu – ursat – ifiiat – ifiiaa – uy."*

Another vision filled his head: an unfamiliar place, opulent, an ebony platform, a huge bed hung with brocade and gauze curtains. Lavinia and the djinni in that bed, making love. A whiff of her lavender perfume wafted on the air. Their voices murmuring, low and seductive. Their desire so strong the air reeked with it. He worked his fists, aching to close them around the djinni's throat.

He had been struggling with this, this fuzzy, dim recollection, but it had remained indistinct, like the nebulous impressions in a dream. A bad dream.

With the memory came a fear so primeval, a pain so intense that Peter uttered a piercing cry and clutched his right arm in agony. His vision dissolved into the impenetrable darkness of the Egyptian tombs. White teeth gleamed with saliva in the flickering light of the torches. With a menacing hiss, a fearsome beast lurched towards him, red eyes glowering.

Peter bent his head to his knees and forced himself to breathe— steady, one, two, three—while in his mind he watched his blood drip onto the dusty stone floor of the tomb as the vision played out.

He raised his head slowly, wincing, found the place in the scroll and repeated the incantation. The last word of the jumbled charm hung in the air, and as fast and smooth as wind blowing clouds away, the pain vanished.

His mind cleared.

He tightened his jaw. His innocent young wife, corrupted by this vile being who had crawled from an ancient urn. *Corrupted by her husband's gift.* Peter squeezed his fist around a Venetian glass paper- weight, then dashed it to the floor. The shattering bauble fountained in a spray of color.

"Damn them." The heat traveled up his neck, burning his face with fury. "Cuckolded by my wife and a . . . a . . ." He turned aside and took a deep breath. How could he accept such nonsense?

"A mythical creature." Putting his fist to his forehead, he forced himself to say it. The words spewed from his mouth. "A djinni, a bloody djinni."

He had heard the gossip, known the victims and laughed at the poor sods whose wives had affairs behind their backs. How foolish and pathetic they were. Now he was one of them. He prowled his study, restless as a wild beast.

His jaw tightened. "By God, I'll get the deuced urn back."

17

aw. *Caw.* Caw.

Lord Peter Bramley recoiled at the harsh cries assaulting him with all the delicacy of an axe. Through the open window, the oak tree speckled black on green.

"Damned flock of crows." No, what was the correct word for a bunch of bloody crows? Murder. A murder of crows. Fitting. He attempted a laugh at his cleverness, then squeezed his eyes shut at the pain in his head.

Murder was too good for the blasted djinni. Peter felt that his memory had returned, but he couldn't be sure there wasn't more. More betrayal. More deceit. Whispers that he couldn't quite catch all around him.

Hands propped on the windowsill, he leaned into the morning air and surveyed his vast estate. All his property, his riches—fat lot of good—for Lavinia had still cuckolded him.

Caw. Caw. Caw. A group of stragglers settled into the tree, setting off the others. The black wings fanned, the ruckus dimmed, as the image of his Lavy and the djinni blocked the sights and sounds in front of him. Bodies as bare as when they were birthed, entwined. Her ivory skin against the djinni's dark flesh.

He flinched and gripped his right arm.

Peter slammed the window sash.

18

At the threshold of the dining room, Lavinia hesitated, putting her hand to her sapphire necklace, the stones still cool as they absorbed the heat from her skin. Had Peter, at the moment draining a glass of wine, heard the rustle of her silks, the pad of her slippers? She glanced at the sideboard. The wine bottle stood half empty, accusing. Peter could well be agitated because she was late, or perhaps, she hoped, in fine fettle after imbibing several glasses.

He set his wineglass on the tablecloth with a heavy hand, almost upsetting it.

"Steady on." He laughed, wobbling as he rose to greet her.

Yesterday, in the afternoon, Peter had sent a note saying that his schedule had changed and he would be able to dine with her tonight. A late answer to her invitation of the preceding day when he had been so obnoxious, batting his riding crop in that threatening manner.

Between his trips to London where Peter stayed at his club, or holed up in his study after requesting a tray, she had not dined with him more than a week in the last month. What had motivated him to take supper with her tonight? She gave him the benefit of the doubt and smiled.

"My dear, you look lovely." He took her hand. Something about his tone made Lavinia incline her head and squint up at him for a passing second.

"Thank you. I am late, Cybelle was—"

"No need to explain." He let go of her hand and pulled her chair from the table.

She sat across from him and watched as he took his seat. The pearl buttons on his blue brocade waistcoat reflected the warm yellow of the candles. She would not turn his good mood. At least, not until she was sufficiently provoked.

"Peter, how have you been?" She touched his arm. She felt his muscles tense. If only he were the same as he had been these past three years, before he appeared in the urn and found her with Yasir, before Yasir cast the spell to make Peter forget. Had the spell worked, or was her feeling that Peter remembered something correct?

"I missed lunch and tea. I am ravenous." He motioned Dobson over. "Serve immediately." He sat there, impatient in his black double-breasted jacket, the soft velvet emphasizing the immaculate white silk cravat tied in a perfect thick bow. His blonde hair, clubbed in a queue, shone in the candlelight and his pale blue eyes, deceivingly innocent, were a ghost of her sapphires.

When Dobson served the pheasant, Peter beamed. He surveyed the mushrooms surrounding the slices of succulent meat tinged with a touch of pink. "It's been too long since I had the pleasure." Dobson poured thick brown gravy until Peter held up his hand. "Just enough." And later, with his second serving of pheasant, "A superb meal. Thank you, Lavinia."

She raised her wine glass in a toast. "Cook conquered challenges and found the perfect bird." *And you, at last, overcame your resistance to dine with me.*

He looked up from his plate, holding his fork poised to slice a bite of pheasant. He had set his knife across the plate and straightened his right arm beside it, his brow creasing as if he were in pain. Did he remember his wound? Remember Ammit?

He saw her looking.

"Deuced arm. Must have pulled a muscle or some such, shooting, or riding. Perhaps you can recall an incident when something might have injured me?" His voice had the undertone of blame. With a piercing look, his eyes met hers.

She held perfectly still. The image of Ammit clamping her crooked teeth on Peter's arm loomed in her mind.

Angels in heaven, did Peter know?

Her eyelids fluttered, then she held his gaze and said in her softest, sweetest voice, "Why Peter, how could I think of anything? I have barely seen you, what with all your projects and trips. How could I know what may have injured you?" She looked down at her plate, forked a piece of browned potato and popped it into her mouth.

"The pain flares when you are around." He glanced at his arm, then ran his eyes up and down her face. "I wonder at the coincidence."

Had she seen a momentary smirk on his face?

"When I arrive home, I look for you. The servants see my carriage from afar. They are waiting on the drive. And where are you?" He took a swig from his wineglass. "I have even come looking for you. In your room. In the garden." He leaned towards her.

She could smell the wine on his breath, a bit sour.

"I wonder if you have a secret lover?"

She almost dropped her fork. How could she let him unnerve her so? She felt her cheeks burn. He would think her guilty from her blush.

And she *was* guilty.

She took a breath, and set her fork down.

"I? I am here with the children. YOU are the one gallivanting around at all hours, tripping off to London and God knows where. Never showing up to dinner." Now her cheeks burned as if she sat before a roaring fire.

"You don't think I've wondered who your mistress is?" There. She had returned it to him with a suitable amount of force.

"There is no need to think such thoughts. I am suitably entertained." He settled back into his chair. "We have had some good years. I would hate to have it spoiled."

Here, he eyed her again. What on earth was he getting at? The superb meal sat hard in her stomach. Was Peter seeing her in bed with Yasir, seeing the djinni's cruel magic with Ammit, remembering he was master first? Had Yasir's spell come undone?

"Dear Peter. I too want the same good years to continue." She reached for his arm, still stiff on the tablecloth, but he slid it away as he reached for his wineglass. The movement sly. Coordinated to seem random.

But it held a message.

19

*P*eter shook his head, feeling the wind further displace the ribbon that held his queue. His hair flowed free, the cool morning air streaming over him fresh with the scent of dewy green grass. He reveled in Palomar's smooth gallop as they sailed through the lower meadow. A hawk swooped in front of them, wings tipping in a graceful curve. It soared into an updraft with a hoarse *kee-eee-arr* as if it were trumpeting Peter's triumph.

He had a plan in place. He would no longer be a cuckold. Lavinia would again be an obedient wife and the djinni would be his slave. Gripping the reins in anticipation, Peter visualized his hand tight around Yasir's neck. He slowed Palomar to a canter towards the stables and watched the sun tip the trees with orange. The onset of a much-deserved good day.

Lavinia tugged the needle. The pink thread held taut and wouldn't come through the linen stretched on her embroidery hoop. She pulled the thread, which promptly snapped. "Pish tosh." She eyed the frayed end.

"An odd day," said Fleming earlier, when she had helped her dress—dropping hairpins, neglecting to set her face creams in order, forgetting to take her linen to the housemaids. As Lavinia made her way through the parlor towards the garden, she sensed an air of excitement about the great manor. A pair of maids rushed down the hallway to the servant's stairs, giggling, feather dusters, mops and buckets in tow. Downstairs, one of the footmen hurried by, stopped before Peter's study, straightened his jacket, then rapped at the double doors. Dobson swept past, studying a sheaf of papers.

"Dobson, whatever is going on?"

He looked up and settled his glasses lower on his nose. "We received our deliveries all at once, milady, rather than staggered through the week. Makes it hard on everyone." Dobson rattled the papers. "Milady, please pardon me . . . I must discuss supplies with the housekeeper." Lavinia studied Dobson for a moment. She rarely saw him emit any emotion, but today he seemed in somewhat of a panic.

"Yes, yes, do continue." Lavinia's voice rang cheerfully. Yasir had been right, there was nothing amiss. What was Alice playing at this time, coming here and causing her to worry so? Yet, the sight of Peter and Yasir together in the mirror still made her uneasy. Did Alice have a hand in what the mirror showed?

After her walk, Lavinia would look into the mirror without Alice around to mastermind the results. Meanwhile, she would try to settle her peculiar feeling about the day's progress. As she turned the corner into a sunny area of the garden, a sweet fruity fragrance floated through the air.

"Ah, the sweet peas." She stood before a fence smothered with wondrous pastel blossoms in as many different shades as sugared hard candies. She should have brought her basket and cutting scissors. As she turned to fetch them, Fleming scurried around the corner.

"Milady, beg pardon, I was running to fetch ye. It's James. Hurry." Fleming disappeared around a bend in the hedges. Lavinia picked up her skirts and rushed after her maid, pressing her lips together as her thoughts raced. Stuart up to his tricks again? She would talk to Yasir once more about his son forever picking on James with his magic. She had told Stuart over and over that James wasn't a little djinni, that Stuart had to treat him like all the other humans.

They burst into a shady glen by the garden pond. Stuart, pale as a ghost, held onto Nanny's skirts while Nanny carried his younger brother and laid him, muddy and dripping wet, on a dry patch of ground. Cybelle sat on a bench with her dolly, eyes big.

"James." Lavinia dropped beside him and ran her hands over his gray face. Nanny turned him on his back.

"Milady, hold his head to the side." Nanny leaned her weight into her hands and pressed hard on the boy's back. Water poured from James's mouth and Lavinia struggled to hold his head steady as he retched. *Dear God help him to recover.* A clammy hand gripped her arm and she glanced into Stuart's blue eyes. He wanted to use his magic on his brother again. Lavinia shook her head and focused on James.

James moaned, faint and weak. "James can you hear me?" Lavinia pushed his muddy hair off his face. "James."

He opened his eyes, the whites pale blue, his skin still gray. Lavinia patted him gently. "Take a deep breath, Jamie, for mummy." She tried to sound cheerful.

Coughing, he blinked and shot up to sitting as if he'd been propelled, just missing banging into Lavinia. She braced him upright. The whites of his eyes cleared. His skin turned rosy pink as if he had a touch too much sun. The water and mud vanished from his clothes and hair.

"James?" Lavinia eyed Stuart who stood behind his younger brother. He crinkled his face and smiled. What was she going to do with that child?

James fixed his eyes on those around him. His high-pitched voice rang out in the dead silence. "Nanny, why are you all drenched?"

Lavinia smothered him with kisses. Everyone laughed as Lavinia helped him up. They ignored the obvious oddness of his recovery, Nanny and Fleming being nicely bribed to look the other way at Stuart's magic.

In a line, they trooped back to the nursery. Nanny carried Cybelle, who had said not a word the whole time. Lavinia held a sullen Stuart by the hand, careful to give him attention, so as not to have him eclipsed by his baby brother. She didn't want a newly disgruntled djinni to jolly along.

Lavinia watched Nanny's clothes dry in a few minutes, in the same peculiar manner as James's.

"A bad day." Stuart jerked his hand from Lavinia's, his face crumpling into a fierce scowl.

"But everything is all right now." Lavinia patted his head. "You made it better." She would encourage him out of this bad mood. Yasir must talk with him before something worse happened. She feared for her little girl.

He twisted away from her. "It's a bad day, even after that. It's a bad day." Stuart turned a corner and ran into the bushes.

.Lavinia crossed her arms. Alice had said much the same thing: *Something is amiss.*

20

Something is amiss. After a day full of calamities, the phrase kept running through her head as Lavinia lay her head on the feather pillow. Why? Yasir was in the urn, Peter was most probably still in his study and, in spite of the odd events, everyone had made it safe and sound into their bedrooms. Thank the Lord, a hazardous day almost ended.

She opened her eyes. Her bedroom dark. The house silent. It must be deep in the night. She had fallen immediately into a sound sleep.

Something glinted in the shadows. Afraid to move, Lavinia kept her gaze riveted to the spot. As her sleepy eyes became used to the darkness, she made out a gilded frame. Just her tall mirror reflecting the moonlight. *Pish tosh*, so jittery tonight. She relaxed into the feather bed, her mind running through the day's incidents.

Moonlight stole through the lace curtains, gleaming off the brass candleholder. There had been a dream she didn't remember, and its distorted remnants trailed through her head. The pond, a pale hand rising from the churning waters; Dobson pushing his glasses up the bridge of his nose, saying, *Something IS amiss, but you'll never find out what*; her magic mirror exploding shining shards into her hand.

Lavinia rubbed her palm, perfectly smooth and unhurt. She had checked on Stuart, James and little Cybelle three times already. Each time the children were sleeping soundly, Nanny in a chair by their beds, calmly reading a book. After the harrowing incident in the garden where James almost drowned in the pond, she never got the full story from Stuart. Of course, it was his magic gone awry.

"My little djinni," she whispered into the night.

Lavinia burrowed back into the covers. As she drifted into sleep, her mind wandered again. Was Peter sleeping well this night? She had only glimpsed him during the day, and he seemed as busy and distracted as the servants. And Stuart . . . When she kissed him good-night he whined,

"Something is wrong, mummy." Cybelle had fretted and fussed, though she usually clutched her doll and drifted off, silent.

"The magic mirror," Lavinia whispered. Barely half-awake, she dragged a match across the matchbox's rough surface. The flame wobbled as she lit the candle on her bedside table. Braving the cold night, she retrieved the silver box, fumbled it open and slid the looking glass from its velvet lining. Without Alice the mirror would have no one to control it. It would show her the truth.

Or perhaps nothing.

Her face, reflected in the mirror, looked puffy, and she pushed a finger into the flesh of her cheek. Her skin felt clammy. She blinked and stared at herself, appearing more awake and a little put out. It was becoming obvious that Alice orchestrated the images in the mirror, for without her nearby, it was merely an ordinary looking glass.

Feeling foolish, Lavinia slid the mirror back into the silver box. Her skin tingled, a faint sensation growing stronger. Yasir's unmis-takable presence. Yet, she hadn't summoned him. She snatched the candleholder with its bright flame, threw off the covers and searched her bedchamber, then her dressing room. Where was he?

He must want to see her. She traced her finger three times across her ruby ring and peered into the shadows in the corners. He wasn't there. She set the candlestick on the night table and slipped back into bed. She would get nice and warm and then . . .

Her head lolled and she jerked awake, bleary-eyed. She had gotten back into bed. *Had she dreamed she stroked her ring, trying to call Yasir?* The candle flame flickered. Lavinia yawned and moved the pillow behind her back. She stroked her ring once. The ruby glowed. Less drowsy, she tried twice more.

He always appeared when she stroked her ring thrice. Alert now, Lavinia opened the silver box and took a breath to calm herself. The mirror's surface had changed from shiny and reflective to mottled blue-black, churning like a body of dark water before a storm. Transfixed, she stared at the undulating mass as the waves grew and suddenly parted. She frowned. A dim image materialized: Yasir and Peter in a paneled room where scores of candles flickered. She looked away from the mirror and peered into it once more. Still the same image, clearer: Yasir and Peter, candles flickering.

Alice had been right. Something *was* amiss.

The mirror forgotten, Lavinia rose from her bed. She slipped into her apricot silk dressing gown, tying the sash with trembling fingers. The candle glowed in her grasp, weakening as the flame quivered. She steadied her grip and opened the door.

Bramley House felt alive tonight. Murmuring voices floated through the air, muffled noises burst into the dark hall and then, abruptly, silence. *Was she imagining these things?* She walked down the corridor to Peter's rooms. If anything were awry, he would probably know.

No light under the door. She pushed on the handle and the door opened to a dark sitting room. Holding her candle high, she stepped over the threshold and crept inside. His bed remained untouched, the thick silk coverlet spread smooth, pillows in perfect order. It must be nearing midnight. Caught up in his studies again.

Upset as she was, her thoughts like leaves in a gale, she trod with care as she navigated down the staircase. At Peter's study she turned the door latch. Locked, with no light underneath. She inspected the rest of the downstairs, all dark and quiet. The first two floors the same.

A current of cold air slid under the hem of her wrapper as she climbed upstairs to the third floor where the Great Chamber and State Drawing Room dominated the formal guest rooms. There was another music room, library, and other chambers and galleries she had surely forgotten about. Her burst of energy began to wane, and she bunched the collar of her wrapper close against a shiver. The polished oak floor creaked in spite of her soft tread, each groan causing her to grip the candlestick tighter.

A loud clap split the air. The candle flame quivered with Lavinia's quaking hand, making shadows leap from the dark. Heart thudding, she stopped and held her hand in front of the candle, shielding the light. She didn't know if she was more frightened by the sudden noise, or by the thought of being stranded on this foreboding floor in total darkness. Her breath came faster but she continued, following the occasional mumblings that rose up then died into an ominous stillness.

Was the floor haunted?

A small white rectangle lay in front of the double doors leading to the Great Chamber. Holding the candle in front of her, she crouched down into the flame's wobbling circle of light.

A letter.

She picked it up. Heavy cream paper. No name on the front. She turned it over. The Bramley House seal—a golden bee with symmetrical wings—had been broken. She set the candleholder on the floor and unfolded the letter.

The engraving at the top stared out with one eye: the head of a jackal in profile, long ears erect, sitting on the torso of a man in formal dress. The jackal's white silk cravat contrasted with its sinister black head. Underneath a spray of leaves and prickly thorns was the phrase, *Anubis Brotherhood*, then the engraved words:

> *The Grand Master of the Anubis Brotherhood requests your Presence at a Special Meeting, Thursday, two weeks hence. The Abode of the Grand Master.*
> *I pervideas in tenebrosam Abyssum.*

Lavinia studied the strange figure. The jackal's eye stared back. *I pervideas in tenebrosam abyssum.* A Latin phrase. *I peer into the black . . .* no, dark. *I peer into the dark abyss.*

What evil was this? She dropped the letter, then picked it up again. The jackal's eye followed her.

Was Peter the Grand Master?

She had heard of these secret clubs from the servants' gossip, the newspapers, Peter's *Gentleman's Magazine* that she sneaked from his study. The goings on at the gatherings. Why, the members were lords and earls. They took pleasure in the notoriety—good and bad—that their excesses garnered. She never dreamed Peter could take part in their roguish behavior, that her practical husband could be such a pagan.

At the distant voices behind the door, she stopped, rooted to the spot. Staring at the dark wood, she could barely swallow for the strangeness of the letter, this new-found Peter, and the mystery of what was occurring in her own home.

She slid the letter into her pocket and picked up the candleholder. Cupping her hand around the flame, she stood, a bit unsteady. She grasped one of the gilded door handles and slowly pushed down. With a soft creaking noise, the door opened onto a long elegant hall with high arched ceilings. The dark marble floor absorbed the light from her lone candle, reflecting it as the mere pinpoint of a star alone in a black void.

Even in the dim light of her small candle, the gold-leafed swags of foliage and fruit shone against the white wall at the end. An ornate pediment, embellished with a golden Bramley bee and flanked by thick columns, framed a set of double doors with knobs in gold roundels. Light flared from the door's edges. Lavinia crept towards them just as a muffled explosion erupted from inside, followed by voices.

Who was inside? The magic mirror lay on her bed. Why hadn't she thought to bring it? She suppressed the urge to flee, and snuffed her candle. With a deep breath, she turned one of the door knobs, dreading a loud click. The door swung open with no sound, thank God.

Lavinia barely breathed as she took in the imposing room. The least sound would give her away to the dozen or so men seated at the far end with their backs to her. Flames flickered inside dimly lit sconces on the walls.

The men murmured amongst themselves, all looking to a brightly lit area in front featuring a naked man, wrists bound onto a horizontal bar suspended overhead. Ugly red lines crisscrossed his back.

Lavinia put her hand to her chest. *Lord in heaven*, what went on here? An odd feeling unsettled her, as if she were in a dream peopled with those she knew in all the wrong roles. Yet she saw no one familiar. Not even Peter.

A tall man with enormous shoulders, face hooded in black, stepped into view. He turned his back to the audience and raised his arm. In a sudden motion he brought it down with great strength and a noise like a crack of thunder.

Lavinia shrieked. The candleholder plummeted to the marble floor. Her cry was encompassed in the resounding snap of the lash, but the clatter of the brass candleholder, seconds after the whip carved another angry gash into the man's back, jarred the eerie silence that followed.

Faces turned towards her, pale, like so many moons. The sharp clang of the metal rang in her ears. Would it never stop? The victim turned his head, his face clear in the light.

The floor rolled out before her. Waves of dizziness rippled through her head as she stumbled her way to the lighted area. Swaying on her feet, she reached for the ropes that held the victim.

"Yasir." She could barely hear herself speak for the din of the men's voices. They boomed louder and louder. She couldn't think how to help Yasir, but she pulled at the ropes.

He groaned.

Something cold splashed in her face. Gasping, she pulled up the hem of her wrapper, swiping at the stinging liquid. A firm hand jerked her away. She looked into Peter's eyes at the same time she realized the racket filling the room was her hysterical screeching, and that Peter had thrown his drink in her face.

"Lavinia, what in God's name are you doing here?" Peter drew her into a shadowed alcove with curtains on either side.

She clenched her fists, nails biting into her palms.

"I live here," she hissed. She wrenched her arm from his grasp, but he seized her and held her fast.

"Why are you hurting Yasir?" She tried to pull away.

Peter looked down at her, his lip curled in scorn. "The creature isn't worthy of a proper name."

This is a vivid nightmare. She would wake, stare into the dark of her room, gather the covers around her—

"What are you doing to him?" Her voice wavered, but she caught herself before it slipped into a sob.

"Only what he deserves, nothing more." Peter forced her arms to her sides. She had never seen such hatred in his eyes. He looked her up and down. His mouth twisted. "What do you mean showing yourself in such dishabille?"

If she could distract Peter. Break loose— She stared at a glimmer on a table in the shadows. A shape emerged from the gloom in a golden glow, light stroking a concave curve, running down a convex arc. She bent forward, breathless, as if she had taken a blow to the stomach. Peter's hands, hot and sweaty, still gripped her arms. She tried to focus on the table. The shape became more distinct.

God in heaven. She sagged, the strength draining from her body as if she had lost all substance.

The urn.

Peter had the urn.

My urn. My djinni. My Yasir.

The room swelled up in one area, dipped down in another, heaving in a great wave. How could Peter have possibly found it? She had hidden it well. Bile rose into her throat. *She would not faint.* Fluttering her eyelids, she feigned a swoon, going limp as she fell against Peter.

Caught unawares, he loosened his grasp as he stepped back to catch her. In a sudden motion, she straightened, dodged his awkward clutching and bounded to the table.

She snatched the urn. "Yasir, help!"

The ropes binding Yasir vanished. He turned, his body blurring, ready to appear before her.

Peter wrenched the urn away.

"My command stands," he yelled.

At Peter's voice, Yasir jerked backwards, pinioned on the scaffolding by the ropes tightening around his wrists and ankles. He struggled, then hung still as the command took hold. The crowd murmured.

"Bloody hell, Lavinia." Peter grasped her by the arm. She threw herself against him. He stumbled into the table, dropping the urn. It hit the marble floor, clanging like a great cymbal. She twisted loose and scrambled towards the vessel, reaching her arms out—

Peter hauled her backwards, spinning her around.

"You slept with him, you whore." He spoke low but fierce into her ear, and gritted his teeth as his hands dug into her arms.

"You gave me every reason. In Egypt you had your dalliances. I heard the gossip. And, after you returned—you beat me, Peter." Lavinia looked him in the eye. He dragged her to the wall and pressed her face against it, holding her firmly in place.

"Best you not look upon what you want most." He spoke in a forced whisper, his breath moist and hot against her neck.

She struggled.

"Be still, by God, or I'll truss you." A brush of cool air hit her back. He must have turned.

"Mr. X, over here," he called out.

She looked over her shoulder. The black-hooded apparition of a man hurried towards them, his long black whip curled in his hand. Lord, would Peter order her flogged?

He wouldn't dare.

"Keep her here. Keep her quiet. I'll be gone only a minute." Peter lifted the urn from the floor and walked away. Mr. X tucked his whip into his belt. He turned her head to the wall. She stared at the paneling, the swirls of the wood grain. His huge gloved hands settled on her back. How could Peter turn her over to this lout? Let him put his hands on her? She smelled blood on him. Yasir's blood. Her stomach roiled. *Oh, God.*

She concentrated on the patterns in the wood. Behind her, chairs scraped, voices murmured, glasses clinked interrupted by bursts of laughter. A party. Showing off his djinni. But why this way? Why not have Yasir work his magic? Had Peter completely lost his mind?

She heard his voice behind her.

"I should give her to you. Set her up at the whipping post. Double the entertainment." Peter's tone carried a hint of amusement, but the strange Mr. X sniggered in a suggestive manner that made her sick. As Mr. X's indecorous snorts died away, Peter spoke again, keeping his voice low. "Perhaps later. Tend to the creature. Make sure he doesn't get up to any mischief. But hold your performance until I return."

Mr. X's hands fell away. She turned and faced Peter.

"It's my urn. You gave it to me."

"Under false circumstances that surely you know of." Peter eyed her with scorn. "Things have changed." He pulled her to him.

As Peter opened the door, she craned her neck to see Yasir through the crowd. His head was turned towards her, but she couldn't make out his expression. All she could see was the blood covering his back. He was helpless, bound to follow Peter's commands, bound to listen to her screaming for his help, bound to have her cries go unanswered.

Peter marched Lavinia inside her room and sat her on the bed. A deep fatigue settled into her bones. Only minutes ago, she had held the urn. Why couldn't she have managed to keep it longer? She would have had Yasir once more. He would've made Peter forget again, dispersed that crowd of perverts.

"Damn you, Lavinia." Peter stood above her, eyes full of disgust. For a moment they softened and filled with a vulnerability, a tenderness. He started, aware she had seen. Would she feel sorry for him? Did she regret all the subterfuge she and Yasir worked against him? She dropped her hand to her side, running it across her wrapper, over something flat and stiff in her pocket. The invitation with the engraving of the jackal, its piercing eye.

The fury radiating from Peter made her wary.

"Who is Anubis?" she blurted.

He jerked his head, and gave her a quizzical look. "After all of this, you want to know about the Egyptian God of the Dead?"

She pulled the letter from her pocket and held it up.

His eyes widened. She could see him put it together—that she knew more about his depraved club than she saw tonight.

"What is it to you, Lavinia?" He sat on the bed and took her hand, leaning close. "If you would think it through, you would know that any scandal that touches me, taints you even more. You would be shunned. No one would give you the time of day. If you left me, there would be no place for you." He squeezed her hand, his breath stinking of his costly wine. "Can you hear them? *She would have had to know.*

Right there in her own house. They might think you were a part of it. A debauched woman. A whore. As you are."

He let go of her hand, scowling. "You have nothing on me."

His weight shifted the mattress when he rose. He turned his back and walked away, his boots ringing on the floor. Before he shut the door she heard him say to the footman. "Keep her in here. Only let her maid in."

Devil take you Peter. All he had to offer were threats. She stifled the hot tears in her eyes. How could he? Peter's best revenge—humiliating Yasir, torturing Yasir. But Yasir's vengeance was Ammit, who had maimed Peter's arm. Lavinia cringed. Would Peter disfigure Yasir, not allow him to heal himself?

She looked around her room. The moonlight had gone, the pitch-black night showing through the lace curtains. The wee hours of the morning, still and quiet, contrasting with the frenzied activity inside the great house. Suddenly exhausted, she lay down, pulling a pillow towards her. She hugged it, her wrists aching.

Peter. Yasir. Who was the most vicious? Brutes, both of them. They bloody well deserved each other. She tossed and turned, unable to forget the hatred in Peter's eyes, the feel of his hands gripping her wrists with no more affection than if she were one of his lackeys.

She sat up and walked to the window, looking out at the night. She gripped her elbow, her hand a fist at her mouth. Was she just as bad? Lashing out at Peter about when they first married, when he had neglected her with his travels, his searching for antiquities. After she first opened the urn, she had grown to understand that she was Thalia reincarnated, that she and Yasir had been betrothed centuries ago. That he had been searching for her all that time.

How could Peter ever comprehend that the djinni was her lodestone?

After she believed Yasir was dead, she and Peter had been good together. Then the djinni had returned. She had gone to him willingly. That was no fault of Peter's.

And now, Peter was taking his anger out on Yasir, being a bit more creative than forcing a duel. She laughed out loud, disgusted with herself, with the three of them.

There was precedent for her actions. She had given Peter three children, more or less, at least for all he knew. No one had known she had broken the rules of her set by not giving Peter an heir before she became involved with Yasir.

 Why, the Duke of Devonshire had even moved his mistress into his home and lived openly with both her and his wife, the Duchess, for 25 years. Everyone in the country knew about it. And the Duchess had given birth to a daughter she conceived during one of her affairs with the future Prime Minister Charles Grey.

Peter's jealousy was out of proportion to what she had done. Perhaps that was the blackness Ammit had seen, if Yasir had been telling the truth. She had seen no sign that Peter had been unfaithful to her these past three years after Yasir's return. Then again, she had seen not a hint of his involvement in the Anubis Club either.

She let out a long breath, becoming aware she was standing in front of the window, the glass fogged. She ran her finger through the condensation, the damp chill of the glass sending her back to the warm covers.

A jumble of passions. Love and hate. Jealousy and trust. Betrayal and deceit.

Was she the cause? Peter had given her the urn. Yasir had come from it. From what Peer gave her. She hadn't known that Yasir had instigated the whole thing. Not until much later. Was she an innocent in this tangle? When had she become a part of the subterfuge?

Suddenly she was unbearably hot. She threw off the covers. Her legs dangled off the side of the bed. She put her head in her hands, the cool air setting on her like hounds on a fox, her cheeks hot under her palms.

What were they doing to Yasir? She pictured him, helpless, at Peter's mercy, and beat her fist against the mattress. Peter could kill him. No one would care. No one could do anything.

Except her.

21

*B*y the Djinn, *I had forgotten the insurmountable horror of the pain that humans suffer. It was days ago that I was summoned, expecting to see lovely Lavinia. I was shocked into silence when I beheld Peter, a smirk on his face, holding the urn.*

'You are mine now, you bloody bastard.' His first words to me, his voice fierce with hatred.

He asked for the usual things my masters first request—what are considered riches in the era (through the ages it has been gold, elephants, camels, slaves, horses, chariots, harems filled with the most beautiful women, amphoras of wine, fertile land, castles, palaces, armies of soldiers as strong as Hercules—I have heard it all).

But what Peter has done! He has commanded me to forego my powers, to be human, the better to experience the pain he is inflicting. I can barely move bound as I am. He has had my back lashed, my skin lacerated so that the blood burns like brimstone as it leaks through my flayed flesh.

I heard screams, then Lavinia appeared in front of me, pulling at my bonds. What did she expect, giving Peter the urn. Foolish woman.

While Peter dealt with her, the whippings stopped. For that I am grateful, but I do not think she planned that. When Lavinia cried help my powers returned. I felt my wounds start to heal, the grace of freedom, but Peter's command nullified my magic like a vicious trap snapping shut.

The pain returned in a blinding swell of agony. I near lost my senses.

All is silent now, except for the shrilling of each broken cell of my body. But the partiers are becoming restless.

Twice betrayed. How could she do it?

Has all I hoped for gone to naught?

22

Peter signaled the footman to wait as he paused at the double doors of the great hall, the glint of the gold leaf vying for his attention like an unwanted conscience. He became aware that he clenched both fists.

Damn Lavinia. How did she find his meeting? He had been firm with Dobson that Lavinia should be kept in the dark. Now she had made him look a fool with her hysterics, fawning over the deuced genie and challenging her own husband for the urn. He shook his head. He had been forced to her level, scrambling for the vessel like a child claiming his toy.

He must keep his dignity. He nodded and the footman opened the door. Peter marched into the hall. Chalmers-Bowles stood next to Yasir, pointing to the exotic markings encircling the genie's waist and hips. "... a tiger's skin is striped, as well as his fur, but this, uh this . . . I say, I've never seen a human with these deep gold bands."

"We ain't been privileged to encounter the likes of *this*, have we now, gentlemen?" Lord Henshawe drawled, intimating innumerable nasty associations with the stressed pronoun.

Gebhardt, Duke of Strathern, leaned closer, cleared his throat and spat on Yasir's waist. He rubbed the saliva with his fingers and looked up at his fellows with a broad smile. "Thought Bramley might have painted these just to flummox us. But," he held up his finger, "no smears here. I even felt a slight raised area where the—"

Peter walked up. An awkward silence fell over the men, who looked at the floor, then at Yasir who was secured so he could barely move. Lord Cavender, snifter of brandy slanting to the left, liquor overflowing in a thin trickle onto the floor, slurred, overly loud, "Bramley, Old Chap, we know why you wanted to flog this fellow."

And there followed self-conscious laughter. Peter saw the smirks in regards to Lavinia. She had made a spectacle of herself. His jaw tightened as he surveyed the men looking at him in expectation. He would give them the show they craved and make it serve himself as well.

"That, my friends, is one point that shall not be contested." Peter raised his glass to his guests and grinned. The tension broke with rowdy guffaws all around. "However, there is method to my madness, which I think you may appreciate." He quaffed a bit of brandy, then gazed steadily at them. "I beg you for your patience."

Yasir stared into the shadows outside the pool of light surrounding him. Peter leaned close to the genie and spoke softly. "Not so brave now, are you?"

Yasir turned his head, face tight with pain, eyes burning as though he had a fever. Peter squeezed Yasir's shoulder, then wiped his hand on the djinni's chest, smearing him with blood.

"I say this again. You may not heal yourself or do any magic unless I command it. You bear your punishment as if you were human." Peter knocked his fist against the scaffolding where Yasir was bound. "Sturdy."

He looked Yasir in the eye.

"I could leave you here to starve, for your wounds to become putrid. No one would hear you scream." He sneered. "Not recompense enough for the spells you put on me."

Yasir's eyes narrowed.

"The beast. My arm." Peter absently clutched his right arm. "My wife." He twisted his mouth. "By God, I should shoot you."

He laughed, a bitter cackle. Years ago he had found Lavinia in the garden with a gypsy. He shot the man. When he discovered the gypsy was the damned genie . . . Peter shook his head.

"I bloody well did shoot you, didn't I?" He jerked a rope, tightening the knots. If he hadn't kept his eye on Yasir, he would've missed the swift facial contortion, the slight wrench of the djinni's neck and chest. He grinned. He had caused him more pain.

"Shooting is too good for you. Too quick. I want it to be slow. Excruciatingly slow." Peter's jaw cracked in the silence. He would have been content to end this punishment now, but that was before Lavinia interrupted. She still cared for this, this creature.

He wiped the sweat from his brow, put his face to Yasir's.

"While you are struggling not to cry out like a damsel, not to wet yourself, not to soil yourself, I will be relaxing in my cushioned chair, sipping an exquisite brandy and sampling sweets. But the sweetest of sweets will be to watch you suffer."

He motioned Mr. X over, who coiled the whip in his black-gloved hand. Peter started to his table, but paused and turned back to Yasir. "I canceled your paltry spells," he said in a low voice and grinned when Yasir's golden eyes grew wide with surprise.

Peter stepped into the light.

"Gentlemen, I think you might take pleasure with me in continuing my sport after the recent unfortunate occurrence."

"Hear, hear." The clinking of glasses and snippets of wagers placed sounded in the hall. A garbled voice rose above the cacophony. "Give the swiving bastard what he deserves."

"Please enjoy." Peter indicated Yasir—muscles tense in his fetters. He nodded at Mr. X.

The whir of the lash stirred the air and Yasir braced himself.

The earsplitting crack of the whip, the dull thud of leather into his flesh. *Ayevalelh.* Each blow stole his breath. There was no getting used to it. He had not been flogged since Rakhshan's soldiers took him, centuries ago. When Peter ordered his clothes ripped off, his wrists and ankles bound, it took all of Yasir's strength not to let the memories of his treatment under Rakhshan force him to panic, to beg for mercy.

Yasir gritted his teeth. Lavinia's histrionics made it worse for him. Peter had been finished with his little game of humiliation then, but now—Yasir flinched from another blow, another strip of skin laid open, like being flayed an inch at a time. He pulled at the ropes, his wrists rubbed raw. *By the Djinn, have pity.* He clamped his mouth tight and prayed he would keep his head.

The whip cracked again. And again.

Peter's little game had turned dangerous. Would Peter, in his fury, go too far and kill him? Djinnis in human form could die. A powerful lord could murder someone, with witnesses, and laugh about it. And then what would happen to Lavinia? Thinking of her, helpless against Peter's rage, he lost concentration and the hurt seared into his body. He exhaled long and slow, envisioning Peter, eating sweets, smirking each time the whip laid into his skin.

Any more and— He swallowed. His parched throat splintered in pain. Blood flowed in warm trickles onto his legs. He had seen men die from fewer lashings than he'd endured this never-ending night. Strong men. His powers were stripped from him as effectively as Rakhshan had done centuries before. He was essentially human now.

And humans were frail creatures.

"Ten more, for my wife." Peter ordered the man in the black hood.

"Hear, hear," the group all but cheered. "Ten more, for the lady."

Yasir had been counting. Thirty lashes. His back was surely flayed to the bone. His jaw so tight he wondered if he could ever unclench it. The jagged shocks of injured nerves flashed through his body. He gritted his teeth to keep from crying Lavinia's name. He thought of Lavinia, his son Stuart, and the baby Cybelle.

He must survive this.

Mr. X panted through his black hood, a wheezy rasp. The leather lash hummed through the air. Yasir jerked forward from the blow. The bloodstained whip slithered down his back and wound around his legs like a serpent or a lover. Yes, Mr. X was talented.

And Yasir waited.

"We have a man who is vulnerable, as you can see here." Peter spread his arm towards Yasir, whose long slow breaths filled the silence. "Come forward and examine his wounds. They are much worse now, I assure you."

For a moment, Peter's smile became a scowl. The men, fond of blood sports, replenished their drinks and surged forward, eager to see the damage done, all agreeing with Peter's base motives.

Young Lord Waverly, a new member of the Anubis Brotherhood stared at the ghastly ruin of Yasir's back. A sly look crossed his face, and he tipped his glass of brandy onto the raw flesh.

Relieved the flogging had ended, Yasir was caught unawares. His screams mixed with Lord Waverly's raucous laughter and caused the group to step backwards, spilling their drinks and guffawing.

"All done?" Peter thumped Lord Waverly on the back. He indicated the men take their seats once more. "Give me leave for a moment and you will see my purpose in this meeting."

Peter turned from the audience and approached Yasir. The genie was still now. His head bent forward, face hidden by his dark hair brushing the muscles in his arm, smearing them with crimson. He smelled of sweat and blood and Lord Waverly's brandy.

"Good God," Peter said under his breath. He kept his expression neutral for the spectators. *Had he killed the genie? Before he got proper revenge?* Peter forced Yasir's head up, startled at the heat from his skin. A shock, like that of static electricity, surged through Peter's body. He caught his breath in surprise.

Yasir opened his eyes. Peter started at huge dark pupils, dilated round with pain, highlighting those odd irises of gold. Yasir blinked, but showed no recognition. He shook his head. His pupils shrank into black vertical slits. Peter drew back as the inhuman eyes fixed on him. *He could hex me with merely a look. But he's powerless now.*

For the first time that night, his anger somewhat assuaged, Peter studied Yasir. He felt the full force of Yasir's physical presence. *By God, he is bloody handsome.* Bound to the crossbar, the djinni hung by his wrists, biceps and triceps strained. His legs, muscled and honed like a Greek statue of Adonis, were stretched and tied by his ankles to either side of the support. Peter watched a trickle of sweat roll down Yasir's chest, the muscles large, defined and exaggerated by his unnatural position. The sweat oozed over his abdomen, sliding onto the hills and valleys across his stomach and downward. Peter tried to control his breathing as his thoughts took a turn of their own. *This powerful creature was helpless under his command.*

Yasir's lips parted as he fought to stay conscious. The genie looked up, and Peter appreciated the expression he had most enjoyed on the faces of his enemies when he was in his majesty's service—resignation to their fate. Something untamed inside Peter awoke and overtook him. A nameless feeling. An irresistible call to the wild.

He grasped a fistful of Yasir's hair, pulled his head upright and placed the brandy snifter next to his mouth. Yasir drank, each sip slow as though it were painful. An odd jolt, like before, ripped through Peter. He shivered, yet he wasn't cold. It was more a burst of intense desire.

As he drank, Yasir's breath warmed Peter's hand, and the sensation rushed through him again. His hand shook. He fought an almost uncontrollable urge to squeeze the delicate snifter until he heard the satisfying sound of glass splintering. With longing, he visualized the sharp pain of the shards bringing his blood to mingle with the sting of the brandy drenching his hand.

Peter jerked the glass from Yasir's lips and drained what was left. His breath came hard as he fought his emotions.

"Do you have enough strength to heal yourself?" Peter's voice, a husky whisper, broke during the short sentence. He was shocked at the gentleness. It sounded like a lover's voice, the intimacy tangible.

Yasir nodded, his half-lidded golden eyes fixed on Peter.

Peter stepped to his table and filled his glass, the gold liquid taunting him with visions of Yasir's gaze. He took a long swig to clear his head and stood in front of his guests.

"Come gather round." The scrape of chairs and excited chatter filled the room. Exclamations as to the condition of Yasir died down as Peter raised his hand.

He turned to Yasir. In the silence, the drip of his blood on the marble floor sounded brutal. Peter felt a rush of dizziness in his head. He took a deep breath.

"Heal your wounds."

Yasir's thoughts swirled like clouds in a windstorm, ragged and torn. The pain that humans suffer, the pain that his master ordered him to bear, had disrupted his reasoning. But his mind registered that he had been given a command. A command that would end his agony.

A command that would further enable his little sport with Peter.

He inhaled, long and slow. As his lungs expanded, his muscles followed suit and his back came alive. Ruined nerves' dying agonies pounded into his torn muscles. Exposed bone throbbed in the cold air. Each slow beat of his heart wracked his flayed skin with agonizing pain. His wrists and ankles pulsated in response. The room spun in great lazy circles.

He closed his eyes as Peter's command released him, letting his magic flow into his body like a soothing balm. A collective gasp filled the room. Yasir could envision the men's amazement as they watched his back transform from a bloodied, swollen mass, ribs exposed, to firm, bronzed muscles, smooth and unblemished.

He shut his eyes at the touch of strangers; he was still bound at his wrists and ankles. He flinched, sensing that some who touched him did so more with a peculiar yearning than curiosity at the miracle before their eyes.

Peter leaned close.

"With my next command, you will use a small amount of magic, no more, to make only your ropes fall away." His whisper became fierce. "No twisting of my words, no outlandish interpretations. No tricks."

Peter stood proud.

"Release your bonds." His voice blared loud and haughty. Yasir had tired of Peter's little game, but with the healing, his strength returned and his resolve firmed. He stood straight and flexed his muscles. *Ayevalelh*, how he would like to—

"Dress properly and shake hands with each of my guests." The arrogance in Peter's voice made Yasir's gut heave.

A wave of his hand, and Yasir stood before them in a starched white linen shirt under a black cutaway coat with gold buttons and long tails. His tight beige trousers tucked neatly into knee-high black boots. He shook hands with each of the men and made a game of guessing whose touches before were tinged with longing, making sure to devil them with a lustful gaze.

A flood of relief filled Peter. The emotion caught him off guard, but he managed to smirk and acknowledge his audience.

"So you see, there was a master plan." He chuckled to himself at his little pun and wondered how many others caught it. "Please, observe for yourself."

Peter held the urn, having retrieved the vessel from the heavy trunk where he had locked it. Satisfaction was his. Yasir had undergone almost suitable humiliation and hurt.

Almost suitable. Peter mulled the words over. Still, he was Master. The men stepped back, widening the circle around Yasir. Peter caught the genie's eye and nodded as he opened the urn's lid. He gave his final command of the night.

"Return to the urn."

Bleary eyes widened with astonishment as the solid form of Yasir gradually faded into an amber mist that rose into the air and, in a sudden and silent motion, was sucked into the urn. Of course, Peter would have the genie make those that attended forget about the main attraction and remember only a night of abandon and drunken carousing with the Anubis Brotherhood and their generous Grand Master, Lord Peter Bramley.

Peter snapped the lid shut. The clink resonated in the small hours of the morning, sounding hollow.

23

The day after the meeting of the Anubis Brotherhood dawned pink and rosy, alive with birdsong as if the world had become innocent overnight.

Propped on fluffy pillows in bed, Lavinia adjusted her shawl and tried to get lost in her needlework. She stole a peek at Fleming, who gazed at her with shiny, spaniel eyes. Caught staring, her maid rearranged her countenance into a careful blank expression. Lavinia forced her needle into the cloth on her embroidery hoop. She shan't pity me.

Fleming had seen how shaken she was after the ordeal with Peter, seen the bruises on her wrists, and other places. Lavinia ached over the whole of her body. Of course, the servants knew Lord Bramley had hosted a party on the third floor, but they only set up before and cleaned afterwards. She heard no gossip about the framing where Yasir had been whipped. Perhaps Peter had made him conjure it. If so, how cruel.

Was she the only one in the household who knew about Peter's little club? It was careless of him to hold the meeting in the house. He could have at least waited until she and the children were visiting Alice, or in London. She set her embroidery on her lap and stared at the flower design. It seemed a relic of the past, irrelevant to anything in her life now.

She was trapped in her secret. Peter had been correct that if anyone knew about the club it would also affect her standing in the community. She was innocent, but no one would believe it. Fuming, she brought her fist down hard on the bed, the impact sliding her embroidery from her lap. She ignored Fleming's abrupt inhale, her stiffened posture.

She and Peter had been happy these three years after Yasir had returned. All this mess with her husband had happened after he found them together in the urn. She couldn't shake the feeling that Peter's crazed actions had been the result of Yasir's spell. It had happened before.

Even so, Peter was master of Yasir. She had lost them both—her husband and her lover.

She wasn't sure how to deal with Peter, and with the loss of Yasir there was no commiseration. She had sent a note pleading for Alice to come forthwith to help her heal from a sudden illness (she couldn't very well state the real reason in writing), but received no reply as yet. Her aunt could save Yasir, she was sure of it.

Nausea made her gasp for breath whenever she thought of Yasir all bloody, Yasir horribly injured. And what had she done? Made it worse for him by trying to steal the urn. Trying to save him. She stifled a sob. Fleming jerked round and gave her that look.

Without warning, she experienced the jolt of cold terror that flashed through her when the brass candleholder had slipped from her hand at Peter's meeting, the crash resonating like the peal of a church bell. The men's faces turned towards her. Her screaming Yasir's name, running to him.

Now Peter knew. Now everyone knew.

Lavinia pulled her shawl closer. The wool enfolded her like a shroud, but that was the closest she would come to an embrace from her husband, from Yasir.

She picked up her embroidery. Silly as it was, moving the needle in and out, building the design, calmed her. She pulled the thread through the linen, starting on the second iris petal. In her wardrobe, she had discovered everything perfectly in place, save for the secret compartment empty of its contents. How had Peter found the urn? How had he stolen it without her having any idea?

She was lost. Peter's secret club, his rough treatment. Oh, she had given almost as good as he had. Her affair with Yasir, her rowdy attempt at stealing the urn back. She bowed her head.

"Betrayer," she said in a whisper. Fleming dropped the pantalets she was folding and stared, but quickly resumed her task when Lavinia returned the look with a glare.

She was a betrayer. She had hurt Peter, deceived him. And she had failed Yasir. Her husband would never have hurt the djinni, never had known about him, if she hadn't been so careless and lost her ring.

Years ago, after Peter had found them in the garden and shot Yasir, thinking him a gypsy interloper, she had walked on pins and needles to be discreet. That's all that was asked of a wife nowadays.

Discreet until now.

Peter had her in the palm of his hand. As well as Yasir. She jerked the needle through the cloth.

"Ow." A glob of blood swelled on the soft pad of her finger.

"Oh. Beg pardon, milady, I forgot yer thimble." Fleming hurried to the side of the bed and rummaged through Lavinia's sewing basket, tossing out skeins of looped thread, patterns, and packets of needles in her haste to placate her mistress.

Lavinia stuck her finger in her mouth, the tang of blood taking her back to Peter's depraved party. There was a real possibility that she might never see Yasir again.

"Milady, I can't find yer favorite silver one, but—"

Lavinia burst into tears.

Her maid stood straight, mouth open. "There, there, milady." Fleming held a thimble in front of Lavinia. "Here's a pretty porcelain 'un wi' pink roses."

But through her tears Lavinia saw only a blur.

24

A whisper floated gently through the air. "Yasir, oh Yasir. I warned you. You didn't listen. You . . ."

Lavinia's eyelids were almost too heavy to open. She must have fallen asleep after her cry. Dark brown eyes with amber flecks peered at her.

"Alice." She held out her arms. "You came." Her aunt leaned over and hugged her, giving her a peck on the cheek. Lavinia inhaled the exotic scent of her aunt's perfume.

"My little Nia." Alice sat in the chair next to the bed. Her hand rested warm on Lavinia's forehead, the delicate strokes of her fingers so soothing. "Shall we have tea? I believe it is just about that time."

Lavinia yawned and pushed herself to sitting.

"Fleming should be bringing it any minute. She's good about those things. Did you say something about Y-Yasir when you first came in?"

"Dear Nia." Her aunt looked down. "Yasir was so sure of himself." Alice pressed her niece's hand.

Lavinia closed her eyes, she would have to say it, say the unspeakable.

"I couldn't mention it in the letter. Couldn't . . . but . . . Oh, Alice, Peter had Yasir flogged." She pulled away. She didn't want her aunt's sympathy. "He was bleeding. His back gashed. Peter wouldn't let him heal himself. I tried to help, but he was bound with thick rope and hurting and I pulled the rope and he winced and—"

"Dear." Alice patted Lavinia's hand. "You're upsetting yourself."

"It doesn't matter. I-I have nothing to lose." She bent forward, heat flushing into her face, the rush of anger giving her energy. "Why didn't you stop Peter? You could have done so. You knew, didn't you? Knew Yasir was being tortured?"

"Nia, don't. Don't go where you shouldn't." Alice put her hand on Lavinia's shoulder and looked into her eyes. "Yes, I knew. I was instructed not to interfere. To let Yasir handle this."

"But, he didn't—isn't—handling it. He's hurt. He's suffering. Peter might kill him. My God, Alice, I thought you loved him. What kind of person are you?"

"Nia." The warmth of Alice's hand radiated through the soft linen of Lavinia's nightdress. "I am bound by a higher power, but our actions or inactions all have purpose. Know that we love Yasir."

Lavinia slumped against the pillows. Inside, she felt herself collapsing bit by bit, and if it didn't stop she would end up merely a fraction of herself.

Alice's words sank in. Lavinia sat up. She brushed Alice's hand from her shoulder.

"Oh yes, you and your mysterious power must love Yasir. You love him so much that you let Peter almost kill him." She leaned toward her aunt. "Right now, Peter's footmen could be carrying Yasir's poor bloody human body away."

She took her aunt's hand, squeezing it in anger.

"Flogged to death, because of your folly." She squeezed harder. "You killed him. Upon my soul, you killed him."

She raised her hand as if to strike Alice.

Alice twisted out of her niece's hold and caught Lavinia's arm with a grip as strong as Yasir's.

"He is not dead. He is healed. And taking care of himself. And Peter." Alice's voice had a peculiar, almost sinister intonation when she mentioned Peter.

Her aunt loosened her hold and stroked Lavinia's hand.

"Nia, underneath what seems folly is a cunning strategy that Yasir has already begun." Alice's voice was gentle and kind, even with the rebuke.

But Lavinia turned away, afraid she might actually slap her aunt. How could it all go so wrong, so fast?

"Dear, you need to clear your head. A hot cup of tea should help." Alice pulled a cup and saucer from the air and snuggled it into Lavinia's hands.

"No." Lavinia tossed the cup away, the tea streaming out, honey-colored with the daylight shining through. It vanished.

"I don't want your poison. I don't—" She winced at the explosion of sound in her head, the image of the whip lacerating Yasir's back, leaving him bloodier, the urn gleaming from the darkness.

Lavinia pressed her hands against her temple. If the sound would just stop.

"I don't know." She groaned. "I don't know how Peter knew, how he stole the urn. He's taken everything. Everything." She was folding up inside again. Soon there would be nothing left of her.

"Alice." Lavinia looked straight into Alice's eyes. "You must get the urn back for me."

Her aunt sat motionless, eyes downcast. Then in a mercurial motion beyond the capability of mere muscles, she raised her head.

Lavinia jerked away. Only Yasir moved like that.

"Nia, I am not like Yasir. He is much too careless, too impetuous. That's why he's in this predicament in the first place."

Alice pressed her lips together and walked to the window. She stared outside, light flooding around her dark silhouette. The sound of her hard breathing filled the room.

Would Alice work a spell right here? Had her aunt locked the door? Lavinia eyed the latch, put her hands to her side, pressing herself up from the bed. She could run out the door, lock herself in the parlor.

Alice loomed above her, her energy palpable. Lavinia suppressed a yelp.

"Yasir should have known better. All those spells. Peter being an antiquary." Her aunt raised her hand.

Lavinia shrank into the pillows. God in heaven, would Alice spell-cast her?

Alice pointed her index finger.

"I warned Yasir. I warned him, and he went into a rage. He did not listen." Her hand fell to her side. The wild look in her eyes softened as she sank into the bedside chair. "There is much I cannot tell you. There are many restrictions on me. I can say this, he doesn't need my help." Alice peered intently at her. "He needs yours."

Lavinia wanted to push her aunt away. But Alice's steady gaze, gold flecks in her eyes gleaming like dew on a spider's web, held her in an almost suspended state. What good was it to have an aunt who had magic if she wouldn't help you? With the same effort that doing sums brought the release of solving the problem, Lavinia broke her aunt's hold.

She stared at the bed covers, her aunt's presence palpable.

How had she thought to find Yasir that night? She had sat right here in bed looking into the magic mirror, which showed Peter and Yasir together. Strength flowed through her. She *could* do this herself. Lavinia picked up the silver box from the bedside table.

She opened the lid. Her fingers rested on the faint circular indentation in the velvet cushion inside.

"It was just here." Lavinia raised her head and stared at her aunt.

Alice sat still, a pensive look transforming her expression. The looking glass rested in her palm. Lavinia reached for it.

Alice pulled the mirror away.

"Nia, I am not confident this is the right time."

"It's my mirror, Alice. You gave it to me. To help me. Now I need help. Would you deny me this gift?" Lavinia snatched the mirror. *What kind of game was Alice playing?* "This is how I found Yasir and Peter. The mirror is mine."

Her aunt made no effort to seize the glass from her.

"I owe you an apology, dear. I meant for the mirror to aid you, but it has only caused you grief." Alice merely gazed at her from the bedside chair.

The glass grew cold in Lavinia's hands. She set the mirror face-down on the velvet inside the case and closed it.

Alice reached for her.

Lavinia pulled back, clutching the silver case against her chest. They regarded one another in the awkward quiet that followed.

Alice folded her hands in her lap, eyeing Lavinia all the while, as if making sure her niece saw each movement.

"Alice, I—"

Her aunt held up her hand.

"Nia dear, remember this well. Magic is much like a child. It finds its own way, no matter the consequences." Her aunt had made her voice melodic, but the words, spoken almost like an endearment, were an icy hand trailing down the back of Lavinia's neck.

She tossed her head, eyes flashing defiance. "No *matter.*" Lavinia emphasized the phrase. "You said getting the urn back is something *I* must do." She held up the mirror case.

"This is how I will start."

25

Peter sank into a chair and rubbed his arm. He felt befogged, as if he had stepped into another time, the same feeling he had when the monster appeared in that strange place. What happened then was hazy. He had been in shock from his injury, from the beast's attack. And he had never thought to ask exactly where all of that had occurred. Revenge had consumed him. Still consumed him.

He sat and stared at the carpet. Turkish. The swirling colors, the intricacy of the design somehow focused him into a place of silence and stillness—inviting the images from his dream. Peter rubbed his hand across his forehead as the sequence played in his head. How could he consider such a circumstance, even in a dream?

He had always, of course, been attracted to women, and they to him. But his ice blue eyes, flaxen hair and powerful build also proved a magnet to those few men of a certain kind who tried to lure him into dark corners, especially when he was younger. If using his charm didn't repel them, then the threat of fisticuffs scared them off.

In his dream, which left him as jittery as if someone had set up his bristles and made him furious, he had been at his wedding, a grand affair attended by royals and the quality. After an excruciatingly long ceremony, happiness rose inside him like champagne bubbles drifting to the clouds. He lifted the Venetian lace veil of his bride. Eyes the color of a blazing golden sunset stared out, pupils a black slit growing round, a beckoning vortex.

The djinni, Yasir.

Peter felt his body jerk. He looked around. No one there. Of course, he was in his room, alone. But in the dream, everyone was there.

The images crowded inside his head, taunting him to review what came next. He took his bride in his arms, feeling a jolt of excitement, and kissed him with a strange, new passion. In a fever of desire, Peter linked his hand with the djinni's. They walked down the aisle, smiling brightly, to the joyous music of violins and the ebullient faces of the huge congregation.

Much to Peter's chagrin, the twinges of anticipation when he brushed those tender lips, when he held Yasir's warm muscular body next to his, still lingered in his flesh. He had never experienced a dream so vivid.

He sat up and slapped his hands on his thighs, resolving not to think on these concerns. By God, he had a wife, but Lavinia was another matter, a matter he also wanted to put out of his mind.

His valet busy preparing his clothes, Peter scrubbed the sodden badger bristles of his gold shaving brush into the bar of Castile soap and dabbed the foamy lather onto his stubble. He shut his eyes, blocking out his face in the mirror, the froth warm on his skin. The golden glow of his dream pierced the dark sanctuary of his reverie and, again, he stared into those hypnotic eyes, glittering like a treasure.

"Milord, the lather goes flat."

Peter opened his eyes. Stevens unfolded the tortoise shell handle of his razor and Peter held it to his chin, the blade trembling in his hand. He felt a clown, smeared with milky, foamy soap, yet unable to scrape his whiskers.

"With your permission, milord?" Stevens held out his hand, steady as a rock. At Peter's slight nod, his valet deftly shaved him. Stevens dipped the razor, obliterated by cloudy foam, into steaming water and the shiny blade emerged clean. The valet toweled Peter's face spotless.

Peter had always preferred to shave himself, uncomfortable with the straight razor in someone else's hands. Yet, his valet handled all else with his usual aplomb, not commenting on Peter's condition, and finished with a perfect knot in his lord's cravat, adjusting it over the stiff white Grafton collar.

Peter stared at himself in the mirror.

How on earth had Lavinia found his secret meeting? She was clearly unsuspecting. It was as though she had happened upon it. But at midnight? His wife did have that seeing ability. He must watch for it from now on; perhaps there was a way to control her.

In the scuffle for the urn, he had manhandled Lavinia, quite possibly hurt her more than he was aware. But it was her own damn fault, running to the djinni where he was bound and bleeding, screaming his name and fawning over him. He could hear it now, the feeling in her voice: *Yasir, oh Yasir. What has he done to you?* Made a fool of herself and him in front of his distinguished guests.

He held out his arms and faced his valet, waiting patiently as Stevens straightened his shirt, then buttoned his coat. His headache, soothed by the warm water from his shave, bloomed again in his temple. Only eleven hours ago he had the djinni stripped and trussed on a scaffold, whipped until he was raw meat. The sharp crack of the lash rang through Peter's head. He flinched.

"Milord? Did I hurt you?" Stevens moved aside and swept his hands behind his back.

"No, it's nothing." Peter looked into the mirror and tilted his head at his reflection. Must have been the tussle with Lavinia that sparked his vivid dream. He headed towards the door. None of it mattered now. He had never held much stock in dreams.

He possessed the urn, therefore the djinni, and he would be damned if he wouldn't make the best of it. Master of a djinni. If anyone had hinted it was possible a week ago, he would've shamed them with his laughter.

26

*P*eter knocked at Lavinia's door. It wouldn't do to burst in after what happened last night.

"Yes, milord?" Fleming kept the door half closed. Peter frowned. What did the silly woman think? It was three in the afternoon, Lavinia should be up and dressed.

"I am here to see my wife."

Fleming looked startled and stuttered. "Why, I-I am sorry sir." She opened the door and scuttled out of the way, announcing him in a disapproving tone.

"Leave us." Peter didn't disguise his irritation. Fleming's face fell. She gathered her skirts and slumped out.

Lavinia's hair shone dark, contrasting with her ghostly complexion, washed of any color. In Peter's mind the image of a pale lace veil falling over the face of his bride faded, then brightened. Yasir's golden eyes, his soft bowed lips, the warmth of his body pressed against him. That damn dream, rearing its ugly head again. Peter reached for the tall bedpost to steady himself.

Lavinia stared, her blue eyes piercing, like lapis inlaid in ivory. The same look she had given him when he found Yasir in her bed. She turned her head away.

He let go of the bedpost and fiddled with the lace of his cuff. It served her right to lose the genie, whoring like that.

Peter walked to the window and stared across the huge lawn to the forest beyond. All his lands, his riches, his accomplishments, and his wife chose a bloody genie over him. How long had Lavinia been sleeping with Yasir? Peter gripped the sill, his face growing hot. If she had opened the urn after he gave it to her . . . If Yasir had seduced her with his jewels and magic right away, it would have been over eight years.

His mind clicked and whirred like the fine mechanism of his tall case clock, rolling an infant's image into the moon dial. *Lord in heaven, how many of his children were Yasir's?*

Peter sat down hard on the pale pink upholstered chair by Lavinia's bed. The pleasure of seeing Yasir flogged and bloody didn't assuage this new possibility. And the incantations in his scrolls hadn't restored his memory all at once. No. Just in pieces. He fisted his hands. Squeezing.

All three children looked like Lavinia. Not a hint of the genie's golden eyes or any magic. But he wasn't with the children all that much, hadn't scrutinized their actions for a hint of whatever might pass for magic. By God, he could have missed any subtle signs. That would have been the furthest thing from his mind. Was it possible they were all his? Or were they all the genie's?

Stuart, his firstborn, had been brought by a gypsy at four months old. This after Lavinia was kidnapped and mysteriously returned, insane and full of lunatic tales. In all likelihood, he was Yasir's child. What about James? And little Cybelle, a strange, serious child, almost fairy-like in her mysteriousness.

After Lavinia stabbed him, Peter had ordered Dobson to destroy the urn. Then his and Lavinia's marriage had smoothed out. Good years with the birth of sweet Cybelle. But when did Yasir return? Was Cybelle his? And how the devil did Lavinia get the urn back?

"Peter?"

Lavinia peered at him from her bed.

"I stopped by to see how you are . . . after last night." Peter turned from the window. He should leave before his anger made him do something he might regret. He had come to apologize, but felt even more justified for last night's actions, his tussle with his wife. His conniving, cheating wife.

"Peter, I-I never wanted this." Lavinia put her hands on top of her coverlet. Her wrists were black and blue. He hadn't meant to hurt her, only the deuced genie.

"I never wanted this either," he said. And that was true. He never wanted to be a cuckold, to confront his wife in bed with another man, to have Lavinia choose someone else over him.

She could have another baby. This time he would definitely see to it that the child was his. Bulls could be gelded. The thought consoled him.

Out of the corner of his eyes, he saw Lavinia narrow hers. But when she met his gaze they were relaxed. What was she hiding? He had the genie. What more could she keep secret?

27

The next day Alice swirled into Lavinia's room, her brown skirts rich with russet in the morning light from the window.

"Good, you're all dressed. I have found the mouse."

"What?" Lavinia yawned, barely managing to cover her mouth. Apparently, all had been forgiven, or set aside, regarding the mirror incident. At least on her aunt's part. Lavinia, however, could have used another day or more as respite from Alice's presence.

"Sit here by me," her aunt patted a place beside her on the small divan. "Let us be quiet and observe." She raised her hand and nodded in the direction of the wardrobe.

Lavinia could see nothing different around the wardrobe. The piece itself was dusted and polished. The roundels, interwoven flowers of ivory, tortoise shell, bone and ebony, surrounded by mother-of-pearl borders, shone in the morning light. A bit peeved with Alice and her intrusion, she looked at the door. Nanny would be here soon with Cybelle, who wandered to find her mother if she wasn't brought to her. Lavinia heaved a long sigh at the mornings spent searching for her daughter before they understood what the child wanted.

Her aunt stared intently at the wardrobe. Following Alice's gaze, Lavinia peered closer. A small furry head peeped out from under the curved leg at the base. She saw a glint of silver before the mouse crept into the shadows underneath. Alice squeezed Lavinia's arm.

Lavinia inhaled softly. The creature had her talisman in its mouth. Was it Meylo or some other mouse? After all, they were savage little things, fighting with those sharp teeth and squeaking from wounds or rage. If the cat hadn't gotten Meylo, he could have been killed by another mouse.

Almost imperceptibly, Alice curled her right hand resting in her lap. As her fingers closed, the mouse came out and turned in their direction. By the time Alice made a fist, the mouse was at Lavinia's feet. The rodent lay the talisman before her. Alice gave a slight nod, and Lavinia scooped it up.

She almost dropped the charm at the shock that went through her when she held the cool silver in her hand. The mouse stood still, its tiny pink eyes boring into her. She had turned this boy into a rodent. It's a wonder he didn't nip her with those sharp little teeth.

What should she do? Yasir had said the talisman fulfilled her wish and made Meylo into a little rat—the last thing she had called him before she summoned the djinni. That was his excuse for not turning Meylo back into a boy, for only she could do the transformation with her talisman. Was it true?

Alice's eyes weighed heavy on her, as well as the mouse's. Both of them expecting her to do marvelous magic. She closed her hand over the talisman, shut her eyes, and wished the mouse would change back into Meylo. After a suitable time, she looked. The mouse and Alice still stared at her.

"Say it out loud, Nia," her aunt whispered. She lay her warm hand on Lavinia's shoulder.

"You are a boy again." Lavinia opened her palm. The talisman had small teeth marks marring the surface. The mouse was still in front of her. It flicked its tail.

"Milady, I have Cybelle." The nanny's voice came through the door. Of course she couldn't knock, her arms were filled with the child. She heard Cybelle whimper.

Lavinia closed her fist on the talisman and turned to Alice, who indicated the mouse with a tilt of her head. Was the mouse larger? Its tail shorter? Before her eyes, the mouse grew, its fur changing to pink skin, its nose flattening. Outside the door, Cybelle whimpered again.

The mouse's round ears shrank, the red eyes widened, whiskers dropped like autumn leaves. The transformation was grotesque, a perfect horror, but she couldn't pull her eyes away. She should have heard creaks from the bones as the legs plumped and extended, moans from Meylo as his eyes moved to the front of his flattening face. But there was only eerie silence in his transformation, his clothes layering on as if they were another tier of his skin. Lavinia felt she would be screaming if Alice hadn't been sitting beside her, her hand placed reassuringly on her arm.

Meylo brushed his hands over his clothes. He looked like he had when he first came into her room and threatened her. Odd how his shirt, pants and shoes appeared as he changed back. But they were a part of him.

"*Criminy!* Took you long enough. I been lugging this jewelry round seems like forever." Meylo towered above them.

Lavinia jumped up, the talisman tight in her fist.

"Shhh. You have to hide. Nanny is coming in." She pushed him behind the bed. "Get down and be quiet. Don't come out until I say."

Alice opened the door and took Cybelle in her arms.

"Little lady, you've grown since yesterday," she cooed to the child. The door closed behind her. Alice was imminently practical with her magic.

The talisman pinged against the ceramic ring holder on the dresser as Lavinia set it down to take Cybelle. The child slipped her fist from her mouth, reaching for the silver charm. She kept her deep blue eyes on the talisman even when Alice placed her in Lavinia's arms.

Lavinia kissed her daughter's dark curls, but Cybelle pointed at the talisman and leaned precariously towards it.

"Cybie, Mother's here. Let me see your smile." Lavinia tried to catch her daughter's attention.

Alice held out a silver rattle with teeth marks much like the talisman. Cybelle snatched it and put it in her mouth as she settled into her mother's arms, drool dripping from her crooked smile.

Lavinia shook her head.

"Alice, I talk to this one all the time. Ask questions. Show her around the garden and the house, pointing out and naming what might catch her interest. She looks, takes it in. But says nothing." Lavinia heard the exasperation in her own voice. She sidled up to her aunt and whispered. "I believe she may be Peter's after all, even though Yasir swears she's his."

The child pointed to the bed and the shock of brown hair rising from behind it. Hazel eyes followed, blinking. Meylo peeped out.

"I told you to stay until I came for you," Lavinia said.

He held out his arms. Spots of gray fur sprouted from them.

Lavinia tightened her grip on Cybelle. Her gasp filled the room like a scream. She stared at his hand. "What's wrong, why—?"

"I'm turning back." Meylo gulped. "I'll be a mouse again." He rubbed the fur on his arms as if he could scrub it away, but most of it stuck, save for wisps that floated in the air like gray dandelions.

"Help!" His voice squeaked. He stood up. As he stood there, his ears grew smaller. His nose elongated.

Cybelle pointed, her mouth a round O.

"Nia dear, I think you must do it again." Alice, fist to her chin, studied him. She held out her hand and the talisman appeared in her palm.

Cybelle widened her eyes and stretched for it.

"Here, you hold Cybelle." Lavinia transferred her daughter into Alice's embrace and took the talisman.

Meylo looked at his arms. The fur covered more of his skin. "It hurts. I almost got eaten by the cat. There was a-a mouse trap." He moaned. "I'll forget everything, won't remember 'bout the bottle, 'bout telling the Lord o' the House."

"Meylo, calm down." Lavinia patted his hand, recoiling at the stiff fur. "It so happens my husband knows about the bottle." She looked directly into Meylo's eyes. "He has stolen it from me."

Meylo's mouth fell open. "He has it now? I thought you guarded it? I figured you hid it well. Thought sure—"

"Yes, Meylo, all those things. And I don't know how. But it's g-gone—"

"Cor, don't cry." Meylo moved towards her, but stopped before he touched her. He had seen how she reacted when she touched his furry hand.

"I'll help you. I don't want the bottle." He stepped closer. "It'll be all right. Bet I can get it back fer you."

Lavinia nodded, then shook her head, words stuck in her throat.

"Lady, I'm sorry. Sorry you lost it." His voice broke. "Can you uncurse me? Then you'll never see me again. I'll never breathe a word." He gripped her shoulder. Hard. He let go. "Uh, please."

"Step away a bit and let me try again." She held her palm open, staring at the silver talisman until it glistened, the glow around it blurring the teeth marks.

"You will become a boy now." Her voice rang out clear and confident. She looked up at Meylo. Long stiff whiskers had sprouted on his snout.

Meylo dropped into the chair by the side of the bed. "That spangly man wot changed me. Please call him. He can change me back so I can leave. I know you wanna get rid of me."

"I can't call him. Things have changed. He answers to my husband now." She heard the raggedness of her voice and held back tears, but the sting in her eyes stayed.

"Has something to do with that bottle, huh?" Meylo tapped his hand on his leg. Slow, then faster.

"You threatened me before." Lavinia eyed him. Could she trust the boy?

"Don't want nothing now, except wot I came with. Jus' me, back like I was." He scratched his head, wrinkling his brow and bent towards her. "I'm sorry fer all the things I did. Please, please help me."

Lavinia squeezed the talisman. "I think we can help each other. Let me try again."

Alice stood beside her, Cybelle in her arms engrossed with the spectacle of Meylo and his changing face and body.

Lavinia held the talisman in her fist.

"You will be not be a mouse. You will be a boy like you were before." She opened her palm.

Fast as a serpent's strike, Cybelle snatched it. The child put the charm half in her mouth and stared at Meylo.

"Criminy, think I might be sick." He held his stomach and rose from the chair. The fur on his body fell off in sheets as if a razor had run over his flesh. His slanted eyes grew wide and blunted, his pointed nose rounded.

Lavinia could see the sprinkle of freckles over the ridge of his nose, the sheen of sweat on his smooth brow. His mouth flattened and spread out as the flesh accommodated his broad chin. Each feature came onto view, slow enough to observe. The features of a boy around fifteen or sixteen.

Meylo held out his arms. "I have my hands! I'm still tall. I'm not shrinking. Am I?" He contorted his face. "Am I?"

Lavinia's stomach lurched. She thought she might be sick. Was he changing back to the mouse? Had she failed again?

"Don't jus' stare. Am I turning into a boy?" Meylo's voice ended in a high pitch, almost a squeak. "Well?"

"You are changing back to a boy." Lavinia spoke in unison with Alice. Surprised, she looked at her aunt, who jiggled Cybelle in her arms and laughed.

Cybelle held out her tiny hand, palm up, the talisman resting in it, mimicking her mother. She closed her fist upon the charm and waved it up and down as if the charm were her favorite rattle.

Lavinia reached for the talisman, but Alice shook her head. What mischief might Cybelle wreak with it? Surely Alice wouldn't allow Cybie to be in danger. When Lavinia cursed Meylo by calling him a little rat, the talisman followed her command, but she had said nothing against her daughter.

Cybie seemed quite attached to the charm. If it were taken away, she couldn't predict what her daughter might do and the effect it would evoke from the talisman. Better to wait until the child lost interest and then secure the charm in a safe place.

She studied Meylo. He seemed to settle into his new body, rather his old body. She held her shoulders straight as a rush of satisfaction replaced her cold fear with a warm glow. She had done it. With the talisman. All by herself.

"That little 'un of yours . . ." Meylo pointed to Cybelle who was sucking on the talisman. "Got magic." He touched her cheek and Cybelle beamed. "I was getting dizzy jus' like afore when my hands got bony as a skelton with claws, when everything in the house grew big as buildings. Then this 'un swiped the jewelry. And poof!" He spread his hands apart as if he were doing magic.

He squinted. "Lady, don't look at me like that. Your mouth is open wider 'n a fish. Your little one's wot changed me back. I'm sure of it."

"I suspect it was a delayed reaction," Lavinia said, crossing her arms.

Meylo raised his eyebrows.

"Guess I should go anyhow." He started to the door, then stopped. He looked back. "Thanks."

"Wait." Lavinia hurried to him. "You have no money. You have no place to go."

Meylo shrugged. "I jus' wanted to be a boy again. It's wot I said. Don't want no trouble, so I'll go."

"We can offer you a job, wages, room and board," Lavinia motioned him to a chair.

Meylo made for the door. "Kind of you, but I think I've had enough of—"

"You said you would do anything if we changed you back. This is what you must do." Lavinia moved closer.

She never knew why Meylo didn't bolt from the room, from Bramley House, at her offer. Yet he ambled back, hands in his pockets. Perhaps he remembered how hard it was being on his own. Or heard the tiny hint of a threat in her voice.

At any rate, he probably never dreamed what was in the bottle.

28

*M*eylo couldn't leave, even though his feet were screaming, RUN, RUN. Those blue eyes of the Lady Lavinia were like a deep well. Something about her just dug into him. That's just the way it happened. Nothing he could do.

The Lady Lavinia said, "You're going to be a footman."

"Wot?" Meylo turned from the door to face her. "I don't have the fancy talk to work here. You know it 'n I know it. Ain't no sense in beating a dead horse. Now let me go. I'll be off fer good." He cocked his head for a last look. She can't say what he said wasn't true. Can't do anything about his way of talking.

The Lady Lavinia turned to the other lady, her eyes full of messages.

"Alice, let me hold Cybelle. As we discussed, this is part of my task, but I've carried it as far as I can. I'm asking one little favor."

Alice walked up to him like one of those brown sparrows you see all over the place. Plump and kind of feathery. He wouldn't have been surprised to hear a squeaky chirp come right out of her mouth.

She put her hand on his arm.

He flinched at her touch. Hot as sitting too close to the fire, but no blister on him.

He would have to say it again. "Milady Alice, at the risk of being tedious I must repeat, I do not have the proper speech for employment—" Meylo put his fingers to his mouth.

Criminy! What was this? Milady Alice? Tedious? Employment? Only gentlemen used those whopping big words. He'd heard them before, but couldn't ever drag them up to use. Didn't know if the words were even stuck somewhere in his mind.

Alice looked up at him, the gold flecks in her eyes sparkling, what gold coins must look like in the sun. The Lady Lavinia smiled like she might eat him up. "Now that you've overcome your objections, here's what you must do."

That was just days ago. And now he was a footman at Bramley House with the fancy liver, uh livery. What they called clothes. A fine jacket of dark blue with a red, claret they called it, collar and cuffs, claret waistcoat and breeches. He had to pull on white silk stockings and black leather shoes with silver buckles. That was what all the footmen wore.

They had him mostly hefting heavy furniture for the maids to clean under. Pretty little things, those maids, and flirty. Have mercy. But the Lady Lavinia said he'd be setting out silver in a few days, she'd heard he was doing so well.

Can't forget his main duty, to find that bottle for the Lady Lavinia. Neither of the ladies ever said what they'd do if he didn't get the bottle, but he didn't ever want to be a mouse again.

"You. What's your name?" Lord Peter Bramley stood beside a grand door in the front hallway. It was him as sure as the nose on Meylo's face. He looked just like the fancy framed painting in the main sitting room, yellow hair, blue eyes and looking down his nose.

Meylo stood there. His head felt like it had emptied out. Cor. The Master His Self. The Lady Lavinia told him his footman name couldn't be Meylo. What was it? His Self would sack him sure as his own name was Meylo if he stood there any longer, mouth open, staring like a dog in the street.

Tindale.

Meylo gave a little bow. "Tindale, milord." In his head, he repeated: tin like the metal, dale like the hill, tin-metal, dale-hill. Tindale, Tindale, Tindale.

"Fine. Tindale. In here, I need a hand." Lord Bramley opened the door.

Meylo angled his head up as he followed Bramley inside. That door was a grand piece of wood, taller than both of them put together, with raised borders carved so rich and fancy.

This must be what the Lady Lavinia called the study. There was a giant desk with stacked papers and a gold penholder, more books than he'd ever seen lining the walls, and fine lamps lit. Enough stuff to study. This Bramley must be smart. But did he have magic like those ladies, the little girl and the spangly man?

Where was that spangly man? The Lady Lavinia said he was with her husband. Meylo glanced at the fine thick rug, the stuffed chairs and polished tables with shiny gold knick-knacks and brass candlesticks and beeswax candles, not those tallow ones that stunk. But he didn't see any sign of that spangly man.

"Can you move this by yourself? Or do you need help?" Bramley tapped on an empty bookshelf that came to his thighs.

"I am able to move it myself, milord." Meylo wasn't sure how his words were changed into fancy ones spoken by that fine voice, but inside he'd said, Sure I can move this, jus' get out the way there.

He put both hands, wide apart, under the top, and lifted the bookshelf, leaning it into him.

Lord Bramley pointed. "Under the window. Mind the curtains."

Meylo set the bookcase down. He heard a rip, moved his foot. One of the curtains bunched limp at his feet, red and gold with fussy embroidery. His first job for The Lord-o'-All and he'd made a mull of it.

Bramley said something under his breath. Cursing in that uppity voice of his.

"Over in the corner, remove the boxes and stack them in the hall beside the front door. Keep the windows clear. Take care, these are fragile. Set them down gently." Bramley walked to his desk.

Meylo watched him out of the corner of his eye as he went in and out with the boxes. His Self opened one of the drawers in his big desk and lifted something up. Meylo pretended to figure out best way to pick up the particular box in front of him, it being bigger than the rest. He kept sliding his eyes over to Bramley who now held a huge key. Bramley stuck the key in a door of the giant cabinet behind his desk. The piece of furniture covered most of the wall and nearly reached the ceiling.

Meylo lifted the box. Cor, heaviest one yet. With the next two boxes, His Self had the cabinet door open. Inside, it was like a treasure chest: fine polished wood with pieces stuck in it all smooth, shining in rainbow colors. And gold fittings like a horse's harness, but fancier. He left the study carrying the next box and piled it on top of the last one in the hall. When he returned, Bramley had closed the cabinet. Nothing looked different around the big desk. His Self must've put everything back.

Meylo took another box. And another. When he went in next, he caught a peek of Bramley setting something in a black bag aside, something that looked the same size as he remembered the bottle. Could he be so lucky?

He hefted another box, hauled it out. Came back. Bramley was moving piles of papers on his desk. Meylo left with another box. Bramley had his pen out, writing. And there were no more boxes. No more time to search the study.

"Tell Dobson the boxes are ready." Bramley didn't look up. "And Tindale, next time don't dawdle so much."

"Yes, milord." Meylo walked out and closed the door with hardly a click.

Did Bramley know he was spying on him? Meylo felt eyes staring as he went down the hall to find Dobson. Eyes from the other servants, from the mice that lived in the walls, magic eyes from Alice and the Lady Lavinia and that little one. His skin tingled. He checked his hands.

No fur. Yet.

If he got sacked, would they turn him into a mouse again?

29

As the light of day faded, Meylo trudged along a path by Bramley House and glanced behind to make sure no one saw him. He'd been a footman for over a week now and hadn't gotten sacked yet. The sun's rays streamed through holes in the thick black clouds building on the horizon, making it look like heaven was coming down to earth. Birds shrieked as they winged to their nesting trees. Probably warning the others about the storm that might come.

He veered onto the grass next to the house, an empty bucket swinging in his hand. Busy looking busy. He eyed the windows, counting to seven, then slipped behind a thick green hedge that reached past the window of Lord Bramley's study.

He set the bucket upside down, climbed on top and hauled himself up to the window. With a good grip on the sill, he peered into the room. A rumble came from the dark clouds behind him, then a boom rang across the sky, as fierce and loud as the trains colliding in that accident near Little Wymondly. The window glass rattled. The birds shrieked. The wind picked up.

Meylo turned to look at the sky and was slapped hard in the face. Caught, he was caught, in the suds for certain. He closed his eyes, thought up an excuse for spying on His Self. Ready to face his accuser, he looked straight ahead. Shocked, he chuckled. Lawks, just the ragged branches of the bush whipping in the wind.

Black clouds filled most of the sky now, only a little streak of turquoise left on the horizon. Cor, must be a big one brewing. As he faced the window, he almost slipped, but latched his fingers onto the wide stone sill. Perfect. He could see the cabinet behind Bramley's desk, even see the gold fittings. A gust of wind slammed the brushy branches into his back. He wobbled on the bucket.

Another burst of thunder. The bright flash of lightning reflected in the glass, making the evening seem darker, scary, like something bad would happen. Lord Bramley lit the lamp on his desk. Meylo hadn't seen him walk into the study, hadn't heard or seen the door open. Best mind what he was about.

He peered from behind the red and gold curtain bunched against the glass at the inside of the window. Bramley paced, then went to the same drawer as before, unlocked it with a key from under the penholder, then lifted up a corner of something in the drawer. He pulled out the giant key. No mistaking that big fancy key, same one as last time.

Meylo could see the exact cabinet door where Bramley stuck the key. His Self opened it and pressed on a spot in the middle. One, two, three . . . Criminy, now Bramley's back was in the way.

His Self pulled out the black velvet pouch.

A howling wind drove a wall of sudden rain onto Meylo's head and shoulders. His breath caught at the onslaught. Colder than bones. He foundered, wheeling his arms to right himself. Branches flailed his back and legs. He grabbed at the window sill, but his fingers slipped off the smooth, wet stone. He went down without a sound. Ass-over-tit. Could have screamed his lungs out and no one would have heard, what with the wind howling and the rain hammering.

His foot kicked the bucket with a clang. He sat up, but something held him down. Was he caught? *Thunder an' turf*, it was the bloody bush again. He thrashed through the branches, slipped in the mud, and ran.

The next day Meylo, scrubbed clean and in fresh livery, moved furniture in the dining room and parlor so the maids could properly clean the floor and carpets. In the afternoon, he helped take grain to the mill and, after waiting for the miller to grind it, delivered the bags of flour to the larder next to the kitchen. Later, he assisted in laying the table for the fancy banquet that night.

While everyone was preoccupied with preparations for the guests, he crept up the servant's stairs, and opened the door just a crack to the second floor. The hall was empty. He hurried out, keeping to the walls. With a gulp, he knocked at the Lady Lavinia's door. The maid answered.

"I have a message for Milady," he said, his proper voice coming from what Alice did to him. He wasn't sure he liked it, but this right and proper talking got him the job. And he wasn't sure that was a good thing. His new voice made him more and more afraid. What else could they do to him?

"Milady, a footman with a message," the maid said as she turned to the inside.

The Lady Lavinia tilted towards the doorway. When she saw him, her eyes opened wide. "Fleming, send him in. Then fetch the two silk shawls from the scullery. Find the satin wrap and bring it up also."

Fleming walked past, and the Lady Lavinia motioned Meylo inside. "Hurry. I must dress. I've only an hour."

"Milady, I—"

"Follow me to my dressing room." Her shiny robe swished as she walked in front of him, the blue flowers so real he thought he could smell them. She stood in front of a tall mirror, held up a fancy gown and turned it this way and that, the rose cloth reflecting the lamplight.

"Milady, I know where Lord Bramley keeps the urn," Meylo said.

She fixed him with those blue eyes. "Where? And why didn't you get it?"

"It is not so easy to procure these things. Your husband is constantly in his study, and he keeps it locked. But I can give almost precise instructions for milady to obtain it. I believe milady should write this down." Meylo followed her to her writing desk.

He told her everything he had seen, adding which cabinet door, the spot Bramley touched and the number of times he pressed on the spot, and a guess on how many more presses after His Self's back blocked the view.

"So you'll get the urn soon?" She blotted the writing paper penned with her careful notes.

Meylo put his finger in his cravat and pulled the cloth away from his neck. Damn thing nearly choked him.

"Milady, I think it might be best if milady obtained the urn. If milady's husband caught me . . ." Meylo couldn't say what would happen, but whatever it was there'd be hell to pay. He looked down at his polished leather shoes. Would he be able to take these? Stash them in a bag and sneak them out?

"Nonsense, Peter knows I want the urn. If he found me in his study, he would hide it in a different place, and we'd be back to where we started." She closed her notes in a drawer. "You need to obtain the urn soon. He might change hiding places often. He has a devious mind, you know." She walked to the corner and yanked the pull cord.

"I am calling my maid. We have guests tonight, and now I must hurry." She gave him a look, her eyes slanting.

Blimey, what did she want him to do now?

"Tonight would be perfect." She curled a lock of her hair around her finger as her eyes shone. He didn't like that look one bit. "You must acquire it tonight. Peter will be preoccupied with the guests—important you know. And the servants will be busy. Since you're inexperienced, and this banquet is formal, they won't expect you to do much." She uncurled the strand of hair from her finger, the red stone in her ring flashing. "Yes, tonight is perfect."

Meylo shifted his feet. It didn't feel like such a perfect night. Something made him uneasy. When he felt this way, he laid low.

She looked at him. "Well?"

"Milady, it is as good as in your hands." Those uppity words again, always agreeing. He wanted to say, *Not on yer life* will I do it tonight. Wot if Peter caught me? No skin off yer back, lady.

Meylo stalked down the servant's stairs. He could go through the kitchen, walk out the back door and be free of all this. But their magic would find him. Like that red moon did. He had changed his mind about the Lady Lavinia and the red moon. Could've been her, that spangly man, or the lady called Alice. They'd turn him into a mouse again, but he'd be a house mouse in the country. Sure to be eaten quicker than here.

He strode down the main hallway, pretending he was on an errand. He was almost to the alcove, halfway to the study, when the door opened and Lord Bramley burst out, followed by his valet.

Meylo slipped into the alcove, trying to quiet his breathing.

"Bloody hell, Stevens, I told you to come for me an hour before dinner. You're late."

"Milord, begging your pardon, it is an hour before dinner." Stevens sounded calm. Probably used to the Lord-o'-All lighting into him all the time. The door clicked shut.

"Synchronize our timepieces. I cannot have this happen again." Bramley's fine leather boots thudded on that fancy marble floor. Angry steps.

"I need a shave. Is all prepared? Hot water, towels warmed? And my deuced neck is bothering me. I'll need a massage. Damn it, I must be in fine fettle for Lord Thompson."

"Milord, all is ready, hot water, hot towels. The wine is decanting. We can start with a massage." Dobson sounded a bit out of breath. Must be hurrying to catch up to his crabby boss. Their voices faded as they turned the corner.

The hallway was clear now. Meylo thought of excuses if he was seen by a nosy servant: *Lord Bramley needed his, his . . . book. Or a satchel. Or a sheaf of important papers.* He tried the door knob to the study. Unlocked. Bramley's bad temper was in Meylo's favor tonight.

He slipped inside.

The late twilight through the open curtains lit the room enough for him to see. He found the key under the pen holder and opened the desk drawer. What had Lord Bramley lifted out to get to the big key? The insides were neat and orderly, extra pens lined up—

Footsteps in the hall, voices.

He closed the drawer, dropped behind the desk. The footsteps passed by and faded down the hall. As he stood, he glimpsed a shape stashed under the desk, almost hidden in the shadows. He crawled under and pulled it out.

The black velvet bag. Heavy. He remembered the bottle feeling like it was made of solid brass. He set it on the floor behind the desk, loosened the pouch and slipped it off. The bottle gleamed golden in the fading light.

Dobson had to have surprised Bramley. His Self wouldn't have left the bottle out like this. He was fearsome neat and the Lady Lavinia said he had a devious mind. And that meant sneaky, along with clever and smart.

Criminy! He was free. He would take the bottle to the Lady Lavinia. Get a reward. Then leave this witchy place. Leave it as a human, not a mouse, with some new shoes and gold coins.

When he touched the bottle itself, a feeling went up his arm like a snake of needles poking into his skin. Was this what all the fuss was about? What had a husband and wife stealing from one another? Maybe the bottle was filled with gold coins or jewels like he saw on the spangly man.

He fiddled with the lid, and pulled back with a gulp when it flew open. As he drew near to look inside, smoke drifted out. More and more, thicker and thicker, a ghost taking shape.

His scalp prickled. Before he could blink, that spangly man stood there in front of him. Like before. Before he turned him into a mouse.

"Please sir, I didn't mean no harm. Please don't turn me into a mouse. The lady sent me to fetch the bottle. It's . . . She . . . she wants it." Meylo shook his head. His old way of talking. It was back. Had this spangly man done magic on him, or was it just being around the man that odd things happened?

The spangly man held both palms up. "Take the urn to her now. Put it in the velvet bag. Do not let anyone see you."

Meylo stepped back. The man came from the smoke, which came from the bottle. If the bottle was empty, would the Lady Lavinia still want it? Was it the spangly man she wanted? He could barely think, but it seemed nearly everyone was strange in this house. Seemed they all had some kind of magic, even the little girl. He'd better be careful to get this right.

Really careful.

"I'll take it to the lady, but you'd better get back in it or I'll get into trouble. Seems she wants more than just the bottle." That stinging started in his scalp again. Criminy! Was he turning? He checked his hands, no fur. But they trembled like an old man's. He looked up.

The spangly man was fading. His jewels still sparkled, but he could swear he saw the window through the man's body. Sweat dripped down his forehead, but he'd never felt so cold. As he lived and breathed, the man vanished right in front of him.

The smoke went into the bottle faster than it came out.

Meylo was shaking so badly he rattled. NO. It wasn't him rattling. It was someone at the door. He snatched the bottle and the bag. The door opened. The bright light from the hall sliced through the dim light in the study. He ducked under the desk, scrambling to the very back.

The scratch of a match being struck made him squeeze his eyes shut as if that would make him vanish like that spangly man.

He clamped his hand over his mouth to stop his moan. A light flickered. Papers rustled. A thud on top of the desk made him curl around the bottle. What? Did he think it would make him harder to see?

The light went out. He heard the door close, the snick of the bolt sliding and catching.

He uncurled. Crawled out from under the desk and peered over the edge, half expecting to see Bramley waiting for him, but no one was there. Meylo slipped the bottle into the velvet bag, unbuttoned his jacket, and stowed the bottle under it. He couldn't fasten the buttons, so he curved his arm around the bottle and slanted his body so the lump wouldn't show so much. If anyone saw him, he could lean to the side and limp, say he had a sudden cramp in his side.

He looked out the window. Still twilight, but darker. The Lady Lavinia and His Self would be in their rooms putting on their showy clothes. The maids and footmen would be busy with the family or their guests or making dinner.

He walked down the hall. Couldn't go too fast. Didn't want to be noticed. He was taking a message to the Lady Lavinia. The truth, for once. Almost in sight, the lady's door. How many pounds would he ask for? No, he should play it down. She wouldn't like it if it sounded like a bribe. Wouldn't want to tip her over *that* edge. The lady could be vicious. He'd say he needed money to start a business. The Lady Lavinia would like to hear that he wanted to make something of himself.

He would say he was going to be a delivery boy, then work his way up. He held up his hand to knock. The door opened.

Those eyes, cold, blue, like winter's ice. Lord Peter Bramley stared at him.

Cor! Meylo felt his insides churn as if they would break out of his skin and run off, but somehow he stood there, feet still feeling the floor.

"What do you want?" Bramley, his lace cravat shining with a big diamond stick pin, still had that temper from when he was keeping on at Dobson. His light blue eyes fell on the bundle under Meylo's arm.

Meylo couldn't find his voice.

"Who sent you?" Bramley said.

"Milord, I have a packet fer Milady." *Cor!* His own way of talking. He thought his proper voice would come back after that spangly man had gone into the bottle. Meylo hadn't said much, but he could hear the way he bent his words.

Bramley jerked his head, a puzzled expression on his face. He couldn't fool the Lord-o'-All. He'd heard the street in Meylo's voice. His Self held out his hand.

"I will give it to my wife."

Criminy! "Milord, Dobson said give it directly to milady." He said the words correctly but they were in that old voice of his. Bramley gave him that owl look again.

"I am sure Dobson would not mind if you gave it to the Lord of the Manor to give to his wife. Hand it over." Bramley held out his hand.

Meylo stood still for a moment.

Then he turned and ran. If he could make it to the servant's stairs he'd be safe, then he would leave out the kitchen door. Leave before anyone turned him into a mouse. He would—

A hand hard as stone gripped his shoulder. Before he knew it, he faced Lord Bramley. The Lord-o'-All opened Meylo's coat and seized the bottle. He held Meylo's arm like the tightening noose that would be put on him if they called the constables.

"You conniving thief." Bramley kept his voice low and soft. But the words were sharp as that knife the robber used to cut the wagon driver's throat. His Self marched him into the Lady Lavinia's rooms, squeezing his arm until the feeling was wrung out. Bramley shut the door. Not a slam, just a little click.

"Lavinia," he said in a low voice, smooth like he was talking to a little pet dog. "Come out here just a moment. There's a footman with a parcel for you."

And there she was, all dressed in a deep blue shiny gown, cut so low her bosoms about spilled out. A row of blue stones glittered around her neck.

"A parcel? I didn't order anything." She stopped, her hand drifted slowly from the hairpin she had been adjusting. Her big blue eyes took Meylo in. He felt just like he did when he looked up at her with his tiny mouse eyes, the talisman between his tiny teeth, wondering if she'd crush him with her slipper.

"Why whatever is it?" She said, her voice all silky and innocent. She was good at this, she was. Because she knew exactly what her husband had in his hands.

"Send Fleming away." Bramley squeezed Meylo's arm.

The Lady Lavinia stood there.

"Send your maid out. Now," Bramley said through clinched teeth.

The Lady Lavinia swept into her dressing room. Her maid scurried out, eyes down.

The Lord-o'-All dragged Meylo with him to the door. He locked it, pocketing the key. *Criminy!* Would he open that bottle? Would that spangly man turn him into a mouse? Meylo closed his mouth tight. Any word could set them off.

The Lady Lavinia strolled out of the dressing room and stood before her husband. "Well, Peter, why don't you give me what the footman brought?" She sounded exasperated.

"You know very well why I will not give it to you. And I'm wagering you also know this lad." Bramley threw Meylo to the floor.

He lay there, almost wishing he were a little mouse so he could scamper through a hole in the floorboards. Disappear.

Bramley slipped the velvet bag off the brass bottle. It gleamed in the lamplight.

The Lady Lavinia just stood there.

"Did you open it?" Bramley gave Meylo a look, his eyes cutting through him like he was butter.

Meylo opened his mouth, but no words came. If he said he had opened it, he'd be doomed. But if he said he didn't, then that spangly man would tell on him. Caught between a rock and a hard place.

"Never mind." Bramley had figured the same as him about the spangly man. He opened the lid. Meylo scuttled backwards on the floor as a wisp of smoke curled out, growing larger and larger.

And there he was.

The spangly man. He looked at Meylo like he'd never laid those hair-raising golden eyes on him before.

"Yasir, did this footman open the urn?"

"Yes, Master."

"What happened?"

Meylo's muscles drew up all by themselves, like Bramley was about to hit him. Now they'd know. Did the Lady Lavinia think he wouldn't open the bottle? With them both mad at him, it would be the mouse all over again. He was done for.

"Without preliminary, he begged me not to turn him into a mouse. And then he sent me back inside the urn." The spangly man smiled at Meylo. Those golden eyes, they were the last thing he saw that time before he turned into a mouse. The spangly man had left out that he told Meylo to take the bottle to the Lady Lavinia. The man had lied. Lied to his master.

Bramley turned to Meylo. "Why did you bring the urn to my wife?"

They all stared at him. Golden eyes, deep blue eyes. Bramley's eyes like frost on a window pane.

"Uh, milord, she asked me to fetch a magazine from your study. And I saw the velvet pouch. It looks like a lady's pouch. So I thought I'd save a trip and bring it here to her." Meylo exhaled. Pretty good story. He wasn't a mouse yet. But his voice hadn't changed to that fancy voice with those fancy words. Was he done for as a footman with his smart buckle shoes?

Bramley studied him. "Where is the magazine?"

"Milord, I forgot it." Meylo tried to twist his words into those crisp syllables.

Bramley seemed to loose interest in him. "Lavinia, do you know this footman?"

"Of course, he's worked here for several months. I know all the servants. A touch that makes for a happier staff, and when I learn their particular talents I can—"

Bramley held up his palm.

"Yasir, make this footman forget everything he knows about the urn."

The spangly man waved his hand.

Meylo grimaced. Couldn't help it. Would this hurt?

The room grew hazy. He blinked. Everyone watched him. He heard their voices, but they sounded far away and he couldn't make out everything they said.

Lord Bramley's voice boomed, "Send him to, hmm . . . mlzmbnex."

He heard the Lady Lavinia reply, "No! I will find a place for him. You dare not *xdncj wzmfzzz* . . ." Then only the sounds of their little spat rang in his ears, the words making no sense.

The room faded just like the spangly man when he had gone into the bottle. Ha! Meylo hadn't forgotten about the bottle yet. Maybe the Spangly man wouldn't follow His Self's orders to the T—like when lied to Bramley and left out that he'd told Meylo to take the bottle to the Lady Lavinia. .

The floor dropped out from under Meylo. He scrambled to hold onto something. Not finding anything solid was worse than the fur and whiskers popping out of his skin when he had turned into a mouse. His gut squeezed tight, spewing the insides from his mouth.

Nothing holding him up or down, he was just falling, winding around like a piece of rubbish caught by the wind.

Meylo took a long breath. Longer than he'd ever taken. Like he inhaled an hours worth of air. He was starved for it. He couldn't feel anything. Was he a mouse like before? Or something worse that could be squashed easier, like a bug or a mushroom? He found his arms, his hands. They looked almost normal, but his seeing wasn't so good. He squinted.

Thunder an' turf. Where was he?

30

*L*avinia sat at her mahogany writing table, chin in hand, staring at the wall. Where had Yasir actually sent Meylo? When she had protested Peter's command, the djinni had given her that look, which meant he was up to something. As Yasir gestured his magic, Meylo had been hunched in fear, his freckles like pepper grains on his shock-white skin. He faded away as if he were a mirage.

Poor boy.

She must persuade Peter to make Yasir bring Meylo back; then she could find someone that would hire him. Until then, she wouldn't forget, ever, that she owed the boy for all she had put him through.

But now she had to deal with what started the whole muddled mess.

Lavinia set her hand on the penwork box next to her porcelain inkstand, the gold-scrolled flowers and vines shining against the black surface. After Meylo had successfully transformed into a boy, Cybelle had clutched the talisman in her fist, opening her hand now and then, staring at the silver charm in her palm. Alice had met Lavinia's gaze with raised eyebrows before she took the child to the nursery.

The next day, Alice presented Lavinia with the lovely penwork box. "For the sanity of the household, keep this locked and, preferably, hidden," her aunt had said, a wry smile lightening her weary expression. "How you could ever think your daughter was not Yasir's I'll never fathom. The child has her father's stubbornness in spades." Alice let out an exasperated huff.

"I made one of her dolls dance. Quite the spectacle. The toy pirouetted, pink skirts ballooning, arms graceful above her head, blond curls bouncing. Cybelle was entranced."

Lavinia had frowned. Had Alice spell-cast Cybie?

"No, Nia, no spells. Cybelle was merely taken with the doll's actions. She set the talisman on the floor beside her and reached for the doll, pulling her dolly close and scooting along the floor with it as it pirouetted.

"I felt a thief when I pocketed the talisman and left Cybelle with Stuart, instructing him to seize the doll if he heard nanny coming." Alice had handed her a tiny key on a gold chain.

That was just yesterday afternoon, yet it seemed days ago. Time must distort with these improbable events—everything else did.

Lavinia inserted the key in the box's lock, and turned, its chain snaking in thin gold coils on the table. She lifted the lid. On a bed of startling red velvet lay the talisman. Rows of indentations from Meylo's mouse teeth marred the surface. Still, it had a presence.

She was afraid to touch the charm. With a firm snap she shut the box, locked it and slipped the key's chain around her neck. Fingering the miniature key, she vowed to hide both in a better place than she had found for the urn.

She set the box in the side drawer for the time being.

These things were incomplete and she despaired at her impotence. The same as she felt when a gift was wrapped and given, but not yet opened, or a letter written and posted, but not yet read. She leaned into her fingers and pressed them to her forehead. Like the gift and the letter, Meylo's whereabouts and Cybelle's magic weren't wholly resolved, weren't finished. They had a life of their own now.

She raised her head.

The magic mirror she had set on the table earlier shimmered, a small round pool situated incongruously on the mahogany surface of her writing table. She inched her hand towards it, the bruise from Peter on her wrist lighter, but still a circle of mottled lavender and cloudy yellow, a muddy puddle.

She touched the cool silver rim of the mirror. Her fingers curled away, reminding her of the delicate fringed-leaf plant that shrinks from any contact.

"Show me Yasir." The words vibrated deep in her throat as if they feared to fully exit.

She lifted the mirror. Looked into the shining surface, which turned murky dark gray, rippling, a pond whipped by the wind. No reflection of her face. No reflection of anything. She held her hand steady.

The glass lightened and smoothed until it shone as bright as the moon in a midnight sky. A dulling fog rushed across the surface. She saw a silhouette, a rounded forehead.

"Mehadeh," Lavinia said out loud. The sorceress looked directly at her, mouth open. Mehadeh turned away. The mirror showed the back of her head, filled with tiny braids, red beads woven into the strands. At an approaching shadow, Mehadeh bowed and stepped aside.

Suddenly, Lavinia stared into pitiless dark eyes. Cruel lips curled under a stiff mustache.

"Rakhshan." Lavinia's horrified whisper made the image in the mirror more fearsome. Her body jerked. Without knowing when or how, she stood by her table, the mirror slipping from her fingertips. She watched as if she were far away, an innocent bystander lost in a crowd, safe in the company of others. Everything happened in a sluggish manner. The mirror fell, a leaf, shiny and round. The air suspending it as it gently glided down angled steps and broad landings, disguising the steep fall.

The crash filled the room with the shattering of glass disproportionate to the mirror's small size. Lavinia shuddered out of her stupor. She stared in horror as the pieces settled onto the polished oak planks. This must be cleaned up immediately.

She hurried towards the pull cord, but halted as though she'd hit a wall. A scream tore from her throat. Her feet, her arms wouldn't move as she told them to. She could only stare at the leering image of Rakhshan floating in front of her.

Alice left her niece huddled quietly in the chair, eyes in a daze, and hurried to retrieve what Lavinia had said was left of the looking glass.

The mirror was unbreakable. The magic should have kept it whole, even if it were thrown into a wall. Surely, Lavinia was exaggerating. These humans with raven black hair and unusually pale complexions were known to become hysterical. Although her niece did have a set of problems that would throw even the most sensible person into fits.

She opened the door to Lavinia's room. The chair by her writing table was lying sideways on the floor. A slight haze marred the air as if someone had recently smoked a cigar, but there was no odor. She looked for the mirror, expecting to find it in a corner with perhaps a dented frame.

The day grew brighter outside. Alice drew in her breath. Hundreds of bits of glass glittered on the floor, radiating streaks of light that transformed into bits of rainbows. The vivid colors unworldly, hypnotic, entrancing. *By the Djinn,* Lavinia had been correct.

The mirror had broken. Impossible, but the evidence sparkled in front of her. The girl must truly have seen Rakhshan. His terrible power had shattered the mirror, not her niece's dropping it.

And what of Lavinia seeing Mehadeh first? Mehadeh bowing, then the Shadow Lord entering. Her niece had been conflicted about the sorceress. Mehadeh helped her escape from the Dark Magician's palace, had tried to save Yasir from the cursed bullet when Peter shot him. Was the sorceress with Yasir or Rakhshan? Another problem, but minor compared to the one in front of her. Alice turned around and around. The glass shards gleamed, beautiful but menacing now, since Rakhshan was the last thing Lavinia saw in the mirror.

They must be destroyed, but with care, with spells far away from Bramley House.

Could he *be here?* Lavinia had asked as she bowed her head, arms folded over her stomach. *D-does he know about my children? Who the father is?*

Alice looked away from the glittering shards. At the very least, the Dark Magician was searching, probing. But the question led her to another possibility that the flurry of recent events had kept her from considering. Did Peter know which children were Yasir's? Yasir could deflect the question if the answer were demanded. If Peter found out, it would be easier for Rakhshan to discover. It would be merely a matter of capturing Peter for a moment via magic.

After Lavinia had told her about the broken mirror, Alice had placed her hand on Lavinia's forehead. "The Shadow Lord is still searching for Yasir. Be calm, you know what I am doing. If you feel anything strange, it is only for your own good." With Yasir stolen from her, Peter her implicit enemy, and Rakhshan on her trail, Lavinia needed a bit of magic help.

"Yasir is with Peter," Lavinia had whispered. "He can't protect our babies. Now, it is up to me. And you. Please?"

Alice had nodded. Yasir had been reduced to the role of Peter's servant, but he was more in control than Lavinia knew. "Dear Nia, the Dark Magician is still thwarted. And we will see that it stays that way."

Her niece had settled into the chair then, her hands in her lap. They weren't shaking anymore.

A wave of menace, like a foul stench, emanated from the shimmering mirror shards scattered around Lavinia's room. Alice whispered the start of a command, raised her hand partway, but dropped it to her side, speaking new words that canceled the half-cast spell.

Her body shrank from the shards, from the magic she almost wielded. Yasir had warned her about the Shadow Lord's mysterious power over him. Perhaps the magician's magic would work on her in a similar way. And her father, Yasir's father, had cautioned her not to get between Yasir and Rakhshan. Bowing her head, she begged a silent forgiveness. How could she forget?

Alice slipped from the room and locked the door the human way. She could do more harm than good here.

"Why, Alice?" Lavinia inclined her head. They were safe in Alice's rooms down the hall. "When I thought of Yasir," Lavinia searched for words, "why did I see the Dark Magician?"

Alice had an idea why, but she was uncertain with regard to this nemesis of Yasir's. She regretted putting the mirror's magic in Lavinia's hands. Still, with Thalia's memories a part of her, Lavinia possessed magic she had yet to explore.

Indeed, Thalia had managed to have the last word. In the urn, the first thing Yasir had found was Thalia's ruby ring with a note telling of the wonders her conjurers had worked to bring them together in their future lives:

> Whenever you are released from the urn, look for me, my love. I will be there and you will know me, no matter the time or the place. Give the one that calls to you this ring, and by and by, she will know that she and I are one and the same. Be patient.
>
> There is now no more time, yet there is infinite time. Remember, our love can only grow as the ages separate us.
>
> Thalia

Alice looked at the ring on Lavinia's finger. Before, if her niece stroked it three times, Yasir would have appeared, but the ruby was duller now, the magic dim. Lavinia was no longer Master.

Lavinia turned her head and caught Alice eyeing her ring. "Why did I see the Shadow Lord in your mirror?"

"Nia, the glass showed him because in that moment he was searching for Yasir. That is all." Alice waved her hand and a delicate painted chair slid across the floor, stopping in front of her niece. She sat down, taking Lavinia's hand.

"After Yasir succumbed to the wound from Rakhshan's cursed bullet, his body vanished. Naturally, his enemies are uncertain that they are free of him. They seek proof he is dead. But soon they will tire of looking." She stroked her niece's hand. "Then we will be safe. Then we will be free."

"But for now, it is best if you stay away from the mirror shards." Alice had jammed the door lock in her niece's room with a subtle spell. Lavinia had agreed to occupy the guest suite and parlor across the hall.

Alice pressed her hands together. Now she must find someone for the task of removing what was left of the magic mirror, someone not threatened by Rakhshan. She must see Zamyad, and he would be most displeased.

31

With a whoosh of thick fabric, Alice closed the curtains in her bedroom at Bramley House, shutting out the daylight, sending constellations of dust specs, fine as sifted flour, to dance in the sunbeams sneaking around the edges of the scalloped green velvet drapes. She would be gone a short time.

The lock on Lavinia's door was unassailable. He niece had instructed Fleming that she would use another suite for the time being. The glass shards inside lay still and, Alice hoped, inert where they had fallen.

In the murky light of her room, Alice walked to the center of the carpet and held her hands out by her sides as if she were about to twirl like a Sufi or take to the air as a bird. But she remained still, hardly breathing, eyes closed. She faded from view, like morning fog struck by rays of the sun.

Floors that were hazy and rippling blue made Alice instinctively stamp her foot to be certain she stood on solid ground rather than water. Silken tapestries woven with exotic creatures, none of which she could name, graced the walls of the vestibule. The magic of Zamyad's citadel was almost tangible, but before it recognized her, Alice sent her spirit outside the ramparts.

The castle perched in a wild mountainous area. Forests grew down to the wide moat. The great tree trunks thick as church towers, ascending into the sky above fast-flowing cerulean rivers foaming in lightest jade green.

This was far-flung from anyone's path.

In a flower-strewn meadow, a creature the size of a cottage lumbered into view, sniffed the air and flashed a long red tongue like a lick of flame. Its thick forked tail thrashed onto a boulder with the ring of a hammer on an anvil. The beast coughed, a startling sound like a felled tree plummeting through the tangles of the forest. Gray smoke belched from its mouth. Leathery bat-like wings unfolded along the creature's ridged back and it sailed, light as a leaf, off the edge of the immense cliff.

The beast soared, bright orange flames roaring from its mouth.

Her father's castle was well hidden, built in a different realm than earth.

Although Alice knew where to find her father, she wandered through the great castle. Truth to tell, she felt afraid. Afraid of facing him with *this* information. She had received only the most polite treatment from her father, but she had heard the rumors. Nevertheless, she was his daughter, as if that might make a difference. She prayed that it would.

The guards at the entrance to the throne room recognized her. The young page whispered to the *Mehmendar,* then on in a line, bowing heads, hands cupped discretely to the mouth, until the King's *Nazir,* adjacent to the throne, bent to the Esquire of the Crown, who received the name with a somber nod, and announced through his golden horn, "Afsoon al Din et Suluyamin."

Her full name echoed in the great chamber whose soaring ceilings rose high enough to accommodate elephants standing on hind legs, their trumpeting trunks to the sky. As the words reverberated, she took courage from the meaning: charm, bewitchment. Her father must have bestowed her name because he had confidence in her power. But her spirit sank at the thought that her mother could have given it in hope that her daughter would inherit the full Djinn magic. Alice had concluded that she had the complete power, but now her confidence waned.

Guards twice her size with muscles like bulls and braided hair coiled around their heads serpent-like, kept close as they escorted her on the long path leading to the dais. At each step, the blue floor rippled, making her dizzy. She looked straight ahead at the guards, and walked to the rhythm of their swords clinking against their mail coats.

The guards halted. In front of her the dais rose impossibly high with no access. Her father's golden throne perched at the peak, the bright metal flaring as if it were ablaze, but dull compared to the King's radiance.

His hair was still black as soot and thick as sheep's wool. His eyes, inherited by Yasir, seeming fashioned from thin sheets of purest gold, King Zamyad al Din sat his throne with majesty befitting his reputation. The years of his long life had touched him with nary a trace. His amazing eyes signaled her welcome under his glittering crown, the room electric with his power.

"*Dagozaar ahn serrde*, Afsoon, my daughter." The King strode through the air, descending slowly, majestically to her. The light shone on sharp angles and straight edges all around him. *By the Djinn's hands*, he walked on a series of clear crystal steps.

King Zamyad stopped before her, dropped his hands to his side, the silk of his robe swaying, catching the light where the embroidery failed to mute it with the impasto of bright threads.

She stared at him and prayed that this would be the sternest expression she would witness. A faint rustling caught her attention. The murmurs of his subjects waiting for audience. She realized she should bow, then greet him right away. How could she forget proper protocol?

"Pearl of Sovereigns, Pearl of my Heart." Alice placed her palms together over her heart and bowed low to the ground. "Afsoon, Djinniye, places her voice on the ether and beseeches The Pearl of Sovereigns, as a favor, lend his ear."

"Afsoon, my daughter, a princess in your own right, I welcome you to Har Medwol." King Zaymad raised his palm, his expression unreadable. At the deep bass of his voice, the murmurs and rustling of the crowd stopped. Apparently, all were in awe of the power of this man, her father.

He led her to a pavilion situated at the far end of the great hall, and motioned for her to go first up the wide marble stairs. She stopped before a door covered with opulent gems, embarrassed to be groping for a handle. Her hand passed through the jewels. As if moved by a breeze, the door wavered and she slipped through the strings of gems, so close together she had mistaken them for solid.

Ebony posts the diameter of an elephant, carved as if they had been twisted by a giant's hands, formed the structure for the rotunda. Fringed tapestry panels depicting the history of the Djinn formed the walls. Alice's feet sank inches into the luxurious silk carpets. She sighed. At times she missed the excesses of the Djinn décor.

She waited until her father had taken a seat, then, at his gesture, sat on a sumptuously padded divan upholstered in a royal purple fabric that glowed. She ran her hand along the soft surface, but stopped when the cloth moved in a wave and bunched next to her leg, emitting a soft purring sound.

Her father's golden eyes flickered like a fire. "What of my son?" Tenderness tempered King Zamyad's tone, a wistful tone that fueled Alice's fear.

His precious son. Stolen. The heartbreak of his life. His Excellency had spent centuries attempting to extract Yasir from the grip of Rakhshan. But what had her father, King Zamyad, the great Djinni accomplished? Yasir was still bound to the urn.

In her father's presence her thoughts clarified. Rakhshan could not reach Yasir. That was why Yasir had found Thalia, Lavinia; that was why they had two children; that was why Yasir was fulfilling the prophecy. Her father, Yasir's father, was succeeding, but subtly. Was it possible that Rakhshan knew nothing about Zamyad's quest? Most everyone had given Zamyad up for dead many years ago.

In quick glimpses so as not to offend by looking directly, Alice studied her father's expression for any indication of his mood, but saw no fleeting frown or smile, nothing to help. She had said the words of greeting. There was no going back.

Zamyad gave a curt bow of his head and crossed his arms, a sign of his readiness, but she felt him close a part of himself, perhaps in preparation for what was to come.

Alice focused her eyes level with her father's chest.

"Your son is . . . your son cast—" She swallowed and started again. "Events are most distressed for your son." Alice glanced at her father, then looked down, then at him again.

Zamyad raised his eyebrows.

Her throat constricted.

"I fear for the fulfillment of the prophecy." Her voice wavered, and though she tried to look calm, she knew her eyes widened as if she were a deer surprised on a forest path.

"Lord Bramley was transported to the urn where he caught your son and his Thalia in a most intimate encounter, which culminated in Lord Bramley stealing the urn." Alice dared look at Zamyad.

"Lord Bramley is master now," she hunched, cowering. This was the phrase she dreaded for him to hear.

Her father stared through her. Why had she bothered to speak it? Now that she was in front of him, Zamyad could see her thoughts, see inside her mind. She could barely take a breath, but pushed on, the effort the same as walking in a muddy wallow.

"The Shadow Lord found his way into a magic mirror I gave Lady Lavinia." Alice heard her voice tremble.

Zamyad glowered. In order to be indiscernible to Rakhshan, her father couldn't visit the small details of Yasir's life. This was new to him. His eyes shone like cat's in the firelight. She attempted to banish the image Lavinia described—Rakhshan as warrior, his deep black eyes searching for a soul to own, peering out of the tiny circle of glass in Lavinia's hand as if he would leap into the room.

"Afsoon. I expressly gave you a task. And you come to me and tell me you are failing." Zamyad's voice rumbled with displeasure. His face remained calm, but his eyes bored into her. "You have the power to direct my son. *You*, Afsoon."

Alice shut her eyes. She felt woozy, her body almost weightless, an insect skating on the water's surface. Her head suddenly hurt. She couldn't concentrate on her thoughts, on what her father was saying.

She opened her eyes. Flowers and vines of brilliant colors filled her vision, growing larger and larger. She collided with a soft substance, faltering in a moment of panic, but in a mad scramble, soared and perched upon a smooth protuberance.

Soared? Perched?

She raised her arm. Her wing unfurled in rows of brown sleek feathers.

"Afsoon." A deep authoritative voice boomed.

She cocked her head, peering downward. Far below, King Zamyad looked up at her, holding out his palm. Without a thought, she swooped from her perch and glided onto his Excellency's hand, fluttering her wings as she came to a perfect landing. She gripped his sturdy fingers with her claws, the glowing stones of his rings making her squint.

"Afsoon." He smoothed her head feathers gently with his huge finger. She warbled at his tender touch, no longer afraid. Zamyad set her on the divan and waved his hand over her tiny bird form.

Alice sneezed. He conjured a goblet and offered it. She sniffed the dark purple liquid and drew back.

"Only *tsuri*, a mild wine from our local grain." He smiled. "Drink."

Her hand shook.

He took the glass after she sipped and placed his hand on hers.

"Afsoon, you must forgive me, I am . . ." he paused and his fierce expression softened, "concerned about my son. But I seem to recall him being, ah, a bit, headstrong and impetuous." He grinned, startling Alice so that she laughed out loud, a scale of unfamiliar notes.

"I realize now that it took great courage for you to come to me." King Zamyad rose from his chair. Alice jumped up, stumbling from the unfamiliar feel of large solid feet, rather than long toes and claws to curl around a perch.

He motioned for her be seated, and, to her astonishment, sat beside her. "You are released from all formalities. Please continue with your message."

Alice reached for the goblet, surprised not to unfurl rows of rich brown feathers, but rather a plump human arm. She flexed her fingers and looked down at her body. No feathers, no claws, merely her own stout form clad in her best gown of sumptuous brown velvet and rust brocade. Glancing up she saw a massive golden sculpture of Ganesha, the elephant god of hearth and home in front of a vivid tapestry of flowers and vines. She had fluttered into the lush silken tapestry and then, disoriented, alit on Ganesha's curled trunk.

Her arm now resting in her lap, she reached again for the goblet. It rose and met her hand. Zamyad nodded and she drank, resting the glass on her thigh when she finished. She straightened. There was worse to impart.

"The mirror, Father." Alice tilted the goblet. "After being polluted by Rakhshan's image, it broke into pieces, scattering onto the floor of Lavinia's chamber." She was surprised at his thoughtful expression.

"It would be dangerous for you to retrieve them, Afsoon." He held his hand up as if to stop her fear. The amazing jewels on his rings flashed. Yasir was so like him, his mannerisms, his looks. It tore at Alice's heart to have them apart.

"I will send one to help you." At the sound of his voice saying those words, the fear left her, but returned seconds later. King Zamyad had not freed Yasir from the urn, had not defeated Rakhshan. She was one of the few who knew her father to be alive. How could he send someone safely?

"Continue assisting your half brother, even if he resists." King Zamyad took her hand, his eyes gentle. "You are a gifted djinniye, but you are forbidden to use your talents on the Shadow Lord. This would not only endanger you, daughter, but my son, Lady Lavinia and their children, as well as myself." A trumpet sounded a regal fanfare and he turned his head. The panel of diamonds in his gold crown blazed like a meteor. She had to shut her eyes.

"Afsoon, be wary." King Zamyad leaned close, his voice low. "This is no game."

To her chagrin, Alice intuited a deep trepidation, flowing like a subterranean river within her father.

She nodded, unable to speak.

32

Peter closed the cover of his inkwell, a gilt bird's head, and placed the quill pen amongst the stiff golden feathers of its tail. He put his hands under his head and leaned back in his chair, surveying his study. The light through the windows faded into gray twilight. Another day's work finished. He would command Yasir to give him knowledge of the scrolls, surely a djinni could do that. Who knows, he might have been around when the scrolls were written.

Feeling satisfied now that he had Yasir under his power, Peter closed his eyes for a moment.

"Master of the manor, once again." He said it aloud, reveling in the strength of the words. "And master of a djinni."

He grinned, broad and expansive. He would never again let Lavinia get the best of him.

"Damned deceitful woman." He unlocked a side drawer in his desk, lifted the lining and slipped out an enormous brass key on a ring jingling with many smaller keys. Facing the walnut cabinet that filled the wall behind his desk, he fitted a small brass key into the gilded keyhole of one of the curved doors. Was his treasure safe here? Once more he checked that the curtains were drawn. Barely glancing at the center medallion featuring two gold peacocks beak to beak, tails inlaid with jewels, he pulled the door open.

Peter reached behind a lapis lazuli column, and pushed twice on the carved image of a solemn Buddha, then pressed hard and long. The huge drawer slid out silently. Scarlet silk lining set off a cache of ancient jewels. Beside them a black velvet pouch held an object about as large as a wine bottle.

He removed the pouch and set it on his desk, adjusting the lamp for maximum effect. He slipped off the black velvet. Not for the first time, he marveled at how such a creature as Yasir could be confined to this metal urn, a vessel Peter could hold in one hand.

The thousands-of-years-old brass glinted as though it were freshly polished. Peter ran his fingers along the incised script. Lord Ewely, of the Society of Antiquaries, after much research, had translated it: *He who is here, resides forever. He that disturbs will play his fortune.* Fingers tingling, Peter jerked his hand from the cuneiform-like characters, and shook it. The back of his neck prickled.

The phrase never ceased to cause him concern: *He that disturbs will play his fortune.* Yet, living your life is playing your fortune. He had chosen to open the urn. Peter stroked his chin, musing on the words engraved into the vessel.

How was that different from deciding to marry Lavinia? Deciding to make his first foray into Egypt for The Society of Antiquities? Choosing to explore Arabia, Turkey, Persia and Hindustan?

He had played his fortune in many ways, but the djinni had skewed his fate with magic spells. If Peter had never given Lavinia the urn, their marriage would not have fallen into disaster. They would have been happy, as happy as these past several years. He wouldn't have been a cuckold. The children would all be his. And he wouldn't have a djinni to deal with.

He rubbed his neck, trying to loosen an aching muscle. He should shut the urn in a strongbox, send it back to Egypt secure in the hold of a ship. Have the captain heave it overboard, burying the urn in sand and barnacles for all time.

A sudden twist gripped his stomach. If he carried out this plan, he would never again behold Yasir's handsome face or his magical presence.

Peter unlatched the urn. Thick mist floated through the study. His hand rested on the open lid. He ought to shut it, hide it away. Be done with this business once and for all. He pushed the lid forward to close it, but it resisted. Just then, through the mist, Yasir appeared, splendidly dressed and bejeweled. Peter stifled his amazement each time the djinni appeared, reminding himself that he—Lord Peter Bramley—had the power now.

Not Lavinia and the bloody djinni.

"Master." Yasir gave a small bow, and fixed his gaze, pupils a black vertical slit in shining gold. Peter couldn't tear his eyes away. A sensation raced through his body, much like the thrill he experienced when his steed Palomar leaped a hedge. He could feel it now, an increase in strength of pace, gaining speed. A heart-stopping moment when he sailed through the air. The ecstasy of flying.

Doing his best to feign indifference, Peter stood helpless as blurred forms came into focus before him. He saw Yasir as he was the night of The Anubis Brotherhood meeting. Hands bound to the overhead beam, muscular back crisscrossed with deep red gashes, blood running down the contours of his bronze body. Yasir's tangy smell invaded his senses, the abrupt crack of the whip exploded in his head. The brute physicalness made him stagger. The rippling muscles of the djinni's body, his half-lidded golden eyes crazed with pain, the surrender in them.

Peter blinked.

He stood by his desk looking directly into those golden eyes.

Was the djinni casting a spell? He would break the creature of this insolent behavior. Peter fought to stand straight, but fell to his knees. No, he was standing, the djinni before him, awaiting his command. These visions were a residue. He had said incantations that rid him of Yasir's curses. Merely residues. He was Master. He was in control.

"Master, how may I fulfill your desire?" Yasir's deep voice was as soft as velvet. The phrasing as subtle as the intimacy in it.

The djinni tilted his head, leaning close. Peter took a quick breath to steady himself. The djinni's spicy scent and his mesmerizing eyes beckoned. Peter stepped closer. The floor vanished. *My God*, he was falling, falling. He jerked straight, the floor as firm underfoot as ever.

Nothing had happened.

The djinni, in front of him, waited for a command.

What had Yasir said? *How may I fulfill your desire?* Pictures floated through Peter's mind, one by one. Oh, the many things Yasir could do to fulfill his desires.

He closed his eyes on those golden ones. Turned his back to Yasir and barked out a command. What had he said? He had no memory of the words that left his mouth. He put his hands to his forehead and pressed hard. So far he had kept his composure. He must stay in control. He was master, by God.

He turned to face Yasir. The remnants of a knowing leer flitted from the genie's face, leaving a somber expression.

Or had he imagined it?

But he had said the incantations just last evening. The magic words from Baruti's scrolls. His memory had returned. He was safe.

He was master.

Peter met Yasir's eyes. He stood alone in front of the djinni. He swallowed.

Merciful God, what had he gotten himself into?

33

$\mathcal{P}$eter stalked through the garden, conscious of Yasir following.

"Da!" Stuart jumped out of the hedge and wrapped his sturdy arms about Peter's legs. His son was strong for a seven-year-old. James, six, always a bit shy at first, crept from the foliage. He put his finger on his chin and stared up at his father.

"James, come here." Peter held his arms open while James backed away, blue eyes wide. Nanny gently pushed him forward and Peter scooped him into his arms.

"So are you two running wild in the garden?" Peter grinned at the nanny who stood waiting in the shade.

"I'm looking for a hedgehog." James said. He squirmed in his father's arms and peered over Peter's shoulder. Had he seen the djinni? Under Peter's command, Yasir, now dressed in servant's clothes, was merely a servant. He was not to do any magic on his own.

"Da, look! I found a toad." Stuart reached into his pocket and held up a goggle-eyed amphibian. Its white-speckled throat pulsed.

"Well, so you did." Peter set James on the ground, who grabbed Stuart's arm.

"Hey, that's my toad! I saw it first!" James reached for the animal.

"I caught it." Stuart lifted the creature away from James, and the toad, taking advantage of a lapse in its captor's vigilance, leapt into the air.

"You stole it!" James jumped for the airborne amphibian, but it flew over Peter's shoulder as if it were a bird in flight. Peter turned to see Yasir snatch it from the air.

James stood transfixed, mouth open.

"What the devil?" Peter said under his breath.

"Give it to me!" Stuart yelled as he ran from Peter to the djinni. He reached up to Yasir for the toad. "You know it's mine, Sam."

Yasir bent and transferred the bumpy creature into Stuart's outstretched hands.

"What are you doing here, Sam?" Stuart turned down his mouth. "Why are you dressed like a servant?" He looked at Peter, then Yasir, who stared at each other, expressions somber. The silence grew.

"Uh oh." Stuart said under his breath, but Peter heard. Stuart backed away clutching the frog.

Peter motioned to nanny. "Take the boys to the pond. They can let the frog go." He tried to keep his voice light, tried to keep the fury from it. When they disappeared along the path, he turned and punched Yasir in the face.

"Damn you." Peter kept his voice low. The boys were just out of sight.

Yasir stumbled backwards.

"Stuart calls you Sam, and asks about your clothes? He KNOWS you?" Peter moved within reach of Yasir. "Stuart can make things fly?" He rifled through what he knew about this djinni and his wife, his suspicions, his formerly spell-muddled thoughts. As scenes fit together, he felt the heat rush into his face. He fixed the djinni with his eyes, wishing he had a spell for this creature. And it would be a fine spell, worse than the torture the other night.

"Stuart is yours and Lavinia's child, isn't he?" Peter pulled Yasir to him and leaned into his face, teeth clenched. He was a bloody fool. The way Stuart arrived from the gypsies, the crazy story Lavinia told him. Why hadn't he seen it before? A damned spell, of course, but the incantation from Baruti's scroll had opened his eyes. The spells had fallen away. Some quicker than others.

"Answer me with the truth." Peter's spittle sprayed Yasir's face. The djinni looked down at the gravel path, and then at Peter. He held his hands out by his side.

"The child is mine. He is half djinni, and because of that, he has powers." Yasir spoke in a soft voice. So he didn't want the children to hear either.

"Master, you love him. Stuart believes you are his father. He only knows me as a friend of his mother." Yasir looked Peter in the eyes. "That he believes, and everyone believes you are his father, is what has kept him alive, so far."

"You talk nonsense. Why would anyone want Stuart dead?" Peter made a scoffing noise in his throat, assessing this outrageous idea. What trick was the djinni trying this time?

"I make this plea for his life. In spite of what you know, please keep being his loving father." Yasir dropped to his knees. "The malicious man who bound me to the urn knows of the prophecy about this child. He will do anything to kill him. But hidden here, growing up as the son of a great English lord, Stuart is safe to fulfill his mission." Yasir let his arms fall to his sides.

To Peter's surprise, the fear in the djinni's eyes was palpable. He had not seen the djinni this submissive unless he had ordered him so.

"There is no reason for Stuart to be in a great family of England. You can conjure anything he needs. Riches, fame, even a title." Peter looked down at Yasir. "It makes no sense."

"If Stuart is known to this man as my son, he will never be safe." Yasir remained on his knees, his face turned up to Peter.

Stuart was seven years old. Lavinia had been in this affair for years and years. Peter's suspicions had been correct. Yasir had seduced Lavinia right after she opened the urn—her husband's gift to her. Damnation, he was a fool! When he found them in bed together, how could he not have put it together? Even then a spell worked on his mind. His jaw tightened as a flush crept up his face. He took Yasir by the arms and jerked him to standing.

"You lie." Peter clenched his teeth, his breath hot on the djinni's face. "I will have you flogged again, but this time you will suffer for a week with your injuries. And I will be there each day, watching your flesh turn purple and green, watching flies lay eggs in your flayed skin." Peter trembled with the effort of controlling his temper. His fists tightened around the djinni's arms.

Yasir opened his eyes wide, his pupils expanding from vertical slits to black spheres in seconds. Peter jerked back, startled, then steadied himself with his grip on Yasir. A noisy hum filled his ears. His body vibrated. Yasir's eyes bore into him. *By God,* Peter had said the words for the spells in the scrolls, had canceled the charms that Yasir had placed upon him. Did it all suddenly come to naught?

"Damn you and Lavinia. She told me Stuart was mine. He looks just like her." Peter could feel his apprehension tightening his chest, guy wires drawing his muscles tight against his bones. *What had he brought into his life?*

"But I see now that Stuart has your mannerisms. Damn the devious woman. She told me straight to my face." Peter tightened his grip and shook Yasir.

Yasir leaned in close, eye to eye, a trickle of blood running from his nose onto his lip from Peter's blow. "Master, you do not want to do this. Think of James and Stuart. If they come running down the path and see you threatening me . . ." He stared into his master's eyes.

By God, if the boys saw they would be upset, most probably at him, not at *Sam.* Peter's stomach turned at the nickname Stuart had called Yasir, the familiar way he'd said it. Peter let go of Yasir and pushed him away.

Suddenly, the djinni was next to him, his body pressed close. His breath, scented with cinnamon, warm on Peter's face. Yasir's eyes, like rare jewels, luminous, enthralling.

Peter breathed in Yasir's musky smell, the pungency of his sweat. "Yes, if I punish you, it must be in private." A strange feeling overcame him, and with it, the outlandish thought to brush Yasir's lips with his, to take him in an embrace, to feel his muscles hard against his own. This, against his desire to see him in agony once more. Peter shut his eyes and drew his body up straight.

He backed away, fighting the force that drew him to the djinni like a swine to mud.

"Heal yourself. I don't want the boys asking about it." Peter kept his voice controlled as he strode down the path.

"Follow me. You will tell me of this prophecy."

With the djinni behind him, he could think of what to do without concern for what showed on his face—the trepidation that worked havoc on his insides, that edged out his clear thinking. He must map out a plan to deal with this creature and his magic. He could feel his face fall as he fought off the voice in his head that tried to subvert his confidence. The voice that kept saying: *You are in over your head.*

34

Alice paused in front of the door to her room at Bramley House and glanced down the hall in the direction of her niece's suite. Lavinia had told Peter that while her rooms were being thoroughly cleaned, she would occupy the guest suite and parlor across the hall. Peter would be satisfied with this innocuous excuse. Besides, he was far too busy being master of his new obsession, Yasir, to bother with Lavinia.

Whatever explanations her niece had given the servants were working. No one tried to fix the lock that Alice had jammed with a barely detectable spell. The room was secure. Rakhshan had been thwarted for the time being.

The Pearl of Sovereigns, Zamyad, knew they were in danger until the glass shards were gathered and destroyed. Alice could do nothing but wait for his emissary. She kept looking over her shoulder. Would these objects with Rakhshan's taint bring more ill fortune?

Well, it wouldn't do to stand in the hall eyeing Lavinia's room where the glass shards lurked. Alice strolled inside her room and closed the door.

"So there you are." A low voice resonated from the corner. Alice turned, knowing she should have prepared for this. *Could Rakhshan have found her?*

A shadow blocked part of the window, light streaming from behind it. Alice was a powerful djinniye. She could handle the Shadow Lord or his minion.

Most probably.

The shape moved, still silhouetted, a sinuous gait. A cape? A long sword? The figure changed direction, altering angles, aligning different planes to the light. A flicker of auburn limned the dark silhouette.

Alice readied her spell. If done at precisely the right moment, it would disable this creature, enabling her to see the threat more clearly. She squinted into the shadows. A faint scent wafted on the air, growing stronger: the heady fragrance of vetiver, like sun-warmed grass drying in a field.

She hesitated before sending her magic strike. That familiar fragrance . . .

"Is it you, Amarja?"

The figure moved closer. Green eyes glinted, high cheekbones with a brush of pink framed a heart-shaped face. "Of course it is me. Who else would it be?"

When the witch kissed both her cheeks, the scratch of rough scar tissue snaking across her velvety skin was almost too much to bear.

"Please sit." Alice kept her voice calm as she offered a chair and took one opposite. Making herself glance at Amarja, she let out a breath of relief at the witch's full ruby lips, her flawless ivory skin glowing with pink. All at once, Amarja's face altered as if a mask had been removed. A pink scar, like a puckered worm, wound from above her left eye down her cheek through the split lips and up her other cheek into her bright red hair.

Alice closed her eyes, steeling herself to endure this.

"You still see them, don't you?" the witch asked.

"You know the answer to that," Alice's voice sounded flat.

She would never forget the day, centuries ago, although she had tried with magic to remove it from her consciousness. They had been thirteen years old when they journeyed to the sacred pool on a spring morning. They managed to elude Amarja's guardian, a Nubian slave called Doi.

"See." Alice had given a silent command to shape-change into smoke. Perhaps this time it would work. Her human form felt lighter. She could have sworn her feet left the ground.

Amarja stared and shook her head, her waist-length red hair swaying from side to side. "Afsoon, I see you next to me, in the same form as you were when we started out."

Alice looked down at her body, that of a pudgy young girl with budding breasts. "What about this?" With a wave of her hand, Alice was gone. She appeared twenty cubits down the path, next to a tree with orange flowers vining up the trunk.

"Impressive," Amarja called out as she walked towards Alice. In a few moments, she stood beside her and plucked three orange flowers, entwining them into her bright red hair.

Alice looked at her dusty sandals. "Djinnis are able to take any shape they wish with a snap of the finger. I am the daughter of the Great Djinn, Zamyad. I should have those powers and more."

She picked a flower and inhaled the clove-like fragrance.

"But mother has stymied me. Why did father ever choose her?" Alice threw the flower to the ground. "She is only half Djinn and her magic never blossomed." She raised her eyes to Amarja. With her sandal she ground the blossom into the dirt.

Amarja leaned against the tree and looked up, half-closing her eyes at the golden sunlight beaming onto her sculptured face. "When I get my moon time, I will come into my full power. Perhaps it will happen like that for you. You can transfer further than you did last time. And even now, I can see my ability to entrance is growing."

She took Alice's hand and led her into the forest. "Afsoon, we will be powerful ladies of magic. That's why we go to the sacred pool."

Yellow Meranti, Manna Gum and Mengaris trees, tall as ancient temples soared over them. They walked in silence, their steps muffled by soft, shaggy moss, the verdant lime green and deep emerald so bright it almost glowed.

Alice mulled over what the young witch had said. "Because of my mother, I have been born into this human form. I do not think what happens to my body affects my magic." Alice ducked under a low branch draped in hanging moss and whisked the orange wisps from her brown hair, crying out at a yellow spider with spindly long legs. She shook it from her fingers.

"Since you are in a human body, human things will happen. Soon you will get the moon blood. Then you will see." Amarja parted a veil of green moss as translucent as chiffon and entered a small clearing.

Alice stopped and cocked her head.

Voices.

She reached for Amarja and pulled her to a halt. When the witch opened her mouth to protest, Alice put a finger to her lips as she looked warily around. The voices grew louder. Where were they coming from? She saw no one.

With a soft laugh, she pointed to the waterfall trickling down an ice-blue crystal wall into a clear pool of aqua, the splashes a symphony of high falsettos—low bass, treble and others in between. A crowd of sound tumbling into quiet. Fringing the pool, ferns of bright red, yellow and rust reflected lavender and jade on the surface.

"I thought I heard voices," Alice said. "But it was the waterfall."

Shafts of sunlight speared through the water illuminating the smooth crystal bottom as clear as if the water lay upon a mirror. Amarja removed her blouse, her skirt, her filmy under-blouse and petticoat. She stood naked, ivory skin and waist-length red hair making her look like a fairy instead of a witchling on the lime green moss.

"Afsoon, if you want your magic, shed your garments." Amarja bundled her clothes and slipped them under a knee-high clump of red ferns. The witch stepped into the water. Her exhale made a furrow of ripples.

"Cold as a witch's tit." She burst into giggles while Alice untied her skirt and slipped out of her chemise and pantalets.

"Shh. This is serious. Do you want to . . .?" Alice gasped as the cold water crept up her bare thighs. "This spring must come from far below, maybe an ice cave where fairies keep rainbows fresh."

They stood before the waterfall. Amarja took a deep breath and submerged, her hair floating on the surface, an exotic scarlet water-weed. Then it vanished.

Alice could not tell anyone else was in the water. Her body felt numb and she worried that the fairies might steal her breath to freshen their rainbows while she was underwater. But she wanted her magic now. She gulped as big a breath as she could, and plunged. Her scalp crawled with the numbing cold, but she focused on her prayer to Anunit, goddess of the moon and battle. Her hands over her heart, she stood on the smooth crystal bottom and besieged the beatific goddess for complete and rightful magic.

When she surfaced, sounds she didn't expect besieged her ears, horses whinnying, their hooves stamping. She opened her eyes and pushed her hair from her face. At the edge of the pool, four men wrangled their frightened horses, long swords clattering against the axes and knives tucked into their belts. Spears and maces were strapped to their horses' saddles.

Amarja surfaced next, startling the horses more. They reared this time, their whinnies shrill as their eyes rolled. With effort, the soldiers calmed their mounts. One said something in a course language and clutched his crotch. The others laughed.

Alice attempted to turn into a column of smoke, but she could still feel the numbness of her legs and arms. Where was the magic she prayed for? The soldiers . . . She had heard the stories of how they treated women, girls. She looked to Amarja.

The witch walked calmly out of the water as if they were alone in the clearing. Had the cold water addled her? Could she not see the men? Alice's teeth clacked together.

Amarja stood on the moss at the lip of the sacred pool, her wet hair stuck to her body like scars. She held out her hands.

The men and horses stared at her, quiet, as if they were trying to decide if she were a vision. Amarja's hair, suddenly dry, swirled around her. A horse snorted, his head and tail held high. Another bucked. A mace thudded into the ferns. The witch started spinning, her hair straight out in a whorl of bright scarlet. She spun faster and faster until Alice could see only a red blur with an ivory center.

Amarja's prayers had worked. Magic radiated from her, each spin generating stronger and stronger power. Alice felt a pang of hurt. Where was her own magic?

The soldiers and horses stood transfixed, eyes distant and unfocused.

Amarja turned to Alice.

"Make haste, we have to escape before they wake." She glanced at the men. "I do not know how long we have." She swept her clothes from under the ferns and ran through the moss veil. As Alice started from the pool, Amarja screamed. Alice moved to the middle of the pond.

A soldier, Amarja struggling in his arms, forced the witch back into the clearing.

"Chronos and kairos. Wind the time to me." Amarja's voice rang out clear as if she had not a fear in the world. The soldier halted, his eyes blank, and she slipped from his arms. In a few seconds, he shook his head, coming to his senses.

He spoke in a rough language as he surveyed the men and horses standing as still as the stones surrounding the pool, then whipped out his curved knife. The silver blade gleamed in the sunrays.

With an inhuman burst of speed, he vanished through the hanging moss veil, coming back with Amarja. He put his curved knife to her throat.

"Witch, with your blood my men will recover their wits and I will gain some of your magic."

Still in the pond, Alice cast her spell. She appeared at the man's side, startling him so that Amarja slipped loose and started her entrancing charm.

"Ishkur's balls." The man pushed Alice to the ground. He seized Amarja and set his knife on her throat. At the first cut, Alice cast another spell.

The knife slipped off the witch's throat, but the soldier, staring at Alice, sliced deep into Amarja's forehead, down her check, through her lips, and up the other cheek into her hair.

Amarja's scream rang through the grove, intensifying as it echoed off the sacred pool and blue crystals. Like a living entity, it cut into Alice as deep as the soldier's knife.

With Amarja's blood spilled, the band of soldiers came to life. They circled around what must be their leader.

"Another little witch?" said the soldier as he reached for Alice, his knife at the ready.

He gripped her arm and pulled her to him. A small pouch, colored symbols burned into the leather, swung out of his shirt on a braided thong. A charm bag. Alice grasped the bag. With her magic she broke the thong.

The soldier cursed and raked his knife down her arm. A sharp sting ran through her flesh. Blood leaked onto her skin. She would vanish and appear in another place, save herself and Amarja, but she still felt the soldier's strong arm binding her to him. He put his knife to her throat. She could only stay still and breathe.

"No!" Amarja stood, and fell back to her knees, blood pouring from her face.

He spat his words. "I will have my pouch and you, little slut."

What good was it being a djinni if she could not save her friend or herself? Her body, her human body, trembled. She couldn't stop the shivering or the bleeding. Her head spun like Amarja's tresses when she entranced the men, blurring her vision as a buzzing sound roared inside her head.

The soldier moved his hand behind her. She felt his bare skin on hers.

The buzzing grew louder. It was all she could hear as her sight darkened. She could not move. She could barely see. The soldier could do anything to her and she could do nothing. New sensations shot through her arms and legs, but she still couldn't move.

Then a manic energy invaded her.

Suddenly she was free, looking down from high in the air on the band of men and Amarja.

The soldier peered in amazement at the soft brown feathers in his hands, then pointed up at the cedar tree and shouted in his clipped language. As one, the soldiers looked up at her.

Alice moved her mouth, but something heavy muffled her. The leather pouch. She set it on the thick branch, her clawed feet holding it in place. She spread her majestic wings. From her beak came a cry, shriller than a falcon's, royal as an eagle's.

She tore into the bag with her curved beak, scattering the magic charms inside—a smooth red bloodstone, a coin of gold, an ivory carving of a bearded man with a sword, a polished wooden horse. Her beak chopped the wood carving into pieces and destroyed the ivory. She defaced the coin and broke the stone into dust.

The soldier gripped his neck and screamed. The men, with cries of alarm, bent their two middle fingers with their thumbs, leaving the index and little finger pointing towards Alice, who perched high in the branches amongst the needle-like leaves. They pulled their amulets from inside their shirts, mounted their horses and fled, leaving Amarja bloodied and naked in the midst of a muddy circle.

As if in a dream, Alice, now in her human form, knelt beside Amarja. She tried to heal the ghastly wound, but her magic only stopped the bleeding. She packed the gash with moss from near the sacred pool and slathered it with mud from the edge of the water to keep it in place.

Somehow they limped back to Alice's mother, who used herbs on Amarja's wounds and gave her a draught to keep her unconscious. Alice and her mother tried everything they knew to heal Amarja, but by the time Zamyad arrived her scars were set.

Alice began the long story of what happened, but Zamyad, seeing his daughter so upset, held up his hand. "No need, Afsoon, I know." Amarja sat still, fear in her eyes, tears running down her cheeks over her puckered red scars.

"My dear, drink this." He conjured a golden goblet studded with jewels and, as Amarja drank, he waved his hand over her. The witch glowed, her now-thin face and haggard body plumped out, returning the beauty she had before. Alice gasped as her friend's drawn face, her gray skin, grew rosy. The ropey scars vanished like a bad dream in morning's clear light.

In a gentle voice, her father explained that because of the ordeal, Alice's magic, of its own accord, had changed her into a bird, saving her. Later, when Alice confessed she still saw Amarja's scars, Zamyad placed his hand on hers.

"I am sorry, Afsoon." His golden eyes shone with an expression so kind Alice wanted to weep. "Because it was your first transformation and happened spontaneously, you will continue to see Amarja's scars, even though they no longer exist." Energy flowed from his hands into her. His special gift. "But, that is a small price to pay for saving your friend's life. No?"

So long ago. How many centuries? Even here in the 1800's, in this strange land of the Angles, she still saw and felt Amarja's scars.

"Afsoon, do not be vexed at me." The witch's green eyes sparkled with happiness. "I am glad to see you after these long years."

"I cannot, Amarja. I cannot be glad to see you. I thought the last time we met would be the end of it, but the curse, it still appears. I saw, just now the scars again—"

"Oh, it is buried in time. And I do not want to think on it. If it was bad for you, can you not imagine how it was for me?" Tears streaked Amarja's beautiful face. The puckered scars glittered through the wetness. "Besides," she sniffed, blotting her eyes, "must I remind you once more that the sacred pool enhanced my powers. Here I am, after centuries, still a young witch. And it taught me never to trust a man. A useful concept, I am sure you agree." She sat straight. "Then and there I vowed never to let a man best me. And you, Afsoon, you transformed successfully. I would think you should recall that day with gratitude."

Alice took Amarja's hands. "Seeing the scars takes me back. The fear. The new magic. All stuff of nightmares. But what you say is true." She blinked, vowing to leave her vision of the scars behind. "Now, are you here for a long visit?"

"Cannot you guess?" Amarja studied Alice, a strange expression clouding her deep green eyes. "I am sent by your father, King Zamyad, the Great Djinni, to help."

"You?"

"Ah, you forget that I am an accomplished witch, famed throughout, even in the world of the Djinn. That's why your father sent me. I am not a djinni, so I can clean up after—"

"Don't say his name." Alice fastened onto Amarja's wrist. "Good magic is tenuous here at present."

"But Lord Bramley, his family, they are human, are they not?" Amarja, looked around, alarmed. "Your father said it was a small task."

"The Bramleys are human, but Yasir is a djinni."

"Yasir!" Amarja gasped. She paled. "He is here?"

35

*N*ight. Best for Zamyad's clandestine task as most of the servants and residents were abed. Amarja strolled down the dimly lit hall of Bramley House, alert for any sign of the djinni Yasir.

She had first met him around eight years ago. After much suffering, Yasir had finally succumbed to his wound from the cursed bullet covertly loaded in Lord Bramley's pistol by Saddani, one of Rakhshan's minions. Yasir's human body had died. His father, Zamyad, snatched him from the afterlife just in time, and sent Amarja to heal him.

Back then, Yasir, so in need of comfort, had languished. She increased his healing immeasurably by bedding him. When her time came, their red-haired son was born dead, his little body and face perfect, the cord coiled around his neck.

They were heartbroken.

Now Lavinia had children by the djinni. Living children.

Alice had told her the whole story, how the urn came to Lavinia, who this girl really was, the children she had borne Yasir. Amarja shrank the swell of jealousy that started to rise within her. Why should she be envious of a human girl? Merely a brood mare for the djinni.

Amarja took a breath. If their son had lived he would have fulfilled the prophecy. But there was still time. Lavinia's children were young yet and they were part human. It would be a wonder if they had any powers to speak of.

She would seduce Yasir and bear another child . . . This time *her* child—part witch and part djinni—would be a hero. Lavinia's children would pale in comparison.

At the sound of footsteps, she slipped into the shadows. A strapping lad in footman's livery walked towards her, fumbling with the buttons on his coat. She wondered who his lover was.

"Who goes there?" he called out, having trouble keeping his deep baritone soft enough not to wake anyone.

She forced a pleasant expression. Zamyad stressed that she must be furtive, to not upset the balance at this manor. Now she had been seen.

Amarja ran her hand over her gown, a modest low neck, rather demure cap sleeves and an empire waist, all in a silk not up to her standards—a dress in the fashion of the time where Alice chose to dwell.

The gown transformed into one of deep rose China silk with gold threads that glimmered in the hall sconce's soft light, her décolletage almost indecent. As she stepped from the shadows her dress shimmered, the translucent silk hugging her voluptuous figure

The young man's gasp filled the hallway.

Amarja glided towards him, her waist-length red hair flowing sinuously around her. The footman, tall and broad with sandy hair, stood still, his expression flickering between fear and lust.

She stopped in front of him. His breath warmed her face. His dark eyes widened. He thought her a spirit, yet she could see the hunger in how he leaned his body close. With a wave of her hand, her gown dropped to the floor.

He reached for her. When he touched her bare breast, she leaned into him. He pulled her closer, her firm body against his. Cupping her bottom, he kissed her. He undid his trousers, and let out a cry as his hands sank through her body.

He jerked back, eyes bulging as she faded before him, her hair swirling about her.

The footman turned and ran down the hall, stumbling as his trousers pooled around his ankles. He bent and pulled them up, his bare bottom ghostly white in the moonlight from the window.

He wouldn't tell a soul. She was safe. A shame though, for he was well endowed—she had made sure of the opportunity to notice before she frightened him away.

Well, now to her task. Fortunately, the night was long. Enjoying the cool air on her nakedness, she sauntered down the hall, and stopped at the white door with gilded molding of putti and ornate flowers. So this was the entrance to the mysterious Lavinia's chamber. What was she like? As an English Lady, she wouldn't resemble Thalia, her former self. Yet she must have enough of Thalia to still attract Yasir.

What a shame Yasir had found this woman Lavinia, before Amarja found him again. Now he would be distracted, engrossed in the prophecy.

Reveling in the sensation on her flesh, she ran her hand over her body and flinched as the gown she wore before the footman interfered covered her. A shame these clothes, these moral restrictions that humans here inflicted on themselves.

Amarja said the words Alice had given her to overcome the locking spell. When she was inside, she held out her hand. A clear crystal globe shining with a firefly's yellow light settled in her palm. She gave the globe a push, and it floated alongside her illuminating the interior.

The room, though large, was welcoming. A pastel carpet, thick and soft, woven with flowers, covered a portion of the wooden floor. Accenting the muted carpet, chairs upholstered in pale peach and pink were arranged in various seating clusters. Over the center of the carpet lay a smaller silk Persian rug depicting the tree of life in strong bright colors, rife with swirls and curls of Eastern calligraphy. Glowing like amber from the globe's otherworldly light, strings of ochre beads hung like a curtain in a doorway leading to a parlor or dressing room. A gold and lime-green sari had been carelessly draped over a chair by the window, seemingly forgotten like the husk of a huge fruit. Thalia was finding her way into Bramley House through Lavinia.

A piece of unfinished embroidery, stretched on a hoop, lay on a table, a black tulip amongst colorful flowers, purposefully placed where it would dominate the design. Hmmm. Whatever Lavinia was like, Yasir must be pleased with her, for Alice said he was in the great manor. A fact Zamyad had left out when he told her only humans lived in Bramley House. She would see to that later.

Amarja shut her eyes and cast the first spell King Zamyad had instructed. When she opened them, she held her breath. The room glittered with unearthly light. Hundreds of tiny glass shards, sparkling like diamonds, peeked from the floorboards. A slight dizziness fought her concentration, attempting to weaken her spell. So this was Rakhshan's magic—each shard a glinting messenger quietly lying in wait to carry out his command—find Yasir.

These pieces of glass could move on their own, but for convenience would attach to a person, animal, rodent or insect, and travel, mirroring what they discovered to Rakhshan. If these got loose, they would find Yasir.

The room weighed heavy on her, as if she sat in a cave, a ceiling of stone overhead, a massive mountain above bearing down tons of granite and earth. She sat alone, protected by Zamyad's magic, yet how strong would it be when set against Rakhshan's needs?

If the Dark Magician found out about Yasir's children, if he knew about the prophecy.

And why wouldn't he? Zamyad knew of the prophecy even before she was born, but kept it close. He hadn't bothered to tell her, but she had heard rumors and finagled it out of him. The prophecy was true.

But like all divinations passed down through the ages, parts got skewed a bit here, a bit there, and arrived changed. She had heard that a child of Yasir's would defeat Rakhshan and free the djinni, but others heard 'child of Yasir and Thalia.'

There could be a surprise.

Amarja was not able to save her son years ago, but she could protect Yasir now. Even his little doxy. With a wave of her hand the winking shards surrounding her scattered. She turned in a slow circle and recited the second spell. A golden coffer appeared on the table beside her, its surface writhing with dimensional figures of animals, plants and calligraphy. A subtle noise, like chattering birds, crowded the room.

Upon sensing the presence of the coffer, the shards squirmed, their chatter fading with their gleam. She tossed her head. The spell would work. The heavy gold lid floated off and, with a muffled thump, settled on the table's marble surface, releasing a silvery light. A beacon of sorts.

Like shooting stars, the glass fragments arced through the room, comets zooming with unerring accuracy into the golden box. The tinkling sound of delicate chimes filled the room as the slivers settled into the coffer. Tiny glinting spies, their evil assignment masked by glistening beauty. She sat still. This task easy, but Yasir, difficult. Always difficult.

The clear crystal globe settled on the table behind her, dimming the room, its light somewhat blocked by the coffer and her body. Details of the room's furniture, windows, and lamps smudged as in a blurred charcoal drawing. As the lid rose from the surface of the table and fitted onto the chest, the squirming figures embossed on the cover moved with less urgency. Amarja reached out, her pale hand high above the coffer.

The sphere glided into her palm, lighting the lid with a soft glow. The embossed creatures on the surface raised up, poised to jump off into the night, but she brought her other hand down onto the lid, sealing it with the closing spell. Muffled screams came from inside.

Amarja let her hand sink below the globe, which floated up to the ceiling, lighting her way. She lifted the golden box from the table. After she had put another, stronger, more difficult spell on it, neutralizing the magic from Rakhshan, she would deliver it to Zamyad. That enchantment must be done away from this chamber.

She looked both ways down the shadowy hall, making sure no one was there, and shut the door without a sound. With a faint series of clicks, Alice's locking spell sealed the room. Amarja tucked the coffer under her arm, checking the hall floor for any stray shards, when a strong power tugged at her.

She put both arms around the box, looked up, and smothered a cry.

He stood there, gazing at her, golden eyes reflecting the residual light from the coffer. Amarja drew back from his overpowering presence. The coffer slipped from her arms.

Only a djinni could creep up on her unannounced.

"Amarja." Yasir's voice wavered. He reached for the box, his magic disorienting her.

"No!" She stepped in front of him, red tresses swirling. "Too dangerous for you."

She bent to pick up the golden box and dropped into a crouch on the floor beside it. The shards still had power even though they were enclosed. She must hurry to add the final spell. The clasp had opened on impact. How could she have been so . . . so befuddled by the power of a djinni? She clamped the lid shut, pressing it tight as she searched the floor.

A few shards of glass scattered on the floorboards near Lavinia's door and caught the light from the trunk. They wriggled away. Would she fail at her task? No, she wouldn't allow this to go wrong. The witch cast a quick enclosing spell on the chest, scraped up the slivers with her hand, opened the lid a crack, and drove them deep into the box. Zamyad's magic should protect her from their sharp edges and Rakhshan's malevolence.

She fumbled with the clasp bent by the fall, then used her magic to repair it, and shut the lid properly, strengthening the closing spell. Once again, she checked the floor. Yasir waited. She felt his presence now, his power mingling with hers, affecting her in ways she couldn't know until later.

A sparkle at the wide molding next to the door. Another shard. She opened the lid again and slipped it inside.

His presence had distracted her from the task. Yasir moved in front of her, his hands out. He grinned.

"I will hold the coffer. You seem to have difficulty with it," he said.

"Only a few words after such a long time and you question my ability?" Tossing her head, she rose and swiveled the box to her side, resting it on her hip and freeing one hand. The coffer must not retain the touch of a djinni. Zamyad could never know Yasir was nearby when she cleared the room. This was a happenstance that should not have been. If the shards that fell from the box mirrored Yasir, Rakhshan would know the djinni was alive.

Yasir took Amarja's hand. A red stain bloomed on her index finger.

"Perhaps you should have used your magic to banish the glass to the coffer, rather than scooping up the pieces." He ran his finger over hers. The cut healed, blood vanishing.

She tightened her hold on the coffer with a shaky hand, fighting the swoon that his touch brought and gazed at him. His pupils rounded from their startling vertical slits.

So, he felt something.

"Amarja, what were you about in Lavinia's chamber?" Yasir eyed the golden trunk. The figures writhed under his gaze.

"In here. We mustn't be seen." She led him into a secluded parlor down the hall. Inside, the globe appeared in her open palm, emitting a warm, soft light. A faint fragrance of spring blossoms haunted the room from the bouquet on a low table. The full, lush pink cabbage roses bent on their stems like women in mourning. Shriveled petals lay strewn on the marble surface. Amarja set the coffer in the midst of them. She reached up and kissed Yasir.

His soft lips, the power of his magic. She had missed him, but had done her best to remove thoughts of the amazing djinni from her mind. After all, she was with Zamyad now. But now she must put her plan into play.

Amarja leaned close, her forehead to his, breathing in his power, so young, so vital. Different from his father's. She stroked Yasir's cheek.

"I entered Lavinia's room to gather pieces of Alice's magic mirror, which the Shadow Lord—" she looked warily at Yasir, "had fouled with his presence." She brushed her lips on his, like the caress of a feather. The slight touch burned.

His hands encircled her waist and she shut her eyes, imagining herself with Yasir all those years ago. He lifted her away from him. Would he reject her so suddenly?

"How did you come to be here?" His voice strained.

"Alice summoned me." She watched the djinni, looking for a glimmer of understanding. *Had Alice kept this a secret from Yasir, that Zamyad was alive and in contact with Alice?* Amarja saw no reaction. Good. Zamyad had stressed that Yasir should not know he was alive, should not know that he kept only a few watching his son. For if Yasir knew, then it was possible for Rakhshan to find out.

"Did you make us safe?" He sounded worried.

She placed her hand on his stomach, his muscles hard under her fingers.

"Of course," she whispered in his ear.

He shivered.

"Can you take us to your urn?" She pressed her body to his chest. Her hand slid down his torso, reaching lower.

"My master wants me back. I am on an errand." He clearly was on his guard.

"Yasir." Amarja called his name like the breeze susurrating through the trees. "Can we not be alone for a time?"

"It is not like it was," he said, his voice stern.

Was he still angry? He had accused her of taking advantage while she healed him after he was thought dead. He had felt like her prisoner. She kept her face impassive, stifling her smile when she recalled his ardor. He had fallen into her arms with such passion.

She veiled her thoughts without him knowing, a delicate task. She must have him. This child would be the one mentioned in the prophecy. *A child of a djinni and a witch.* Much more powerful than a get from that human, Lavinia.

"I must give you a warning. Though, here, we may not be as *protected* as in another place." She peered around the room.

Yasir whirled his hand around his head. Twinkling sparks encircled them in a ring of silver.

"No one can listen now." His golden eyes reflected the silver flecks spinning around them. Silver and gold. Such magic.

"You are in danger still. From another than the Dark Magician." She ran her hands through his silky hair.

Yasir frowned. He took her hand and pushed it away.

"It is the Blue Sorceress, the one who heals." Amarja narrowed her eyes at the djinni. Had the Blue Sorceress been his lover? But she saw no telltale flicker in his expression. "She is looking for you. Or your body. She knows not that you live."

"Mehadeh?" Yasir tilted his head, staring into the distance. "But she tried to heal me. She assisted Lavinia."

"But she did not heal you, did she?" Amarja saw doubt cloud his expression. "Things change, Yasir." She ran her hand down his arm.

He nodded. Considering.

"She is working for someone. One whom you know well. One who is your nemesis."

Yasir caught her gaze without a waver. Had her revelation surprised him, or did he already suspect Mchadeh?

Armarja closed her eyes, breathing his essence. "I wish he could have lived. He would be . . . like you."

"Please, do not speak of it. I— " Yasir's voice caught and she felt his chest convulse. "I cannot bear it."

"I must take the coffer away." She embraced him and smiled to herself as she heard his breath quicken. This would happen, if not here at Bramley House, then another time. But she would have her hero child.

36

Yasir lounged on the divan in the urn, sinking into the soft silken pillows of cloth of gold and silver, of intricate weavings and embroidery.

Waiting for the betrayer.

At Peter's side as his manservant, Yasir had not been to the urn in weeks. He grinned. His plan was going well. Peter had developed a reticent, but growing, liking for him. It had been difficult, but Yasir had been submissive and obedient while stretching the bonds of the curse.

A sinking feeling overcame him. The warning signs were there, a decline of his magic at twilight, a thinning of his spell on Peter portending imminent release. If he wasn't careful, the urn's curse would mitigate his enchantment, reduce his powers and foil his plans. He was so close, only days from the spell's completion.

He would take the chance. That decided, he must deal with the problem brought up by the witch Amarja.

He lifted a golden cup from his opal table, spilled the bright jewels into his palm and savored the light playing through them. Waiting had always made him restless. A ruby fell on the table, smaller than the apple-sized ruby Mehadeh, the Blue Sorceress, used to rescue Lavinia and him from Rakhshan's palace.

Mehadeh had tried to save his life after Peter shot him. She shepherded Lavinia when he could not. Mehadeh the good. But he had his suspicions. She was at Rakhshan's palace before Lavinia became a prisoner. What was the sorceress doing there? Would she betray him after all they had been through?

Mehadeh the bad would be formidable.

He clutched the faceted jewels in his palm at the disturbance in the ether. This intimate room, like a private area of a Seraglio, was Mehadeh's favorite place in the urn. He waved his hand over himself, his human body fading as the ether thickened.

A vague gray form shading to deep blue spun before him, then metamorphosed into a curved shape much like the contour of his urn. The figure, gaining substance, became defined like a master artist might craft a painting if he were removing, rather than adding, brush strokes.

Mehadeh appeared before him. She blinked, her eyes as dark as her blue-black skin.

Yasir took his human shape, standing directly in her path. If he found her guilty, his face would be the last she saw.

She took a step, then halted as if she had run into a wall, her slanted eyes so wide they looked round. With this swift surprise, he had hoped her guard might drop, allowing him to discern her loyalties, but the sorceress kept her strength.

"Yasir, *dabekan*, every sign indicated that you were dead. I thought, with sorrow, never to see you again." Tears glistened in her dark eyes.

"Nor I you." He was glad to see her in spite of his suspicions. They shared a long, long history.

She looked thin, her dark eyes disturbed. His memories of Mehadeh featured a woman confident, haughty with a taunt in her eye. This worked to her advantage with her enemies, most of whom were intimidated by her strong presence and rumors of the Nubian Sorceress's powers.

As if she were a long lost sister, he embraced her. She rested in his arms, head against his breast, her thick black hair in long tangled funnels brushing his face like sheep's wool. There was something unfamiliar about her, some vague threat that grew stronger.

Scenes flashed through his mind. He slowed them, seeing the almond-eyed Bishan Shaman drowning the sorceress, Rakhshan saving her, making Mehadeh beholden to him. He felt the Dark Lord's evil threats, Mehadeh's fear, Rakhshan's hunger for his power, for him.

Soon, he knew the entire story. The sorceress was tasked to find him, dead or alive, and bring whatever she found to Rakhshan. Mehadeh had purposely opened herself to him, her way of answering his unasked questions. Of saying he should trust her.

Satisfied that he had seen enough, she removed herself from his embrace, fixing him with a haunted look so familiar from his own reflection when he dared confront himself in the mirror. In a graceful motion she folded her body onto the divan, spreading her indigo blue skirts like the night sky.

"I have wondered through the ages how a mere court magician had such a hold on you," said Mehadeh as she picked up the golden bowl on the table and ran her fingers through the sparkling gems.

"The Shadow Lord has your secret name. How?" She let the stones fall through her fingers, a river of colored light.

He looked to the heavens, the glow of the stars. They were there, infinite, somewhere outside the urn. At last, an explanation for Rakhshan's power over him. He had buried his ignominy so long, so diligently, that he never saw his secret name as a piece of the puzzle.

The revelation flummoxed him. He felt his human shape fading, but worked to keep it so he could better feel Mehadeh's reactions. Should he confess?

He sat next to her, wrestling with what he should reveal. But the need to speak of his shame, like the urge to worry a sore pustule throbbing in one's flesh, could only be massaged by the telling.

"Mehadeh, I am calling up a memory that I have buried. A terrible disgrace I brought on myself. Something I never resolved until just now." He held out his hands, palms up, giving himself to the tale.

"Like a cobra drawn to the motions of the man playing the flute, I stood in front of a soothsayer's hut in the souk. I turned around, looking for Afsoon."

He squeezed his hands into fists and looked at Mehadeh. "You know Afsoon as Alice." Lost in his story, Mehadeh stared at him for a moment, then nodded. Yasir continued.

"She had been tasked to watch me, but the jostling crowd of shoppers streamed on, oblivious. No tumult in the flow of bodies, animals or conveyances. No frantic voices, or even distant calls of my name. Alice was not seeking me yet.

"At twelve years, I had become adept at my magic, and often vanished from the house to wander as I pleased. This worried my mother no end. But now I was free for the time being. The soothsayer, gowned in a brilliant garment of purple silk woven with bright gold patterns, appeared in the doorway and tossed her head. Her long dark tresses shone in rival to the diamond in her nose.

"'You,' the lady said. She pointed her hand, painted in red swirls, in my direction.

"I shrugged. 'Yes, you, little one with the curls and golden eyes. Come closer.'

"She moved her head from side to side. Her eyes, lined in kohl, looked like the enormous false eyes dotting a butterfly's wings. I could see the red paint of the bindi between her eyes glistening on the pores of her dusky skin.

"She smelled of sandalwood and jasmine. Her thick hair, hanging to her waist, shimmered, a dark waterfall in brilliant sunlight. She took my palm. I pulled back from the shock of her touch—like a bee sting—but she held on and drew me into the dark interior of her hut.

"I wanted to jerk my hand from her cold grip. Run from there, but my muscles, under a different command, followed. She sat me in a chair and knelt before me. The place was cloudy with incense, the smell so overpowering I felt as if I would smother.

"In a lilting voice she said, 'You show great promise.' She looked up, still holding my hand. Her eyes, glistening with tears, drooped in grief. 'But you will be thwarted before you can bloom. Nipped in the bud.'

"I can still recall the staccato clip of her words. The intonation of her phrase, nipped–in–the–bud. Spoken so fast that it took me some time, after she spoke, to decipher what she said.

"The lady's dark eyes filled with compassion. 'I can help you to stand it. I will assist such a beautiful boy, but first you must tell me your secret name.'"

Yasir sprang from the divan after he spoke the soothsayer's words. He shook his head, trying to rid the image of her sinister dark eyes. He looked around. He was in the urn. Trapped. A slave of his own making.

"How could I have been so foolish?" His voice, loud and angry, startled Mehadeh. She came to his side and shook him as his breath hitched.

"Yasir it is done."

He felt her hands go through his body as he faded into the faint smoke of the Djinn.

"This is where I could have stopped it. Stopped this terrible course my life has taken." With effort he brought himself back to his human form, slammed his hand on the opal table and swept the golden bowl away. The precious jewels clattered on the floor like common pebbles.

Mehadeh's hand rested hard on his shoulder.

"Best continue. For your sake, you must finish this tale." The calm tone of her voice soothed him.

He sat beside her, anxious to finish. Could he bear the rest of the telling?

"I was a foolish and proud youth. Flattered and stupefied and, perhaps spelled by the dusky wench, her bosom squeezing out of her gold-threaded blouse.

"I sat still, the noise of the ever-busy souk outside isolating me with this lady from the land of Rajas. I was shocked that the woman even knew I had a secret name, and anxious from what she foretold. I stood to leave. She rose halfway, took my arm and gently dragged me back into the chair.

"'You will be sorry if you go without my gift. Every day, you will wish I had helped you.' The soothsayer leaned close to me. I inhaled the voluptuous woody fragrance of sandalwood underneath the sweet jasmine of her perfume. My fear evaporated.

"Of course she knew about my secret name, she was a soothsayer, they would know these things. But I was young enough to forget to reason further. With me before her, my mind there for the taking, if she were a competent soothsayer, she would *know* my secret name.

"I can feel my slowed, spelled movements to this day. My mouth to her ear, her golden earring cold on my lips, her spicy scent, combined with the incense, cloying.

"I spoke the scarce-said word.

"She smiled and rose to her feet, towering above me. Her dark eyes hardened as she turned and shoved aside the beaded curtain, leaving me alone in the small room. A feeling of dread snaked through me, that I had done something horribly wrong, something that could never be undone, something that could be my undoing.

"I sat there in the dark, choking on the pungent smell of the incense, horrified at what I had told her.

"I would force the soothsayer with my magic. I would make her forget. Rage rose inside me like my powers when I summon them.

"I strode towards the beaded curtain.

"Someone grabbed my arm and spun me around. I faced an enormous thickset man. Below his dusty blue turban a thick red scar, like a new-plowed furrow, ran down the left side of his face, broken by a malicious grin.

"'The lady has no use for you now, *Dosti-drety gundnam.*'

"Taken by surprise, I was too slow gathering my magic.

"He picked me up, walked out of the hut and tossed me into the crowd. I landed on my face in the dirt. Spitting foul dust, I staggered to my feet to the raucous laughter of an amused throng. I dodged legs and robes and hands that shooed me with slaps, then ran as fast as I could.

"I ran from the man's evil grin, the harsh stare in the soothsayer's eyes when she had her prize. A terrible cold coursed through my blood, even though the sun blasted down upon me. The midday heat rose from the ground as though the underworld were seeping through the floor of the earth."

He stared straight ahead, seeing only the soothsayer, the man's scar, feeling the shame. Mehadeh sat beside him. He felt her strong presence, her slow breathing. Did she judge him? He pulled his legs to his chest, tucked his feet close, the jewels on his curved slippers dull in the shadow of his body.

Still not looking at Mehadeh, he said, "I have searched for, but never found the soothsayer. At random times, a sense of unease devours me. I glance over my shoulder, sure that someone is poised there, hands formed in a black magic gesture, ready to overtake me with a wicked spell. I take the smoke form of the Djinn, only to shudder as though my very essence will be overcome by a depravity so terrible it defies descriptions of the most egregious evil in legends and myths."

At last he turned to Mehadeh. She sat, spell-bound. Or perhaps shocked at his foolishness.

"Never have I told this before." He surveyed his opulent prison, silently cursing the innocence, insolence and pride of his budding youth.

"The soothsayer procured my secret name for the Shadow Lord. For a pretty price I wager." He swallowed his pride in his extraordinary powers, laid low by his own folly so many centuries past, and forced himself to ask the sorceress.

"Is there a way to fix this curse?"

She put her hand to his cheek. "My dear Yasir, my blood-sworn brother, know that this is said with love and empathy."

The tears in her eyes made him uneasy. He braced himself for her answer.

"That is why the prophecy says that one of your children will defeat the Dark Magician." Mehadeh said it with dignity, without judgment, without pity. He silently thanked her for that.

"But, Mehadeh, I promised Lavinia I would not let Stuart fight the Shadow Lord. That I would face him myself."

Mehadeh looked deep into his eyes. He had not recognized until now the sadness that had been lingering there. She sagged into the pillows. The rich embroidery and weavings made her troubled face look even more haggard.

"You should let Stuart fight, Yasir. The prophecy says he will defeat the Shadow Lord."

"But it doesn't say at what cost," Yasir said, his voice quiet, spiritless, the tones vibrating in the air like the muted strike of a gong.

He knew he would have to fight. After all these revelations, could he find a way to foil Rakhshan? He snuck a glance and met Mehadeh's dark gaze.

Yasir reached for the golden bowl, but saw it upturned on the floor, the gems scattered like spilled secrets.

Was it possible that his destiny had been set in stone when he was but twelve?

37

Yasir had been free for a time. At least, he had pretended so as he traveled the earth, procuring scrolls, tablets, statuettes with inscriptions and moldy Medieval books for clues about the prophecy regarding Stuart. Egypt, Indos, the Land of Shin, Turksland, the Deserts of the Middle Sands, and old realms whose ancient names had been relegated to the dust since he last visited.

Yasir kept from smirking. His master sat at his desk, bent over a cuneiform tablet. Peter was deficient in deciphering this language, but would not admit it. His eyes scanned the tablet as moved his lips, the telltale sign of a beginner. He would be mortified if he knew Yasir had noticed. Wisps of blonde hair escaped Peter's tightly bound queue, framing his face as he studied the incised wedge-shaped marks in the hard gray clay.

The intensity of Peter's expression when he became lost in studies heightened his beauty, which made the spell Yasir had worked easier to perpetuate. An ugly victim was repugnant to seduce.

This slow, subtle spell was hard to detect, even by Peter, who had scrolls containing instructions and enchantments about how to deflect the Djinn—and had used them to thwart him. A smooth glow of satisfaction warmed Yasir's insides. The spell enthralled the victim, and, while the charm fully insinuated itself, the enchanter had to be entirely subservient.

Peter, thoroughly in the spell's grip, was beyond saving. He looked up from the tablet, his mouth curved into an inviting smile that lit his face like a pearl in candlelight, like an angel from paintings in the great cathedrals on the continent. The image of the huge panel behind the altar of the ancient Basilica of St. Janustacia the Lame rose in Yasir's mind, the dark background broken by brilliant beams of light and incandescent wings, Peter's luminous countenance in place of the visage of some hapless model hired off the street. His master was almost fully taken by the spell. Yasir answered Peter with a smile of his own.

Only a few more days, and he will be completely mine.

Peter motioned him over.

"Look here, you must assist with this particular cuneiform." He cocked his head, a pleading look in his pale eyes. "The languages I know, even the most arcane, are no help in translating." He rapped his fist on the desk in frustration, the soft thud muted by the stack of documents on which it landed.

Yasir placed his finger on the ancient slab of hardened clay. The power of the words inscribed thousands of years ago flowed through him. A crisp sheet of paper covered with precise calligraphy appeared on Peter's desk.

"A complete translation of the cuneiform, in your language," said Yasir. "This tablet is a survivor of many that were made quoting the prophet Ulan-e-al Seimn. The important part of the prediction says, 'He will turn back the tide of evil that is to take the world.'"

Yasir slid his finger to the line before. "The word *du'jiiâiti* means *bad life* in this instance and refers to the perpetrator of evil." Yasir pointed to the fifth line of the incised glyphs, "You can see here that this scroll is dated *adjeo 29s.*"

Peter looked at him, puzzled. "I don't understand that date."

"Humans do not know that we have our own way of marking our time. This date is in the time you call 'before Christ.' This would be approximately 2,000 years before your Christ," said Yasir with authority, as he stood nearer to Peter than studying the tablet warranted.

For a human, close proximity to a Djinn is a noticeable experience, some fall in love immediately, some become ill, some become fearful. Being spell-cast and standing close to the conjurer strengthens the spell exponentially.

His master caught his breath, and pressed too hard on the quill pen, spattering ink on his notes. "Confound it." He covered the splashes of India ink with blotting paper.

Yasir moved away. He watched Peter, who shook his head as though that motion could remove the web Yasir had woven around him like a spider encasing his next meal.

Peter set the blotting paper aside and indicated the stained papers beside the tablet. "Can you clean these?"

Yasir beamed, pleased with the spell's progress, Peter asking rather than commanding. With his magic, the dark stains vanished. The papers were again pristine.

Peter held his hands up, smeared with black. "These as well." After Yasir obliged, Peter rubbed his fingers against his palms and examined his unsullied hands.

"Yasir, your scholarship impresses me. You will assist with more of my studies." Peter rose from his chair and stretched. "I say we have a respite. Have one of the servants bring us lunch."

Peter stood straighter, eyes stern. Of course, he realized what he had said. He had admitted out loud that his feelings for his djinni were different now. Yasir was not any more an object of retaliation with respect to Lavinia.

"If I find out that this knowledge is just some of your hocus pocus, well," Peter laughed and affected a formal tone, "you know I am creative in my punishments."

"You will find these sources genuine, I assure you." Yasir, his face suitably somber, bowed. "Thank you, master, for your consideration, but I am not too fatigued to bring you lunch."

Yasir was careful to be accommodating. It would not do for Peter to go into a fury this late in the spell, things could slip out of balance, and magic gone awry could be dangerous.

Strolling into the kitchen, Yasir pondered his plan. *It was working beautifully.* This time he had gotten off easy, so far only a flogging, complete humiliation and a few beatings.

38

$\mathcal{L}$avinia wearied of avoiding her husband. These last weeks, she had taken supper in her room on a tray, or dined in private with Alice when her aunt was at Bramley House. Other than his visit after the night of his club meeting and a few passing courtesies, she and Peter hadn't spoken since she stumbled upon him and his cronies flogging Yasir. Neither of them acknowledged that Peter had caught Lavinia in bed with Yasir, had stolen the urn, had tortured Yasir and was probably still doing so.

Tonight, she had dressed in a silken gown the color of lapis lazuli. A cascading diamond necklace and matching earrings sparkled like stars to the deep blue heaven of her dress. Fleming had pinned her hair up, arranging diamond combs so they would glimmer in the candlelight.

This was her house too. She could go to dinner as she pleased. Why should she be afraid of her husband?

The footman opened the dining room door. Peter was already there. She walked to her seat. The footman pulled out her chair.

"Lavinia." Peter looked up, startled. Good, she had succeeded in surprising him. Perhaps she could glean information about Yasir.

"Have some wine." Peter slurred his words, his visage brightening with a smile. Lavinia pressed into the back of her chair as he held the bottle over her wineglass, his hand shaking. The burgundy missed spilling by a hair, but Peter bowed with a flourish, oblivious of the near calamity.

"Thank you, Peter." She kept her voice formal, hiding her disdain. She took a sip, the wine a bit bitter, and scrutinized him as if she were a coiled serpent eyeing a juicy beetle. Her husband, drunk and handsome in a light blue velvet jacket and tight brown breeches with white hose that showed his figure to advantage.

Peter, master of the urn—her *urn*, her *djinni*.

Lavinia's stomach suddenly felt heavy, weighing down her insides. These aches and pains that had plagued her since she came upon the Anubis Brotherhood must be part of her grief for the Peter that used to be, for Yasir's absence.

"Bring in the supper." Peter addressed the footman in the corner by one of the great arched windows, the drapes, even the muslin sash curtains, open to the deepening twilight. In footman's livery, Yasir stepped from the shadows, a purple bruise like a generous splash of paint on his left cheek.

Lavinia gasped audibly, then put her hand to her mouth as though she could take back her expression of consternation. Peter shot her a look of triumph.

Yasir didn't seem to notice her as he left the room at Peter's command. What other injuries were covered by the djinni's clothes? Other footmen appeared with dinner. She glanced about, spotting Yasir standing off to the side, almost hidden by a great ceramic vase. A good servant awaiting his master's summons.

"How are the children?" Peter asked as if inquiring about the weather.

Did she catch a look of wistfulness flitting across his face? Was he sorry for the dastardly things he did to Yasir? To her?

"They ask about you." Her voice sounded normal and didn't ring with anger. Good. She had controlled it well. How she wanted to say, *I forbid you to see them.*

Peter waved his soup spoon. *Could he hear the deceit in her voice?*

"Ah, I've been so busy. Musht shee them more often." His words ran together so she could barely understand them. He raised his glass, tipping it to the right. "To Stu, James and Cybelle."

Lavinia lifted her wineglass, joining the toast. She nodded, attempting to behave as though nothing untoward had happened between them, as if all were normal, when ghastly things, completely out of the ordinary, had occurred. Prickles ran down her back and shoulders. She felt the djinni's golden gaze on her, as if it were a physical thing, like a hand laid on her flesh. If only she could look his way. See how he was. Talk to him.

She considered it her failure that Peter stole Yasir. *How had her husband found the urn when she had so carefully hidden it? Did Yasir blame her?*

Lavinia nodded at her wine glass, and, to her horror, Yasir obediently refilled it. The soup bowls had been removed and the youngest footman served her plate with roast duck covered in berry sauce and potatoes in rich cream tossed with greens. She finished her wine and motioned for more. If Yasir answered she was prepared to try to signal him, but the footman with the brown hair poured this time.

Peter, in the middle of a rambling tale, described Palomar tearing the skinny stable boy's trousers. She forced herself to laugh.

"More wine." Peter motioned to the footman and continued his tale, stopping for the arrival of dessert—pastry filled with cream and pears, sprinkled with powdered sugar. Lavinia's favorite.

Much to her dismay, she found herself gradually enjoying the evening with this imbibing Peter. When he was drunk, he lost his newly acquired priggishness and became his old self, clever and funny.

"Yashir," slurred Peter. "Ready my chambers."

Lavinia watched Yasir leave. Her thoughts fuzzed, imagining the djinni telling her he missed her, scheming with her to steal the urn away, holding her for a forbidden moment behind the folds of curtains or a partially opened door. Peter was drunk. She could get away with this.

"Lavy. Accompany me." Peter wobbled as he rose from his seat, but steadied himself, holding onto the back of the chair. He lurched over, stumbled, and helped her to standing.

"Peter, I am weary. Tonight I would go to my own room." Lavinia spoke in as sweet a voice as she could manage. She had drunk at least four glasses of wine, maybe more. Perhaps, that's why she enjoyed the meal with her husband.

Peter took her hand and led the way. When he was in his cups it was best to indulge him. This drunk, he often had trouble in bed, which would make her protests unnecessary.

In the bedroom, her husband called for Yasir to bring them brandy and extinguish all the lamps but two, so the light glowed low and romantic. Peter pulled Lavinia close and kissed her, long and slow. Lavinia responded in spite of herself. She must have had more wine than she thought. Five, no, six glasses?

"Peter, dear, I do think it best I go to my room now. Perhaps, another night," Lavinia said gently.

"Nonsense, nonsense. All is forgiven and forgotten about the little incident." He sipped his brandy and looked her up and down, sloshing his drink, a curve of gold captured in the snifter's balloon glass.

"Yasir, remove my boots." Peter flopped in a chair, extending his legs.

Lavinia paced as Yasir knelt before Peter. She took this chance to slip out.

"Yasir, be a good man and grab my wife for me," Peter said. Yasir suddenly stood before her, barring her way. He looked through her as if she weren't there.

"Move," Lavinia whispered angrily. "I mean to leave here." She whipped around Yasir and out the door. In the hall, the djinni appeared in front of her and took her by the arm.

"Let me go!"

His eyes gleamed. She tried to pull away.

Yasir's eyes stayed cold as he said, "You gave him the urn. How could you betray me?"

"What?" Did she hear him correctly?

"You gave him the urn." Yasir practically spat the words.

"No, no. I don't know how, but he stole it." She tried to see some compassion, some empathy in the djinni's eyes, in his posture. Anything. He divulged nothing. She would make him understand. "Believe me, I hid it well. I don't know how he knew. About you. The urn."

"YOU told him, remember? In the urn, right after he struck me." Yasir spoke to her as if she were a naughty child.

"He could have killed you," Lavinia whispered. "I had to do something."

Yasir kept his grip on her arm, eyes dispassionate.

"Bring her in. Now!" Peter garbled his words.

"I am bound to do what he says." Yasir's shoulders slumped, his eyes, colder, if that was possible. And angry. He blamed her. For his flogging, for his humiliation in front of her, for his servitude. He blamed her.

"God in heaven, are you going to do it?" Lavinia struggled to free her arm. "You know what Peter means to do. Will you stand for it?"

She placed her hand on Yasir's face. The shock of his smooth skin, his magic, almost made her acquiesce. "Look at me, and tell me it's what you wish."

"It is what *you* wish. You set this in motion when you told him of me. When you gave him the urn." Yasir stopped in front of the door. "I try to draw his rage away from you to me. It works. He tortures me. He beats me. He does not allow me to heal myself." Yasir set his jaw tight, but it quivered. He looked away. "In that small way, since I am under his command, I can protect you, protect Stuart and Cybelle."

He looked her in the eyes and she saw the anguish filling his dark pupils. It pierced her soul.

"But what if it is not enough? What then?" He broke their gaze and took her by the wrists. "I beg you. Do not resist me, or he will order me to hurt you."

He escorted her into the room and closed the door.

The heat from the flush of her cheeks spread into her neck and arms. She had been churlish and childish. Yasir bore his humiliation valiantly. Peter was his master. Yasir had to obey.

She gathered her words, the right ones to show Yasir that she knew all this, to show compassion. As she opened her mouth, Peter's ice blue eyes bored into her. Anything she said to Yasir would bode poorly for the djinni.

"Lock it, and bring me the key." Peter scowled. His mood had turned foul. He had shed his shirt and sat on the bed, anxious and, Lavinia noticed, all too ready.

As Peter unbuttoned his trousers, Lavinia stared at Yasir. Now would be the time. The djinni could work a small spell on Peter and make him unable to perform. Then she'd be understanding, say the right words—*it was her fault for being so tired, for not being cooperative.* She would plead that she felt she was coming down with something and leave for her own bed. But could she soothe Peter's humiliation in front of Yasir?

"Bring her to me." Her husband looked from her to Yasir. She could see Peter's mind working, suspecting betrayals from them both, already accusing her of sending messages to the djinni, sneaking off with him. At that very moment, Peter was probably devising new tortures for Yasir.

Yasir took her by the waist and led her to the bed. This could so easily go wrong. Peter could turn violent, take it out on her, forbidding Yasir to interfere. Better to have it this way.

"Ah, what a good djinni you are." Peter lounged against a pillow and grinned at Yasir. "Now use your magic and remove her gown. I am impatient, and these damned dresses with their laces and buttons and frippery—" He belched.

Lavinia instinctively raised her arms to cover her bosom as her clothes vanished, leaving her bare in front of her husband and Yasir. She let her arms rest at her side and closed her eyes. If she lashed out and tried to run, Peter would order Yasir to bring her back again—or worse. Yasir was right. She had to acquiesce.

Peter pulled her towards him. "For God's sake, man, don't stand directly over us. Go over by the wardrobe." And he laughed. Then he kissed Lavinia hard on the lips.

She glimpsed Yasir as he stood there, silent, staring, like a cat, calm and collected. If he had a tail it would have twitched.

Through the window, daylight flooded the room. Lavinia shielded her face with the covers. It must be late. A throbbing pain ripped through her temple. She pressed her fingers, cool from the chilled air, into her forehead, and moaned.

Where was she? Lavinia pulled the covers down just below her eyes. Warmth radiated from somewhere on her left, and she turned to see Peter sprawled on his stomach beside her, lost to slumber. A peaceful scene. She snuggled into the bedclothes, drowsy, ready to sleep some more, but something nagged at her, dragging her more awake.

Moving only her eyes, she searched the room, stopping at a bulky shape in the cold blue shadows of the corner. It wasn't a piece of furniture. Too big to be a bunched, discarded piece of clothing. She clutched the covers in alarm, breathing hard. She would wake Peter and—

Lord in heaven, it was Yasir. In a blur of motion, he stood beside her as if her thoughts had commanded him there.

She couldn't think why she hadn't seen him for a while, why he was in the bedroom, on the floor, with Peter there beside her in bed. Her head throbbed. Through the pain, scenes from the night before flooded her mind and she sat up, covers sliding down as the horrid phrase rang in her head as loud and bright as the daylight—*Peter was master now.*

Lavinia shut her eyes, the intensifying daylight almost as unbearable as the memory. Pain hammered in her head, a blacksmith banging at his anvil, and her wrath at Peter gathered like gray smoke above a roaring fire.

She slipped out of bed. Wrapping the knitted shawl from the bedside chair around her, she glared at Peter, still in the same position, sound asleep. It would be intolerable to be here when he awoke. The farther away the better. She wanted nothing to do with either Peter or Yasir.

She hurried towards the door, the floor smooth and cold, like ice under her bare feet. Yasir shadowed her, his magic enveloping her, but she wouldn't look at him, not after last night. The latch wouldn't go further than midway. She remembered. The door had been locked from the inside. A stab of pain jagged through her head. She couldn't deal with Peter. If she had to talk with Yasir to leave this prison, so be it.

"Quick," she whispered trying not to look into the djinni's eyes. "Give me the key." What was she thinking, why hadn't she asked him to open the door with his magic? But perhaps he couldn't use his magic at her command now. She had to leave. Now. She adjusted the shawl around her, wishing she had her slippers. Fleming would fetch her clothes later.

Yasir produced the key with a flourish. "I will say I was asleep when you left."

Lavinia couldn't face him. The full memory of last night flooded her brain. Standing naked in front of them both. Yasir watching Peter make love to her. Her head throbbed. The key shook in her hand. She could only be glad that Peter hadn't made Yasir join them.

"How could you, Yasir?"

The djinni stared at the floor. "You know very well the why and how of it." She heard the resignation in his voice. "You allowed Peter to obtain the urn."

"I did not. I didn't know." Curse his foolish stubbornness. Why wouldn't he believe her? She guided the key into the lock, but it slipped from her hands, clattering onto the floorboards. Hearing Yasir sigh, she turned to him.

"You were careless. The urn is a treasure," he said. "Throughout the ages—" The key appeared in Yasir's palm, but he looked at it in exasperation, and waved his hand at the door. The lock clicked. The door swung open. Cold air from the hall rushed into the room. Lavinia gasped and pulled the shawl tight.

You were content to stand by while my husband . . . She couldn't say the sentence or even finish it in her head. Her body shook. She turned away. Blinded by rage at what had occurred, at her helplessness to make Yasir understand, at his helplessness under Peter's command, she lurched through the doorway, catching the shawl on the door handle, baring her shoulder and breast. Flushing, conscious her movements were awkward, she tried to unhook the shawl, painfully aware that Yasir watched her every move.

He waved his hand. A brocade taffeta dressing gown covered her from neck to toe. Warm slippers wrapped around her feet. Lavinia clutched at the neck of the gown and scurried down the hall, seething with fury and shame.

39

*P*eter sat up, his head pounding. He set his hand on the mattress, searching. Lavinia should be here. He tried to focus. The blurry bed was empty. Where the deuce was she? Or had he imagined her here, because he wanted her to be with him? Because he wanted them to be together like they were before he found her with the blasted djinni? He squinted at the light coming through the window.

The djinni sprawled on the small divan, asleep.

"Yasir," Peter mumbled. *Bloody hell*, he shouldn't talk. He put his hand to his head and let out a moan. The djinni, faster than a thought, stood at the bedside. Peter's head swam with the creature's inhuman speed and movement. This flitting so fast from the divan to the bedside—part of a spell Peter hadn't excised? He pushed his tangled hair from his eyes and pressed his thumbs into his temples, the ache in rhythm with his pulse.

What was the djinni for if not to help with this?

"Remove the pain." His words sounded slurred as if molasses had stuck his tongue to his teeth.

With the touch of Yasir's hand on his head a rip of pain surged through his body. Peter drew back. Was the djinni taking his revenge for the Anubis Society meeting? For him being Lavinia's husband?

Then, like a fresh breeze, an amazing lightness replaced the muck clogging his body. He could almost see the mess draining away, a mud-colored sludge writhing with ghastly brutes, their long snouts and sharp claws struggling to rise from the mire.

After a moment, Peter sat straight and rubbed his eyes. The open window let in the fragrance of sweet grass and jasmine blooms on the vine crawling up the outside wall. He felt as if he could leap out the window onto Palomar's back, and gallop into the burgeoning day.

"Splendid. Splendid," he said.

He scraped the razor through the lather mounding on his face as Yasir stood by with a bowl of steaming water, towel draped across his forearm. Peter rinsed and rubbed dry with the warm towel. He felt fine. Better than fine.

He stared into the mirror. The expression in his eyes caught him off guard. Cagey, as if he were guilty of something. Lord, he could barely remember last night. Hazy images floated through his mind: Lavinia in bed with him, Lavinia struggling with Yasir, both of them angry. Yasir always peering at him, at them. What the hell?

"Yasir, what happened here last night?" Peter turned to the djinni, who looked away. "Tell me, now."

Yasir faced him, his round pupils closing into vertical slashes.

Damnedest thing.

"Well?"

The djinni gave him an incredulous stare.

"The truth, tell me the truth." Peter heard the shaking in his voice. He walked towards Yasir.

"Master, you made me bring your wife to you. Made me remove her clothes—"

"Devil take it." Peter took Yasir by the throat. "You know what I can do to you. Why would you lie?"

"I do not lie."

Peter ground his teeth. An explosion of pain in his head made everything go black for a moment. With great effort he took his hands from the djinni's throat.

"Go on." His voice was barely audible. The djinni didn't want to say it any more than Peter wanted to hear it.

"By your command, I brought her to your bed. You bade me watch." Yasir's jaw clenched, his voice tight with anger.

"And Lavinia?" Peter watched the djinni closely. He seemed as upset as Peter.

"She was angry, but decided that if she didn't acquiesce, you would order me to make her. You might order me to harm her. She feared you might hurt me." Yasir stopped.

Peter saw him put his hands behind his back as if he couldn't control them if they were nearer to his master.

Peter sat on his bed. He did that to Lavinia? Well, he was drunk, very drunk. Angry at being cuckolded. Jealous. Yes, he was jealous. And that hadn't changed. Yasir had just told him that the reason Lavinia let him bed her was because she was afraid he might hurt Yasir. Peter winced. The pain pounded in his head, the effects that Yasir cured had returned ten-fold.

He could command the djinni to make Lavinia love him, but he knew first-hand that a spell could have adverse effects on the one who had been spell-cast, like bad medicine. Peter still hadn't completely comprehended the foul deeds he had committed under Yasir's spells— spells that made him forget he was master first, that he gave Lavinia the urn.

He was Lord Peter Bramley, master of a djinni. Able to command magic. Yet, he had completely lost his wife.

Peter looked askance at Yasir. Something sinister in those golden eyes. Well, he had tortured Yasir near to death the other night. And, apparently, had forced him to watch him swiving Lavinia. It would take even a djinni a bit of time to get over all that.

He stared at the floor. He felt his wife in his arms, moaning with pleasure, kissing him with soft kisses. He glimpsed her deep blue eyes staring into his, eyes without hate, a new bond between them that he felt from last night. She had responded to him, by God. He remembered that. But she has been drunk. As had he.

Early morning sunlight, skimming the tops of the trees, burst into the room, illuminating Yasir, his servant's clothes transformed into a radiant palette of golden yellow, amber and tawny orange. His face and eyes, glowing unnaturally, revealed him in all his supernatural glory.

Peter's arms lay stiff at his side. He could barely breathe. The djinni glided to him. As if drawn by a lead, Peter rose to meet him, eye-to-eye, blue to gold. The djinni's breath mingled with his, warm on his flesh. Peter wanted to bash his face in, but he couldn't move. Like a gulp of brandy, the light reached deep into his body, stinging, flooding him with desire. His breath came ragged. His fingers numb, paralyzed, but bursting with the need to touch and explore.

The light shifted. Yasir's clothes became that of a valet on an ordinary morning, his countenance handsome, but human. Peter blinked a few times. He couldn't have said how long he stayed transfixed in that one spot. These bloody daydream episodes, the after effects of the incantations to shuck off Yasir's spells compounded by the drink and Lavinia.

Always Lavinia. Was she a bloody spell-caster as well?

Peter took a breath and traced the purple bruise fading to yellow on Yasir's cheek. "What a shame, this bruise mars your handsome face." He pushed hard on it, silently daring Yasir to grimace. The djinni winced, but Peter's twinge of smug gratification was spoiled by an instant of awareness that the djinni only did it for show, for some ulterior motive.

"Heal it. Now that Lavinia has seen it. Go ahead and heal them all." Peter seized Yasir by the shoulders, looking him in the eye. "And don't let me catch you near my wife. Ever."

40

Over the back of the chair in the corner lay the sumptuous brocade wrapper, the soft velvet slippers. Lavinia had pulled them off as soon as she returned to her room, burning with embarrassment, shame and rage, replacing the wrapper with a cotton nightdress. But she couldn't replace her thoughts—roaming around her head like a cat on the prowl.

Fleming would wonder where on earth she'd gotten the exotic wrapper and slippers, but the woman wouldn't say a word. Lavinia smiled, picturing her maid's consternation.

But that was the only thing humorous. She sat on the bed, arms tight against her chest, keeping the fury and shame away for a brief moment.

At some point in the night, she had dreamed that her husband commanded Yasir to cast spells on her. If so, Peter would be paying her back, tit for tat, for the spells Yasir put on him, for her collusion with the djinni.

Would she be able to tell she was spell-cast, or would she become victim to the magic as Peter had? She twisted a strand of hair around her index finger. Saints help her, she didn't know.

Lavinia peered into the full-length looking glass. Her hair undone in disarray, circles under her eyes, her complexion as pale as her white nightdress. She pulled the cord for Fleming, who breezed in moments later with a stack of clean chemises.

"Fleming, I must dress." Lavinia indicated her hair and clothes. "I want to look enticing."

She pinched her cheek and tilted her head as she compared it with the other side of her face. Her headache, after hot tea with lots of lemon, came and went now, as transient as her thoughts.

Fleming turned from the wardrobe, holding up an elegant gown.

"This one milady? Since your fitting the other day went so well, I thought you might want to show it off."

She helped Lavinia slip on the white muslin dress, the stylish empire waist tucked high just under her bosom. Blue ribbon lined the tiers of lace ruffles at the hem. A triple row of ruffles framed her neck and another set trailed onto her hand from the long full sleeves.

"Slower, it's tangled like brambles." She flinched as Fleming combed through her hair, a result of her tossing and turning from her troubling dream. Would she feel it if she were spell cast? Or go through her day blithely doing things she would never normally consider?

After pinning Lavinia's hair up, her maid slanted a miniature top hat a bit to the side, a jaunty look.

"Well?" Lavinia patted the ruffles on her hat.

"Lovely, milady. You'll turn heads," Fleming said as she fitted blue leather slippers over her mistress's gleaming silk stockings. Eyeing herself in the tall mirror, Lavinia ran her hand over the soft muslin of her gown, turned sideways and fluffed her skirts.

Tucking a loose curl under her hat, she pressed her lips together. She would get her revenge: find Yasir alone, steal him back.

The heavy paneled door to Peter's study frequently made Lavinia pause. Foreboding. That was the feeling it evoked. She never knew what she would find behind that door. She had encountered a brightly painted Egyptian sarcophagus, lid set to the side, the brown mummy partially unwrapped, its desiccated face staring sightless at the ceiling. A set of canopic jars, one opened, the shriveled organ—a heart—sitting in a place of honor on her husband's desk. Saddani had been in this very room before he kidnapped her in the garden.

She shut her eyes. This was *her* house. Just a room in her house. And Peter was her husband. She crossed her hands over her chest. Last night, the cold air on her flesh as Yasir made her gown vanish, her husband and the djinni staring at her . . .

She would act as if the incident hadn't occurred. Taking a breath, she put last night from her mind. Peter had meetings and assignments where he couldn't take Yasir, and Tuesdays he usually left in the morning, not returning until late in the day. She had heard the carriage in the front, the horses nickering. Peter was probably out, and he might have left Yasir here by himself to search through scrolls and manuscripts for whatever arcane information they were seeking.

It was out of the question to ask Dobson or any of the servants if Peter were in the house. Lavinia wanted them to think she and her husband were as they used to be. She didn't want them nosing around, finding Yasir. Peter could be careless. She hoped to use that to her advantage.

She grasped the door handle and turned it.

Unlocked, thank the angels.

Peter's papers and books lay stacked on his desk next to a scroll held flat with paperweights, a manuscript opened beside it. Just as she thought. Peter must have left, intending to return and resume his studies. He and Yasir had been immersed in the history of the Djinn and the prophecy involving Yasir's offspring by Thalia. That much Lavinia had gleaned from having Fleming interrupt on pretense of retrieving something important that her mistress left, then eavesdropping after she pretended to leave. Of course, Fleming was puzzled by her mistress's interest in her husband's strange studies. And she repeated the foreign words and names, mispronouncing most of them, but Lavinia knew what they were, what they meant.

The study was unusually dark with the heavy crimson and green-striped drapes drawn over the gauzy sari-fabric sash curtains. Strange, even when he was out, Peter normally didn't have them closed until night had darkened the view. Lavinia hustled over to open them when she heard murmuring from the corner.

She crept up to the immense painted Oriental screen of black lacquer. She had always been fascinated by the delicate water birds inlaid with mother-of-pearl, their long legs planted in flowing river rushes delineated by sweeping brush strokes. The screen sectioned off a corner of the study containing a table, a wingback chair, footstool and a couch large enough for Peter to stretch out on for naps. When Peter needed to ponder something or just rest undisturbed, he retired to this refuge.

She peeked around the screen.

There, on the couch were Peter and Yasir, clutched in a passionate embrace, their clothes scattered on the floor below them. Yasir's dull servant's attire mixed with the superfine, glossy silk and tightly woven linen of Peter's.

How could they?

Lavinia bit her fist to quiet her cries and struggled to keep upright. Her breath almost a pant, she slowed it with effort, and pinched her arm so hard she almost gasped aloud.

She would burst in. Tell Peter what she thought. Curse him. Curse Yasir. Insist they had to choose her. But Peter could simply command Yasir to make her forget. To spell-cast her. Then she would start on the long road that Peter had traveled—struggling to remember, deja vu episodes, becoming angry, raging, stabbing her husband again, perhaps killing him. Would she go mad once more?

And all the while, Peter and Yasir would continue their love affair, paying the waspish, furious woman she had become less attention than they paid the nanny.

No. She mustn't let on she had discovered them. They wouldn't, couldn't, find her here, face burning red with jealousy.

A jilted lover.

She shut her eyes and willed her stupefaction begone so she could slink away without a sound. When she could stand it, Lavinia opened her eyes, the pit of her stomach leaden. They were beautiful together. Yasir's dark smooth skin entwined with Peter's paleness. Black curls entangling straight yellow tresses. Muscles rippling with their slow rhythmic movements like waves cresting in an ocean. Her breath caught as Peter's hand stroked the length of Yasir's long back, imagining his hand on her.

Here were the two loves of her life and they were . . . not with her. Her husband and lover in their fascination with each other had forgotten about her. Yasir cried out, a familiar long low moan, signaling his passion spent.

The sound shook her to the core. She pressed her elbows tight against her sides, her hands hard against her cheeks as she watched Yasir seek Peter's mouth with his. The feel of the djinni's lips soft on hers as if she were the object of his desire. She felt flat, divested of any trace of her former desirable self.

Yasir lay in Peter's arms, his figure slack from their exertions.

They were lost in each other, their beautiful bodies given freely. And she was alone.

Lavinia turned away and stole from the dark study, moving like a phantom. The patterned carpet, sinking beneath her feet, muted each step as she escaped. She swung the huge door shut with a whisper of a click. The small noise made her jump.

She strolled leisurely to her room, her face plastered with a pleasant expression for the servants, for Alice, for anyone else in the great manse that glimpsed her. But inside, she screamed in outrage, picturing the lovers, her husband and Yasir, their bare bodies tangled in a torrid embrace.

41

So the djinni was good for other things also. Peter stretched and yawned, getting the morning of a new day. The day after. By God, if he were a rooster he would have crowed. First Lavy, now Yasir. He'd been deprived, hunching in his study, suspicious of everything, when it was just his wife cuckolding him, and a djinni's hexes.

They'd put him through the wringer. But he had shown them one better. And now his reward. A man needed amorous congress. Better than a physic. Invigorating.

"Yasir." The name escaped his lips, unbidden. Yesterday in the study, he had ripped off the djinni's shirt, pulling him close, his bare chest, his taut muscles hard against him. He could feel the magic now, pulsing through him.

"Master?" Yasir stood at his bedside.

Peter started at the intrusion on his thoughts, but smiled at how even his subtle wishes were met. He threw off the covers and rose to meet his djinni. As if in a dream, he ran his fingers down the soft skin of Yasir's cheek, inhaling his cinnamon-and-cloves breath, sweet spices of the mysterious East. A prickle, like the sting of an insect, flowed down each finger and spread through his body. His breath quickening, he gripped the back of Yasir's neck and pulled him closer.

The kiss was soft. Tender. Yet there was a greediness in Yasir's response, a hunger that Peter relished. He watched someone else go through these motions, yet these were his lips, his hands, his body. Yesterday in his study, he hadn't meant to do it. He was taken by surprise, his strong passion sweeping him into the djinni's arms. But today he was eager.

The softness of Yasir's lips. A surprise each time.

Yasir's accepting him, opening to him with no command to that effect, always a shock.

Yet, in a brief moment of clarity, Peter suspected he was being manipulated, a marionette oblivious of the strings controlling him to some purpose. He tightened his jaw and summoned his will. He would step away from this djinni.

"Damnation, Yasir." The words rushed out, a half whisper. In a burst of energy, he drew back, attempting to push the djinni away, but his hand fell to his side. The yearning, the longing, the intensity of this sudden wave of desire, his need to be next to this fantastic creature, dissolved his will as if it were a feeble whim.

Yasir, illumined by some inner light, stayed still, but for a hint of a smile.

The sensation that Peter had first felt at the meeting of the Anubis Brotherhood coursed through his body like blood, but faster, hotter. With the triumph of a win, he saw the reciprocation of his own feelings in Yasir's faint smile.

For a split second, Peter looked hard at the djinni. Was it his imagination? He thought he saw, in a space of time as brief as the blur of a hummingbird's wing, a triumphant smirk on the djinni's face.

Peter took Yasir in his arms. Chest to chest, hip-to-hip, thigh to thigh, the djinni's flesh jolting an awareness into Peter. He shut his eyes, conscious of Yasir's every movement.

Somewhere deep in his mind, Peter observed himself. The things he did were unnatural to him—ripping Yasir's shirt in his haste, fumbling with Yasir's trousers. His breath caught at the djinni's body so close, stripes curving around his waist, dark on his glowing brown skin. Different from when the djinni was bound naked to the scaffold at the meeting, because Peter had nothing to prove, because no one could see his desires laid bare. Different from yesterday in the dim study when he fell into the djinni's arms without time to peruse his beautiful body.

"You are mine, mine alone," Peter whispered into Yasir's ear, biting his earlobe, caressing his raven curls, kissing his bow-shaped lips. He kissed Yasir's chest and ran his hand down the muscles of his abdomen, appreciating once more that, truly, the djinni's body worked much as his own.

Peter put his tongue to the peculiar stripes encircling Yasir's waist, his fingers tracing them with a feather touch. As he continued his exploration, the djinni raised his face to the ceiling, shut his eyes and softly moaned, a husky murmur from deep in his throat like a cat blissfully purring.

Peter stood, placed his hand on Yasir's shoulder, and kissed his djinni full on the mouth. Yasir smiled, a teasing look dancing in his animal eyes. Peter thought of those eyes entrancing Lavinia, his young wife seduced by the very gift from her husband.

He punched Yasir in the stomach.

The djinni's eyes widened, his pupils a mere scratch of black. He doubled over with a grunt, black hair swinging over his head as he grabbed his middle with his hands.

"Wouldn't want to hurt your beautiful face again." Peter pushed him onto the bed.

Yasir landed on his back in the disordered bedclothes and Peter pinned him by the chest. He straddled his waist, kissing him, seeing his own pleasure reflected in the djinni's eyes—burning into him as surely as if he had been branded then and there. The morning light played on their flesh, and he saw as if from above, pale and dark entwining, flaxen and raven locks tangling.

Peter poured two glasses of wine.

"For your delight." He raised his drink to Yasir as he handed him a goblet, the burgundy liquid sloshing.

"You are quite the valet." Peter clinked his glass against Yasir's, and kissed him a wine kiss to the ringing of the crystal goblets.

He touched Yasir's cheek tenderly. "I see you are well-skilled in the art of Turkish love." Peter fashioned the statement more like an inquiry, for he was curious about this djinni.

"Master," Yasir drew out the word slowly, making it an almost physical thing, "I am accomplished in most activities." He leaned in close.

"I found ours most gratifying," Yasir purred, running his fingers down Peter's cheek to his chest, tweaking his nipple delicately with his thumb and index finger.

Peter gasped in surprise, and cuffed the djinni on the arm.

Yasir grinned and relaxed against the pillow. He sloshed his wine in the crystal goblet, the light building a fire in the crimson liquid. Peter narrowed his eyes and snaked his pale arm around Yasir.

"You must tell no one, of course. But you must indulge me again and again." Peter smiled up at Yasir, caressed his flowing hair, and kissed him.

The spell has taken my prey unaware. I let my master think it was his idea, let him believe that he, the great Lord Peter Bramley, is truly in control. The spell I first planted in him at the meeting of the Anubis Society has flourished like wildfire in a parched forest.

How can I feel gratification with a man who humiliates me, enslaves me, flogs me? With a man I hate. Yet, as we took our satisfaction in one another, I forgot where I was, who this man was, and gave myself to desire—the craving that through the ages has been my downfall.

Satiated, I glance at Peter, his warm flesh next to mine. With a flash of his blue eyes, my master brushes my lips with his. It has not escaped me that Peter, with his blonde hair, those azure eyes and pale skin, is as desirable a man as Lavinia is a woman. I was not sure until now that English men enjoyed the pleasures of one another.

In some cultures I have known, this expression of love is casually accepted, in others it is a death sentence.

42

Bare bodies intertwining, pale and dusky, a slow ocean of flesh mounding and swelling, cresting in a moan of ecstasy. Peter and Yasir, together, in that way.

The images and sounds, seared in Lavinia's mind, endlessly repeated. A torment she couldn't escape. Hands over her ears, merely closing her eyes—how she longed for a simple way of shutting them out.

She had avoided Peter for the last few days, spending her time with the children, taking supper in her room. He hadn't inquired about her, and she was glad of that. How could she ever face him?

She glanced at the arrangement of white gladiolas on the gilded table by her dressing room. In the middle of each blossom on the sword-shaped stalks was a blotch of red, like a kiss or a stain. Their clean fresh smell had sustained her these endless days, but the red centers increasingly made her uneasy, reminding her of the blood on Peter's white silk cravat after she stabbed him years ago. She pressed her fingers together, feeling the penknife in her hand, the swift movement of her arm as she plunged the short blade into him, the shock on her husband's face. Oh, how she wanted to see that expression again.

She picked up the tall crystal vase, heavy in her hands. The white swords swayed as she walked to the open window of her room. She held it outside and turned the vase upside down, watching with satisfaction as the flowers plunged to the ground. From the garden, she would gather only the bright-colored gladiolas and arrange them herself.

A short time later, lemon yellow, sunset orange, rose pink and royal purple gladiolus lay in her basket, swords of brilliant color. The bright shades reminded her of happier times. She snipped another purple one, the snick of the scissors supplanted by *thunk, thunk, thunk.* She turned at the sound.

It was only Peter, practicing his archery. Lavinia picked up her garden scissors and started towards the practice area. She squeezed her hands together, the scissors warm. She wanted to, oh she wanted to, but what would happen to her if she went through with this? What would happen to the children? She turned back, tucked the scissors under the blossoms and picked up her basket to leave.

Thunk, thunk, thunk. Then murmuring. Voices? Was Peter talking to someone? Would Yasir be at his side? Before she knew it, she was at the thick privet hedge which fenced the practice area. She peered inside.

Peter had filled up the target facing away from her and was setting up to shoot at the one at the opposite end. She noticed that only one arrow was even near the bulls-eye.

Peter glanced over and gave her a look. Lavinia rested her basket next to her stomach. Good to have a barrier between them.

He nocked an arrow, drew his bow and let the arrow fly. *Thunk.* She flinched at the impact. Bulls-eye. Peter faced her, bow at his side, a smug look on his face. "So, you finally came out of hiding."

"After recent events, why would I want to be in your company?" Lavinia stepped inside the hedge. She didn't see Yasir, but she couldn't check thoroughly without Peter noticing.

Her husband pulled another arrow from the standing quiver. She looked around, taking in the covered area, the empty chairs in the shade, the green hedge wall enclosing them. Yasir was not there.

"*He* is back where *he* hides. Safe from prying eyes." Peter nocked the arrow to his bowstring. "Care to join in? You sound a bit wound up. This might do you some good."

The nerve of him. He knew what he'd done. All of what he'd done. She envisioned setting up her bow, aiming the arrow straight at her husband's heart. A different kind of cupid.

Lavinia set her basket down in the shade of the hedge. From the supply box, she buckled a stout leather brace on her left arm, her bow arm, just above the wrist to prevent the string from chafing. She slipped the shooting glove on her right hand and buttoned it around her wrist to protect her fingers. Holding the bow horizontal to the ground, she nocked her arrow. Aiming, she pretended the target was Peter, took a breath, pulled back and let go. *Thunk.* She didn't flinch this time. Two stripes away from the bulls-eye. She should practice more.

"You surprise me, Lavinia. I assumed you'd be in more of a shambles, as lately."

She nocked another arrow. "Peter, do you expect me to continue bantering with you? Did you think I would so easily forgive you?" Her arrow landed a bit closer to the center.

"Darling, whatever are you referring to?" He turned to her, genuinely puzzled. Could he have no memory of the after-dinner incident? He had been drunk, slurring-words drunk. His eyes widened, a softer look for only a second. So he did remember, at least enough to have a minuscule bit of conscience.

Still. She couldn't talk about it. She felt that damning flush of heat on her cheeks. Her feelings laid bare for anyone to see.

"You know what I mean." She glared at him, but was too ashamed to bring up details of the after-dinner incident. The bow shook in her hand. She was in Peter's room, the cold enveloping her body as Yasir conjured her clothes away, as the djinni and Peter—she blinked, stopping the scene playing out.

"You stole MY urn." Her voice was hard. That was one other thing she was angry about, and that was easy for her to discuss. She aimed her arrow and let it fly.

Bulls-eye!

Peter raised his eyebrows. "Ah, just a small revenge for you sleeping with him, don't you think?" He gave her a lopsided smile. His eyes, though, were angry, and he strolled over, leaned in close and brushed her cheek with a kiss. "Would you have preferred I flogged you, rather than him?" Peter looked her up and down and Lavinia raised the bow to her chest, attempting to deflect his indecent gaze.

"You couldn't have healed your welts, alas." Peter mocked her.

"You had Yasir watch." She blurted the sentence like it was one long word, her anger flaring. There. She had said it. She looked at the ground, again feeling bared before them both, before Peter now. It was as if his shameful treatment of her had made her the guilty one.

"I was drunk," Peter said flatly, he held his bow at his side.

"Many husbands get drunk." Lavinia snarled, the pitch of her voice rising. Anger again. Anger which gave her strength. "But they don't usually take their wives to bed and have their lover watch."

Peter dropped his bow in the gravel.

"Lover? Hmmph." He scowled at Lavinia. "You still want Yasir. It's all over your face." Peter swooped to the ground and retrieved his bow, his eyes bright blue patches of accusation. "You look at him with a hunger."

Lavinia gave him a glassy stare, her knuckles white around the polished yew wood of her bow. How dare he say that?

"I walked into your study the other day." Her voice came out low, pointed like a sword. She leaned forward, her eyes hard. She looked directly at him. "The curtains were drawn. I thought you had left, but I heard a sound from behind the screen."

The blood drained from Peter's face.

"And I saw you and Yasir."

Peter's cheeks colored with pink splotches. He breathed hard while he stared at her, his eyes hollow, his mouth a straight line. A bird landed on the target, ruffled its feathers and trilled a long string of notes. Her husband was quiet for what seemed like minutes.

"THAT is none of your business." Peter curled his upper lip. He threw his bow on the ground, knocked over the metal quiver of arrows and stomped off, the exaggerated crunch of gravel fading as he trudged further away.

She listened for other sounds nearby. The faint footfall of an eaves-dropping servant, the rustle of skirts or clank of gardening tools, the titter of two voices shushing one another. But she neither heard nor saw anyone. In a daze, she gathered her basket. Her exchange with Peter had been loud enough to hear several hedgerows away. If anyone eavesdropped, if rumors got out about Peter and Yasir's antics, Peter could be ruined. As his wife, she would be ruined along with him. And Peter could be executed, hung by the neck.

She let out her breath, her bow in her hand at her side. No one was there, as far as she could tell. They were most probably safe, after all, how could anyone find the mysterious Yasir? They would blame her for this, and refer to her former madness. Still, if anyone had actually managed to see Yasir . . .

She clapped her hand to her mouth. All the men at the Anubis Club. They had seen Yasir.

They knew.

43

The room, lit by moonlight shining through the window, appeared unfamiliar. Peter had found refuge in a high-backed chair, hands set stiffly on the polished walnut arms, his fingers wrapped around the curved wood. If he let go he would be lost, his sanity gone as surely as Lavinia's when she stabbed him. The hard brass of the urn pressed into his left calf, sending an uncomfortable tingling, like an injured nerve, all the way to his fingers. He found it impossible to separate his leg from the vessel.

"Master, what is wrong?"

Peter dropped his gaze to the floor.

"She knows." He put his head in his hands. "Lavinia encountered me this morning at archery. She saw us, when we . . . "

Peter pushed against the back of the chair, tightening his fingers on the padded arms. He flinched from the prickle that flashed through them.

"It is a hanging offense here in England, you know. I have seen men tried for it. Attended their execution. Seen them writhe when the rope didn't snap their neck immediately. Their families are ruined." He shook his head as if to clear it.

"Lavinia . . . she looked disgusted. I left. Ended up here." Peter arched his neck, looking up at Yasir, his djinni. "I remembered when I found you in bed with her. I was incensed that she dared break her vows as my wife." As if he had been released, he stood, clenching and unclenching his fingers.

He wanted to punch Yasir. He wanted to kiss Yasir.

Peter took the djinni in his arms. "It all started with you." He closed his eyes. Nothing in the world felt like this embrace, not the wind caressing his hair as he rode Palomar, not the exultation of excavating a new tomb in Egypt, not the thrill of finding the golden crown in Persia. Making love with his wife was what it should be, but making love with the djinni was magic, like how flying must feel.

All of this was hidden. And of hidden things he was well aware. Aware how they could eat into you, destroy parts of your life with the cravings they left behind. How the obsession blossomed, seeded and grew and grew.

"If the urn hadn't come into my life, Lavinia and I would have children that were ours—no question. My wife would be in love with me only, and I would be in bed with her right now instead of embracing a . . . creature that lives in a bottle." Peter pushed Yasir away with a look of hatred. What was he doing? It was all he could do not to stagger with the sense of loss. Still, he forced himself to sound stern.

"Yasir, go to the urn. Stay there. You, out of sight, will keep us safe from that damn magician." He turned and walked out, slamming the door.

Peter made his way to the nursery. He couldn't get Yasir out of his mind, those golden eyes fixing him, luring him—the feel of the djinni's flesh, his hungry kisses. Perhaps looking in on the children would remove his agitation, thrust Yasir from his thoughts.

The window sashes, raised a few inches, let in the cool night air. Moonlight flooded the room with the ghostly gleam of a fairy tale. Stuart and James lay in their separate beds, lost in sleep. The canopied baby bed, with see-though caned sides like a miniature fence, held little Cybelle. From his vantage point, the child was a lump under a blanket, her dark curls spilling out like flourishes of calligraphy.

Stuart had thrown off the covers, but James remained tucked under his. The languid hold of their deep sleep permeated the room, and Peter forced his own eyelids open against the drowsiness. James's dark hair spilled around his face, his mouth hung open with his rhythmic breath, eyes darting under his eyelids at the behest of some dream. Oh, to embrace sleep that way now.

Peter reached out and touched James's perfect hands, the child's fingers curved on the pillow like petals of a flower. The brothers were remarkable in their resemblance, but James was his.

Would Stuart, with Yasir's blood, bring even more trouble than his father? Peter eyed the eldest child in his family. He picked up the soft pillow at Stuart's feet, cold with a night chill, the one that should be under his head were he not such a restless sleeper, and held it in his hands like a shield. The boy turned over onto his back, a garbled word escaping his lips.

A word of magic?

Lavinia had brought the toddler to him one stormy day, the boy's black curls framing lapis eyes, the same odd blue as Lavinia's. She insisted that the gypsies had drugged her after she gave birth. Then they stole her baby. In her grief and confusion, she had run away from the Roma. The gypsies' superstitions made them return Stuart—so Lavinia had said.

Peter ran his hand through his hair. *God's blood*, how could he have been so blind? He still couldn't fathom how he accepted Lavinia's excuses, how he dismissed the fleeting recognition of his uncharacteristic and immediate acquiescence. After he started working with the scrolls, nothing untoward came up about Stuart as it had with Yasir, but gypsies had their own arcane magic—so he had heard.

He clutched the pillow.

In front of him lay an innocent child, sleeping, a child he had given his name, a child he had raised. Yet, Peter couldn't shake the sense of doom and foreboding that Stuart could be his family's downfall. A shadow flitted over the boy's face. Did his eyes open, glinting with malice in the darkness?

Unnerved, he placed the pillow over Stuart's face. Now he couldn't see those evil eyes.

"Hold the pillow down hard," spoke the insistent voices in his head. "End this threat to your family."

"No!" A shriek careened over the clamoring voices.

What the devil? Peter let go of the pillow and drew back as Lavinia ran towards him, her face twisted, her screams preceding her. Wide awake now, Stuart wheeled his arms and struggled to sit, batting the pillow, which flew from his face and bounced off Peter onto the floor.

"Mommy's here, mommy's here." Lavinia ran her hand over Stuart's hair.

He whimpered.

Peter blinked. *Why had Lavinia screamed?* He looked around. *Why the blazes was he in the nursery?*

Peter unlocked his study, slipped into the darkness, closed the door and locked it. He bumped into a table. "Bloody thing." Soft thumps signaled that some of his treasures had landed on the thick carpet. He felt his way to the window and opened the drapes, letting in the bright moonlight.

What had he done? The question loomed from the chaos of his mind, like rays of sunshine through dark clouds. He poured a brandy, swirling the liquid in the glass. His mind churned like the liquor. He gulped it, sloshing his shirt.

Were his darkest thoughts turning into reality? Creeping from his mind, pinchers feeling the way, spilling from his nightmares? Only the insane and the criminal acted upon these impulses. Normal people pushed their evil glimmerings back into the darkness, and when that didn't work, they prayed to the good Lord to take them away.

Or went mad.

But he had attempted it. Actually attempted it.

The black thought acted upon.

Peter threaded his way through the deep shadows to the gold-framed painting hanging above a side table. He flicked a knob on the frame's left edge and swung the painting out from the wall. After turning each of the four sets of rings embedded in the horizontal lock, the engraved metal door set behind the painting opened. In a flash of gold, he held the urn.

He had commanded Yasir to the vessel, and had sworn to leave it rotting in the safe. Keep the djinni and all his turmoil out of his and Lavinia's life. Keep the djinni's bloody friends and enemies from harming his family. He thought of Ammit, of Rakhshan, of others he didn't know about. He started to put the urn back.

But he needed help and didn't know who else to turn to.

The beautifully worked lid lifted easily. His study filled with mist. A dim memory arose in him of a time before he knew djinnis existed. He was in his house in Cairo, haze obscuring the room, when a deep resonant voice spoke: "Master, what do you wish?"

The same voice that spoke just now with the same phrase.

A dark form, silhouetted in the window's moonlight loomed in the mist and walked towards him. Peter seized Yasir by the shoulders.

"Take this burden from me. I don't—I didn't. She saw. I don't know. He could have been dead. I killed him. I killed—"

Yasir slapped him. The force of the blow, the sharp sound of Yasir's hand on his flesh made Peter's ears ring. He put his hand to his face. "What the devil? What do you think—?"

Yasir forced him over to a grouping of chairs and pushed him down. A golden goblet appeared in his hand and he set the rim at Peter's lips.

"This will calm you, Master."

Peter drank, coughed and shoved the goblet away, sloshing the contents.

"Gods above. Are you trying to poison me?"

Yasir jerked him by the shoulder. "Do you wish me to hit you once more?"

"No, Yasir. Stop. Let me go." Peter swallowed hard and cleared his throat.

Yasir raised his hand—

"No! No spells. I can barely think now." Peter ducked.

"Master, you commanded me to take a burden—"

"I know what I said." He looked up at Yasir, his face drooping.

"I-I almost killed Stuart." Peter's voice broke.

Yasir flinched, then stared into the distance. "I see him with his mother. The child is fine, unharmed."

"Thank God." Peter put his head in his hands. "I heard a scream. It was Lavinia. I-I didn't know where I was. Somehow, I was in the nursery. Lavinia seized Stuart and ran out.

"But now, I . . . I remember. I watched Stuart sleeping. A shadow passed over his face. His eyes flew open. I saw their evil gleam. A threat to our family, like Rakhshan. A voice . . ." Peter gazed up at Yasir. How could he put this into words?

"A voice told me to cover his eyes, cover the evil gleam. I put the pillow on his face. Lavinia stopped me." Peter hung his head, his body limp.

"God in heaven, what is happening to me?" He put his fist to his forehead, squeezing his eyes shut. Maybe he had dreamed this. "I've never done a deed so foul."

Yasir leaned forward. *By the Djinn*, had Peter lost his mind in the space of a day? His master's eyes glittered with the haunted cast of madness. And in answer to his statement, yes, this man *had* done a deed so foul, in fact several deeds: beating Lavinia almost to death, disfiguring her, but for Yasir's quick healing and restoration; ordering Yasir's brutal flogging and putting him in mortal danger. But Yasir said nothing. The former had been caused by the spell Yasir had cast on Peter to hurry things along and possess Lavinia for himself. The latter, a malicious ploy by Peter to humiliate Yasir for stealing Lavinia.

Peter was a selfish man, but that didn't make him evil, not evil enough to kill an innocent child. A son he had raised to the age of seven. A son he loved. An innocent, djinni child—that was the crux of the matter.

Yasir waved his hand, lighting several lamps in the room.

"I'd rather sit in the dark," Peter grumbled.

"Master, to help you it is best to have a bit of light." Yasir ran his fingers over his rings as he studied Peter, the gems calming his master with their penetrating energies. Bramley stared into the room, tapping his foot, running his hands through his hair, restless in his unhappy realizations. There was something off-putting about the man's eyes, even now, after he had taken the potion. But Yasir couldn't place it.

He threw a subtle spell onto his master to see what would happen. A glow of orange light flared when the spell hit him.

It didn't take. Peter sat up. "Wha—?" His eyes widened and he gripped the chair arms. "What the hell was that? I told you, no spells."

"Master, you gave me leave to use some power when you commanded me to take the burden from you. I see in your eyes—"

"Stop yammering and get on with it. And fill my glass." Peter took a long sip of the potion and tapped his fingers on his thigh. "Well . . ."

Yasir raised his palm and moved his hand back and forth. Peter sank into the chair.

"That's it? That's all you're going to do? Just a slow wave of your hand?" With a sneer, Peter mimicked Yasir's movements.

Not a good sign. Peter had become more agitated. Yasir tried a stronger spell, one that would free a minor enchantment. A humming sound, droning louder than the locusts of old Egypt, filled the room. Peter vanished, then wavered back into his chair surrounded by an eerie greenish glow. Mouth open, he held his arms out and looked down at his body.

Yasir put his finger to his lips, indicating for Peter to be silent.

By the Djinn, Peter had been enthralled. It is a wonder that he remembered the deed at all. If Lavinia had not happened by the nursery to check on the children, Peter would have carried out the task with no memory of it. And there would be a small corpse in the nursery, waiting to be discovered in the early morning by the nanny or Lavinia.

Yasir placed a counter spell, careful to make it look as though Peter had accidentally walked through a power spot or some other inadvertent magic that had broken the spell. It was untraceable and not unusual for something like that to nullify one's magic.

Peter held out his glass. Took a drink after it was filled.

"I feel different. What did you do?"

Yasir held out his palm. "I must ponder this." He rested his chin on his hand, repressing the urge to leave his human form while in front of Peter.

Was this spell from the sorceress? By his invitation, Mehadeh had come to the urn looking for him, and willingly shared what had happened with Rakhshan, seemingly an open confession as befitted a blood-sworn friend. Could that have been a ruse? Had she attached the Shadow Lord's spell when she pressed her body to his, knowing it would transfer to Peter?

Or had a glass shard from Alice's magic mirror somehow found Peter and entranced him? A spell to kill Yasir's sons and then Lavinia. That way he would have no more children by her, voiding the prophecy. Peter, murderer of his children. Of his wife. His fate—to be jailed, perhaps hanged. James, orphaned and raised by some relative.

And Rakhshan would never again let the whereabouts of the urn slip from his grasp. Yasir would be forever a slave, broken from the loss of Lavinia and his children, with nothing else in his future. And Rakhshan would be safe from destruction, the prophecy merely a harmless tale.

"Master, I have a suspicion about what happened. I will search your study then your room." Yasir eyed Peter, looking for any other clues.

Bramley sagged into his chair. "Go ahead. Get rid of it, whatever it is."

The shard would only need to be near Peter to have an effect. Yasir searched his master's desk and his chair with his magic. He paused, hand to his chin. When Amarja spilled a few shards in front of him, he had not noticed. They must contain a spell that made them undetectable to djinnis—the reason Amarja was sent to destroy them. She had warned him that they were from Rakhshan and dangerous to him. With his proximity to Peter, had he already been exposed? With his powers heightened, he explored the study, Peter's rooms, the stables, the tack and gear. Nothing.

"Why are you still here? I thought you would go to my room, roam about the house." Peter indicted the glass. "I'm feeling peculiar again. More potion."

Yasir idly waved his hand as he made his magic strong and searched the study once more.

"Master, remove your boots."

"I have my valet do that. You are my valet, Yasir."

"This would be dangerous for me. You must call Stevens. I will vanish. Have Stevens take the boots and remove the shard of glass in the bottom of the left heel. Then he must give it to the blacksmith, have him crush it, taking care to contain each bit of glass. The smith must fire the crushed glass until it has completely melted. I will have a container ready when Stevens fetches the residue. The boots likewise must be burned."

"Damn it all. These boots took months to break in, not to mention costing a bloody fortune." Peter stamped his foot.

"Here, Master." Yasir held out a handsome pair of boots.

Peter ran his hand over the leather. "Fine finish, soft, yet firm." They faded away.

"What the—?"

"Master. These must not be, how would you say, infected. We will wait until yours are gone from the house and destroyed."

So Amarja missed at least one shard. Was it purposeful? It would be to her advantage for Peter to kill Yasir's children and Lavinia. Then Amarja's child would be the One. The only one. Could she be that ambitious, that cold?

44

$\mathcal{L}$ate the next evening, Lavinia sat beside Stuart who was finally sound asleep in her bed, trying to negate the what-if's plaguing her from the night before. What if she had checked on the boys earlier? Later? Not at all? She slipped under the warm covers and shivered, trying to banish the scene in her head—Peter, a stark silhouette against the nursery window, attempting to kill Yasir's son.

Peter had been cruel the way he dealt with Yasir, but he had gone only so far. She caressed Stuart's dark curls. Her hand stopped. The time Peter had beaten her. If Yasir had not saved her then, she would have died. And he had shot Yasir.

So, Peter *could* murder.

She twirled a strand of her hair around her finger. How could a person's character transform so completely? But, a small voice persisted, the common factor was Yasir. Her husband's personality had changed after the djinni first appeared to her. Then after Yasir supposedly died, and she returned to Bramley House, it was just Peter and the children. He was different and she had fallen in love with her husband again.

Why would Peter try and harm Stuart? Her husband loved that boy as much as she did. Her son had told her that when he made the toad fly, Peter and Yasir locked eyes with *that peculiar stare,* as Stuart put it. The stare must have marked Peter's realization that Stuart was Yasir's son.

From what she had seen in the past few weeks though, Stuart being Yasir's child wouldn't constitute a negative in Peter's eyes. Lavinia yawned, but her weariness wasn't enough to let her fall asleep. The harrowing events of last night had put a stop to that.

With a cry, Stuart thrashed and threw off the covers. Just what did her son recall of the pillow over his face, her screaming, Peter staring as if he had lost his mind?

She needed to sleep, to end her mind's ramblings. The moon, full the night before, filled the room with a harsh light, illuminating Stuart's face deep in slumber, his mouth half open, drooling onto the pillow. Lavinia adjusted the covers, feeling the drag of his heavy sleep. She turned her pillow over, put her head down on the cool underside, and watched the lace curtains sway slowly in the night breeze.

From the shadows of the headboard, two slanted green eyes stared at her. Her breath caught in her throat. A black cat sat on her bed, unblinking. What were they called? Familiars, here in England, but Yasir had used another word to describe Rakhshan's beasts.

With the glass shards gone, had the Dark Magician sent his minion to spy on them once more? Or was this just another black mouser that had slipped inside past the servants? She lay still, addled by lack of sleep, confounded by the things that had happened.

She wouldn't take a chance.

With a deep breath, Lavinia sat up. The cat didn't move. Its eyes locked on her. She picked up the sleeping bulk of Stuart, a blanket trailing in her wake. As fast as she could, she stumbled down the hall and leaned her weight against the door to Peter's rooms. Somehow she turned the handle. With a distinct click, the door swung into the room. She gained momentum as she lost her balance. They fell, a dream sequence.

She saw each movement as if she were watching from above. Her hands tightening around Stuart, head bowing towards his as her body slanted. Feet scraping the floor for balance, then slipping from under her, her body airborne, floating. The abrupt joining of her above self with the one that fell, the instantaneous hard landing. The loud thud. Stuart's body pressing into hers. His cry as he awakened.

"Peter!" Lavinia cried. How could her husband have slept through that?

"Huh?" Peter jumped out of bed. Caught his foot in Stuart's blanket. Flew headlong over them, and landed with a sickening thump a hand's breadth from her on the wooden floor, just missing the carpet.

Peter groaned. He staggered to his hands and knees, his blonde hair tangling over his face.

"What in God's name, Lavinia?" He sat back on his heels and swept his hair out of his eyes.

She saw Peter scowling in front of her, shadowed by the figure from last night smothering Stuart. A wave of fear fluttered over her, but her husband was the only way to Yasir. And she was more afraid of Rakhshan than of Peter.

The cat!

"Shut the door and lock it," she shrieked.

Peter scrambled to his feet, stumbled over Stuart and slammed the door. They stared at one another in the silence.

Her husband paced, his attempts at questions stopped by her gestures and piercing looks while she settled Stuart in Peter's bed. As the boy dropped into a restless sleep, Peter hustled Lavinia to a sitting area near the window. She nestled into a crocheted coverlet on the divan and tried to reassure herself that the cat hadn't made it into the room. The moonlight gleamed on the wooden floor, then faded into shadows. She yawned. Still the middle of the night.

"Well," Peter said, his eyebrows raised. He leaned forward, elbows on his knees. The combination of the pose, his general disarray, and his sleepy expression, making him look boyish.

She explained about the mysterious black cat with green eyes, Rakhshan's minion searching for Yasir. She left out that it had appeared in her room, eight or so years before, when she had first learned that the Dark Magician sought the djinni.

"The cat was in my room on the bed." She could hear the fear in her voice, could Peter?

Last night after the horrible incident with her husband and Stuart, Lavinia had insisted that a footman guard the nursery door, while Nanny slept next to Cybelle and James. Would they know not to let a cat inside with the children? But nanny was particular. She would be strict about keeping anything different out.

Lavinia watched her husband's expression change. He looked annoyed. Why had she thought that Peter, after his appalling actions, could help them?

"Call Yasir, he will know what to do." She placed her hand on Peter's arm. If need be, could she could somehow persuade Yasir to protect her and Stuart from her husband, even though Peter was master?

Peter took a deep breath and stared at her, the pastel blue of his eyes sparkling in the moonlight like ice crystals. He stayed quiet, unnerving her.

"Lavinia, have you given any thought to how our lives changed after you opened the urn? After Yasir took hold of you? After he took hold of me?" He spoke in a low voice as if he were afraid that Yasir, wherever the djinni was, could hear.

He dropped his gaze to the floor, then looked her full in the face. "Do you think I've ever—" his voice broke, "been with a man before?" He held his hands out, palms up, the moonlight making his rumpled nightshirt a map of an impossible terrain. "The things I have done . . ." Peter clasped both her hands in his. "Almost done."

"If not for Yasir . . ." Peter clenched his jaw. "I wouldn't have done such a thing. I would never hurt—I could never have hurt—our son." He looked up at the ceiling as if there were something placed high in the corner he needed to see at that very moment.

"Could you forgive me?" He bowed his head in her hands. His hot tears dropped onto her fingers. He sat before her, disheveled, clearly puzzled at the turn his life had taken, as if he had played no part in it. A wave of pity for him washed over her, pulling at her heart. When they wed, they had been so happy, her knight in shining armor, his lady love.

She took Peter in her arms, hugged him hard, his body familiar and safe. She leaned back to look at him, to see him in this renewed feeling they had for one another. The sounds of Stuart's breathing and his occasional moans were the only thing bringing her back to the complications of her life.

In the moonlit side of Peter's face, Lavinia could see the blue of his eye, the tears staining his cheek, the curve and color of his full mouth, the blonde of his hair.

A small glint caught her attention in the shadowed portion: the eye's sinister red gleam. In the dark shadows, did she see that half of his mouth twist into a deformed smile? Were those dark locks, instead of blonde, falling in curls on his forehead? She blinked. Jewels gleamed in darkness from the gold band decorating his hair. She put her hand to her mouth. That half was Yasir's face, distorted with evil.

She jerked away, unable to find her voice. Peter turned and, for a moment, she saw clearly—half Peter, half Yasir. Then Peter, his face his own again, leaning towards her.

He helped her to stand. "What is it now?" He braced his legs against the floor, ready to act if threatened, and checked the room.

"Peter." Lavinia turned his face towards her. "Yes, it's just you now," she said, her voice soft with relief. She took his hand. "What I saw in your face. Half yours, half Yasir's. But his—his, terrifying."

"Just as I was saying, Lavinia." Peter viewed the chamber. When his eyes met hers they held confusion. "Things have changed, and not for the better, since Yasir has come into our lives. And now we have Stuart as part of our family, forever associated with the djinni."

The sky framed in the window glowed with the deep blue of pre-dawn. Peter grasped her shoulders. "Now that we have our little Cybelle, our precious daughter. Perhaps we should somehow put Yasir behind us." Peter looked into her eyes, his expression calmer.

Her husband hadn't called Yasir. Peter wanted to betray him. She prayed her husband hadn't felt her flinch when he mentioned Cybelle, who Yasir claimed as his, despite the fact that the child had no magic.

This hadn't turned out as she planned. She wanted Yasir. Yasir could fix these things.

They were still in danger from that cat. Those eyes alive with cunning, the eyes of Rakhshan seeking them out. She knew that Peter had heard from Yasir how the Dark Magician could harm them, about the prophecy and the danger they were in. But he didn't know the evil of the magician's gaze, the horror he had put Yasir through, had put her through. Somehow, he had sectioned this in a compartment that didn't really affect him. He couldn't comprehend that she, Yasir, Stuart and Cybelle could be taken. Murdered.

Would he be left with only James?

He had made his decision. Now she had to make hers.

45

Ahead, outside the sunroom, the rain descended in torrents. Through the French doors, Yasir could see the garden dissolving in a curtain of gray-blue, almost the same tone as Amarja's gown, so that at first glance he beheld only a cascade of red floating by the window. The witch's tresses. The rainstorm beat down the plants surrounding the patio, stealing their flower petals, the streams of water vivid magenta, orange and purple.

Amarja turned to face him. She was attuned to his presence now.

"I thought you would have left since our last encounter," said Yasir as he strolled into the room.

"And I thought you would be imprisoned in your urn by the master of the house." Armarja fondled a pink rose in the bouquet on the wrought iron table near the doors. The heady fragrance filled the air.

"My master neglected to send me to the urn last night. He is becoming less conscientious. But what can one expect from a human caught up in my subtle spell?" He grinned at Amarja.

"Yasir, do not mess up their lives." The witch brushed her hand through her hair, arcing those amazing tresses behind her, a red flag of warning. "Do you truly believe Lavinia's child will be enough for the prophecy? She is merely human, with nary a bone of magic in her body." Amarja's slanted green eyes probed his as if they could, by their silent inquiry, discern what he was up to.

He sat facing the garden on a blue damask couch and ran his hand along the smooth surface, the fabric slick like water.

"You may not taunt me about my Thalia, my Lavinia." Yasir pushed his hands together, working the muscles in his upper arms. "Thalia was in a time far before yours. Let it be."

The matter was settled.

With a wave of his hand, a tray laden with food and drink appeared, filling the room with the inviting aroma of fresh-baked bread.

"We will break our night fast together." Yasir put his hands behind his head and leaned back, watching as the teapot rose in the air and filled the two cups. He forsook his magic, layering *tabrizi*, sweet yellow butter; feta cheese; his favorite, *sarshir*, heavy whipped cream sweetened with poppy flower honey; and apricot jam on *naan-e sangak*, golden triangular bread. He licked his fingers, lifted the messy concoction to his mouth, and consumed it in one bite.

"Those were not meant to be used all at once Yasir," Amarja said with an air of disdain. "You lose the subtlety of the flavors, jumbling them so." She spread a thin layer of *sarshir* on a piece of *naan-e sangak*, topped it neatly with a thin slice of feta and held it for him to see.

She took a delicate bite. "A burst of sweet and sour."

"Ah, so unlike your other appetites," Yasir muttered, mouth full, a glob of apricot jam dripping down his chin.

She made a face and sipped her chai.

"And so like yours." Amarja indicated his full mouth. Her scarlet hair rippled as if a zephyr had lifted it, though the room was dead still and stifling with the close atmosphere from the rainstorm.

The gentle pull caught him off guard. He gripped the couch arm as the sensation of his body falling made him press his feet firm to the marble floor. He scowled at her. The faint vibration of her magic suddenly stopped.

"Do. Not. Start. Amarja. All you have is your poor witch's magic and your womanly wiles. I am bonded to Lavinia." Yasir started assembling another concoction.

"Such a shame she already has a husband. And a handsome, rich one at that." Amarja's laugh tittered over the drum of raindrops. "And he is your master, Yasir. Is it worth being so faithful, when, by her very situation, Lavinia cannot be?"

A flash of lightning brightened the room in a blinding glare, and he glanced outside at the garden. Caramel-colored eyes peered through a pane of the French doors.

Yasir rushed over and put his face to the glass. A crash of thunder rattled the doors. He could see nothing but the blue wall of water and the occasional smear of the drowned garden.

"I saw him also, Yasir." Amarja stood close beside him. Too close. The rain thrummed harder, making a great noise, as if the house had suddenly situated itself beneath a colossal waterfall.

A black shape zoomed by the doors, blurred both by speed and the rain. Yasir turned to check the other windows and stared into Amarja's eyes. Deepest green, like a perfect emerald lit from within.

He looked away.

"I think we will win this one." She tossed her hair. That haughty bearing, even after he had refused her.

A figure lumbered onto the patio, becoming more distinct—a huge black hound, easily as large as a calf. The creature waited patiently at the French doors, gripping something in its mouth.

Yasir motioned in the direction of the great hound. The door opened in a whoosh of pattering rain, the sweet smell of ozone gusting in on the cold wind, mixing with the aroma of the breakfast, confusing the senses.

The dog trotted over the threshold, rivulets of water rolling off his body. In his mouth he held a limp black cat.

"Release," said Yasir as he waved the door closed.

The dog set the poor creature on the floor at the djinni's feet. Yasir sent a burst of healing energy to the animal as the huge hound shook water from his coat with a loud slap, drenching Yasir and Amarja in a shower of cold rainwater.

"Yasir, you look rather like something the dog brought in." Amarja's peels of laughter sounded eerie against the pounding of the worsening storm.

He couldn't help his broad smile. Her dress, soaked and near transparent, clung to her body, delineating the curve of her hips and breasts, her nipples hard from the cold. A deep tint of scarlet graced the "v" between her thighs.

He was falling, falling like the rain outside, falling to Amarja. She had nerve, the witch, plying her meager skills against his magic. He took a breath and shut his eyes, shut out her beauty.

In a swirling gesture, Yasir restored all that the dog had soaked, evaporating the water in a blue mist. Flames of the hearth fire blazed, consuming the chill in the room as Amarja sat beside him on the couch. The black dog yawned, its mouth a great pink cavern, and settled beside the fire with a satisfied groan.

The lump of fur at Yasir's feet stirred. He studied the creature, his senses tingling in alarm. Rakhshan had frequently used black cats as familiars to attend his needs. Perhaps Yasir could turn this one.

Yasir reached for the cat, but jerked backwards. The animal's shape funneled upwards, thinning and growing as it twisted and turned like a waterspout. The funnel spun back on itself, becoming darker and denser before collapsing and transforming into a man, supine on the carpet.

His body stretched long and slim, bare skin the color of charcoal. He stared, impassive, but intent, with rounded green eyes. Moving his muscular body in a graceful flow, he sat upright.

"Join us for breakfast," Amarja said as if he were a good friend who had just been announced.

The man leapt to his feet, so fast that Amarja started. Wary, he squatted on the floor, all the while staring at the witch, his eyes unnaturally wide.

She set a plate of *naan-e sangak* before him on the table in front of the divan. Cats should be fond of butter and cheese. Next to the plate, she placed a bowl of *sarshir* and took her seat across from him.

The man sniffed the food. He dipped his finger into the bowl, shook it, and drew back, eyeing the *sarshir* suspiciously. Then he lapped at the heavy cream, the kiss kiss of his tongue discernible as the rain lessened. His black hair, braided into countless tiny plaits across his pleasingly shaped head, bobbed up and down.

"What is your name and your task?" Yasir enunciated as though he were talking to a child.

The man looked up from the bowl, licking his mouth with his pink tongue, eyes unblinking. His dark complexion made it hard to see detail in his face, but his nose sat long and straight and his high cheekbones tapered into a small rounded chin.

"I am Xiphilinos. I am here to find if the djinni called Yasir is truly alive, where he is, and if he has any children," he rumbled in a curiously languid voice. "Then I am to tell Master." As if he had just noticed he had no clothes, he ran his hand down his body, covering himself with long black trousers and a black tunic.

"Who is your Master?" asked Amarja, trying unsuccessfully to capture his gaze.

The man arched his back, graceful, his chary eyes closing for a moment as he leaned his head towards the sound of the rain. Then he stared at Yasir.

"They call my master Dark Magician, Master of Magic, Rakhshan." His thin voice cracked. He snatched a small chunk of *tabrizi* with his right hand, holding the white cheese to his mouth as he nibbled it.

Yasir tried to hide his wince. Amarja saw it. Xiphilinos had not noticed. Or had he?

"Have you reported to your Master yet?" Yasir studied the creature. The room suddenly brightened as if someone had lit hundreds of lamps. The next instant they were plunged back into the morning's gloom. A crackling sound ratcheted downscale into a low hum, growing progressively louder. Each looked about, seeking to identify the source of the strange noise.

Xiphilinos jumped up, eyes wide and round, his braids stirring like living creatures. A deafening crash resounded through the glass into the room. Yasir jerked to his feet in unison with Amarja. The boom echoed through the great house, rumbling louder as it ricocheted from library to hall to parlors. Simply an unusually loud peal of thunder. They sat down as the rain rattled down harder than before.

"Master doesn't expect me for half a fortnight. Then I will report to him," purred Xiphilinos as he licked another chunk of *tabrizi*.

Amarja strolled to the dark man, her hips swaying. Xiphilinos sat straight, half-rising as she stepped behind him and placed her hands on his head. His low snarl became a yowl. His braids standing on end, he transformed back into a black cat, trapped in an ornate wire cage. He arched his back and hissed, his tail undulating like a snake.

"We can send him to the Dark Magician. He will tell the Dark Magician what we want him to." Amarja held her hand above the cage and it disappeared. "I will take good care of our little pet as he is readied." She rubbed her hands together, a self-satisfied look in her eyes.

Oh yes, she would take care of him. Yasir smirked. The man was well-formed and exotic, to Amarja's tastes. Now she had another target, thank the Djinn. He would not have to put up with her constant seductive shenanigans.

"Not like that, Yasir." Amarja chastened him.

He gave her a sideways glance. She would take her fill of her new toy before she sent the creature back to Rakhshan. Would she think to warn him when the cat was returned?

"When will you realize that you are special to me? It has always been that way." Amarja slipped beside him on the divan. Her fragrance filled the air around them. Vetiver. Earthy like just-turned soil awaiting planting.

Her hair rippled. Yasir got caught in her deep green eyes, a bottomless pool. She put her hand on his.

He pulled back and turned away.

"Amarja, our time has passed," he said gently.

The witch looked down, her face impassive, hands in her lap,

He felt the side of his lip curl with satisfaction. Amarja was not used to being thwarted. Yasir faced the hearth where the hound had been napping. The rug lay empty.

"Where is he? How could such a gigantic beast have left without us knowing?"

Amarja took a breath and raised her head, her neck pale and smooth. She gazed into the distance, then her expression changed, eyes bright, and she gestured to the vacant space before the fire.

"The creature is running to the moors where he will meet his mate and live on in a work of literature to be written much later." Her voice rang low. She was a siren, a prophetess.

"Is anyone aware of how much we contribute to the great writings of the world, Yasir?"

"You know that Yasir fancies me," said Amarja. With a tilt of her chin, she turned her head to the side. Her red hair spun out behind her like a satin cape. Alice remembered being jealous, with her plain brown hair, her plumpness, but she had learned that love goes beyond the color of hair and the slant of green eyes.

"I would be careful. Yasir has other priorities now." Alice dared to conjecture what had happened between Amarja and Yasir. Yet there was a restlessness about the witch, signaling that she had not obtained what she wanted, or that she wanted more of it.

"Yasir and I have a very long history, you know." Amarja reached out to take Alice's hand. "It is time now for me to take leave of you, old friend."

Alice clasped the witch's hand, sending her mind searching Amarja's, but was met with nothing. A flash of reproach from the witch's green eyes was all that Alice would get, which merely confirmed Alice's suspicions.

"Go in well-being," said Alice. Presented with one last glimpse of the horror of scars crisscrossing Amarja's beautiful face, Alice let the witch's hand slide from hers. She felt as if she were releasing a wild animal from a cage.

The early morning brightened. Perhaps Amarja's exit lifted a weight from the burgeoning day.

Amarja readied herself, masked her feelings.

Zamyad al Din, Yasir's father, would be waiting. She had succeeded with her task and Zamyad was generous when he was pleased. She knew how to increase his generosity in many ways. It would take no effort at all to veil her plans and schemes from him—her plotting to seduce his newly prudish, but, oh so, enticing son.

46

James arced his pencil point on the paper as he finished the last button on the uniform. He looked at his soldier doll propped against three of Cybelle's blocks set near the edge of his table. Almost finished. He tapped the pencil against his lips. *Hmm, might need to rub out the drooping side of the soldier's mouth, make it more of a smile.* But now he would draw the feather in the hat. That would be harder than the buttons.

"This soldier doll is magic, Jamie. Now you can have your share. Keep this a secret from your father. *Our* secret," his mom had said as she placed the cloth doll in his open hands. She had kissed him on the cheek.

He rolled his pencil on the paper. He and Stuart were stuck in the nursery, watching Cybelle until Nanny, who wasn't feeling very perky, returned from the necessary. He stared out the window. From the corner of his eye, he saw something dark move along the wall.

Or had he?

"Did you see that?" he asked his brother.

"What?" Stuart faced him, his arm raised, hand level, fingers manipulating the dance of the miniature dolls he had created. Yellow, pink and blue hair, hats laden with flowers, birds, cakes and sugar-plums. Frocks covered in lace, gold brocade, fancier stuff than Mum's. The dolls twirled and bowed and pirouetted to an orchestra of flutes and drums. James wanted to cover his ears, it sounded so odd. But now that he had his brother's attention, the music had stopped.

Cybelle let out a frustrated cry and pointed to the dolls as they hovered in place above her.

"What?" Stuart asked him again, beginning to sound angry.

"Behind the toy chest." James laid his pencil down and slid from his chair. A black tail snaked above the chest.

"Here kitty, kitty." James held out his hand. "Stuart, give me a sugar biscuit. Quick!"

"Cats don't like sugar biscuits, silly," Stuart said. "Besides, you ate all yours and you may not have mine."

A shriek made them both turn at once. Cybelle pointed at the dolls. With a beaming smile and a flick of his wrist, Stuart set the dolls spinning in a figure eight, accompanied by trumpets this time.

Wincing at the off-key tune, James squatted by the edge of the chest. The cat peeked out. "Don't be daft, sugar biscuits have cream in them. I saw Cook make them. Come on, give me one." He held out his hand, fingers beckoning, and Stuart dropped half a biscuit into his palm.

"That's your half," said Stuart.

James presented the crumbling biscuit to the cat. The creature's bright green eyes locked on the confection.

"Kitty, kitty. Come get some biscuit," James said in a high, sweet voice.

The cat came closer, tail switching. It sniffed. With its rough pink tongue, the cat licked the biscuit, then gulped it down, sharp teeth flashing white. With a meow, the feline curled around James's trousers, brushing against him.

"It likes me." James held still.

His brother leaned over, holding out another biscuit. "Come on kitty. You can like me too." The cat sat about a foot away and licked his paw.

"Ha! He's ignoring you. He knows which one of us is best." James tilted his head, giving his brother an exaggerated grin.

"He knows which one can best him." Stuart raised his hand.

James grabbed it. "No! Don't do anything mean to the cat. I—" He straightened, eyes bulging, as the cat's fur stood on end, the edges trailing a smudgy black haze into the air. The dark smudge rose in a spiraling mass, transforming the cat into a shape taller than James, taller than Stuart.

"I told you not to do anything to it." James threw himself on his brother, knocking him to the floor. "I'm sick–sick–sick of your stupid magic." He hit Stuart on the arm, then started pummeling him on the chest. "You can't leave anything alone. Always with the magic. Why don't you just—?"

He choked, the collar of his shirt closing around his neck as he was dragged off his brother. His hands pulled at the collar but it was too tight, he couldn't get them under it. He would choke, he couldn't get air— Then he was on his feet, his collar loosening.

He gasped, panting, face burning with fury, and faced his assailant, fists ready to pound.

A cry, like a girl's screech, poured out of him at the peculiar creature that had grabbed him. A very thin man with no clothes, his skin as dark as the black smoke still drifting around his bare body. Before James could punch him or run, the man grasped his upper arm and lifted him into the air as if he were as light as his soldier doll.

The creature batted at his chest with his other hand.

"Stuart, help!" James swung his free arm, trying to deflect the man's pointed fingernails. One ripped into his skin, scratching down to his elbow.

He screamed at the pain.

"Stuart, do something!" James squealed. He would get him for this. His sodding coward of a brother used his magic and then didn't help him. James hated magic. Hated it.

His brother stood in front of him, mouth gaping.

"Why are you standing there like that?" James waved his arm trying to get his attention. "Help!" He tried to wriggle loose, but the man still dangled him in the air. "Stuart what did you do? WHO is this?"

Stuart moved his mouth, but nothing came out. Then he stuttered.

"I – I don't know. I didn't do this." His voice sounded small and strange.

The man set James down. James stumbled to his brother, his arm bleeding. "Look what he did. Make him go away. This isn't funny." He hid behind Stuart, peeking out. If the man made a move, he'd push his brother straight into him. See how *he* liked being pummeled.

But they all stood there, assessing one another.

The man stroked his fingers on his pointed chin, his bright green eyes darting between them. Those slanted eyes reminded James of someone. Who? The cat behind the toy chest, that's who. He poked Stuart in the ribs and said in a low voice.

"You changed the cat into this–this thing. This cat man. He's mean, Stuart. Mean. I wanted a real kitty and you made him into a big mean man. I'll get you for this, I will."

"Shh, I didn't do this. I couldn't do this. Something strange is going on. Be quiet." Stuart sounded scared. He wouldn't fake that. And it was odd he didn't take credit for the magic. He was always bragging about his magic.

The man stepped closer. They both moved back.

The cat man ran his hand down his chest. As they watched, a long black shirt and trousers covered his naked body. Black velvet shoes grew on his feet.

He held out his hand. Two small cakes frosted in pink and dotted with sparkling sugar candies appeared in his palm. The sweet smell of sugar and rich cream floated to them on the murky air that surrounded the man.

James's mouth watered. Maybe the man was sorry for the way he treated him. For the scratch. He grabbed one of the cakes. "Come on Stuart, don't be a fraidy cat. See, he's thanking us for the biscuits we gave him."

"I'm not afraid." Stuart took a cake and bit into it. "Hey, this is better than Cook's." He took another bite and studied the man, his eyes squinting. "Will you turn back into a cat?"

The man licked a blob of pink icing off his finger. He stretched and walked out the door, his gait peculiar as if he were sliding on ice.

"Wait!" James called. He looked behind him. Cybelle stood by his desk on tiptoes, pointing at his toy soldier.

Stuart waved his hand. The dolls and music vanished and the toy soldier appeared in Cybelle's pudgy little hands.

"Nanny should be here any minute to take care of Cybie. Besides, we won't be gone long." Stuart closed the door to the nursery and they followed the cat man down the hall.

"You're not tricking me are you, Stu?" James walked alongside his brother. "I mean, I kinda believe you, because you've never made an animal into a man."

Stuart shook his head and pointed to the cat man. "Don't let him get away."

The man stood in front of the tall window at the end of the hall, his back to them.

"What do you think he's doing?" James whispered.

"Looking out the window, dum dum." Stuart crept closer until he stood directly behind the man. He beckoned for his brother.

James followed. Down the hall a door creaked. A figure hurried out. Hard to tell who. The lady was silhouetted against the brightness from the window at the corridor's end. Mum! Most definitely she should not see this peculiar man. They would be in big trouble. He tugged at Stuart's shirt. His brother pushed his hand away.

James beat on his back.

Stuart whipped around, his face red with anger.

"Don't—" He raised his head. "Mum!"

James scrunched his face at his brother. Now what?

"Sir. Who are you?" Their mum said in a loud voice, her angry mother voice. She marched up to them. The cat man put his arms around James, then Stuart.

"Let go of my boys!" His mum looked in the man's face. "You are trespassing, I'll have you thrown out."

The cat man's arm shot out and pushed her, curved nails ripping the sleeve of her dress. Mum screamed as she fell to the floor, her head hitting with a thump. It was such a fast, unexpected move, that when the man let go of him, James hadn't realized he was free until the man's wiry arm clamped around him again.

"Mum!" James struggled and felt the cat man's hold loosen, but before he could slip away, the man bundled them off down the hall, Stuart's head banging into his. The man glided down the stairs faster than they slid down the banister the other day.

"Peter! Dobson!" Their mother screamed. The thud of footfalls and voices grew as the servants hurried to help his mum.

"Do magic, Stu," James pleaded.

"I have. I am," Stuart rasped, his cheeks red, sweat on his forehead.

The French doors to the garden opened by themselves as the man approached. Bushes and trees and flowers whizzed by. The man went so fast, they could be speeding in a train, looking out the window. But they weren't.

James closed his eyes.

He vowed he would never own a cat. Never!

Lavinia staggered to her feet. A bit dizzy. And that buzzing sound. She could hardly see for the fuzzy black spots gathering in her vision. She bowed her head, groping for something to support her and made it to the wall, leaned hard against it. If she lost consciousness, she would simply slide to the floor.

"Peter, Dobson!" She winced at the pain in her head. Her hand touched a hard surface by her side. She was sitting on the floor. She must have blacked out for a moment. Had she heard Fleming and one of the footman talking nearby?

Lavinia raised her head. The hall seemed to be enclosed in a dark halo. Where were the servants? Where was Peter?

A sharp pain in her temple made her close her eyes. Was it the blow to her head, wishful thinking, or had she seen Yasir in front of her?

Strong hands grasped her arms, lifting her. A warm pressure on her forehead dissolved the ache and dizziness. She opened her eyes.

"Lavinia, be still, let me heal you. I sent the servants away. They will not remember seeing me here with you." Yasir touched her arm. The blood welling from the deep scratch vanished along with the burning sting.

She looked up at the djinni. "Yasir. The boys! A-a peculiar man. Tall, dark skin, took them."

"Green eyes?" Yasir still held her. She couldn't pretend it had no affect. She grasped his arm and nodded, trying to work out what was so familiar about the dark man.

"He is the black cat. Rakhshan's minion, Xiphilinos." The anger in Yasir's voice made her shrink from him.

"Hurry. Save them." She let go of the djinni, hoping she could stand by herself.

He scowled. "I am not free. I am bound to return to Peter. When I inform him, he will command me to rescue the boys." Yasir clasped her hand. "Come with me. Then we will save them."

Now his touch felt different, as if every hope she held had been sucked away, leaving a desolate hollow space. She stifled the impulse to pull her hand from his.

"Oh, Yasir." How many times must he remind her of his helplessness as slave to Peter? Her eyes filled with tears, for her boys, for her djinni. "I must go find the boys."

"You will put yourself in unnecessary danger. If you will but stay for—"

She wrenched her hand from his. "I will be there for *them*. Waiting for you."

"He what?" Peter rose from behind his desk. He slammed down his ledger, papers flying. "I thought you secured this place with your magic."

Damned djinni. Had he lied about his protection spell?

Yasir narrowed his eyes, his gold pupils glinting with anger. "This is a creature who shape changes. He came as a cat, but can project the illusion of a man. Soft-witted, he is given the little magic he can handle from one greater. I know now that what he receives is too weak to trigger my protection spell."

"And he took my James and Stuart? Why?" Peter strode from behind his desk and stood face to face with the djinni.

"Because he is a dullard and cannot tell who has magic and who does not. Do not worry, I will save them."

"Bloody hell, Where are they?" Peter took Yasir by the shoulders. "Where?"

"Master, they are nearby, at the river. I cannot leave until you command me to save them."

"Damn it, Yasir. This should never have happened. Are they hurt?" It was his own fault. Something should have been done before this.

"No, master, but I must go now."

"I will come with you."

"No. Beg pardon. You will only hinder me. Please, master." By God, Yasir was near as agitated as he was.

"Hinder you?" The damned djinni was becoming too uppity.

"The one behind this is powerful, I mean to save the boys before he appears. If you are there I must protect you, as well as the children. This is no ordinary man."

"Don't expect me to wait long. If they're not here soon, I'll summon you." Peter ran his hand through his hair, then made a shooing gesture at Yasir.

"Go. Save them." He seethed as Yasir vanished. The damned djinni had put his children in danger, as well as his wife.

Like an automaton, Peter sped through the motions of unlocking his desk drawer, withdrawing the huge key, and choosing the specific door from the many that cluttered the front of the huge cabinet behind his desk.

"Bloody djinni. I should have done this long ago."

He stuck his loaded holster pistol in the pocket of his blue tailcoat. Clutching the urn, he ran upstairs to one of the third floor bedrooms, pressed a wooden rose in the decorative panel next to the fireplace, and entered the secret tryst chamber where he had hidden his favorite treasures.

He pulled the urn from the black velvet bag and set it upon the mantle. By the grace of God, it would stay there for eternity— unopened, undisturbed.

After Yasir brought his boys back, there would be no magic threats against them.

Ever.

47

*Y*asir stayed in his ethereal form, a wisp of translucent smoke wafting through the forest to the riverbank. He would find Xiphilinos, the wretched servant of Rakhshan, and wrest the boys from him. Then the cat man would face his destruction.

The story he and Amarja sent with Xiphilinos—that there was no magic and no djinni or any sign of one at Bramley House—had worked. Now Rakhshan was checking to see if the children were Yasir's.

Cybelle hadn't been touched, perhaps because she was so young. The spell he had set around her, as well as the footmen in and outside the nursery, nanny and several maids at her side, should keep her safe for the time being.

"Ah, there you are." The voice came from inside a grove of dense trees.

"Quick, assume your human form. I must speak with you." Mehadeh swept the cascading leaves of a willow aside and looked in the direction of the river. "We have little time."

He had no warning that Mehadeh was there. Was she helping Rakhshan? Even after her visit to the urn where she let him inside her head, proving she was faithful, doubt rose in him.

She motioned him into the grove, where she faced him, her red skirt surrounded by the thick undergrowth of bright green ferns.

Yasir took his human form, making sure the shimmer of light around him reminded the sorceress of his power. His white kurta and cloth-of-gold trousers glowed in competition with the jewels in his gold headband, earrings and finger rings.

Mehadeh started to speak, but drew up as if she were stricken by a sudden chill. She leaned close, her breath sour with fear. "You are too late. *He* is here."

In her dark eyes he saw terror. "I need your help, Yasir."

"I cannot indulge one who has betrayed me." Yasir started to walk away.

Mehadeh clutched his arm. "No. Do not go. I was bound. I did my best to balance my obligation to him and my love for you. I stayed as loyal as I could."

She moved closer. "How can you forget that when I searched for you, the Shadow Lord coerced the Bishan Shaman to drown me in her scrying bowl? Then the Shadow Lord swept me away before I died. By our law, I owe him. My task is to find you, dead or alive, and bing you to him."

Was that a moan that floated on the breeze? Yasir looked towards the sound, as did the sorceress. He had to find the boys. This delay was intolerable.

She took his head in her hands. "We are blood brother and sister. I have never broken my blood oath. You can feel my truth." She put her forehead to his.

The images came fast: Mehadeh held underwater, her eyes bulging in terror; Rakhshan's guards dropping her on the floor in front of him, her limp body crashing into the hard marble; the Shadow Lord screaming at her in a rage as she retched. Yasir closed his eyes against her humiliation. He moved his forehead from hers.

"Please." She held onto his arm again. "I need to present you to the Dark Magician as if you are my prisoner. I will create the aspect of a spell that convinces him you are held by my magic. You will be close enough to give him a fatal blow with your full power. And Stuart should be there to compensate for the Shadow Lord having your secret name.

"Yasir, If you do not do this, the Dark Magician will destroy me, for good this time. Then I can never help you."

Yasir looked past Mehadeh. The leaves shimmered in the breeze. He was in a quiet copse in a wood by a river, but he could feel the darkness gathering as if there were thousands of soldiers massing for a great battle. Now Rakhshan would know he was alive. All this time keeping it from him, all the effort would be in vain if he acquiesced to Mehadeh's plea.

Could this be a trap, the images he saw false? But with his blood mingled with hers, the sorceress was not quite powerful enough to deceive him in that way.

Would this be the fight for his freedom? So soon? Yet this ruse of Mehadeh's would give him an advantage over confronting Rakhshan and Xiphilinos. At the very least, he could save the boys, even with the Dark Lord present.

"So be it." Fate had led him to this moment. How he had dreaded it.

"I will present you, then leave, but I will not desert you, Yasir. The Dark Magician cannot know I am with you." Mehadeh looked him up and down. "Dim your aura."

"Now, we go."

Lavinia bent over, hands on her thighs, chest heaving, her eye on a tiny metal soldier in the brown dirt and pebbles. She had followed the candies and small toys that she knew Stuart kept in his pockets for Cybelle. A clever boy, he had left her a trail.

Almost there. But she must catch her breath. It wouldn't help the boys if she were to arrive only to faint. The river was close by. She could smell the sharp scent of decaying leaves in the still pools by the bank, feel the damp in the breeze. Voices, distant, muted. She straightened and hurried towards them.

A man's voice rose above the others, clear and distinct. She stopped, her scalp prickling.

Rakhshan.

She crept up the grassy rise, keeping to the edge of a thicket of trees and ferns. When she glimpsed the figure in the cobalt robe and indigo turban, she slipped behind the largest oak, peering from the girth of its trunk. A woman in red held Yasir in front of Rakhshan, her skin as black as the cat man's.

Mehadeh.

How could it be Mehadeh? She had labored to save Yasir in the urn. The sorceress had helped her return to Bramley House to honor Yasir's last wishes.

"He is yours now. I have put a spell on him, saving you the trouble." Mehadeh's deep voice dripped with pride. She let go of the djinni and walked away.

Yasir stood there, facing Rakhshan. She didn't see the cat man or the boys. Lavinia looked around for something to throw, to distract them, but only saw thin twigs and dead leaves, not even a pebble. But if she did throw something, it would only let Rakhshan know someone was there. He would draw her out with his magic. Then she would be a hostage, or worse.

Why did Mehadeh leave? Why not stay and help Rakhshan? Lavinia crept deeper into the thicket and followed the sorceress, trying to keep her footfalls silent. When they were at the bottom of the hill, she rushed ahead and met her face to face.

Mehadeh stopped, her dark eyes wide.

"Lavinia, what were you doing spying on us? If the Shadow Lord had not been so transfixed by Yasir, he would have taken you as well."

"Traitor!" Lavinia slapped her. "You betrayed Yasir," she hissed. The wind blew her voice away from the river, away from Rakhshan. Still, the crack of her slap gained in volume as it resounded through the thicket and off the hillock.

"Quiet." Mehadeh dragged her into the copse, the red beads in her hair clicking together as she moved. "I have not betrayed the great djinni. He is helping me. And I will help him now, but the Shadow Lord cannot know. I gave him a chance to surprise the Dark Magician and strike a fatal blow."

Lavinia stifled a groan as the sorceress squeezed her arm.

"Listen. I give you a powerful spell. It can heal only. Anything stronger would harm you, even with your bit of magic." Mehadeh put her hands together. "To use it, cup your hands like this, and say the recipient's name. Then speak these words clearly: *der bedn, rewh w rewan, shema ma shefa khewahed.*"

"Now. I put the words in your head and send you the power." The sorceress's palm on her forehead felt hot.

Lavinia flinched as the spell flowed into her. She staggered when it stopped, her head spinning, held upright only by the power Mehadeh had given. The sorceress held her by the waist, steadying her with a firm grip and a bit of magic. Lavinia could feel the strength of the spell grounding her to the earth.

"Use this spell wisely. I will not abandon you or Yasir. But I must not be seen in your company by the Dark Lord." The sorceress stared into her eyes.

Lavinia leaned closer, anxious for more instruction, more of anything that would help her save her children, save Yasir. She saw glimpses of the djinni as a lad with a young Mehadeh, rainbows of colors surrounding them. The colors surged into a swirl of red and Mehadeh was gone, the click-clack of the sorceress's beads still in the air.

In a daze, Lavinia gaped at where Mehadeh had stood. The breeze trailed her own tresses in front of her and brought the stagnant smell of the river's shallows along with voices. She straightened, feeling the strength of Mehadeh's gift.

Would she dare to use it?

48

*L*avinia stalked through the grove, following the voices. She stopped where the trees thinned, and hid behind the trunk of the same oak where she had spied upon Mehadeh and Yasir. When she peered out, she choked back a gasp of surprise. From what Mehadeh told her, she had surmised that Yasir, who Rakhshan thought was under the sorceress's spell, would attack the Dark Magician with his magic and kill him. This was his chance.

She held her breath as she watched Yasir dodge a blow from the Shadow Lord. With a roar like an enraged beast, the magic plowed into the ground behind the djinni, throwing clods of dirt into the air. The dust scattered, blowing towards her. She put her hand over her mouth and nose, fearing breathing in the magic.

The two were far enough apart that if each had a sword they would have to move closer to fight. But the rules of magic were different from normal combat. Lavinia searched for the cat man, for the children. Where were they?

"Set the boys free." Yasir held his hands out. A burst of gold light flared from his splayed fingers, glancing off the ruby aigrette in Rakhshan's turban. The repelled light fell on the Shadow Lord, surrounding him. He raised his arms, struggling inside the gold sphere, then stepped forward as it faded.

She heard Yasir curse.

Lavinia pressed her body against the tree trunk. The djinni had promised that when the time came, he would fight in place of Stuart. He was true to his word.

"Ah, the boys." Rakhshan gestured and the cat man appeared by his side in a smudgy haze of dark smoke. As the haze dispersed in the breeze, she saw that the man held Stuart and James, one at each side as if they were inconvenient bundles.

"Sam!" the boys called out in unison. The name they used for Yasir, the same name as the under-groom, so Peter wouldn't suspect anything if they let it slip. Now she felt guilty for not sharing the djinni's real name with them.

"Help!" James's high voice screeched over Stuart's low cry. He looked up, eyes lit with fear and tried to wriggle free. The cat man's face distorted as he hissed at James.

Lavinia scraped her nails on the bark of the oak, imagining it was the man's face.

Rakhshan didn't look at the children. He kept his dark gaze on Yasir, the ruby in his aigrette glittering like an evil eye. "Why should I let them go? One of them is prophesied to kill me. I take that as a serious threat."

Yasir seemed to grow in stature, the gold light from his eyes making a mask around Rakhshan's eyes that she could see even from her hiding place. The djinni and the magician were silent, like wolves circling.

Her skin tightened as if a north wind gusted around her. Surely djinnis were more powerful than a mere human magician, but Rakhshan had bested Yasir over and over.

A phrase flickered in her mind, faint, then bolder, so that she almost comprehended. She shivered as the words, unbidden, became clear: *Yasir knew the secret of Rakhshan's power over him. But the djinni could do nothing about it.*

The realization hit her hard. Why hadn't this occurred to her before? It had been staring her in the face for years.

Lavinia felt the magic from Mehadeh build in her. She had power now, and could use it to save Yasir and her children. The magic surged up her spine. She stood straight. No one had seen her, a human woman, worrying over her children, her lover.

Yasir's light still shone on Rakhshan's eyes, but now the shadows of the magician's magic almost obscured Yasir's features. Was the magician growing stronger? Was he gaining over the djinni?

A flare from one of Yasir's rings burst through the darkness surrounding him, chasing away Rakhshan's shadows. Lavinia saw the fierce determination in his expression. The djinni kept his focus on the Shadow Lord, but lay his finger on the brilliant diamond in his ring that shone in splendor from the last burst of light.

The magician and Yasir still circled, tension building along with their powers, waiting for the time when they could do the most damage.

Yasir stumbled. A flutter of fear riffled through Lavinia's flesh, but he righted himself. The magician's aigrette glowed, delineating the shadows on the djinni's face.

Lavinia's body ached from her rigid stance, and she craved to be near Yasir, but dared not creep to a closer hiding place. Anything could set them off.

Slowly, slowly, she cupped her hand, Mehadeh's spell words writ large in her head as if they were floating before her. She hesitated, but the magic screamed from her pores.

You can do this.

She took a breath and whispered as softly as she could, "Rakhshan *der bedn, rewh w—*

Yasir vanished.

She almost strangled on the next words of the spell, but managed to keep them unsaid. She had forgotten. How could she? The spell would only heal. Not kill. What if she had completed it? The healing spell could have made Rakhshan stronger.

Lavinia clapped her hand to her mouth. She didn't know what the words meant. Mehadeh hadn't translated them. There had been no time.

Had she already used the magic? Did her misuse make Yasir vanish?

She had seen the flash of the djinni's diamond, felt the outpouring of power. He had been about to attack the magician with something ferocious and strong. Why would he disappear?

Rakhshan's magic encircled her like a noose. He must have sensed at least some of Mehadeh's spell, and traced it to her. She turned to flee, but instead, stepped from her hiding place into the open where he could see her—this was the Shadow Lord's doing.

Rakhshan's fathomless eyes held hers.

"We know now in what esteem the djinni holds you. He left you and your sons at my mercy, which I find in short supply at the moment." The Dark Magician's voice was close, as if it he were beside her, crooning into her ear. He curved his hand, beckoning her nearer.

She turned, meaning to put distance between them, but in seconds was transported up the hill to Rakhshan's side.

"Mum!" James cried out as he struggled in the cat man's wiry arms. Stuart raised his head, face flushed. He glowered at the cat man.

She would claim Yasir's disappearance as her deed.

"Just now, you saw but little of the magic I have, hatched and matured since we last met." She was a kitten facing a lion. Still, she had made her voice bold and strong, and didn't flinch when she met the magician's gaze.

When he had imprisoned her in his palace, he acknowledged she was his daughter Thalia reborn in this life, and rued the fact she was with the djinni once more. There was that connection. She would either make the most of it, or be destroyed by her gamble.

"I will use all I have to save my sons."

"You need only send the one with magic to live with me. I will foster him and see that he is well nurtured." Rakhshan sounded fatherly. So that was his plan. To take Yasir's son and turn him against the djinni.

She kept her eyes on Rakhshan, enduring the feeling that washed over her as it had when she was his prisoner: that of a daughter yearning for her father's embrace. Resisting the impulse to go to him, she crossed her arms over her chest.

"I would have both my sons to raise until they reach the age of consent. You would give that to your true daughter who stands before you." Out of the corner of her eye, she saw Stuart's mouth gape. She would have to answer questions when they returned home.

If they returned.

"Ah, Thalia, you were always my difficult princess." He ran his fingers down his multi-stringed necklace of luminous pearls. The arc of a brilliant rainbow spilled from each one, the colors bleeding into the next display, so subsequent hues shone brighter and brighter. Colors she had never seen before, so vivid— She pulled her attention to his face again. She must not be lured from her mission.

"I would keep my sons safe, only that."

"Then use that great magic of yours and give me the djinni." The ruby in his aigrette glowed, pulsing as if it had a heartbeat. Her eyes were drawn to it, the throbbing light soothing her anguish, luring her to his side.

If she said yes, she would have her sons. They would be safe. Giving Yasir to the magician would only set the djinni before the evil lord, just as Mehadeh had done, and Yasir had agreed to that. Then Yasir could fight Rakhshan as he intended, as he promised.

With great effort, she wrested her gaze from Rakhshan's. Free from his hold, a thought burst into her mind like a needle piercing its length into her skin. The prophecy said that one of Yasir's offspring would defeat the Dark Magician. Stuart would do it because Yasir could not. In fear that Stuart would be killed in the fight, she had made Yasir promise to go against the prophecy

What had she done? Her body seemed to shrink, the inside a desiccated ruin sparking in terror.

Yasir's promise to her doomed him.

Yasir had glanced away from Rakhshan for less time than it took a thought to form in the human brain. Just long enough for him to amplify the strength of the diamond in his ring. He then sent his potent magic in the Shadow Lord's direction. An explosion and the crash of glass shattering broke the silence as he looked to see his nemesis destroyed.

But he saw only the jagged remnants of glass stuck in a window frame.

By the Djinn, where was he?

A breeze billowed the curtains at the window's edge, spreading a thin haze of dust from the tall Egyptian bronze of Isis and Horus, revealing the hint of long-ago gilding. Instead of the sandy riverbank, he stood on a soft Turkish carpet.

He turned from the broken window, only to face his irate master.

"Are you ignoring me? I asked a question. Why don't you have my boys with you?" Peter came closer.

"Master, I was preparing the final salvo to save them . . ."

"Salvo? You put them in more danger? Bloody hell, Yasir . . ." Peter rambled on.

Yasir shook his head, attempting to dispel the confusion from his untimely displacement. Rakhshan's strength had been formidable, but the Shadow Lord's magic had been weakening. Yasir would have bested his nemesis. Peter had said he would summon him if he weren't back with the boys soon. *Ayevalelh*, how could his master have such ruinous timing?

"What's wrong with you? Take me to them. Now!" Peter stepped in front of him, glaring.

Yasir placed his thumb on his first two fingers, curling the other two into his palm—setting in motion their eyeblink transfer to the riverbank. He could feel the ether enclosing them, see Peter fading away. Through his master's body, he saw his urn on the mantelpiece next to a Roman bust.

All the while he prayed that his reappearance would work to his advantage and not Rakhshan's.

49

*L*avinia tried to say it. Tried to say, *Yes, you can have Yasir*, even though she knew full well she couldn't deliver him. She stood in front of Rakhshan, her mouth partly open, her insides a battlefield.

Rakhshan glowered. "Neither my helper nor I can tell which of these boys has magic, so I will—"

"—give them to the djinni Yasir." Yasir's voice boomed as he appeared beside her, Peter in tow.

Lavinia let out a cry. *Lord in heaven*, why did he bring Peter? They ignored her. Yasir fixated on Rakhshan, and Peter glared at the cat man holding James and Stuart. She slipped behind them, relieved to be out of the magician's spotlight.

"Father!" James called as he caught sight of Peter.

"I will take this one. The one that speaks." Rakhshan's ruby aigrette marked James with its eerie glow.

"I don't have magic!" James yelled. His face was bright red, made even more livid by he magician's ruby. He looked directly at Rakhshan.

Why, her son was angry, not fearful.

"I hate magic. You let me go. I'm no good for you." James kicked at the cat man, but he couldn't get any traction, and his legs fell short of his target.

An explosive bang made them all jump. The smell of rotten eggs fouled the air in a cloud of smoke. A strong gust of wind off the river blew the smoke back onto Peter who held a pistol, aimed at Rakhshan. As he swung the gun down, his smug expression became a grimace. He dropped his pistol and clutched his arm. A stain of red appeared on the sleeve of his jacket.

"You think a mere pistol can penetrate my magic? That is YOUR bullet in your arm. It is a shame it did not pierce your heart."

"It's only a scratch." Peter put his fist to his chest.

Rakhshan signaled the cat man, and James, arms askew, sped through the air. He struggled to get down, but hung like a ripe fruit next to the magician.

Rakhshan directed his focus on Peter. "I take this to be your son. A little something on which to whet my magic, an appetizer for the main meal."

"He is innocent," Peter said. He gestured frantically at Yasir.

Yasir made a motion with his head and the boy appeared by his side. He set James on the ground and embraced him.

Lavinia hurried to them in time to hear Yasir whisper, "Do not be afraid, you are going to Bramley House. Stay there with Nanny." With a little squeal, James vanished. She stared at the spot where he had been, occupied now by an agitated Peter who kept pointing at Stuart.

Thank God, her younger son was safe. She watched Stuart, still in the clutches of the cat man, eyes hollow, seeming to focus on nothing. Did he even see what was going on? She didn't think he had used any magic. Why not? He was competent, especially for a seven-year-old.

At a burst of light, she flicked her gaze from Stuart in the cat man's wiry arms to Rakhshan, who clutched his chest, head bowed. Yasir had attacked the magician. Behind him a black cat arched its back, hissing.

"Mum!" Stuart collided with her, almost knocking her off her feet. She hugged him. Peter loomed over them and motioned for Yasir.

In a blur, the djinni appeared beside Stuart and whispered in his ear, his hand in the same position as when he sent James away. In a few seconds, her son would be safe.

She saw Rakhshan raise his head. Slip his hand up his sleeve and whip out a wand. .

"Yasir!" Lavinia screamed.

The djinni shielded them with his body. He spread his hand. A flash of gold shot from his fingers, meeting the red burst of light from the Shadow Lord's wand.

Each levered their magic, muscles straining as the power receded on one side, surged on the other. The magician's light grew deep red, held from going further by the djinni's glowing gold. Was Yasir winning? She couldn't tell.

Stuart stood transfixed.

Yasir brought down his hand.

Spots of light appeared on the ground next to the djinni, ringing around him in a complete circle. Before Lavinia could blink, the lights grew tall and broad, and over a dozen Yasirs stood in the circle, all identical. By his position, she could tell which was truly Yasir.

The djinnis traded places, moving as if in a waltz. She tried to keep her eye on the one that had slipped from Yasir's spot. Clasping her hands in frustration, she felt a slow smile spread on her face at the magician's puzzled expression.

As one, the djinnis stared at the Shadow Lord.

"By God, I can't tell which is Yasir." Peter squinted at the circle. "We are too close. Lavy take Stuart."

Lavinia pulled her son away and they fled behind a tree at an angle to the circle, just as Rakhshan raised his wand again.

Red light shot out at every djinni. They sidestepped the rays. In unison, each one faced the magician. Each one raised his hands. Each one recited the same spell. Gold rays grew from their fingers, meeting in a concentrated beam that sped towards Rakhshan, tearing into him.

"Well played, Yasir," Lavinia whispered as she exhaled. The Shadow Lord crossed his arms above his head, howling in rage. Bright red flared into the golden flames. The searing heat and glare made her turn her head. She held Stuart tight, cowering behind the tree, Peter taking them both in his arms.

When she saw the reflection of the light dim, she dared look. A receding wall of flames roared where Rakhshan had stood. The magician couldn't possibly have survived. Yet the djinnis peered into the blaze, a crease between their eyebrows.

The flames changed color, growing higher. Then, without warning, they erupted into a fiery ball of red, which roared into the djinnis, engulfing the front three.

"Yasir!" Lavinia screeched, her voice lost in the ear-splitting roar of the conflagration.

The djinnis flung out their arms, writhing in silence as they twisted into grotesque burnt shapes. Horrified at the gruesome scene, she put her hand over Stuart's eyes, but he pushed it away. She heard Peter, behind her, breathing hard. He had already used his pistol. There was nothing he could do.

Looking through her fingers, she saw the fireball recede into a small deep blue sphere. The remaining djinnis stood still, faces and tunics reflecting blue as they closed the gap in their circle.

He had to be alive. Lavinia clutched Stuart to her side as Rakhshan strode through the cold blue glow.

Peter inhaled, abrupt and short. He gathered them close. She felt his chest muscles tighten. He was afraid, and Peter was no coward. She wished she were in the urn, in her bedroom, even in Peter's study, anywhere away from this brutish magician.

Rakhshan chanted, an ominous rhythm that blackened the sky as if it were the deep of night, not mid-morning. The sound droned into her, making her mouth dry with the terror of what was coming.

The ruby in his turban flared. The djinnis faded in and out, their gold rays diminishing. Rakhshan's chant grew louder. The djinnis became mere ghosts, fleeting gold shadows.

All but one.

Yasir stood alone.

She staggered, and felt Peter lean into them, felt his long exhale of relief.

Rakhshan held out his wand. In the broad path of the wand's red light, the grass waving in the wind wilted into dry stalks and blew away, bushes shriveled into brittle sticks clattering in the breeze. Thinning into a point, the light pierced Yasir in the shoulder, the same place Peter had shot him with the cursed bullet.

Lavinia's cry caught in her throat.

Stuart yelled, "Sam!" and pulled away from her.

Peter let go of them both. He ran to Yasir, who stood still, a stillness that was all wrong, as if he had left his body then and there. The djinni's pupils grew round and black with only a small edge of the iris's gold. He arched his back, his head almost touching the ground.

"Yes, gather round to see the djinni's demise." Rakhshan took in Yasir's suffering with a perverted eagerness.

Reeling at Yasir's inhuman posture, Lavinia clutched the tree trunk, praying that the djinni would recover and blast the magician. Yasir's round pupils contracted to the thinnest vertical slits. He fell to the ground.

"Yasir, Yasir," she whispered over and over. When she reached him, his golden eyes had dulled. Stuart and Peter knelt, touching Yasir, murmuring to him, to each other, looking lost.

Cupping her hands as Mehadeh had shown her, Lavinia said the words: "Yasir, *der bedn, rewh w rewan, shema ma shefa khewahed.*"

A force moved through her body, even stronger than when Mehadeh directed it inside her. She saw it flow into Yasir. She didn't know how, the magic was truly invisible, yet she saw the waves of energy penetrating the flesh of the djinni's human form.

Then, so fast she couldn't grasp it, everything happened at once. She couldn't have told which occurred first or last or middle, the events became such a jumble.

Yasir's eyes fluttered open, the gold shining like a newly wrought coin.

Lavinia glimpsed Stuart running in front of Rakhshan. In a blur, her son held out his hands. She remembered seeing his face distort in concentration, seeing Stuart's magic in the same way she had seen Mehadeh's spell work on Yasir. All of it happened faster than she could take in, like the mercurial speed of Yasir's incomprehensible moves.

"So it is *you*," Rakhshan rasped. He fell to his knees, his hands at his throat.

Stuart puffed out his chest. She saw a cloud gathering before him. Fear took her breath until she realized it was a cloud of magic pouring into him—strong magic. His eyes shone. He made a quick gesture, so like his father, Yasir.

Rakhshan raised one knee, planting his foot on the ground. He was trying to stand, but she could see in the paleness of his face, his weakening. His chest met his thigh, his head hanging like a wilted flower on a limp stem. *Had she glimpsed his hand—shaking—reach out, raise his wand slowly?*

Puzzled, she bit her lip and studied him carefully. But no, the magician was in the same position, his head still bent in defeat. No wand in either hand.

With a burst of pride, Lavinia beamed at her elder son. He was so brave.

Stuart held out his arms. She could see the magic building. He opened his mouth, his eyes staring. Grasping his stomach, he lurched towards Rakhshan who still knelt on one knee.

Stuart crumpled before him.

She must've called Stuart's name. She was still kneeling by Yasir, when the djinni rose, strong magic surrounding him. Had Yasir been running to his son when the boy sent Rakhshan staggering from his first blow?

Lavinia saw the energy leave Yasir. A golden beam encircled Stuart, who rose like a phoenix, glowing in his father's magic.

Yasir gestured.

Stuart vanished.

The djinni sought her with his eyes and stared into hers—his promise that he would fight Rakhshan in place of his son. Stuart, who was prophesied to defeat the Shadow Lord, would stay out of this battle.

How could she tell Yasir this was all wrong now—that his son should stay? But Yasir's magic proved strong enough to save Stuart. Perhaps the djinni could be victorious.

Yasir turned his gaze to the magician, who stumbled to his feet.

Now would be the time to attack Rakhshan. If only she had another spell from Mehadeh, a spell without limitation. No one would expect anything from her. It would be a complete surprise.

The djinni's chest rose and fell as he brought his arm up.

Lavinia scrambled to her feet, hand upon her heart. A pain lurked there, a fist slowly compressing inside her. An awful foreboding. She inclined towards Yasir. Was that a slight tremble in his arm? An odd slouch to his shoulders, his stance somehow off? She squeezed her hands. Then she understood.

When she had healed Yasir with Mehadeh's spell, it gave Yasir a surplus of strength so he could defeat Rakhshan. But the djinni had used all of it to heal Stuart.

Now Yasir was weak.

And Rakhshan knew it.

The magician was on his feet, a bit unsteady, but his hand grasped his wand—a firm strong grip. Stuart's magic had only temporarily weakened the Shadow Lord.

In a rapid motion, Rakhshan pointed the wand at Yasir.

That moment, the sunlight disappeared. The shadows darkened. Birdsong ceased.

Lavinia could see every detail of those left, as if each one had become a statue, as if she were leisurely viewing them in a museum. Rakhshan, the ruby glinting in his aigrette, the cold hard determination in his dark eyes. Yasir, the weakening glow of his golden aura, the clench of his jaw. Peter, standing to the side in the shade of the trees, the bloodstains on his blue coat darkened to black, mouth in a grim line as he stared at the standoff.

Like a hawk plunging for prey, Rakhshan brought down the wand.

A blur of blue shot from the side, pushing in front of the djinni, pushing Yasir out of the trajectory.

Peter!

Lavinia watched in horror as Rakhshan's magic struck her husband. Thin wavy lines of red light encircled his leg, crackling like tinder catching on the hearth.

Peter screamed. He landed crossways over Yasir, his leg twitching.

What in heaven's name was her husband thinking?

Heedless of Rakhshan, Lavinia rushed to them. Peter lay face down on top of Yasir. He had taken only part of the magician's blow, magic meant for a powerful djinni. Was her husband dead?

She could see Yasir's face, and part of his chest. His eyes were closed.

"Peter." She shook her husband. He felt hot. He didn't move. She put her fingers on Yasir's neck—a faint pulse, irregular as always.

"Peter." She shook him again. He turned his head to her, his light blue eyes as blank as Cybelle's dolly's.

A rustle, a ghostly touch, the breath of a phantom—Lavinia looked behind her.

Rakhshan held his wand above his head. The Shadow Lord could destroy Yasir now with only a paltry spell. Could destroy them all in one arc of his hand.

"Peter, command Yasir to the urn," she said in a desperate whisper. Could Peter understand her? Could he speak?

"Now!"

"Ya-Yashir." Peter slurred the words. "Go. Urn." His eyes fluttered closed.

Yasir's body faded, then vanished from underneath her husband, and Peter sank slowly to the ground.

50

*S*omething drained out of Lavinia when Yasir vanished before her eyes. She couldn't put a name to it. Only that the hollowness inside her dulled the sheer terror she should have felt at being left alone with Rakhshan.

Her husband, unconscious, possibly dying, was the only one in the whole world between her and the Dark Magician. She could feel Rakhshan lurking behind her.

"Peter." Lavinia heard the wobble in her voice. He didn't respond. He lay as he had fallen, on his stomach. The cloth of his trousers on one leg was torn and the flesh was raw and cut in a fashion she had never seen. She knelt and put her cheek near his mouth, his breath a ghost touch on her skin.

With a grunt, she heaved him on his side, his arm, pierced by the bullet, facing up. Avoiding touching his sleeve where his blue coat was bloodstained, she slid both her arms under his back, and lay him down as gently as she could. He breathed easier, but didn't open his eyes.

The front of his leg and part of his chest were covered with cuts and burns, some deep and clotted with blood, cloth and dirt. She wanted to brush the dirt away, but needed soap, water, medicine and bandages.

She closed her eyes, trying to feel for the magic from Mehadeh's healing spell. A wisp of something rose in her like a curl of smoke. She formed her hands in a cup and said the words again, using Peter's name this time:

"Peter, *der bedn, rewh w rewan, shema ma shefa khewahed.*"

His complexion dulled, his face becoming a shadow.

She exhaled, feeling herself deflating, growing smaller as Rakhshan's presence loomed large behind her. Mehadeh's spell wasn't working. The sorceress had implied that it was limited when she had said, 'use this spell wisely.' It had only worked once. Done and finished.

She looked past the stretch of barren ground next to her husband, inwardly flinching at her thought that it looked like a patch cleared for a grave. Beyond, the trees tossed in the breeze, while behind her she could still feel Rakhshan's sinister magic like a gathering storm. Any minute his hand might grip her shoulder and take her prisoner—or worse.

She brushed at her torso, her head, trying to bat away the midges that swarmed around her in a twist of black funnels. When she blinked, they vanished, but she still felt them sucking at her thoughts, at her hollow insides. She sighed, weary and worn. Of course, there were no midges, only the malicious power of Rakhshan. Oh, how she wanted to flee. But she wouldn't abandon her husband to the Dark Magician.

Peter hadn't moved. Lavinia feared to check his pulse or his breath. She couldn't bear it if he had . . . She wouldn't even think it. At least her children were safe. That is all she would have asked, had she known it would come to this. And Yasir was in the urn, but the last she saw of him, he was injured as badly as Peter.

She would have to face Rakhshan.

Alone.

In her panic, she had demanded that Peter send Yasir to the urn. How could she have been so foolish? She should have had Peter command Yasir to take all three of them to the urn. Dear God, had she killed her husband by her rash, unthinking request?

It was too late now.

The enchantment of the Shadow Lord coiled slowly about her, a serpent readying to shape her to his ends. She lurched to her feet and faced him. He stood tall, broader than she recalled, his indigo robes blowing in the breeze, a majestic figure in his silk brocade turban, his dark ruby aigrette, his ropes of luminous pearls.

"What shall I do with the both of you, now that Lord Bramley is master of the djinni?" He set his mouth as if he were choosing delicacies for his meal. So, Rakhshan had heard her tell Peter to send Yasir to the urn.

Rakhshan wouldn't need to work to obtain what he wanted. He could easily force Peter to call Yasir. She fingered her ruby ring from the djinni. If only she could summon him, but she wasn't master anymore. Her ring was merely a keepsake. Useless now.

But Peter had no ring.

Lavinia could barely breathe for the weight that pressed her chest with this realization. Peter needed the urn to summon Yasir. Why hadn't she remembered this before? She blocked her mind as she did with Alice to keep her from prying; forced her alarmed expression, her tensed body into a normal pose, but saw a flash of recognition in Rakhshan's eyes. Had he read her thoughts, even as she put up her defenses?

The magician gazed at her, disgust souring his expression. "Your husband has made you useless to me."

Apparently Rakhshan still thought Peter could call Yasir. She knelt, put her hand on Peter's chest. Thank God, he was still breathing. She slipped her ring off and put it in his pocket. Bending down, she whispered in his ear. "Peter, you were transported to the urn with my ring. The ring is in your pocket now. Do the same as you did then and call Yasir so he can save us." She kissed his cheek because she cared for him, because Rakshan would be more suspicious otherwise.

She looked the Dark Magician in the eye. He had just said that Peter had made her useless to him. She summoned what courage she could, replying. "And you have made my husband useless. Heal him, or he's no good to anyone."

Rakhshan pulled his wand from his sleeve. Lavinia cringed. He waved it over Peter. Would he heal him or do some dastardly magic?

"Lord Bramley will fetch the urn. It might be his last act. He is not looking well." The Dark Magician's lips quirked into a semblance of a smile as he watched her husband.

Peter rolled onto his hands and knees. He retched, then looked at her and shook his head.

Yasir hadn't answered his call.

She prayed it was because she wasn't master as when the ring worked for Peter. The other reason, that Yasir wasn't healed, or worse, she put out of her mind.

"If you heal him, I will come with you," she said to Rakhshan. That was all she had to offer. Herself. She had refused Peter's plan to put the djinni out of their lives. If she had accepted, they would be at Bramley House enjoying luncheon, the urn banished for good, the little ones safe.

Peter opened his mouth, tried to form words, but no sound came, and she couldn't tell what he wanted to say.

Rakhshan scowled at her. "You offer me nothing I cannot easily take. When I finish here, you will come with me, happy to be by my side." He flicked his wand at her husband.

Peter stood, jerking like a marionette. He hung there, arms at odd angles, feet turned out as if he were indeed dangling by a puppet's strings.

The Dark Magician mumbled something. Peter stood straight. His complexion grew pinker. He blinked. Shook his head.

"You will bring the urn to me. Do you understand?" Rakhshan looked into Peter's eyes. Peter nodded, but his face stayed stiff, the expression still dazed.

"When you are holding the urn, you will not open it. Yasir is your enemy." Rakhshan's voice was mesmerizing. Lavinia focused on Peter, trying to keep the magician's words from going round and round inside her head, working their malicious magic.

"When I wave my wand, you will be at Bramley House. Find the urn. When you have it, you will be transported back to me. Do you understand?"

Peter bobbed his head. He stared at Lavinia. With his puzzled expression, those fish eyes, he resembled a ghoulish version of himself.

The Shadow Lord had gotten into Peter's mind. He would destroy him. She thought of Yasir. It had all seemed so wonderful, a tale of true romance and magic. But the urn both blessed and cursed. Did it take vengeance on anyone who was master?

Rakhshan flourished his wand over Peter, then suddenly leaned forward, eyes intent on something behind her. Had Yasir returned? Relief flooded through her, but she feared to look. So many disappointments.

The Dark Lord could be tempting her, deflecting her attention from Peter so he could commit some horrible act. She kept her eyes on both of them.

"Mother, tend to father." The words rang out, familiar. Words spoken to her. Words that could not, should not be in this place.

Filled with dread, Lavinia dared look to the voice.

Stuart stood there, his dark curly hair mussed, his shirt untucked. Here where he should not be. He must have revived, found his magic again, for him to appear at the river so soon after Yasir had sent him to Bramley House.

She glanced at Rakhshan, who moved closer, eyes glittering with intent, focused on her son.

"H-help," Peter cried as he walked with stiff jerky movements to Stuart. Legs and arms twitching, he vomited, spewing bile and blood.

She saw her son's energy surround her husband. In seconds, Peter's face slackened, the awful distortion gone, and he slumped gently to the ground.

"He can't be your errand boy now." Stuart met Rakhshan's gaze, eyes defiant.

The magician reached into his sleeve.

"Run!" Lavinia pushed her son away.

Stuart moved like Yasir. His body almost obscured by his speed, he tore down the slope and vanished into the woods. As she turned to face Rakhshan, she saw a blur from the corner of her eye. Her son appeared on the hillcrest, hands on his hips. He looked down at Rakhshan.

"Come and face me." Stuart's young voice boomed over the riverside.

"I'm here to avenge my true father."

51

"So you have returned." Rakhshan spoke in a measured tone, which didn't match his suddenly straight back, his piercing stare. Was he concerned that Stuart could harm him? The magician knew of the prophecy, had said it amounted to little, but took it as a personal threat.

"It is my calling to be here." Stuart vanished from the hilltop and appeared next to Lavinia.

She placed herself between them, and considered carefully what she would say. "You want the djinni, not my seven-year-old son. Wake my husband, he can get the urn—"

"Enough of your words. The boy is clearly magic and he will be ruined by it." Rakhshan's bitter inflection surged with power, scrambling her thoughts, her schemes to save Stuart. He leveled his wand at her son.

Saints and Angels, this vile magician intended to fight Stuart.

"He is merely a boy, being brave for his mother. Surely you don't mean to harm a child? Why, he . . ." Lavinia gasped for breath as Rakhshan's magic sucked the air from around her. A green glow appeared on the scuffed dirt separating them and the magician. She took Stuart's hand.

The glow expanded like the molten bubble on a glass blower's stick. She could see Rakhshan distorted through it. He brandished his wand.

At a brilliant flash, she shut her eyes, the green luminescence coloring the darkness inside her lids. A pain zagged through her head, fierce and penetrating. Stuart's hand fell from hers. Had Rakhshan struck her? Had he hit Stuart?

She opened her eyes.

Cybelle stood before her, her little pink shoe untied, the matching shoelace trailing across the bare dirt. She hugged a soldier doll to her pink pinafore—James's only toy with magic. Somehow the toy must have transported her here.

Lavinia glanced at Rakhshan. His mouth had turned down. He hadn't moved, and held the wand in the same position. So he saw Cybelle as well. Surely he wouldn't hurt a three-year-old.

Cybelle held out her arms and walked to her. Eyeing Rakhshan, Lavinia scooped her daughter up, her knees almost buckling in relief.

"Mother, take Cybelle home. I will tend to father." Stuart positioned himself in front of her, his black curls blown behind him in a burst of breeze, so like Yasir's.

"Stuart, come with me. Your father didn't want this. He promised to fight in your place. You need to know that." How could she convince him? How could she save him with Cybelle in her arms? *Oh Lord, please don't make her have to choose between her children.*

"My father, Lord Bramley, cannot fight this magician. He is not magic." Stuart's voice dripped with disdain.

Lavinia felt as if she were shrinking. She and Yasir had been careful, too careful, so Peter wouldn't suspect. And they had neglected telling their son the truth, but now Stuart knew. "I am not a fool. I suspected. After this you *will* tell me why you lied to me all this time." Stuart kept his eyes fixed on Rakhshan.

Lavinia startled at Rakhshan's voice blaring through her thoughts, so much so that she missed his first words. "—that is perfectly fine. Spend as much time as you need to untangle your family problems. I will wait and take your son when he understands fully who he is." The Shadow Lord crossed his arms, his mirth evident in his light tone of voice, his almost gleeful expression.

Lavinia ignored the magician and spoke directly to Stuart. "We didn't lie, we did all this to save you—"

"Save me from this moment? Well, here I am, all alone, doing what you lied to try and save me from." Stuart didn't turn, didn't look at her, which was wise since she saw Rakhshan preparing to strike.

"Before you and Yasir muck things up any more than they are, take Cybelle and leave." Stuart made a swatting gesture behind his back.

Her body was forced backwards, so that she and Cybelle ended up downhill from Stuart. The boy's magic had grown. She didn't have any idea what he could do.

Rakhshan, a broad smile creasing his face, called out, "Yes, leave with the baby. Stuart will come with me and learn great things. He will be famous for his deeds and magic." She heard the Dark Magician as clearly as if he stood before her. And, as if she were still close by, saw him bend to his knee and lean forward, the ruby in his aigrette eye level with Stuart. The gem detached and floated in front of her son.

"Take it. The stone will give you greater power than you ever imagined. Now that you know who you are, you can choose who you will be." Rakhshan's voice had the same hypnotic quality that had affected her before. What must it do to a young boy?

Stuart spat on the ruby. It sped back to Rakhshan and reset into his aigrette.

"So it will have to be a grander gift." The magician stood and gestured. A magnificent white stallion appeared before him, tossing its long mane. With a loud whoosh, great wings of white feathers unfolded from its back. The creature trotted to Stuart, who scowled and held up his palm. The stallion faded before it reached him.

Fumbling, Rakhshan plucked at the ruby in his turban, but jerked his hands away as if the stone were on fire. His face twisted into a grimace of pain.

"You poisoned my ruby," the Dark Magician said through gritted teeth. With great effort, as if some force resisted him, he raised his left hand to his turban, grasped the ruby, and plucked it from the gold setting. He threw it to the ground.

At the sharp cracking sound, Lavinia clutched Cybelle and yelled a warning to Stuart. The jewel broke apart into hundreds of glinting red splinters.

"You dare spurn my gift and turn it upon me." Rakhshan inclined his head at the winking shards. They rose in an arrow formation and shot into Stuart's chest. He screamed. Dots of blood stained his shirt. Squirming in agony, he splayed his hand on his chest and sank to the ground.

"Now, you will come with me." Rakhshan gestured and Stuart sat up. The boy slumped, bracing his hands on the dirt and looked away from the Shadow Lord.

Cybelle wriggled in Lavinia's arms. The little girl threw the soldier doll down, thrashing wildly in her mother's grip.

"Cybie, no!" Lavinia held onto her child with all her strength, but Cybelle wrenched loose and tumbled out of her arms. The little girl picked her doll and darted up the hill to her brother.

Would Rakhshan dare hurt a toddler? *But this was Yasir's toddler.*

"Leave them alone. She's just a baby," Lavinia shrieked as she ran to Cybelle. She reached for her child, but suddenly found herself further down the hill than before. She couldn't see any of them. The forest on either side crept closer, dark with shadows from the sun high overhead.

Lavinia ran her finger across her ruby ring. Three times. If she wished for Yasir hard enough, he might appear. The wind ruffled the trees, the shadows moving as if they were reaching for her. A noise buzzed in her ears, that of thousands of feet marching. She shook her head. The sound vanished into complete silence. She looked up the hill. Were her children dead?

What could she do? How could she save them? She looked for something to use as a weapon while she ran up the incline, her feet sinking, the ground siphoning her strength. Running, running, yet still in the same place. When she at last crested the hill, Stuart was standing alongside his baby sister, both of them facing Rakhshan.

Stuart looked at Cybelle. Their blue eyes locked. Their little faces tightened, and they thrust their chests out. The wind blew hard from the river, roaring as before a storm, bringing the biting smell of rain. With a banshee moan, a cloud of dust foaming with bits of leaves and detritus gusted through, propelling a black scarf, which snaked above their heads, a harbinger of doom.

She saw her children as they were in other times, as they progressed in age: twelve, eighteen, thirty, forty, sixty. Their changing faces shimmered into view, then faded into new versions: older, wiser countenances with exotic headdresses, jeweled crowns and tall polychromed hats from other lands, other eras.

She could sense them communing, feel centuries of wisdom, of power, emanate from their aspects. But something pulled her away from this radiant vision. She looked past them at Rakhshan. The magician's eyes fell on her youngest and oldest. Menacing evil eyes that showed no mercy.

Why wasn't Yasir here to save his babies? A pall spread over the riverside, shrouding them in dead air, stagnant and musty, as if they had been entombed. Not a leaf or blade of grass moved.

Lavinia found it hard to breathe. Would this be the end of her children? She tried to run to them, tried to throw herself between them and Rakhshan, but was pinioned to the ground, heavy as a stone statue.

Stuart raised his hand. Cybelle mimicked him.

Stuart dropped his arm. As though she were attached, Cybelle's arm went down simultaneously with his.

Lavinia moved her eyes from her children to Rakhshan. A flash of red sparked from his wand. She screamed.

Stuart jumped in front of Cybelle. The light penetrated her son. He jerked, more blood stained his shirt. Cybelle rushed to him and placed her pudgy fingers on the wound.

Her brother straightened, face beaming. They held hands, swung their arms out, meeting Rakhshan's next volley. Green light slammed into red, an emerald shaft breaking away from them and extending to the magician.

Rakhshan clamped his hands on his solar plexus. His mouth hung open. With the thunderous crash of an ocean smashing against a seawall, his body bowed as if blown by a gale. But his arm reached out, wand extended, red light flaring.

The muscles in his face clenched, then relaxed as if he had exhaled. Arms askew, he flew backwards towards the river, chanting his evil magic.

Lavinia saw Cybelle hunched over, hands across her chest, mouth open in a scream, Stuart wrapped in swirling red light. Then everything distorted, and Lavinia was swept away by the same force as Rakhshan.

She called to her daughter and son, but her cry became lost in the clamor of wind and magic. It took all of her strength to remain upright and not to be tossed head over heels in the gale. In spite of her struggle, Lavinia was dragged after Rakhshan. She saw him fall off the edge of the bank, plunging into the river, arms and legs straight by his side as though he were bound. He vanished underwater.

Still fighting, she was pushed to the river. No! She couldn't swim. The water had swallowed the magician. It would engulf her as well. She would drown, her body swept downstream. Before she reached the drop off, Lavinia flung herself onto the ground, landing hard in the dirt at the edge of the bank. She dug her fingers into the soil, but the wind had died and the earth held her to its bosom.

From her position, she could see where Rakhshan went under. The water fountained—rising, splashing, louder and higher, magnified by aberrant forces, then fell back into the swirling surface. Gray bubbles erupted from the spot, blowing towards her on the breeze where they burst, letting off a foul smell. As if heralded by the odor, the Dark Lord bobbed to the surface like something rotten repelled by the river bottom.

He floated, face up. Pale, rigid and unmoving.

A cloud of green light hovered over the Shadow Lord. With a weak flick of his wrist, a fiery red beam shot from his wand, but ricocheted off the green cloud.

Lavinia lay on the ground, transfixed. The red shaft, Rakhshan's own magic, stabbed into his chest without a sound.

His mouth opened, as soundless as the beam that pierced him. Then the scream reached her. She scrambled to put her hands over her ears, but the shrill cry dove into her as if she too had been pierced by the red bolt of magic. The cold mud on her hands made her shiver when she covered her ears.

Rakhshan's face distorted in agony, his mouth frozen in the rictus of his scream as he floated into a stronger current. Faster and faster he circled, blue robes trailing in his wake until she could see only a blur of indigo and muddy foam.

Then nothing was there.

Only the river flowing past, glinting jade and turquoise, dark cobalt patches where the current ran deeper, as if Lavinia had imagined the entire scene.

She exhaled, not realizing until then that she had held her breath. Slowly, slowly, she lifted her hands from her ears, wincing at the memory of the harrowing sound. Stepping back from the ledge, she watched the river—flowing as it had for centuries, witnessing lovers on the bank, witnessing the urn sinking into the turquoise and aqua of its depths, witnessing her fight with Meylo for the vessel.

The flowing river, mute through life's impossibilities.

Small white crests rose and fell in the swift current in the middle. A chill shivered through her. She wrapped her arms around herself, fingers scraping through the cold dirt on her clothes.

Was Rakhshan truly gone? A string of birdsong brought her to her senses. Peter lay back there somewhere.

Then she was running.

Her baby girl! Her son!

She rushed down the bank and up the hill, but they were nowhere to be seen. She turned around and around. Only the green grass blowing in the breeze, the dark forest, silent but for the birds, the dull sound of the river flowing, flowing. Always flowing.

Please no, they have to be here. Rakhshan couldn't have sent them to his palace. Couldn't have killed them.

The ground moved away from her before she realized she had been lifted off her feet. Had the Shadow Lord returned? She tried to get her bearing as her speed picked up, but she was moving too fast.

Not for the first time, she empathized with James—enough of this magic. Was Rakhshan taking her prisoner again, only this time with her children by Yasir?

She stopped moving, but all was a blur around her. Gently, gently she was set down upon a grassy bank. Two forms fuzzed into shape. Was there a third, dark figure?

The two shapes became blobs of color, then gained in size, sharpening as they came nearer. Cybelle, her other shoe untied, held out her arms.

"Cybelle, Cybelle." She lifted her little girl in a joyous embrace, pressing her sturdy body close, smelling the bird's nest scent of her midnight-black curls. "Cybie, did you do magic?"

Cybelle leveled her gaze at her mother, her lapis eyes unblinking, her Cupid's bow mouth neither turned down nor up. She rubbed her eye with one chubby fist, the other still holding James's doll.

She hadn't had her nap today. Lavinia shook her head at the nonsensical thought.

Her son had hung back, waiting, but now Stuart ran to them, and threw his arms around her legs. "Mother, do not think we left you. We watched. Made sure you were safe. We brought you here."

"Stuart." She shifted Cybelle to her hip and ran her hand over his bloody shirt, his head, searching for wounds. "Are you hurt?"

He puffed out his chest. "Good as new, Mum."

They stood on the hillock facing the river. Cybelle lay in Lavinia's arms, head upon her shoulder, thumb in mouth, cuddling the soldier doll. Stuart leaned against her, his hand on his little sister's arm.

Lavinia studied her children. Both watched the water, a glum expression on their faces. What went through their minds? The minds of these magic beings who defeated their father's nemesis.

52

anny, I'm keeping her with me." Lavinia didn't know if she'd ever be ready to let go of her little girl. She almost lost her today, along with her brother.

She looked down at Cybelle, cradled in her arms, deep in a dream. Her tiny pink mouth puckered as she suckled at an imaginary teat. She slowed, sucked vigorously and stopped, mouth parted. Her face stayed smooth and soft, no frown marred her brow or cry disturbed her lips. It was a wonder the child wasn't thrashing about and screaming after what she'd been through.

Stuart had tried to transport them to Bramley House, but the poor boy was simply too exhausted to work that kind of magic, or to heal Peter. He confessed that when he first returned to the river, he made his father pass out rather than send him home because he didn't know how much magic he had, or how much he needed to fight Rakhshan.

Her son insisted on walking back, getting help. She and Cybelle stayed to watch over Peter. Lavinia had tried to wake him, but hadn't gotten so much as a mumble or flicker of an eyelid.

As she waited, her mind explored different scenarios if someone didn't come for them soon. Peter dying right at her feet, Rakhshan somehow returning, finding them helpless and finishing Peter off, then Cybelle and her. She tried to stop the thoughts, but they kept worsening. Cybelle squirmed in her arms.

"Do you want down, Cybie?" But the child gestured and frowned in the direction of the forest. A puff of dust rose over the trees.

Had Stuart revived, magjicked his way to Bramley House, and sent a coach for them, so soon? Or was this Saddani or another of Rakhshan's minions? She shifted Cybelle's weight to her left arm. If it came to it, she would abandon Peter to save Cybelle. Perhaps she should run deep into the forest now. Rakhshan wouldn't hurt Peter, for Peter was master and knew the location of the urn.

A dusty brown cloud appeared in front of them, brightening in the center. Lavinia backed away, tightening her hold on Cybelle, but the shape, growing larger, followed. Cybelle thrust her arm out, index finger straight. A burst of green light shot from her fingertip.

The brown mass shifted and Cybelle's magic passed to the side.

"Cybelle, it is I, your Auntie Alice," a voice said. The brightness scattered into the golden flecks of Alice's brown eyes. A shiver rippled through the brown shape like a bird shifting its feathers, and Alice stood before them. She offered her great niece a plump white rabbit with pink ears, breathtakingly real looking, although Lavinia saw that it was painted fabric, stuffed and cleverly sewn. Cybelle hugged her soldier doll and turned her head into her mother's shoulder.

"Well, we have our preferences now, do we?" Alice patted the child on the back and whispered to Lavinia. "A bribe to stop spontaneous, fear-induced magic. Unfortunately, a bit late. Luckily, I am agile." She pitched the rabbit into the air, where it turned into a dandelion puff.

Cybelle stretched and held out her hand, opening and closing her fist as the seed heads floated through her tiny fingers like feathery inverted umbrellas.

Alice cocked her head, her expression a bit aghast. "Nia, you two look as if you've been wrestling in the mud." She squinted, her eyes glinting under her lids.

Lavinia shivered at the cool breeze on her bare skin as her tattered clothes vanished, then flinched as a corset and petticoat bound her again. A light blue dress, tucked and gathered in the latest fashion, replaced her dirt-covered, ripped gown. Cybelle wriggled, then grinned as she admired her new pink dress and matching ruffled pantaloons, her pink shoes tied neatly. "Now that little trifle is out of the way."

I was half-way home in my coach, which is now almost to Bramley House, and experienced the most distressing vision." She glanced down at Peter. "I see that it was accurate."

Alice knelt beside him, her hands moving above his body, their shadows on his coat and breeches changing from purple to orange to yellow. "What made the man think he could take a blow meant for a djinni?"

Lavinia started to answer, but realized Alice was just muttering to herself. But then, why *did* Peter jump in front of Yasir? Could it be her husband truly loved the djinni? Just as she did.

"It is a wonder he survived," Alice continued in that low tone. "Breathing better than a few seconds ago. Brain working, but barely, and in a hidden realm. An imprudent action. A departure from our old Peter."

Alice reached into her reticule, pulled out a red stone—a ruby?— crushed it in her palm and sprinkled the dust on Peter. Each speck flashed bright red when it landed on his body, then in a whoosh that sent Lavinia a step back, the specks flared as one.

"Peter!" She hiked Cybelle further up her hip, and reached with one hand to the flames covering his body. Alice knocked her arm away.

"No, Nia. Just for Peter." Her aunt stood between them, blocking her.

Lavinia tried to push Alice aside. "He's burning. What are you doing? He tried to save Yasir. He didn't—"

"This is a healing light, not truly a fire. It just takes the form of fire in this demesne. Harmless." Alice looked down as the flames subsided. She marched Lavinia a few yards away.

"Here, I'll take Cybelle." Her aunt braced the child on her waist, and held her in place with one arm. "Now, sit beside Peter and lay your right hand on his chest. We must join my coach when it arrives at Bramley House. Whatever happens do not move your hand. We cannot lose your husband in the ether." She watched Lavinia closely. "Nia, you have the most peculiar expression."

Of course she had a peculiar expression. Alice had terrified them with her dramatic appearance, then stated that Peter's consciousness was in a hidden realm. She hadn't mentioned Yasir. And now these odd instructions with a threat of losing Peter in the ether. Lavinia held her hand in place on Peter's chest. She could barely feel the faint rise and fall of his breathing.

All that had happened pressed upon her. She inhaled long and deep with a keening noise, but still couldn't get enough air. She dared not move and be the final cause of his demise.

"The Shadow Lord found out Peter was master," Lavinia said, wondering if her aunt already knew.

"How did he discover that?" Alice sounded worried.

"I-I asked Peter to send Yasir to the urn. He-he . . ." It all became a jumble, what each person had done, why they did it, where they were. Where was Peter? He was here, but not here. If only he would open his eyes.

She felt a pull. Alice. Staring at her. Lavinia opened her eyes and continued, afraid Peter might worsen if they didn't hurry to Bramley House.

"Yasir was hurt. Hurt horribly by the Dark Magician. It was the only way I could think to save him. Peter barely got the words out, but Yasir vanished. And the Shadow Lord heard." Lavinia bowed her head.

Peter's complexion had paled.

Alice gave a little harrumph. "Never mind all that. When I raise my arm we will appear inside my coach, which will just have arrived at Bramley House. The footman will act accordingly. Keep your hand on Peter."

Since yesterday, when they arrived from the riverside, Peter had been in his bed, unresponsive. Lavinia insisted on staying in his room, and had Dobson serve their afternoon tea, with enough for Peter in case he woke up.

"He is not improving, but he is not worsening, either." Alice took Lavinia's hand. "I have not remarked upon it, but I must see Yasir."

Lavinia turned away, pretending as she looked out the window that things were as they had been days before—no cat man, no confrontations at the river. She hadn't wanted to ask, was afraid to even broach the subject of Yasir with her aunt. But Alice didn't know the most important thing.

"Alice, Stuart and Cybelle killed the Shadow Lord."

"I saw that in my vision. I am surprised you did not mention it earlier. The strong magic bandied about delayed my coming to assist." Alice placed her teacup on the table amongst the cucumber sandwiches and sugar biscuits.

Lavinia tapped her fingers on her mouth. Alice had a no-nonsense manner today, more than usual, which meant she would be terse and stingy with answers. Still, Lavinia had to know.

"Shouldn't Yasir be free, now that the Dark Magician is dead? Shouldn't Yasir be here with us? He could heal Peter." Lavinia watched Alice for any sign that might show she was keeping secrets.

Her aunt tapped her foot on the floor, staring at her brown satin slipper.

"Yes, Nia, that is how it was supposed to happen. That is what Yasir believed. That is what he kept saying. Kill the magician and the curse will be nullified. But things change." Alice's eyes filled with the despair in her voice.

Her aunt had almost whispered the last three words, as if she didn't want to put them into the world, to make them come into the realm of possibility.

Alice leaned close, her eyes bright. Did her aunt have a solution, a special magic for this? "What did you do with the Shadow Lord's body? Did Stuart and Cybelle destroy it?"

Lavinia sat still. Her face burned. The heat traveled to her neck, her arms. The feeling that she had done something terribly wrong, something that ruined everything, poured over her. "The magician was in the river. The current took him. He started spinning and . . ."

Angels in heaven. There was no body. No proof that Rakhshan was dead. "And he just, his body just . . .vanished. It happened so fast. He was there. Then he wasn't. He must have sunk into the water, drowned. He had to be dead." She had seen the green light pierce him. She had heard him scream.

What was her aunt insinuating when she asked about Rakhshan's body? That he wasn't dead? That he was alive? That her children risked their lives and failed? That they all failed?

Lavinia's own ruby ring wouldn't summon the djinni. Peter was master. Would he ever wake up? Yasir was sorely wounded when he was sent to the urn. Had he survived?

Both of them, Peter, Yasir, unreachable. They could die. She was alone.

"Nia. Stop!" Alice was shaking her. "Stop. You were gibbering."

Lavinia closed her eyes. The phrases she had been muttering, according to her aunt, continued inside her head, a litany of terror. The words collided, slid onto one another, combining into nonsense.

Alice's palm lay warm on her forehead. The voices stopped. Lavinia's throat caught in an abrupt inhale, a clawing-your-way-to-the-surface breath. What with the horrible battle, the casualties, she had used every excuse not to think of the urn. Not to think the unthinkable.

"Nia, here. Drink this." Alice put a glass to her lips.

Lavinia took a big swallow. Her eyes flew open, tears streaming out. She pushed the glass away, choking.

"Wha—?" She lapsed into a coughing fit. "I thought it was a-a potion. Not . . ." More coughing.

"No dear, just plain Scotch whisky. Good for bringing the stray mind around." Alice held the glass up.

The colors shone as vivid as the jewels in Yasir's rings. Lavinia raised her eyes to the figure of Jesus, who held a white lamb, the brilliant red of his robe striking her in the eye as a beam of sunlight angled with the changing light. Her prayer finished, she rose from a cushion on the chapel's marble floor. The peaceful quiet, the figures in the stained glass—old friends from when she first arrived at Bramley House, a new bride so in love with Peter—all imbued her with a serenity she hadn't experienced since those days.

She wouldn't think of anything before this moment. She basked in the calmness, the stillness. Only the light altering, subtle and slow like a soft breeze playing on water. Colors crept across the floor, sidling onto the altar. She should come here every day and pray.

Lavinia kept repeating her prayer as she walked up the stairs, down the hall, even as she entered Peter's rooms. She stopped, unable to believe what was before her.

Peter smiled. He sat in bed, propped up with pillows, eyes open, hair combed. Her prayer answered.

"Peter." She spoke softly, almost afraid her voice might cause this vision of him to revert to Peter lying in bed, eyes closed as he had been since he jumped in front of Yasir and suffered a portion of Rakhshan's blow.

But Peter smiled a new smile.

She sat in a chair beside his bed and took his hand. Warm. He turned to her, his expression pleasant.

"How do you feel?" She leaned towards him.

He smiled again, his eyes clearly taking her in, recognizing her.

"Peter, dear, can you hear me?" She enunciated each word carefully.

"Yes." His voice was scratchy.

"Are you feeling well?"

"I feel a bit peculiar." He swung his legs over the side of the bed. "I want to go—Palomar."

She put her hand on his arm. "Perhaps tomorrow you can ride, dear. Have you eaten?" Best to deter him, like she did with the children.

"I'm not sure." He moved his legs back under the covers and settled in. "I could use a bit of tea."

She hurried to the corner and pulled the bell pull. Stevens rushed in.

"Bring Lord Bramley a full tea. Scones—"

"—and sausage with mashed potatoes, bacon and brandy." Peter interrupted, his voice stronger.

Peter slathered raspberry jam on the scone and took a mouthful. Nothing was wrong with his appetite, and they had done enough small talk to fill a whole evening's party. He took a swig of brandy.

"Peter, darling, have you seen Yasir?" She tossed the sentence out casually, in spite of her insides quivering.

He sipped his brandy and pushed his plate back. An odd expression clouded his face. He cocked his head.

"Who?"

Dear me, was he being deceitful? Why? At this point they both knew about Yasir. *Lord*, Peter knew him even in the Biblical sense.

"Yasir." She repeated the name.

"Yes, I heard you. Is he a new footman?" The blank expression in his eyes frightened her.

"Peter, where is the urn?"

"Urn?" He started to scowl.

"Never mind. I fear I'm overtaxing you." She patted his hand. "Let me have your tray removed. Stevens can help you get ready for the day. I shall check on the children."

He looked up at her with a bewildered expression as she walked to the bell pull. Did he not remember the children either? He had been upset that Stuart was Yasir's child, and old wounds could surface easily after a trauma. She shouldn't have mentioned them. But she found it peculiar he didn't ask. And of course, she shouldn't have brought up Yasir, but she had to know.

Was the devious Peter fully returned? Was he hiding something?

Or had he truly forgotten?

53

*Y*asir pulled her close, his chest warm, his body spent from their exertions. She looked over his shoulder. Sheer silk inner curtains covered the gap in the brocade bed hangings, distorting the dark figure that stared at her. She drew back.

A gloved hand wrenched the bed hangings away.

"Lavinia." The way Peter said her name, squashing the letters together as if he would crush her in the same way, made her bristle in anger. Then she saw the glinting metal of his sword.

Yasir pushed her behind him.

The sword glimmered as Peter raised it. He brought it down hard on the djinni.

Screaming in rage as Yasir's blood soaked her, she lunged at Peter. His face deformed. Glinting evil eyes. A shimmering ruby aigrette.

Rakhshan.

The Dark Magician clutched her wrists. His eyes grew wide with horror and with a sharp exclamation, he let her go. He tugged at his blood-soaked gloves. It took her a moment to realize that Yasir's blood hurt the magician.

She tried to rouse Yasir but he wouldn't move. His blood gushed from the horrific wound. It dripped from her hair, covering her body like sticky warm wool.

Rakhshan threw his last glove to the floor, smearing the djinni's blood from his hands onto the sheets.

She rushed to him, slipping on the djinni's blood that dripped from her body. Rakhshan backed away, fumbling in his sleeves for his wand.

The Dark Lord had been weakened. When she embraced him, Yasir's blood would destroy the last of his magic.

Gasping for breath, Lavinia threw off the covers. The sticky warmth suffocated her. Shaking her arms to rid the blood, she looked down at her nightgown.

No blood anywhere. Her nightgown was white in the dim light of the morning.

She was alone. In her room at Bramley House.

Fleming rushed in.

"Milady, what happened? I heard you scream." Her maid surveyed the room. "Another dream? Shall I send for the master?"

"No, leave Lord Bramley to his sleep. And leave me." Lavinia heard the weariness in her voice. Peter would be no help. The poor man was under a doctor's care now.

Under her instructions, the servants had looked high and low throughout Bramley House and its environs for the urn.

Nothing.

Stuart fretted in his room, angry with her because he hadn't gotten to acknowledge his real father, Yasir, and now no one could find the djinni. Cybelle still didn't speak, and roamed the house at all hours as if she too were searching for Yasir. It was almost impossible to keep her properly watched.

And dear James, Peter's son. She let out a heartfelt sigh. James had found her crying in Peter's study, clutching one of her husband's precious scrolls. Her son had climbed into her lap. He traced the tears running down her cheek with his finger.

"Mum, I cry about the magic too. *I hate it.*" His face had flushed in anger.

"Stuart has it. The lady that looks like the cat man has it." James had tensed, his eyes bulging. He turned to either side as if he feared the cat man might snatch him straight from his mother's lap.

Lavinia had hugged him close. "Dear James, you and your father are safe from the Dark Magician. You have nothing to fear from him and his terrible magic."

Peter was fighting his demons, brought on by Rakhshan's powerful strike. She desperately hoped her husband would win, for she needed him more than ever.

He held the key to their fate.

He knew where the urn was.

If Yasir had the strength to heal himself, if he had survived his wound, he was now imprisoned in the vessel. Her arms trembled with the sheer helplessness of their predicament.

"You saw the dark lady with me in the parlor?" Lavinia had lifted James's chin so that he faced her.

Her son nodded.

"Her name is Mehadeh. She is a friend of ours and isn't mean like the cat man. Mehadeh is helping us find Yasir." James had slumped and looked down. He mumbled something she didn't understand, then spoke louder.

"I think Cybie has magic, also. And Auntie Alice." He had sat up and stared at her. "I heard you tell the nasty man with the turban that your magic had grown." He leaned away.

Afraid he might topple off her lap, she had put her hand against his back. His blue eyes met hers. Bless his little soul, he was afraid again.

"Mum, is this magic like a cold? Catching?"

54

I assume my human form in the urn. The ethereal meeting the corporeal. I welcome the binding of flesh, a grouping of the tenuous. The flow of blood, a concentration of my freedom of movement. The strength of bone, a solid grounding of the diaphanous.

This taking shape is slow even now. Rakhshan's possession of my secret name combined with his last attack weakened me. This compounds his curse. I have not found a solution.

I recline on the divan, my solid body sinking into the silken cushions. I reach into my gold cup of jewels, and view the mound of glimmering colors, a rainbow resting in my palm—the gossamer into the material—like my body.

I let the jewels fall through my fingers, the feel of their smooth surfaces slipping over my flesh. Oh, the sensation. The colors flashing in the light of the urn. Brilliant red from the glowing rubies. The green of a woodsy glade a gift from the emeralds. The glint of fiery sunlight from deep inside the bright white diamonds. How I miss the loamy earth, the pure blue sky of Lavinia's world. Lavinia. My children. Even Peter, bless his soul.

Yet today, it all seems more real than the many times I've slipped into my body here. It is as though a veil has been lifted, and I am able to face what has happened.

I have survived what was to be the final fight with Rakhshan.

I lost.

The burning torment of defeat starts in my solar plexus, rising through my chest, blistering, until I cannot bear it. I jump from the divan, silken pillows scattering, and fling the jewels in rage.

Another day of waiting.

I have counted three hundred sixty-five days and five hours, a little more than a year by the current human calendar. In that time, I have pondered what befell that day at the river when Rakhshan brought down his wand. I was ready. I countered with my magic, but the Shadow Lord's power consumed mine as effortlessly as a carp snapping up a water mite.

Peter had jumped in front of me.

I heard his scream through a haze while my body convulsed in a spasm of agony. I tried to leave my human form, but it was as if I were locked in a torture chamber, flailing at the walls in vain.

Then nothing.

When the blackness left me, I found myself here, in the urn.

In the background of Peter's scream, I thought I heard a voice. Lavinia's? But after all this time, I still cannot make out what she said. The words tumbled out fast, overlapping. She sounded frantic.

The last I saw of the urn, Peter had moved it from the depths of the monstrous cabinet in his study to his secret room with his favorite treasures. He likes to bask in the midst of these. His own private museum.

My urn sat on the mantelpiece next to an ancient Roman bust. I thought nothing of it then, but when I found I was trapped here, I realized what it meant.

Peter alone can find the urn.

Magic powers cannot locate it, so Alice, Mehadeh and Stuart will have to search like any human. And by design, Peter's treasure room is almost impossible to discover.

But Peter has not summoned me. I am certain he suffered from Rakhshan's magic. Is Peter dead? At the end there was Rakhshan, Lavinia, Peter and myself, the great djinni.

I failed them. Left them to Rakhshan and his cruelty.

At least, I spirited James and Stuart to Bramley House with Cybelle. I assume they are safe. But I puzzle as to why I feel little Cybelle's presence most of all.

At times, I hear Lavinia's voice from that last moment. She called Peter's name. The rest is difficult to decipher. But today I closed my eyes and heard her, desperate, distraught, the words clear for the first time as if she were here with me.

Peter, command Yasir to the urn. *Those were Lavinia's words.*

Ah, so that is how I came to be here.

Peter, *wounded as he was, sent me to the urn. My heart warms, my eyes flood with tears. My Lavinia, my Peter.*

I was saved by their acts of love.

55

And so I speak these words once more:

I am Djinn. I am abandoned.

My lament through the centuries. I thought to never use this phrase again after I found my Thalia, my Lavinia. After our son and daughter were born, I knew we would be saved from the curse of the urn. But I have learned that in this world every tide has its ebb, so I must remain in readiness.

Whoever finds the urn and opens it will be my new master. It could be one of my grandchildren, a cousin, one of the servants, or a new owner of Bramley House. Perhaps soon, or decades or centuries from now, when my Lavinia and our children are not anymore on this earth.

The one thing I know without doubt—Rakhshan is alive, or I would be free.

END

Also by Claudia Herring

Novels of the Djinn Chronicles

Obsessions of a Djinni
Book One of the Djinn Chronicles

Ties of Smoke
Book Two of the Djinn Chronicles

Claudia Herring writes romantic fantasies. Her Djinn Chronicles novels are set in a world of mysterious powers and tumultuous intrigues fraught with subterfuge. They begin in Regency England where sensible mortals encounter djinnis, magicians, sorceresses, and soothsayers.

She would live in a library if she could.

She's afraid of her cat.

For more about her novels, and special previews, visit claudiaherring.com.

Sign up and be the first to hear about new releases and exclusives.

Acknowledgements

The author's grateful thanks to: Barry Smith, go-to reader. Chris Rogers, my editor. My writer's groups and Scott, Jay, Robin, Heather, and Karen.

For her opinions on writing and law, Kate Alsina.

For all you wonderful readers who have taken the time to read my novels, thank you. Please know that writers thrive on reviews.

www.ingramcontent.com/pod-product-compliance
Lightning Source LLC
Chambersburg PA
CBHW020215260626
47156CB00002B/386